Krissy broke free from her father and sprinted across the lawn, screaming, "Jayson, Jayson, please don't let him take me." She flung herself into his arms, clinging to him with all the might of a scrawny eight-year-old.

"Krissy, I'm so sorry." He buried his head in her short blonde curls, remembering the countless times she'd run next door to him when her mother was drinking. He'd been her protector, her hero, since she was born. And now he had no choice but to let her go. How would she ever make it without him?

Krissy's father stalked towards them and pried her weepy body from Jayson's arms. "This is your fault," her father spat at him, then turned on his heel and hauled Krissy, flailing and screaming at the top of her lungs, to his car.

Jayson struggled to free himself from Mitch's iron grip. But at sixteen, his strength was no match for his twenty-year-old brother's. His last memory of Krissy, the memory burned into his very soul, was her panic-stricken face pressed against the car window, and her blood-curdling screams of, "Jayson!"

DEDICATION

To my mother, who fostered my love for reading and writing by introducing me to my favorite place in the world as a child—the public library. Forty-two more days, mama, and you could have read my book.

Nine Million Minutes

Leigh Ann Lane

CHAPTER 1

KRICKET WALKED AROUND THE lime green Jeep Wrangler for the hundredth time. Yes, it was an obnoxious color, and yes, someday she would wonder what on earth she'd been thinking—but a lime green Jeep, along with her new auburn hair color and the cricket tattoo on her butt that still stung, screamed 'goodbye shy'–and that's exactly what she was aiming for. Before she talked herself out of it, she gave a quick nod to the salesman. "I'll take it."

Two hours later, the Jeep was hers. Her first stop was Starbucks for a skinny vanilla latte to keep her warm while she did something crazy, something she'd needed to do for a long time. For once, she didn't mind that the drive-thru line wrapped around the building. The storefront window provided the perfect opportunity to stare at the reflection of her new Jeep. She waved at a little boy tugging on his mother's jacket and pointing wide-eyed at it. Maybe the color only turned the heads of boys under the age of ten, but she didn't care. She liked it. And Brock would hate it. Not that he'd ever see it. But just knowing that made her like it even more.

Nothing could ever replace Pepper, the little red Wrangler she'd driven since her sixteenth birthday. She could kick herself for allowing Brock to convince her it wasn't the *proper* vehicle for a professional. Apparently, it hadn't occurred to him that sleeping with your girlfriend's roommate wasn't *proper* either. Never again would she let a man run her life.

She ran her hand across the smooth leather steering wheel, then gave the dash a loving pat. "Starting today, you and I are going to kick life in the butt."

Keeping her eyes on the line of cars in front of her, she blindly dug through her mammoth purse for the journal her best friend Becca had bestowed on her a few weeks ago. She winced when a brush bristle jabbed under the nail of her pinky before her fingers finally found the soft bound book. She tugged it out and surveyed the cover. *The So-Awkward Journal* certainly seemed to have been created for her. That pretty much described her to a T. The cover even had an image of a redhead on it. Some of its steps to overcome shyness were way outside her comfort zone, but apparently that was the point. New Year's Day seemed the perfect time to begin, and that was tomorrow. But since 'Do something spontaneous' was the step on the first page, she'd go ahead and get that one out of the way. Buying a lime green Jeep seemed pretty spontaneous and hadn't been painful at all. Maybe this journal wouldn't be so challenging after all.

She glanced up from her journal to check the progress of the line. A big black Jeep covered with mud was queuing from the other entrance. Whoever drove *that* had to be hot. She counted the cars ahead of them. He would fall in line right behind her when they reached the point where the two lines converged. Jeepers wave at each other, that's the Jeep Code, so she had to wave at him, no matter how red her face would turn. Okay, who was she kidding? If he was a hottie, there was no way she would wave at him.

The cars inched forward until finally it was her turn to merge into the single line. Just as she pressed the gas pedal, he jumped in front of her, barely missing the front bumper of the Jeep she'd had for all of twenty minutes. She sucked in her breath. "You jerk," she yelled to the universe and blasted her horn. "I guess we'll start by kicking *his* butt," she said to her Jeep.

Her journal beckoned from the passenger seat where she'd dropped it. 'Do something spontaneous,' it taunted. After pondering for about two seconds, she flipped him off over her steering wheel. "There's a Jeep wave for ya." She quickly sunk down in her seat. Nice job, Kricket. Brandish your middle finger for the very first time in your life when you're trapped. It said *spontaneous*, not stupid.

She busied herself with the stereo buttons to avoid eye contact with him when he rolled down his window to order. But after he pulled up to the window, she cautiously surveyed him in his side mirror, laughing and obviously flirting with the Starbucks girl while he paid for his coffee. His scruffy whiskers and curly dark hair said 'I just got out of bed.' His face was obscured by sunglasses and a ball cap. But from what she could see, he definitely fit the name 'Mud Ninja' painted on the fender of his Jeep.

He caught her eye and held up his coffee in a toast before squealing his tires as he drove away. Big fricking show-off.

She pulled to the window and held out her credit card.

"Oh, I don't need that," the cashier said, handing Kricket her latte. "The guy in front of you paid for it. He said he likes your Jeep...and your hair."

Kricket touched an auburn curl that fell just above her waist and gaped at the girl. He paid for her coffee? He hardly seemed the sunshine and rainbows pay-it forward type.

"And he bought you a muffin." The girl handed her a small paper bag. "He comes through every day. Definitely makes *my* morning."

"Does he always pay for the person's coffee behind him?"

"Nope. Guess you're the lucky one," the girl responded with a raised eyebrow. "I'd chase him down if I were you."

That wasn't happening. Kricket sipped her latte as she headed north about five miles until the gated neighborhoods on the edge of Edmond, an Oklahoma City suburb, turned into cow pastures. Even though the air was frigid, she had to do it, just for a few minutes. She turned up the stereo full blast and lowered all four windows. Until summer, this was the closest she could get to driving with the top off.

She pulled her ball cap tighter over her head and cranked up the heater, kicking herself for not going home to grab a coat first when she saw her dream Jeep perched on risers in front of the dealership on her way home from the gym. Her hoodie did little to keep her warm, but there was no way she was going to roll up the windows yet. The exhilaration of her hair whipping about to the thump, thump, thump of music booming from the stereo, and the sturdiness of big knobby tires grabbing the road made her feel alive…and brave. She filled her lungs and let out a liberating yell.

Red lights flashing in her rearview mirror popped her arctic bubble of freedom. She jerked her foot from the gas pedal and glanced at the speedometer, willing herself not to hit the pedal and flash her brake lights like a neon sign that said, "Yes, I'm speeding."

Her fingers fumbled for the stereo volume control while her eyes kept a vigil in her rearview mirror. Please go around me, please go around me. The motorcycle cop drew up beside her and motioned to pull over. No such luck. Her heart sank as she slowed to a halt on the side of the road.

One stinking mile in her new Jeep? In nine years of driving, she'd never had a ticket. She glanced at her journal lying innocently on the passenger seat. So far, breaking out of her safe little introverted world was not working out so well.

She poked her escaping curls back under her ball cap. Her heart pounded as he swung his leg over his motorcycle and walked towards her Jeep. Of course he was tall and broad shouldered, just like she pictured a motorcycle cop would be, which made her even more nervous.

"Good morning, ma'am," he said, with a tip of his chin. "May I see your license and registration?"

Naturally her wallet was buried under all of the dealership papers in her purse. After what felt like three days had passed, she finally dug it out, but her panicked fingers weren't cooperating and she fumbled it onto the floor. She grasped it from the floor mat and bonked her head on the steering wheel as she raised up.

His face showed a hint of amusement when she finally accomplished the seemingly impossible task of placing her license in his hand.

"Ms. Taylor, are you in a hurry to get back to Dallas, or did you just steal this Jeep?" he asked, noting her Texas license. His mirrored sunglasses masked his eyes, so she couldn't gauge if he was joking.

She stuck her hands under her legs to keep from fidgeting. "I just moved back home a few weeks ago. I grew up here…well from the age of nine until I went to college. After college, I moved to Dallas. That didn't work out so well, so I'm back." she babbled. Why on earth was she babbling? Normally conversations with men completely eluded her.

"Then you should understand that, in Edmond, we like to think our speed limit signs are here for a reason."

She looked down at her lap. "I guess I got a little carried away in my new Jeep. I'm sorry."

"I can see why, Sparkles," he said, obviously referring to the big rhinestone "K" on her pink camo ball cap. "But if you have a speeding habit, lime green probably wasn't a good color choice."

"I think I'm already sorry I chose it," she said, relieved by his humor. "I was just ready for a big change."

"Aren't we all?" He surveyed the license, then glanced at her. "This doesn't look like you at all. Are you sure you didn't accidentally hand me your fake ID?"

"Hardly. I'm twenty-six." She nervously toyed with a lock of the auburn hair she still wasn't used to. "I changed my hair color. And it's kind of an old photo."

He handed back her license. "My sister's name is Kristen, too. I call her Kris though."

"I go by Kricket."

He smiled. "Well, Kricket, I'm going to let you off with a warning this time. But keep your foot off the pedal. If you're speeding, I'll see you." He touched the tip of his hat. "Have a good day. And welcome home."

CHAPTER 2

KRICKET SWUNG IN BECCA and Kevin's driveway and honked the horn twice. Becca, her diva best friend, would scowl at her appearance. But her *spontaneous* morning and unplanned chat with the cop had left her with no time to change or put on makeup. Besides, she'd just have to redo it tonight for the New Year's Eve party Becca was dragging her to. She was still trying to figure out a way to get out of going. But Becca was intent on getting her back into the dating world, and when Becca set her mind on something, there was no stopping her. So today, she was stuck with an agonizing day of shopping for something 'hot' to wear for a disappointing night.

A sudden pounding on the window made her jump. "Kevin, you almost made me wet my pants," she said, lowering the window.

"Sorry, Kric. Becca's still primping. She'll be out in a minute." He stuck his head in and pecked her on the cheek. "Love the Jeep! Becca's going to cringe when she sees it, isn't she?"

Kricket nodded. "She'll probably have to change her clothes to make sure she doesn't clash with it."

They both laughed, then sucked in their cheeks when Becca appeared and sashayed down the sidewalk like it was a fashion show runway. Kevin darted up the walk to meet her. His sandy-haired boyish good looks and lanky frame contrasted starkly against Becca's pixie body and long dark mane as he escorted *Her Highness* down the sidewalk. Becca didn't bother hiding her look of disapproval as she surveyed the Jeep.

Kevin opened the passenger door for her.

"How on earth are you going to hoist yourself up in this thing when you have on a short skirt?" Becca asked.

"Mmm, I wish you had on a short skirt," Kevin said, boosting Becca up and smacking her on the butt.

"And why on earth did you buy lime green? You'll have to be careful about the color of clothes you wear," Becca said, frowning at the yoga pants Kricket was wearing.

Kricket exchanged a knowing glance with Kevin. "Bye, ladies," he said, then planted a big kiss on Becca's mouth.

Becca wiggled her butt in the passenger seat as Kricket backed out of the driveway. "Mmm, I don't even have heated seats in my Beamer." She cocked an eyebrow at Kricket. "And speaking of warm butts, has anyone besides me seen that new cricket tattoo on your butt?"

Kricket shifted her mouth into a sly grin. "Maybe."

Becca's mouth flew open. "You had sex and didn't tell me?"

She bit the inside of her mouth to keep from laughing out loud as she nonchalantly fiddled with the stereo just to torture Becca. She might get to the count of five before Becca's impatience spewed like a shaken can of soda. One, two…

Becca punched the off button on the stereo. "Spill it, missy!"

Kricket threw her head back in laughter. "You should see your face." She mocked Becca's gaping mouth. "Okay, it was a massage therapist who saw it. But it was a guy."

"That doesn't count. Starting tonight, we're going to work on getting something else massaged. And I don't mean with something battery operated." Becca fished a pen out of her purse and reached into the back seat for Kricket's journal. "Have you started this yet?"

"Sort of. I think I've got the 'Do something spontaneous' challenge covered."

Becca raised an eyebrow then flipped through a few pages. "Set some goals. Let's see…" she said, chewing on her pen. She scribbled something on the page then turned the journal towards Kricket. "Get laid. That's your first goal."

"Funny." She turned the stereo back on, hoping to avoid the conversation she knew was coming.

"I just want you to be open to meeting someone." She flipped the visor down and fluffed her hair. "And you know, actually talk to guys when they approach you. Several of Kevin's hot single friends will be at the party tonight. We'll have no trouble getting you laid."

"I'm not interested in getting laid. And for your information, I had a conversation with a hot guy this morning."

Just as she anticipated, Becca flipped up the sun visor and gaped at her. "Really? You talked to a guy?"

Kricket savored the moment again before bursting Becca's bubble. "An extremely nice cop pulled me over this morning," she said, holding up her warning notice.

Becca's face deflated. "Let me guess, he was fifty and pudgy."

"He was maybe thirty, and as far as I could tell behind his sunglasses and a helmet, kinda hot."

"So, did he ask you out?"

"Of course not. He's on the job. That's probably against cop code or something. I was just happy he gave me a warning. And I didn't have to flash my boobs at him or anything."

Becca flipped the visor back down to finish primping. "I wouldn't flash my boobs to get out of a ticket." She leaned towards Kricket, squishing her boobs together with her elbows. "All you have to do is show a little cleavage and hold your mouth like this," she said, opening her lips seductively.

"Yeah, worked like a charm for me too." She had no cleavage

to speak of and if she tried to hold her mouth like that she'd look like she'd just been to the dentist.

The sweet scent of magnolia welcomed them into the boutique. Even though it was the dead of winter, stores were beginning to switch out the dark tweeds and cozy wools with wispy florals in spring colors. They made their way to the back of the store where the sale racks were bound to be bursting with winter bargains.

Becca thumbed through a rack and held up a slinky low cut zebra print dress. "How about this one?"

"There's no way I would wear that. I'd feel like a slut. It's perfect for you, though."

Becca held it up in front of the mirror. "You're right, it is perfect for me." She tucked the dress under her arm with a sassy head bob. "Now I'll work on finding something utterly boring for you to wear."

Kricket perused several racks until, finally, her eyes locked on an emerald green and black geometric dress with long bell sleeves. She ran her fingers down the thick knit fabric. "How about this one? Sort of a 70's throwback. And I can wear boots with it." She would *not* stand around all night in heels she could barely walk in, no matter how big of a hissy Becca threw.

Becca eyed it carefully. "The green goes great with your hair and it's short enough to be sexy, but straight enough not to show your coochie on the dance floor." Becca touched her arm and smiled. "And I know what you're thinking. The sleeves cover your scar."

Kricket rubbed the scar that ran the length of her arm from the top of her bicep to her wrist. She wasn't terribly bothered by her scar anymore, but being at a party full of strangers would be awkward enough. She certainly didn't need anything else to be self-conscious about.

The dresses fit each of them perfectly, so their shopping trip was short and sweet. They grabbed a salad at Zoe's Café before heading home.

"We'll pick you up at eight," Becca said when Kricket dropped her off. "And no boots."

❦

Kricket had three hours before she had to be ready for the party, so she grabbed her journal and flopped across the bed. With Becca hovering over her tonight, there was no chance she'd be able to hide in a corner, so selecting a few journal challenges to knock out at the party would keep her mind focused on something other than her own awkwardness. She found several easy ones to start with, like 'smile at a stranger,' 'give someone a compliment,' and 'ask someone their opinion about something.' She would definitely save 'starting a conversation with someone you find attractive' for a much later date…like never.

Her phone chirped, and she grabbed it to read the message. Of course it was Becca reminding her to wear heels, not boots. Her eyes froze on the next sentence. *Guess who just emailed me a link to her engagement website. Bet she's preggo!*

So, Brock and Sutton were engaged. Well, they certainly hadn't wasted any time. Her cheeks burned as she grabbed her iPad off the nightstand. She knew better than to look, but it was like driving by a car accident. You didn't *want* to see blood and gore, but no matter how hard you tried not to look, you *had* to peek.

Against her better judgment, she clicked on the link. The moment their glowing faces appeared on the screen, a knife sliced through her heart. Sutton, in a demure pale pink dress, looked uncharacteristically angelic. And Brock probably custom ordered that tie to specifically match his eyes…his steel blue eyes that delved deep within to uncover your flaws.

How many people had visited the site, cooing over the perfect couple? And how many knew the perfect little bride-to-be had stolen her future husband from her friend, roommate, and co-worker? Everyone at Pinnacle Consulting, that's how many.

Kricket's stomach knotted just thinking about it. She should have never let Sutton talk her into moving to Dallas after college. But they'd both received offers from Pinnacle Consulting, so they packed their bags, rented a small two-bedroom apartment in Dallas, and set out on an adventure together. *Cocky Executive Pounces on Shy Intern*, the headline could have read, when, within a month of their arrival, Brock descended on Kricket.

Nearly everyone in the company had known about Brock and Sutton. Everyone except her. And if she hadn't gone home at lunch that day, she might still be wasting her life with that jerk. She'd never get the image out of her mind. When she walked in, Brock and Sutton were on the couch going at it like it was mating season for swine. Sutton had grabbed an animal print afghan and sprinted into the bathroom, but Brock just sat there, wearing nothing but a smile…as if she'd walked in and caught them playing Scrabble instead of hide-the-weenie.

With that disgusting image burned into her retinas, Kricket fled from the apartment. She'd never really made other friends in Dallas, so she had nowhere to go that night. She had no choice but to stay in a hotel near their office with no makeup, no change of clothes, nothing.

The next day, she'd nearly vomited when she was summoned to the CEO's office. Although Brock hadn't done anything technically wrong from an HR perspective, the CEO suggested it might be best for all involved to remove Kricket from the environment. Those were his exact words. They offered her an equivalent position in any of their satellite offices. After enduring five agonizing weeks of co-workers staring and whispering while

HR worked out the transfer, she moved back to Oklahoma City with her tail between her legs, only a mile away from Grandpa and Dot.

The flash of her iPad screen saver jolted her back to reality. Although her gut warned her against it, she couldn't help but click through page after page of stereotypical engagement photos. Seeing Brock's smile repulsed her. His constant criticism still reverberated in her head.

She studied Sutton's face, trying to find a remnant of her childhood friend. Becca had been the ringleader of their friendship trio since the third grade. They were inseparable. But one man sliced through their friendship. She despised Brock, but a friend's betrayal cuts through the heart.

But six months of licking her wounds was long enough. Tomorrow was a new year and things were going to be different. She closed the cover of her iPad and rolled over on her back, resting her head on her hands. She stared at her new dress hanging on the bedroom door. New Year's Eve in a room full of strangers, mostly couples, was less and less appealing as the time to get ready grew closer. She'd either be dodging some drunk guy trying to kiss her at the stroke of midnight, or be standing alone trying not to look like the only person who had no one to kiss as the confetti fell. Neither was appealing.

She'd promised Becca she would follow the journal. And she would. She hated being shy, so she was willing to try anything. Tomorrow. She would start tomorrow.

She texted Becca that she had a headache, then turned off her phone, grabbed her keys, and climbed into her lime green steel cage of courage for a long drive. She would end this year on her own terms. Alone.

CHAPTER 3

JAY INCHED FORWARD HIS Range Rover in the Starbucks drive-thru line, chiding himself for glancing around the parking lot for the lime green Jeep and the feisty redhead who'd flipped him off last Saturday. He didn't know why he was looking for her. Life was easier without women. Well, without any *specific* woman, anyway.

"Ooh look, Uncle Jay. I want a Jeep just like that when I turn sixteen." Madi aimed the pink covered iPhone she got for her eighth birthday out the back window and snapped a photo.

Jay glanced in his rearview mirror just as a lime green Jeep whipped into a parking spot. He banged his hand on the steering wheel. Now? She's here now when he's stuck in the drive-thru line with his niece and nephew? He watched her bend over to retrieve the iPad she dropped when she hopped out of her Jeep. God bless whoever invented yoga pants. Hopefully Madi caught a photo of *that.*

He drummed his fingers on the steering wheel, waiting for the cars to move forward so he could maneuver out of the line and into a parking spot. C'mon, c'mon people, move, move, *mooove.*

Madi stuck her phone in Miles' face. "I'm putting this in my bulletin board app so I can show Mom and Dad when they get back from the Carmen Islands."

"Cayman Islands, stupid," Miles said, looking at the photo. "Wow, she's hot."

"Whatever, Miles. She's way too old for you. Besides you can't even get a girlfriend."

Jay watched the color creep up the back of Miles' neck. "That's enough, Madi." At fourteen, Miles was in that awkward self-conscious stage of puberty. And his little sister was no help.

When the cars moved forward, Jay deftly maneuvered the Range Rover out of the drive thru line. "Change of plans, guys, we're going inside."

"Why are we going in, we were almost to the order thingy," Madi asked, unbuckling her seat belt and poking her head between the front seats.

He nodded towards the photo Madi was holding. "Because *she's* inside."

Miles' eyes widened in awe. "Are you gonna ask her out?"

"You don't even take girls on dates, Uncle Jay, 'cause you're a man-whore," Madi stated matter-of-factly.

Miles burst out laughing and Jay whipped around to glare at her. "Madison Shea Hunter! Never use that word again."

Madi threw herself against the back of her seat and crossed her arms. "Mom said it. She told Dad it's been long enough since your divorce that you should quit being a man-whore and start dating."

Jay glared at her. "I don't care what your mom says. And you shouldn't eavesdrop on your parents." Why couldn't his mom and sister-in-law quit worrying about his relationship status and let him live his life in peace?

Madi rolled her eyes. "I can't help it if their room is right below mine."

Jay mentally filed away Madi's revelation that she can eavesdrop in her parent's bedroom. He'd find the perfect moment to drop that bomb on his sister-in-law, Meg. Probably when he had his chat with her about the man-whore comment.

Jay opened his car door and winked at Miles. "C'mon...it's time for you to learn the Hunter technique for picking up ladies." Jay grabbed Madi's hand before she could dart across the crowded parking lot. "The key is to catch her eye, twice. What she does the second time reveals whether or not she's interested." He gave a quick nod to Miles. "Watch and learn, Grasshopper."

Jay bent down and looked Madi in the eyes just outside the door. "Keep your big mouth shut or you'll blow it for me."

"I don't have a big mouth," Madi blurted loudly as they walked in. Everyone in Starbucks looked up at her and grinned. Everyone except the red-head in the corner facing the window, with earphones stuck in her ears and intently glued to her iPad.

Jay counted six people in line ahead of them. Normally standing in line annoyed him, but not today...the longer the line, the more opportunity to catch her eye. He watched her, plotting in his head ways he'd like to wrap himself in that long red hair and make her scream louder than her green Jeep. He mentally unleashed her ponytail and watched her curls cascade like a waterfall down her back.

"May I take your order, sir? Sir?"

Miles poked him. "Oh, um...whatever they want plus a venti bold," he said, handing over his credit card without taking his eyes off his prey. Did he really just say "um?" As a professional conference speaker, he'd trained himself to completely eliminate that word from his vocabulary. Or so he'd thought.

He surveyed the room of tables filled with soccer moms and sorority girls getting their caffeine fix before their day of shopping. The cream and sugar station was right beside her. He didn't like cream or sugar, but it was his only chance to catch her eye.

Her phone rang just as he picked up his coffee and headed her way.

"Hi, Grandpa," she answered. After listening for a moment, she responded. "I'm just having some coffee, so tell me what you and Dot have done so far on your trip."

Jay poured a bit of cream in his cup and stirred. Please let it be a short trip.

"Me first? Okay, that's easy. The only thing exciting going on here is I'm having fun driving my new Jeep. And tonight I'm meeting Becca and some of our high school cheer squad friends at Club 100. It's the first time we've all been together since I moved back."

Jay popped the lid on his coffee and walked towards the door. "C'mon guys, let's go,"

"But you didn't even talk to her," Miles said, following Jay out the door.

"Hold this, Uncle Jay, while I go get a napkin." Madi thrust her hot chocolate at him and darted back in.

Miles face was crestfallen. "That's your big Hunter technique? Why didn't you talk to her?"

"She's preoccupied. Timing is everything. Besides, I overheard where she's going tonight, and now, I just happen to be going there too."

"You dog." Miles slapped Jay on the arm, nearly knocking the hot chocolate out of his hand, then held up his hand for a high five.

Madi pranced out the door and danced in a circle around them, chanting, "I talked to your *girlfriend*, I talked to your *girlfriend*."

"You did what?" Jay glanced in the window, but only saw his own reflection. "Here, Miles, hold her hot chocolate while I throw her in front of a moving car." Jay snatched up Madi with one arm and hoisted her over his shoulder, hanging her upside down with her arms dangling down his back. She squirmed and giggled as Miles followed them to the car laughing.

CHAPTER 4

"GRANDMA KAREN, WE'RE HOME," Madi shouted, barreling through the front door. "Are Mom and Dad back yet?" Jay followed Madi and Miles into his brother's ridiculously perfect home for his ridiculously perfect family, Mitch, Meg, Miles, and Madi. Even their names were perfect together.

Jay's mom marked her place and laid the book she was reading on the coffee table just as Madi dove in her lap and planted a big hot chocolate-covered kiss on her cheek. "I know you miss them, sweetie, but their plane arrives in just a few hours. Just enough time to get your rooms cleaned up."

Miles hung his backpack on the circular staircase by the front door and plopped down on the white couch, flinging his legs out in front of him. "My room's always clean, but Madi's will take three weeks to straighten."

"Feet off the couch, Miles," Karen said.

Jay leaned over the back of the couch and gave his mother a one-armed hug, being careful not to spill his coffee on Meg's designer couch. Why Meg would buy a white couch was beyond him. Apparently, design takes precedence over practicality when your home serves as your interior design business showroom. He had to admit, Meg was extremely talented. After his divorce, she'd insisted on redecorating the rental he moved into, spending a small fortune of his money. He knew she was trying to make it homey for him, but her ulterior motive was using it as a showroom, which frequently resulted in a phone call from her yelling at him for leaving his boxers on the floor.

"Thanks for taking the kids for the night, honey. I caught up on my reading and picked up a little so it doesn't look like a tornado hit when Mitch and Meg get home. Although I must admit, this house is so big it was lonely by myself."

She had a little more color in her face than yesterday. He could tell that watching the kids for a week while Mitch and Meg celebrated their fifteenth wedding anniversary in the Caymans had taken its toll.

"Sorry my conference schedule was so heavy, and I couldn't help out more. After this week, you and Dad may change your minds about moving here."

Madi climbed off her grandma's lap and sprawled out beside her. "We had pizza and cupcakes and we made a fort in the living room, and Uncle Jay let us stay up until two in the morning watching a Harry Potter marathon."

Jay gave Madi a shut your mouth look, then put on his best innocent face when his mom frowned at him.

Madi stuck her phone in her grandma's face. "And look at this Jeep picture I took. And see that girl? Jay has a crush on her." She batted her eyes and made kissy face lips at him.

Madi's mouth never stopped. His mom smiled and took the phone from Madi. "She's very pretty."

"She looks just like my red-haired Barbie, doesn't she, Grandma? Uncle Jay was afraid to talk to her, so I did for him. And guess what her name is? Kricket, with a K. I'm going to change my Barbie's name to Kricket. And when I turn sixteen, I want a green Jeep and I'm going to name it Grasshopper. That's what I told her she should name her Jeep, and guess what? She's going to," Madi said with her chin in the air. "And she doesn't have a boyfriend, but she said she doesn't want one either."

"Enough, Madi," Jay said, walking around the couch towards her. "Your grandma doesn't need a play-by-play of your conversation with a stranger."

His mom seemed amused. "Since when are you afraid to talk to a girl?"

"He wasn't afraid," Miles answered for him, rolling his eyes at Madi. "He was going to show me his technique for picking up girls, but she wouldn't look up from her iPad so he could catch her eye. That's the first step, catching her eye."

"You let them stay up until 2:00 a.m. *and* you showed Miles how to pick up girls? In front of Madi?" Karen raised her eyebrows at Jay, doing a poor job of masking a smile.

Madi bounced up and down on the couch. "So he put cream in his coffee, even though he doesn't like cream and he heard the girl say where she's going tonight and now—"

"End of story, Madi." Jay swooped down and began tickling her.

"You don't scare me, you big baboon," she giggled, pretending to struggle.

He tickled her relentlessly. "Are you finished with the story yet? I'm not stopping until you say yes."

"No! And so now…." she said between giggles. "He's going to…follow her there."

His mom was smiling, but her eyes were somewhere far away.

"OK, into the fire you go." He picked up Madi by the ankles, hung her upside down, and walked towards the fireplace.

"No, don't …let…him…Grandma," she shrieked. "No, Jayson!"

Jay's head felt like a meteor crashed inside it. He tossed Madi on the couch and stumbled into the kitchen.

"Madi, you know better than to scream the name "Jayson" at him."

"But, Grandma, *you* call him Jayson sometimes and he's not a big stupid meanie about it."

"Just hush, Madi."

Their voices sounded like echoes as Jay leaned over the kitchen counter trying to stop his head from spinning as the memory flooded back.

Krissy broke free from her father and sprinted across the lawn, screaming, "Jayson, Jayson, please don't let him take me." She flung herself into his arms, clinging to him with all the might of a scrawny eight-year-old.

"Krissy, I'm so sorry." He buried his head in her short blonde curls, remembering the countless times she'd run next door to him when her mother was drinking. He'd been her protector, her hero, since she was born. And now he had no choice but to let her go. How would she ever make it without him?

Krissy's father stalked towards them and pried her weepy body from Jayson's arms. "This is your fault," her father spat at him, then turned on his heel and hauled Krissy to his car, flailing and screaming at the top of her lungs.

Jayson struggled to free himself from Mitch's iron grip. But at sixteen, his strength was no match for his twenty-year-old brother's. His last memory of Krissy, the memory burned into his very soul, was her panic-stricken face pressed against the car window, and her blood-curdling screams of, "Jayson!"

The touch of his mom's hand on his shoulder jolted him back to the present. He grabbed a bottle of water from the refrigerator and stood at the big picture window that overlooked an endless edge pool in his brother's backyard. The pool was covered now, but in the summer it gave the illusion of overflowing directly onto the eighteenth fairway of the golf course. He watched a pair of geese fly over the house and land in the pond on the other side of the fairway. Geese mate for life. What a concept.

The chair scraped on the tile floor as Karen sat down at the breakfast table behind him. He felt her eyes boring into his back.

"I sent the kids upstairs to tidy their rooms before Mitch and Meg get home," she said softly. "Do you still have nightmares about Krissy?"

He hoped she would take his silence as a hint that he didn't want to discuss it.

"I'm sure she grew up to be a fine and happy young woman," she said a little too cheerfully. "Meg helped me search for her on the Internet once. We searched under Kristen Beckett and Krissy Beckett, but we didn't find anything." The spoon clinked in her mug as she stirred her coffee. "Did you ever try to find her?"

"It was a long time ago, Mom. If it weren't for her damn scar, she wouldn't even remember me. I wish she didn't have to remember." He rubbed his identical scar as he watched the flight of a ball hit by a lone golfer sail across the fairway and land on the brown grass. Hopefully her scar had faded with time.

"Sometimes I still hear her screaming too," his mom said softly. He turned to see a tear roll down her cheek.

"Aw, Mom. I know it broke your heart too." He walked behind her chair and wrapped his arms around her. "You were much more of a mom to her than Tara was. I know she remembers that."

Krissy had spent more time at the Hunter's house than her own. Tara constantly dropped Krissy next door for free babysitting while she went clubbing, frequently leaving her for days at a time. And Karen had treated Krissy as one of her own.

An image of Tara seeped into his mind. Tara got pregnant with Krissy when she was seventeen, so she wasn't that much older than Jay, maybe eight or nine years. All his friends thought she was hot, with her thick lined eyelids and red mouth, and her tight dresses that showed everything she had going on underneath. But she disgusted him. He shook his head to force the image from his mind.

His mom wiped her eyes with a napkin and smiled grimly up at him. "Let's talk about something else, shall we? Help me turn on this iPad. I told the kids I'd be watching them on the monitor to make sure they are cleaning their rooms. Meg showed me how to use it before they left, but I was afraid to turn it on in case the kids could see me in the bathtub or something."

Relieved to see her smile, he sat next to her at the table and punched the code into the security monitoring app. "There you go. See, you can view both rooms on the same screen. And of course Miles is watching TV and Madi is playing with her Barbie dolls."

"Of course." She shook her head and smiled. "So, tell me about this girl you saw at Starbucks. Do you know her?"

He stalled with a long sip from his water bottle before answering. "No, Mom. Madi's just flapping her mouth, as usual." That answer wouldn't satisfy her, but he had to give it a shot.

And of course, his mom used one of her famous high school counselor tricks—maintaining eye contact while silently waiting for the real answer.

He closed his eyes, sighing in resignation. "Poor Miles is so awkward around girls. I was just trying to show him how to tell if a girl is interested when you catch her eye." He gave her a cock-eyed grin. "You're not the only one who knows how to read body language."

His mom smiled. "Well, honey, if anyone knows how to catch a girl's eye, it's you. I just wish you would let a *nice* girl catch you, instead of all those…" She took a sip of coffee.

He smiled, thinking of the numerous words he could use to finish her sentence to elicit a smack on his cheek. But none of them would be accurate. They were all professional business women who wanted the same thing he wanted—a little sexual diversion with no strings. There was never a shortage of conference attendees wanting to hook up with the eligible bachelor keynote speaker. He took a sip of water and shook his head. "Mom, I travel too much to worry about a relationship."

"I just want you to be happy, honey. Don't let what Rachel did to you chart the course of your life. What she did was unforgiveable. And don't even get me started on Tara. I really wish you'd go see Dr. Rhine. He could help you let go of some things."

Jay pushed away from the table, muttering some choice language under his breath. "I have to go." He snatched up his bottle of water and headed towards the front door.

"Jayson Kyle Hunter, you will not use that language around me and then stomp out the door."

He stopped in his tracks, like he was twelve years old again. He held up his index finger to indicate *wait a minute*, then walked out the kitchen door. He slammed his water bottle against the side of the house. Water spraying all over his clothes, his hair, and the patio as the bottle burst open intensified his anger. What a stupid move. He stood on the patio, dripping, while he regained his composure.

"Feel better?" his mom asked, stifling a smile, as he walked back in the kitchen with his wet hair hanging in his face.

He grabbed the kitchen towel off the counter and dried his face and hair. When he pulled the towel from his face, he caught the gleam in her eye and they began laughing.

"I'm sorry, Mom." He pulled her into a hug, intentionally rubbing her face against his wet shirt.

She grabbed the towel out of his hand to wipe her face. "I'm sorry too, honey. I didn't mean to dredge up your demons." She rose up on her tiptoes to ruffle his damp hair. "You and your dark curly hair. You look just like your father did when we met. That young lady in the Jeep won't know what hit her. Are you really going to try to meet her tonight?" Her eyes were wide with hope. "She looks sweet."

He wrapped her in a bear hug. "I doubt it, Mom. I wouldn't know what to do with a sweet girl." He plucked a candy bar out of a bowl and winked at her before heading towards the stairs. "Peace offering for Madi. After I tickle her until she forgives me, I'll tell them to get busy on their rooms."

CHAPTER 5

THE DANCE FLOOR HUMMED like a hormonal beehive. Kricket and Becca watched their friends dance while they caught their breath with another round of flirtinis. They laughed when some guy flinging his arms around like a drunk pledge at a frat party wormed his way into their friends circle.

"Now aren't you glad you didn't bail on me again?" Becca asked with a satisfied look on her face.

"Would you get over that already? It was New Year's Eve and you were trying to set me up. I wouldn't miss *this* for anything. It's been too long since our whole group was together."

"Our *whole* group will never be together," Becca reminded her.

She held up a hand to shush her. "You promised no more Sutton trash talk." As she'd expected, Sutton had been the primary topic of conversation during dinner.

"Have you danced with anyone tonight?" Becca asked. "Besides us I mean?"

Kricket gave her a 'don't start' look.

"Just humor me. Pick some guy in the crowd who looks nice and make eye contact with him. Then I'll leave you alone about your journal."

Kricket scanned the tables scattered near the dance floor. She'd rather just dance with her friends.

Becca nudged her elbow. "Don't look now, but there's a ginormous hottie on the other side of the dance floor who can't take his eyes off you."

When Kricket turned to look, he smiled. Her cheeks grew warm and her breath caught. She swung her head back around to look wide-eyed at Becca.

"I told you not to look, silly."

"That's him."

"Who?"

"He was at Starbucks this morning. His niece talked to me. She was adorable." She snuck another glance. He tipped his chin and flashed a grin at her. "Ugh. He saw me looking," she said, jerking back around.

Becca eyed him approvingly. "He's definitely in the AP category of men. If you're brave enough to cut your teeth on him, I give you permission to burn your journal. You will have graduated magna cum laude."

"I can barely even talk to you right now my heart is beating so wildly." She didn't dare look at him again.

Becca watched him for a moment. "Well, you'd better calm it down, because he's making his way over here."

Kricket jumped from her barstool and rushed back on the dance floor to find her other friends, who'd been sucked into the middle of the bee hive. She'd dance with the arm-flinging frat boy before subjecting herself to becoming a mute tomato-face in front of that guy.

Becca followed her into the middle of the dancing mass of people. Shielded from the eyes of Hot Starbucks Guy, she lost herself in the music and laughter of her friends as they danced to song after song. It felt good to be carefree with her girlfriends again. Even though her curiosity nagged at her, she dared not glance towards his table again.

When their favorite cheer song, "Ice, Ice Baby" began, Becca dared the girls to dance their high school cheer routine. At first, Kricket was hesitant to join in, but their laughter and the two glasses of liquid courage she'd slammed loosened her inhibitions, so she fell into step with them. Some of the people dancing around them tried to follow along, but eventually gave up and stood back to watch. It was surprising how well the girls remembered the routine after eight years.

Suddenly, the crowd parted to the edges of the dance floor, like a UFO had landed in their midst. It took a moment to register, but when Kricket looked up, the six of them were alone in the middle of the dance floor. The familiar grip of anxiety began closing in on her, so she slipped off the back row into the crowd.

Her mouth felt like cotton and her head spun from the pounding music as she fought her way through a sea of elbows, sweaty bodies, sloshing drinks, and lewd looks. She just needed to make it to the less crowded bar area in the back for a glass of water. Pausing to lean against the wall for a moment, she blew out an exasperated sigh. She'd only made it halfway. She placed a hand against the wall while she leaned over to fish her phone from her boot. Becca would try to find her if she was gone very long.

A hand touched her elbow, as if to steady her. "You okay?" Electricity surged up her arm, causing her to suck in a breath. She knew without looking, it was him.

Willing herself to exhale slowly, she turned towards the husky voice, looking up to his towering height. Deep brown eyes gazed down at her with a sympathetic grin. Up close, his good looks weren't as intimidating as they were from a distance. Oh, he was heart attack hot, but something about his eyes softened his chiseled face and she found herself drawn to them. They were kind, like deep pools of melted chocolate inviting you to jump in and take a relaxing swim. His smile drew her eyes down his sleek jawline to his full, soft lips. Her breath faltered as she wondered what it would be like to be kissed by them, followed by a warm flush that crept slowly up her neck.

"I'm…I'm just trying to get some water." Her voice cracked from dryness and nervousness.

"Come with me." He laced his fingers with hers, pressed them against his back, and headed into the crowd. Pinned so close to him, she had to concentrate on matching his steps one by one to keep from tripping, but it kept them from being separated or strangling someone with their linked hands. His stride announced he meant business, so the crowd readily parted as he forged their way through. Upon reaching the bar, he hoisted her onto the single empty barstool.

"Water, please," he called out, holding a twenty in the air. She took the opportunity to glance at his left hand. No wedding ring or tell-tale sign of one.

The bartender with fake boobs popping out of her blouse like goggle-eyed goldfish leaned over the bar and seductively grazed his fingers as she took the bill. She eyed him lustily while she filled a glass with ice and shot it full of water with her bar gun. She smirked at Kricket as she sat the glass in front of him.

"Here you go," he said, sliding the glass towards her with a gentle smile.

Kricket laid her phone on the bar and thrust the water glass to her mouth, reminding herself to demurely sip instead of gulp the water.

"Better?" he asked after she emptied the glass.

"Better, thanks"

"I'm Jay, by the way."

She forced herself to glance up at him. "I'm Kricket…with a K." She was surprised and thankful her voice didn't shake.

"Nice to meet you, Kricket with a K."

"Nice to meet you, Jay by the way." The second she realized how corny that was, he caught her eye and they burst into laughter.

She liked his boyish grin. It made his eyes twinkle like he

had a secret. Oh, what she'd give to reach up and brush that dark curl off his eyebrow. The small scar on the corner of his eye, along with just the right amount of stubble, made him look rebellious instead of just a pretty boy. Why did scars look sexy on guys and ugly on girls?

His voice jolted her out of la-la land. "Would you like another water, or can I get you a beer or drink?"

"Just water, please. I've already had two martinis and I'm pretty much a one-and-done kind of girl." She cringed. Nice job, Kricket, why don't you just write 'I'm drunk' across your forehead?

He laughed. "Another water and a Guinness please," he called to Fishboobs, who was hovering nearby. He pulled a twenty from his wallet.

Fishboobs grabbed an icy mug and filled it from the tap, then seductively leaned over the bar as she placed the overflowing mug in front of him. "Sorry, I got a little too much head on it," she said, looking directly in his eyes.

She did *not* just say that. Kricket glanced at her own barely B-cup chest, demurely covered by the green geometric dress intended for the New Year's Eve party she'd skipped. Boobs always win.

From the corner of her eye, she saw that instead of smiling or fixating on Fishboobs' chest, his jaw was set. "And a water for the lady," he said, resting his hand on the back of Kricket's barstool. He held Fishboobs' gaze until she picked up the bar gun and filled Kricket's glass, then put the twenty back in his wallet and pulled out a ten. Kricket pressed her lips together to stifle a grin when Fishboobs stuck the bill down her shirt and stalked away.

When he turned towards her, his face was soft again. "I'm sorry for that."

She shrugged, not knowing how to respond to his chivalry. Undoubtedly that was a common occurrence for him. She fought for something to say. "Haven't I seen you somewhere before?" she blurted out, instantly appalled that the world's most infamous pick-up line just came out of her mouth.

He raised one eyebrow and grinned. "Does that line work for you often?"

Before she could respond, her phone lit up with a text from Becca, *'r u with hot starbucks guy?'* Kricket snatched her phone from the bar and dumped it in her lap, glancing sideways just in time to see his grin. She propped an elbow on the bar and rested her face against her palm, hoping to spontaneously combust before she had to look up.

"So, you *did* see me this morning." He nudged her shoulder with his. "You think I'm haw-awt," he said in a sing-song voice.

She blew out a puff of breath. "At least quit smirking while you watch me die of humiliation," she said into her palm

"How do you know I'm smirking? Your eyes are covered."

"Because you sound like you're smirking."

He laughed. "So now we're even."

She popped up from her posture of shame. "How's that?"

He took a sip of beer and offered the mug to her. "This morning, I was going to show my nephew the subtle technique of picking up chicks, and you completely ignored me. And for the record, my niece and nephew will never let me live that down."

"I'm sure that was a new experience for you." His teasing made her feel oddly cocky. She took a sip of his beer, then slid it back to him.

He picked up the mug, turned it around, and took a sip from the side she drank from. He did not just do that! She swallowed hard, hoping her eyes weren't bulging out of their sockets.

"I'd say it worked out in my favor. This way I got to see your special performance with your friends. You girls pretty much shut down the dance floor with that one."

Heat rose in her cheeks. Either he hadn't noticed her running off the dance floor, or he was being kind. "That was our favorite routine when we were cheerleaders in high school. I didn't realize everyone on the dance floor would stop and watch."

"You don't seem like the cheerleader type." A small crease formed between his eyes as he tilted his head to study her.

"Okay, true confession. I was on the squad, but I was too embarrassed to actually cheer at games, so I was the cheer manager. Basically a glorified water and equipment girl." Why did she just tell him that? She glanced down for a moment to escape his brown eyes that seemed capable of seeing inside her mind.

"Just so you know, you were the best one out there tonight." His smile made his eyes crinkle. And made her heart feel warm.

"So do you come here often?" she asked, grimacing as the second-most infamous pick-up line spewed from her mouth.

"Hardly," he said with a chuckle, but thankfully let it slide. "Dancing is definitely not my thing. Actually, I'm here because I overheard a cute redhead say she would be here tonight."

She nearly spit out her water. Not only because he touched her hair, which caused her to practically die on the spot, but he followed her there? She chewed on a fingernail, deciding if she should be flattered or scared.

"The look on your face right now is worth any regret I might have for admitting that," he said, chuckling. His perfect white teeth were straight out of a toothpaste commercial and she tried not to stare at his mouth. "I probably should have kept that a secret. I'm not a psycho stalker, I promise."

"Just your everyday run-of-the-mill stalker then," she mocked, with the best cocky attitude she could muster given her state of shock.

"I just had to meet the girl who drove that Gecko Jeep."

"You know the color is called *Gecko*?"

"I know a little bit about Jeeps."

"I've only had it a week. It's the catalyst for the new me." She immediately regretted admitting that.

He placing his hand over hers, tilted his head, and looked directly in her eyes. "I don't see anything wrong with the current you." Her heart stopped beating in her chest, and she had to remind herself to breathe.

"Hey, girlfriend. I've been looking all over for you," Becca said, giving her a hug from behind. "Who's your friend?" she purred. "Hmm," she said, blatantly appraising him. "TAG watch, no wedding ring mark, clean nails…" She stepped back to check out his shoes, then smiled with approval. "You'll do."

Kricket gaped at her. He chuckled, seemingly unaffected by Becca's natural seductiveness nor her rudeness.

"Jay, this is my best friend, Becca, who I'm going to strangle later," she said after finding her voice.

He raised from the bar to shake her hand. "My pleasure, Becca."

Becca craned her neck to look at him. "I don't know whether to climb you or what. How tall *are* you?"

"Six-five. How short are you?"

She straightened her spine and smirked at him. "Exactly five feet of something you couldn't handle."

"I'll just take your word on that." His eyebrows revealed his amusement.

So, what do you do, Jay?" she asked, resting her arm on Kricket's barstool like a mama bear. Here she goes with her inquisition. She would find out more about him in thirty seconds than Kricket had in thirty minutes.

"Management Information Systems," he said, before taking

a long sip of his beer without breaking eye contact with Becca.

"Where did you go to college and what was your major?" she fired.

"OSU. Masters in Entrepreneurship."

"Entrepreneurship. So either you have big dreams of developing the next Google, or your daddy gave you a nice corner office in his company when you graduated." She gave him the once over again. "I'm going with the corner office."

Kricket cringed. If she had even the most miniscule chance with this guy, Becca had just ruined it.

The way he leaned against the bar with his arms crossed indicated he was more amused than insulted, and thoroughly enjoying the Becca challenge.

"What kind of car do you drive?"

"Mini-cooper."

Kricket burst out laughing.

"Very funny, Jaynormous. Your foot wouldn't fit in one."

Kricket nonchalantly poked Becca in the ribs with her elbow, which did absolutely no good.

"How old are you?"

"Thirty-three."

"Ever been married? Kids?"

"Married once, no kids."

"How long have you been divorced?"

"A year and a half."

"Did you cheat on her?"

He narrowed his eyes. "Nooo," he drew out.

Becca thrust her hand out, flashing a smile of approval. "Very nice to meet you, Jay." She turned to Kricket. "You have my permission to stop shopping and add him to your cart."

Kricket sucked in so much air she nearly toppled off the bar stool.

"Easy," Jay said, grabbing both sides of the seat to steady her.

She made a deliberate attempt to shut her gaping mouth, trying to ignore the fact that his hands rested on the outside of her thighs. She couldn't look at Jay, but she could glare at Becca. Sometimes, actually most of the time, Becca went too far.

"C'mon guys, we're wasting some great music, let's go dance," Becca said, grabbing them each by the arm.

"I don't dance, but I'll come watch." He held Kricket's arm as she slid from the bar stool, then took her hand and headed towards the dance floor. As they filed through the crowd, Kricket looked back and gave Becca the stink eye. Becca mouthed "yummy," and winked at her.

The pulsating beat slowed to a sleepy ballad. Her heart pounded as he passed by their friends' table and led her onto the dance floor. Dear Lord, her body was going to be pressed against him. Without releasing her hand, he whirled her around to face him, locking her arm against her back. She sucked in her breath as he jutted her waist forward, forcing her to look up. His warm brown eyes were now piercing, and she had to look away. He raised his palm, beckoning for her to take it. When she lifted her hand, he slid his palm down her hand until their fingers locked, then rested their hands against his chest. They began swaying to the beat of the music, which was much slower than the slamming beat of her heart. "I thought you didn't dance," she choked out.

"Small sacrifice," he said in a husky voice. His hand slid down the curve of her back, melting her skin in its path. He exhaled slowly in that sexy loud way men breathe, before pulling her into his chest. When he rested his chin on her head, all cognitive thought escaped her.

She breathed in his scent, committing every sensation to memory. The tautness of his chest against her cheek. His hand alternating between whisper-soft strokes in her hair and firm pressure on her back when he pulled her closer. The scratch of his whiskers as he nuzzled the top of her head with his chin. The rise and fall of his breathing. Every slow and deliberate move made her tingle all over. Holy Joseph, she was going to have an orgasm right there on the dance floor.

As the song came to an end, he brushed his lips over her ear. "I wasn't ready for you, but here you are," he whispered, then surrounded her with both arms.

His confession paralyzed her. She felt the blood seep from her face as anxiety bubbled up to consume her. No, please not here, not now. She had to steady her breath or it would suck her in. Tears welled in her eyes, and her heart pounded as she looked around for a way to escape. She had to get away before she curled up inside herself. Don't let it suck you in, Kricket. Don't let it suck you in. She blinked to clear the fog from her head that nearly blinded her as he led her from the dance floor.

"Hey girlfriend, come to the ladies' room with me." She couldn't see her, but felt Becca grab her arm. "I promise I'll bring her right back. Watch my drink, okay?"

"I'll hold your drink hostage until you bring her back," she heard him say through the fog.

Becca's voice was dim. "Look at me, Kricket. I'm right here. Just look at me."

She felt a hand on each shoulder and forced her mind to follow the voice. Please let them be alone, she thought as she broke through the fog. She opened her eyes, thankful to see they were in the ladies room.

"Your face was as white as a sheet coming off that dance floor. Good thing I was being a creepy overprotective friend," she said when Kricket's eyes focused on her. "You guys had a moment out there, huh?"

Kricket nodded, blinking rapidly to keep a tear from rolling down her cheek. These attacks she'd labeled as 'freezing' were horribly embarrassing. But, as opposed to an anxiety attack, at least she didn't feel like she was dying. She'd always presumed the two were related since both stemmed from too much attention.

"Don't move," Becca said, grabbing a piece of toilet paper out of the stall. "Let me dab your eyes so you don't look like a raccoon. Kric, I'm sorry I pushed you. You don't have to go home with anyone. I just wanted you to have fun."

Kricket sighed. "It's not your fault. That was the sexiest four minutes of my life. It was just so intense…I wasn't ready for that. And what he whispered in my ear just overwhelmed me."

"What did he say?"

"He said he wasn't ready for me, but here I am."

"Whoa. That's intense. That might have given *me* an anxiety attack."

"His every move was so deliberately slow and sexy. I swear I nearly had an orgasm on the dance floor. That would have been more embarrassing than a stupid anxiety attack!"

Laughter burst from Becca's mouth. "*That* I couldn't have helped you with. But you know what they say…you can tell a lot about how a man is in bed by the way he dances. Sounds like he'd take it nice and slow, making you beg for mercy." She slowly rotated her hips back and forth and they buckled over in laughter.

"Jay is definitely sexy. But he's also really nice. And oddly, he makes me feel somewhat comfortable. Well, right up until the near-orgasm part." Kricket checked her face in the mirror. "And guess why he came here tonight? He overheard me on the phone at Starbucks this morning saying where we were going. He came here to meet me." She knew she had a ridiculous grin on her face.

Becca's eyebrows furrowed. "Are you sure he's not some creepy stalker dude?"

"Would a creepy stalker tell you he stalked you? And seriously, someone who looks like that probably has women stalking *him*."

"Good point. C'mon then, let's get you back to your next big mistake. By the way, did you see the size of his hands?" she said with a smirk before strutting out the door.

❧

Jay leaned against the bar, keeping a vigil on the ladies' room door. He slowly rubbed his fingers together, recalling the feel of her hair sifting through them. She made him feel... Yeah, that's it, she made him feel. And he wasn't at all sure he liked that. He'd kept women in his bed and out of his head for almost two years and had no plans on breaking that streak.

When he glanced back towards the ladies' room, he couldn't keep from grinning at the sight of her walking towards him, laughing with Becca.

When she reached them, he pulled her into a sideways hug. He slid Becca's drink towards her. "Becca, your drink is safe, minus a few sips by that guy over there with a sore on his lip."

Becca scrunched up her nose. "I am not drinking that."

"I'll take it, drama queen." Kricket picked up the drink, downed it, and plunked the empty glass on the bar.

Becca looked at her wide-eyed. "Thirsty?"

Kricket blushed when she realized what she'd done. As he was ordering her a water, two of their friends ran over and begged them to come dance. He was glad to see Kricket hesitate.

"Stay and talk with me," he said, lightly touching her on the arm. He caught a quick exchange of glances between the two girls, followed by Kricket's nearly imperceptible nod. Becca gave Kricket's arm a quick squeeze before sashaying off to the dance floor.

After Becca left, Kricket seemed a bit withdrawn. She stood with her arms crossed, rubbing a hand up and down one arm, obviously avoiding his gaze. Something about their dance had made her uncomfortable. "Come stand in front of me, and we'll watch them," he suggested, extending a hand to her. She placed her palm in his and moved towards him. He leaned against the bar and eased her shoulders against his chest, encircling her tiny waist with his arms. "Good?"

She nodded and rested her arms on his. He remained silent for a while, letting her grow comfortable with their closeness.

"Becca's a bit of a watchdog, isn't she?"

"She's always watched out for me. In case you haven't noticed, I'm not very good around strangers."

"You're doing just fine. But we'll let her off the hook for a while and you can let me watch out for you." He leaned around and looked at her with squinted eyes. "If you see a ninja in the crowd, get behind me."

Her body relaxed in a laugh. When she let her head fall back against his chest, a warm glow seeped through his body, dissolving every single muscle. They stood in silence watching her friends dance. The fresh scent of her hair made him wish his chest and arms were bare so he could feel the tickle of it cascading over his skin. He rested his chin on her head and closed his eyes, fighting what the feel of her tiny frame pressed against his body did to him, fighting the urge to whirl her around and consume her mouth with his. The way his heart felt when she was wrapped in his arms, he never wanted to let her go. And that wasn't good. It wasn't good at all.

CHAPTER 6

BEFORE AGREEING TO LET him drive Kricket home, Jay thought Becca was going to require a blood sample. But Kricket lived near him, and her friends lived the opposite direction, so it made sense. After leading them to his freshly detailed Range Rover, Becca's guard weakened. Thankfully, his Jeep had been too muddy to drive. Becca made a show of snapping a photo of his license plate with her phone before she finally acquiesced.

He grabbed his jacket from the backseat and put it around Kricket's shoulders before opening the passenger door for her. In her eyes he saw a hint of fear. "I'm just taking you home, okay?" Her shoulders relaxed as she nodded.

They chatted easily on the drive home. During a lull in their conversation, her stomach growled loudly. He laughed when she grabbed her stomach with a horrified look on her face.

"Don't worry, I have just the thing for that." He spotted a church parking lot and turned in, pulling to a stop under a light.

The box he presented from the back seat lit up her eyes. She gasped. "German chocolate? That's my absolute favorite."

"Wait until you try these. The bakery near Club100 makes them just right. I'm rarely on this side of town, so I stopped and picked up a few on the way to the club. You have no idea how hard it is for me to share these."

Her face glowed as she selected a cupcake. "When I was little, I always had a German chocolate cake for my birthday."

"Me too. Still do, actually."

He watched her lips sink into the gooey frosting. "Pretty

good, huh?" The only thing he could think of that was better than German chocolate cake was German chocolate cake on her lips. He reached over and wiped a bit of frosting from her mouth and stuck his finger in his mouth.

She stopped chewing for a moment and watched him, then fumbled out some words when she realized she was staring. "Um, yeah," she said, wiping her hand across her mouth. "Almost as good as my childhood birthday cakes. Maybe it's just the memory, but I haven't found one yet that compares."

"Your mom must be as good a cook as mine."

In the glow of the parking lot lights, he saw a flicker of darkness cross her face. He led her wrist towards his mouth and sunk his teeth into the cupcake. Her eyes grew wide at his enormous bite. "I didn't say you could have it," he said, after swallowing his mouthful of chocolate. She stuffed the rest in her mouth, laughing as it spilled out.

He couldn't keep from staring as she self-consciously wiped the frosting from her mouth. If he kissed those lips, he'd be toast. And as much as he'd like to, he was *not* making out in a church parking lot. Nor was he going to be toast.

After tucking the cupcake box in the backseat, he resumed the drive home. Two points for self-control. Within just a few miles, her alcohol buzz turned into an alcohol nap. In the glow of a stop light, he studied her. Her tilted head exposed a slender neck begging his lips to meander down the length of it. He brushed a tendril of auburn hair from her face with his thumb, envisioning himself cupping her face in his palms and kissing every single freckle scattered across her cheekbones.

At his touch on her cheek, she sighed and stirred in the seat, causing her dress to inch up to a delicious level on her smooth taut thighs. And causing his crotch to hijack his mushy daydream. She'd sigh when he kissed those too.

She was nothing like the women he'd been with since the divorce; or actually ever for that matter. A typical girl-next-door. The kind of girl who would get hurt by someone like him. An odd sensation flickered though his mind but was gone before he could grasp it.

At the entrance of her apartment complex, he touched her shoulder. "Kricket? Wake up," he whispered.

In that semi-conscious moment between sleep and wake, she buried her nose in his jacket that surrounded her, breathing in deeply with a little smile before her eyes fluttered open. "Are we here?" she asked sleepily, sitting up straight and pulling the hem of her dress down where it belonged. She rubbed her eyes then smoothed her hair with her hands. "Sorry I fell asleep. You know how it is when you have a good buzz going...everything's fine until you sit still and then bam, lights out." She glanced sideways at him, then quickly studied her hands.

"Lightweight," he said, giving her shoulder a playful shove, knowing she was mentally kicking herself for announcing to him she was drunk.

"I'm in the last building, facing the street. You'll see Grasshopper parked in front of my door." Her face lit up. "Hey, your niece is the one who suggested that name. I thought it was perfect."

"Absolutely perfect," he said, swinging in beside her Jeep. "Stay right there so I can help you out." As he walked around the Range Rover, his body missed her presence next to him. Shit, he was already toast.

When he opened her door and extended his hand, her brows furrowed. "Dresses and SUVs don't mix well. Turn around and I'll slide out myself."

"Duck your head." He reached in, plucked her out, and planted her solidly on both feet before she could open her mouth to protest. "Problem solved," he said, amused at the shocked look on her face. She tensed a little when he put his hand on her back during their walk to the door. He could tell she was out of her element. So was he for that matter. This was nothing like walking to the hotel room of a willing conference attendee who knew the score.

At the door, she grasped his arm to steady herself while she unzipped her boot to fish out her key. "Ta-da," she said, holding her key in the air with a triumphant grin.

When their eyes locked, her grin vanished into a look of apprehension. Her nearness triggered something inside him and without a moment's hesitation, he swept her into the circle of his arms. His heart felt as though it were reaching through his chest for hers. He couldn't recall a time when the pull in his heart was stronger than the pull in his crotch. Sure, he wanted her. But what he really wanted to do right now was to hold her and never let go. He stroked her hair while he steadied his breath.

Pulling slightly away, he tilted her face towards his. Her cheek was smooth under the brush of his thumb. His lips hovered near her mouth, hesitating. Of all the women he'd kissed, these lips frightened him. He knew the moment their lips touched, he'd be sucked into an abyss from which he'd never emerge. An abyss he had no intention of entering again.

His lips won the battle and found hers. He forced himself to drink slowly, to savor this first taste of her mouth. Her body melted against his as his tongue descended leisurely, exploring her mouth as tenderly as he would explore the secret parts of her body. Her tiny sigh erased every care, every hesitation, every sense of anything beyond her sweet German chocolate mouth.

"You're intoxicating," he whispered, reluctantly coaxing his lips away to rest his forehead against hers. Her soft intake of breath was his undoing and he buried his hands in her hair and kissed her again, losing all sense of time and space in her returned passion.

When their kiss slowed, he cupped her cheeks in his palms. Her green eyes reflected the way he felt inside.

"Do you want to come in?" she asked in a barely audible whisper when their kiss slowed. He could tell from her deer in the headlights look she was battling between 'please say yes' and 'please say no.' She was frightened of the deed. He was frightened of how the deed would make him feel. And even though he wasn't ready for that, the thought of letting her go seemed insurmountable, while the thought of taking her inside and learning everything about her seemed inevitable. He held her tightly against him while his heart pleaded, 'Walk away, Hunter, just walk away.'

He forced his body from hers and gently brushed a curl from her face. "Goodnight, Kricket," he whispered, then softly kissed her forehead and forced himself to turn and walk away.

CHAPTER 7

Sunday, January 8
...two flirtinis and one random drink is too many.
...eating half a carton of mint chocolate chip ice cream at 2:30
a.m. doesn't restore your inner sexy.

Today's goal: *Keep myself from ripping this stupid journal into a*
million tiny pieces.

KRICKET BLEW OUT HER hair sultry straight, which took forever, slipped on a V-neck sweater that showed a little cleavage, and tugged on her favorite jeans that made her butt look good. And here she sat, watching her fourth Lifetime movie of the day, hoping he'd drop by for his jacket. She stared at her journal peeking out from under the couch where she'd thrown it. Quite possibly, she'd gone a little overboard on stepping out of her shyness box. Right now she felt like curling up inside and duct taping it shut. She wasn't sorry she'd bought the Jeep, and her auburn hair color was pretty sexy, but never, ever, ever, would she shamelessly throw herself at a man again. Ever!

Admittedly, she was relieved he hadn't stayed, but he could have at least asked for her number before he scampered off, leaving her standing on her doorstep. She puffed a breath against her hand and sniffed. Was her breath atrocious? Does she kiss like a walrus? She'd only kissed three guys in her entire life, and one of them didn't count because they were fourteen and didn't know what to do with their tongues so they just mushed their mouths together like people did in old movies.

His jacket hung on a coat hook by the front door. She intentionally put it way over there so she'd stop torturing herself by smelling it. Much like a trout who'd just latched on to a fisherman's hook, her body was reeled towards his jacket. She plucked it from the hook for the hundredth time today and breathed in his scent. When she closed her eyes, it almost felt like they were still dancing. Swaying to the sultry background music in the Lifetime movie she'd just abandoned, her mind drifted back to the feel of his strong arms surrounding her. She touched her cheek where his whiskers had brushed against it.

The sound of pounding on her front door startled her, and she threw his jacket at the coat hook but missed. Her eyes darted towards the window to see if her make-believe dancing had been visible from her porch. Thankfully the blinds were closed. Her heart pounded as she hung his coat, then grabbed the remote and flipped off the television. He was not catching her watching a Lifetime movie. She paused a moment to slow down her breathing while she checked her face in the entryway mirror. After taking a deep breath, she opened the door.

"How's my girl?" Grandpa asked with his arms open wide.

Kricket quickly hugged him to hide her disappointment. "I thought you were coming home from your trip tomorrow."

"A week with Dot's family is five days too long, so we left early and drove straight through."

"Your grandpa is having trouble with his bowels," Dot stated matter-of-factly. "Here hon, we brought you a souvenir from Santa Fe." Dot proudly handed her a gift bag that would undoubtedly contain a T-shirt designed for a twelve-year-old or one with a suggestive saying on it, depending on who picked it out.

Grandpa motioned towards her Jeep. "She's a beauty. I'm glad you got the four-door. Better for kids when you have them."

"I honestly don't know how you're going to get your sexy on in that thing," Dot said, obviously trying out some reality TV lingo.

"She doesn't need to get her sexy on, Dot."

"Well she certainly isn't going to attract a man if she's driving a tank, now is she?"

Their banter made Kricket grin for the first time since last night. After being raised under Grandpa's strict rules about how a lady should dress and talk, she found it comical that Grandpa had met and married such a colorful woman. When Kricket left for college, Grandpa still hadn't told her about the birds and the bees, but Dot managed to work sex into nearly every conversation.

"Looks like someone's going on a date," Dot said, giving her the once over. "No girl pours herself into jeans like that just to sit around the house. Who's the lucky fellow?"

Humph. Nice choice of words, considering he had chosen *not* to get lucky. She started to say she wasn't going anywhere, but Dot would be suspicious, plus they might decide to stay. "I was just going out to meet some friends at the brewery."

"We won't keep you then, sweetheart." Grandpa smoothed back her hair to peck her on the cheek. "You go have fun."

Dot winked at her. "Put on some bright red lipstick. Turns men into tigers."

Kricket grabbed her coat and purse off the hook and followed them out. She pretended to fiddle with something in her Jeep until they drove out of the parking lot, then went back inside. She stared at his jacket hanging on the coat hook, glad that Dot hadn't noticed it. She would *not* pick it up again. She would *not* pick it up again. She would *not* pick it up again. Nor would she sit waiting for him like a loser. She bundled up in her winter running gear and went for a run.

CHAPTER 8

JAY'S HEAD THROBBED. THERE was no way he could tell his biggest client that he'd done the very thing he cautioned conference audiences against—never make a promise to a customer that you can't keep. And he certainly couldn't tell his dad that he'd violated a key principle in the business management model that made their family legendary. The model his dad masterminded from the school of hard knocks after starting his own business at the age of twenty-two. The model his dad taught his sons when they each started their own companies after college. And Jay's success in turning his dad's business model into a profitable e-book, which led to conference gigs and eventually his business software solution, D-A-S-H, would mean nothing if he failed at this latest endeavor. How could he stand in front of an audience and tout a business model he'd failed to follow?

It wasn't like he'd made the promise blindly. Yes, he'd agreed to a tight deadline, but when a large national client wants to implement your software in all fifty states in ninety days, you simply hire a reputable consulting firm to help get it done. Luckily, the CEO of Pinnacle Consulting Partners was his dad's fraternity brother and was eager to become involved with Jay's new client. Pinnacle's reputation was top-notch, so Jay had the utmost confidence they would do whatever it took to meet the deadline. And everything had gone like clockwork, with the exception of the staff interpersonal skills training courses his new client had requested.

"Jay, Cecil McKnight from Pinnacle is on line one," Gayle's voice blared through his intercom.

"Thank you for returning my call so promptly, Mr. McKnight. Dad told me you came inches from hitting a hole-in-one at Pebble last week." He gracefully listened to Cecil's excruciatingly detailed play-by-play description of the shot, then gushed appropriately before jumping into business. "With all due respect, sir, the course designs presented to me last week were unremarkable," Jay said, pacing across his office during the call. "Staff personal development training must be engaging. We have to create interactive material. Your team has excelled in every other aspect, but I'm extremely disappointed in the lack of effort put forth in this particular area. If anyone had read my list of requirements for the courses, they would have known these were unacceptable."

He stared out the window, rubbing his throbbing temple while Mr. McKnight promised to speak with Pinnacle's Vice President of Client Education and ensure they sent their top course developer from the Dallas headquarters to present a new suite of designs.

"Have them in my office first thing Friday morning. This project is already weeks behind schedule. And Cecil, ask your V.P. why he didn't send his top developer the first time," he snapped before punching the End Call button on the speaker phone.

"That was a little harsh, don't you think," his dad said from the doorway.

Jay ran his tongue along the back of his bottom teeth to keep from responding in a way that would only worsen his headache.

"Just remember who you're speaking with, son." Thankfully, his dad left without waiting for a response. He did not need his interference today.

"Gayle, do we have any ibuprofen?" he snapped into the intercom. His fingers drummed impatiently on the desk as he eyed the long list of unopened emails on his computer screen. "Gayle?"

His cellphone buzzed with a message, which he ignored, but once again, he found himself pulling up the photo of Kricket and her Jeep that he'd secretly texted himself from Madi's phone. He leaned back and propped his feet on the desk. When would he stop thinking about her lips, her legs, her hair? And the way her eyes were so hesitant, yet sprung to life when she laughed. "What am I going to do about you?" he said to her photo.

"What are you going to do about who?" Gayle asked.

He grabbed the edge of the desk to keep his chair from tipping over. "You scared the piss out of me, Gayle! Don't sneak up on me like that."

Gayle stood beside him with one hand on her hip and the other holding out three tablets in her palm. "I did not sneak up on you. You asked for ibuprofen, so I walked my happy butt in here to give you some. And you're welcome," she said with a head bob.

"You didn't answer on the intercom, so I figured you were either in the break room living vicariously through Sylvia's love life, or doing your nails in the ladies' room again." He tossed the tablets in his mouth and took a swig of cold coffee.

Gayle snatched his phone off the desk, nearly causing him to choke on ibuprofen as he grabbed at the phone.

"Mmm, mmm, mmm, who's this sweet young thing?" she said, gazing at the photo.

He held out his hand and glared at her. "Give me my phone."

"She's a little young, don't you think?" she asked, leaning over his head. "See look, I'm starting to see a little gray in here."

He slapped her hand out of his hair. "Gayle, give me my phone."

She perched her expansive hindquarters on the edge of his desk and crossed her arms. "Not until you tell me who she is. I've seen you staring at your phone for weeks now, and I know it's not this fluorescent Jeep that has your loins all in an uproar."

He turned to his computer, signaling their conversation was over. "Shut my door on your way out, Gayle. And please try to keep your mind off of my loins in the future."

She made a production of leaning his phone against the computer monitor so the photo of Kricket stared at him. "You know you can't keep secrets from me. I have my ways," she called over her shoulder on the way out the door.

CHAPTER 9

Friday, January20th
...I wonder if he still thinks about the kiss. I have to stop thinking about the kiss.

Today's goal: Practice eye contact with someone non-threatening. That would mean someone I wouldn't want to kiss. And quit thinking about the kiss.

KRICKET HIT THE ALARM button and stretched one arm, then the other over her head like a cat. After a quick shower with the bergamot scented stress-relieving bath gel she bought yesterday, she scanned the closet for something comfortable to wear on casual Friday, trying to ignore the crumpled dress she'd thrown in the floor two weeks ago. She'd left it there to fulfill the 'do something outside your comfort zone' task in her journal. She was a certified card-carrying neat freak and never left things on the closet floor, not even a pair of shoes. Plus it was a reminder of why she should take this whole journal thing a little more slowly.

Her cell phone rang as she tugged her favorite boots over black leggings. No one called her this early. Sprinting to her phone on the nightstand, she prayed something wasn't wrong with Grandpa.

A breath of relief flew from her mouth when she saw it was her boss, Deidra.

"Kricket, we have a situation. The Director of Client Education Services in Dallas was flying in today to present some course ideas to an important client. His flight was delayed and he won't be here in time. Brock needs you to step in for him."

This had to be a joke. Brock wanted her to meet with a client?

He knew better than anyone she couldn't do that. She was a course designer. She didn't know the first thing about meeting with a client. And why her? She didn't work for Brock. She didn't even work for Client Services. Since moving home from Dallas, she'd had no need to interact with Brock whatsoever, and intended to keep it that way. She had to get out of this without sounding like a baby. "Surely one of his staff in our local Client Services department would be better prepared to fill in."

"They're all out on a large assignment. Trust me, this was not my idea. I would never ask you to do something like this, but Brock has a lot of pull—"

"But, I—"

"My hands are tied, Kricket. Brock stressed how crucial it is to satisfy this client and insisted you are the only person for the job. The client was dissatisfied with the first presentation he received and wants something totally different. Something interactive and fresh. You, of all people know that Brock's group doesn't know the first thing about designing interactive courses. The ones you've been working on are perfect."

Brock had always scoffed at her course designs, saying they were fine for training Pinnacle new hires, but would never pass muster with his external clients. And now he wanted her to present one to a *picky* client? This smelled like a setup.

"The appointment is in forty-five minutes. I'll text you the address. The name of the company is H-Tech, and you're to ask for Gayle Anderson." Her voice softened. "Kricket, I know this is way outside your comfort zone, but you can do it. And you're not doing it for Brock. You're doing it for Pinnacle...and for yourself."

She held onto the bedpost to steady herself as the blood drained from her face. *This is not real, this is not real.* The chirp of her phone with the address text snapped her out of the trance. She had just enough time to change into a suit.

Kricket wheeled into the H-Tech parking lot with fifteen minutes to spare. She grabbed her iPad off the seat and walked towards the building like she was walking to her own funeral.

H-Tech was in an older warehouse district near downtown, so she was surprised when she walked into a lobby that looked like a wonderland. Sun streamed thru a triangular glass ceiling that appeared to go up for miles. Pop art prints brightened the walls, and an enormous aquarium with every color of fish imaginable separated the lobby area from what appeared to be a conference room.

After providing her name to the security desk, she perched on a sleek tangerine leather chair in the reception area to wait for Gayle. The full-wall mirror in front of her provided an unwelcome peek at her appearance. Would she always look fifteen? She adjusted the collar on her white blouse and smoothed her jacket. Breathe, breathe, breathe.

A large black woman appeared around the corner, wearing a pair of khaki pants and a purple H-Tech polo. "Kricket Taylor? Hi, I'm Gayle," she said, shaking Kricket's hand. "Let's get you checked in and I'll take you to meet the CEO. We're big on security around here, so the guard will need your driver's license and a urine sample."

When Kricket tensed, the woman laughed. "Gotcha, didn't I?"

Kricket laid her iPad on the counter to fish her license from her purse. After studying it, the guard swiped it on a reader attached to his computer. "Now I just need a description of your car, ma'am."

"It's a Jeep Wrangler. Lime green."

Gayle, who had been fiddling with her nails during the check-in process suddenly perked up. She looked Kricket up and down, then walked towards the front window. "Is that your Jeep?"

"Yes, am I parked in the wrong spot? I can move it." Kricket followed her, fumbling in her jacket pocket for her keys.

"No, you're fine." Gayle rubbed her palms together and grinned. "Let's go meet the CEO."

Kricket turned back towards the security desk and slammed into a dark blue shirt that felt like a brick wall. Something hit her mouth, and she squeezed her eyes shut as lukewarm coffee showered her face. If a large hand hadn't gripped her arm, she would have lost her balance on her heels. "Ow!" She doubled over, holding her mouth with one hand and wiping coffee from her eyes with the other.

"Look what you did, you big moose!" Gayle shouted.

A deep voice snapped, "Don't just stand there, Gayle. Get some napkins from the security desk."

That voice. She'd never forget that voice. She slowly raised her head, opened her eyes, and looked into the face that had been whirling through her head for weeks. Jay's eyes were wide.

"Oh shit. I'm so sorry. Let me see your mouth. It's bleeding," he said, prying her hand away from her mouth.

She slapped at his hand. "Stop it."

He lifted her chin to tilt her head towards him. "Stick out your tongue and let me look."

"I am not sticking out my tongue!" She grabbed the napkins Gayle offered and turned away from him, wiping coffee from her eyes. "Jay, please just leave me alone. I have coffee all over me and I have a meeting with the CEO, and—" She spotted a ladies' room across the lobby.

"Go on, Jay. Let the poor girl get herself cleaned up," Gayle said as Kricket darted across the lobby.

She pulled the bloody napkin away from her mouth and stared in the mirror at her busted lip and coffee stained blouse. The moistened paper towel she used on her stained blouse resulted in making it see-through. Her black blazer was damp, but didn't show any coffee stains, so she pulled it together and buttoned it. After taking a few moments to calm herself, she opened the door. Please let him be gone, she prayed.

Gayle stood alone, waiting for her. Her eyes were sympathetic. "Don't worry, I waved my magic wand and transported him back to his office."

"Is the stain terribly obvious?" she asked Gayle, fussing with her jacket. "What a great first impression I'm going to make on the CEO."

Gayle's expression instantly changed from empathy to intrigue. "I'd say you made a fine first impression," she said with a sly grin.

"I did?" she asked, seconds before realization swept over her. "Wait, Jay's the CEO I'm meeting with?"

Gayle nodded. "You didn't know that? You called him by name when he was trying to look at your mouth."

"We met a few weeks ago at a dance club." She probably shouldn't have told his employee that.

Gayle lifted a single eyebrow. "A dance club, huh?"

"He said he was in management consulting, but he didn't say where he worked. And he certainly didn't mention he was a CEO."

"I'm not surprised. He gets enough attention at his speaking engagements, so he likes to keep a low profile here in town."

"What kind of speaking engagements?"

"You don't seem to know very much about him. Didn't you do any research for your meeting?"

Kricket shook her head, wishing Gayle would wave her wand and make her invisible too. "My boss just called me this morning to fill in at the last minute."

Gayle raised her eyebrows as she handed Kricket her iPad and a visitor's badge. "This day is just getting better and better."

Actually, this day was getting worse and worse.

After swiping their badges at the door, Gayle led her down a brightly lit hallway with all-glass offices on one side like colorful aquariums lined up in a pet store. On each door was a small dry-erase board with the employee's first name. Apparently they decorated their own, because some had smiley faces, while others had elaborate drawings on them. It reminded her of an adult kindergarten room. Employees wearing jeans and H-Tech polos or T-shirts glanced up from their computer screens and smiled as they walked by. In her black suit, she felt like she'd shown up at a picnic dressed for a funeral.

At the end of the hallway, Gayle led her into a non-glass corner office with 'Jay' written on the dry erase board. Below his name was a sword wielding masked ninja.

"Gayle, knock please?" Jay said, frowning as he walked out of a private bathroom in the corner of his office, buttoning a black striped shirt he'd changed into. Even in her current state, Kricket's mind flashed to something completely non-work related as she watched him button the last few buttons.

"Have a seat." He held out a sleek yellow chair at a triangular conference table, then sat across from her. "I'm sorry about the spill...and your lip. I had no idea you would turn around so quickly." His sheepish smile was unexpected. "It's good to see you again."

She crossed her arms, resting one hand over the wet blouse clinging to her cleavage. "You too," she said, avoiding his eyes.

"So you work for Pinnacle. Cecil McKnight is a good friend of my father." His brows furrowed. "He said they were sending someone from Dallas."

She explained her workshop designer role at Pinnacle and the last minute phone call to fill in for Brock, tastefully leaving out the part that he was her ex, who apparently was trying to set her up.

Jay's jaw tightened as her story progressed.

"Would you mind waiting at Gayle's desk for a moment? I need to make a phone call, but I want to talk to you afterwards."

He led her to the door and shut it behind her. Kricket sat quietly across from Gayle, avoiding her gaze. Who was he calling in the middle of their meeting? What did he want to talk about after the call? Please, please, please don't bring up that night.

Jay's door opened abruptly. "Mr. McKnight isn't available. Kricket, who's your V.P. of Client Education?"

She closed her eyes and choked out the name. "Brock Strickland." She couldn't say his name without the image of Brock and Sutton naked on the couch flashing in her mind. And why was Jay calling senior management?

He must have seen the terror in her face. "This is not about you," he said, before shutting the door.

Gayle raised her eyebrows questioningly. "What's not about you?"

Kricket's explanation to Gayle was interrupted by Jay's voice booming through the door. "Mr. Strickland, we are in a critical time crunch and you send me a last minute replacement who is completely unprepared, and knows nothing about my company or the assignment?"

Kricket needed to vomit. How could he do this to her without even giving her a chance?

"Don't blame this on Ms. Taylor. For a 9:00 a.m. meeting, you should have taken a flight last night, not this morning. I've traveled to over 150 speaking engagements all over the country and guess how many times I took a flight that arrived right before an engagement? None. I would never risk the reputation of my company to save a few dollars on a hotel."

Jay was silent, so Kricket presumed Brock was still trying to throw her under the bus. "I'm not interested in excuses. The other

Pinnacle departments working on the D-A-S-H project did a phenomenal job. Your department is the only one that can't seem to execute."

Kricket would have thoroughly enjoyed listening to Brock being lambasted if her job security wasn't smack in the middle of it.

"As of this moment, you are off my project. I'll be meeting with Mr. McKnight early next week to discuss how we'll move forward."

After several minutes, Jay opened his office door. His expression was soft again. He invited her back in and they sat at his conference table. She picked at a fingernail while he explained his situation with D-A-S-H and the type of training modules he wanted built. He reiterated not to take it personally, but it was obvious that Pinnacle's Client Education group was not going to be able to deliver what he needed.

When he finished, she forced herself to look him in the eye. "I'm in the Human Resources department. Employee development is what we do. You could at least let me show you my stuff."

"Well then, show me your *stuff*." His eyes twinkled, causing her face to grow hot. Why did things always come out of her mouth wrong?

He brewed two cups of coffee in his Keurig while she fired up her iPad and sifted through her latest course designs. When he brought two steaming mugs back to the table, his ninja coffee mug caught her eye.

She quickly opened a different course and turned the iPad towards him, watching his eyes grow wide as he read the title.

"How to be an office ninja is the title of your workshop?" That's wild!"

She nodded, secretly thanking the hot guy at Starbucks in the black Jeep named 'Ninja' for not only triggering her hormones, but for triggering the theme idea. He looked at his coffee mug and she could tell he was biting down a smile.

"What?"

"Nothing," he said, moving to the chair next to her so he could see the screen better. "Show me the rest."

He paced and sat and paced and sat as she described the activities, video clips, and team competitions included in each workshop. He loved the Appropriate/Inappropriate game where she showed video clips of employees in sticky situations and asked participants to discuss the employee's reactions. The ideas he shot out fueled her enthusiasm and before they knew it, the morning was gone.

"Let's demo this one this afternoon. I'll have Gayle gather a small group of my staff."

Stress churned in her stomach. She stared at him, willing herself not to run out the door.

"What's wrong?"

"I've never conducted one before. I'm a course designer…hardly facilitator material."

"But haven't you always wanted to? Even if the thought of it scares you senseless?"

She shrugged. Brock had laughed when she mentioned her dream was to be confident enough to actually present the workshops she designed.

"You don't have to do it, but I know you can. I can tell you're passionate about your content, and that's what matters. My staff has no expectations, other than getting out of work for an hour, so it's a low-stress environment." He put a hand on her shoulder. "Everyone has to start somewhere."

The thought of embarrassing herself in front of him made her want to run out the door, but his eyes were so encouraging, he made her want to try. She took a deep breath and nodded.

"Yes!" He jumped out of his chair and punched the air. His excitement made her laugh. "We're going to have to do something about that suit though so my staff doesn't think you're an auditor or something."

"I have other clothes in my car." Thankfully she'd brought her skinny black jeans and boots to change into tonight for Happy Hour with Becca and Kevin.

"Great, I'll give you a tour as I show you the way back to the lobby. We have three separate companies housed in this building," he said, leading her down the hallway. "Dad is the CEO of H-Tech, the alarm company he started. He has staff here and in Tulsa. The second floor houses H-Vault, my brother's data security company. Hence the security cameras covering every centimeter of the building." He pointed at the cameras in the ceiling. "H-Strategy, my management information systems company, is on this floor. We have a few consultants and sales reps, but most of my staff is dedicated to the D-A-S-H software. And that's where you fit in."

Where she fit in. She liked the sound of that. "What does D-A-S-H mean?" she asked, struggling to keep up with his long stride.

"It's an acronym for Define, Assess, Strategize, and Humanize. It's the business model our dad taught us. The D is 'define your goals,' A is 'Assess your progress,' S is 'Strategize any changes needed,' and H is for 'Humanity.' The most important aspect of any business is the people...the staff and the customers. D-A-S-H is my most requested conference speech, so I had our developers create a software program to capitalize on its popularity. It's taken off like wildfire." She could see the excitement in his eyes. "You and I have a similar eye for presentations. People love to hear real stories. It helps them relate to the concepts." He flashed her a grin. "We're going to make a great team."

When they reached the main entrance, he continued talking while he followed her outside. Although he'd been fairly talkative at the club, he chattered non-stop now. Obviously he was passionate about his work.

"Nice lift and wheels," he said, when they reached her Jeep. "When did you add those?"

"Last week. I have a long list of things I want to do to her."

He opened his mouth, but then swallowed what was most likely an inappropriate response.

She opened the back of her Jeep and rifled through her duffle bag. "Perfect. I have boots and leggings, but I was in such a hurry this morning, I forgot to pack a shirt."

"What's this?" he asked, holding up a plastic bag.

"There's no telling. My grandpa and his wife, Dot, brought it back from a trip." She opened the bag and pulled out a long sleeve T-shirt that said 'Am I Hot or What?' on the front, and 'Man, that's Cold' on the back.

"It's perfect," he said, bursting into laughter.

"There's no way I'm wearing that in public, much less in front of your staff."

His eyes danced excitedly. "Oh come on. We can work it in to the Appropriate/Inappropriate activity." He eyed her gym bag. "Do you have a workout jacket in there? If not, we can use the blazer you have on."

She nodded, unsure where this was headed, but caught up in his enthusiasm.

"Here's my idea. You can zip up the jacket and every time the video clip is deemed *Inappropriate*, you turn around and flash your T-shirt. Get it? *Man, That's Cold!* It's perfect!"

She gaped at him. "I'll be lucky if I can even talk in front of them. I'm definitely not going to be a flasher in front of them."

His face fell. "You're right. I suppose that's a little over the top for you. I'd do it in one of my speeches though. I get a kick out of shocking my audience to drive a point home."

After she changed clothes in the lobby restroom, he led her down the hallway into a large room filled with colorful sling chairs, low couches, and large throw pillows. "We call this *The Pit*. We use it for brainstorming sessions, meetings, and training classes. This is where we'll do the demo this afternoon."

She surveyed the room in awe. Even though it seemed more like being in someone's living room than in a classroom, it did nothing to calm her nerves. Nothing could overcome the dread of standing in front of a group of people trying not to puke.

"We have four projectors, so presentations can be shown on each wall." He turned to her with a wicked grin. "I have an idea. I want you to meet Brandon, the creative designer of the D-A-S-H software," he said, leading her down the hallway to a group of offices. "He can do miracles with video."

After introducing her to Brandon, Jay explained his idea of replacing Kricket's standard Appropriate/Inappropriate activity video clips with clips of their own staff from the security cameras.

He glanced at his watch. "I have a conference call in ten minutes. Hopefully you two can find some *appropriate* examples. The *inappropriate* ones will be easy. And you know exactly who I'm talking about, right Brandon?" Brandon smiled knowingly.

"Let's meet back at The Pit in two hours to practice."

Brandon was one of those guys who never stopped talking, so she immediately felt comfortable with him. He and Jay had been buddies since college, so as they searched through video clips, he regaled her with stories that Jay would probably prefer not be repeated. After selecting a few clips, Brandon said he would piece them together while she grabbed some lunch. When she confided to him how nervous she was, he promised to sit on the front row and be her 'friendly face' to focus on during the presentation.

The way her stomach felt, eating wasn't an option, so she spent the next hour working herself into a frenzy by analyzing all the things that could go wrong during her baptism by fire. Accidentally belching, puking, farting, or fainting beat out 'forgetting what to say' by a landslide.

And apparently, she had no hidden magic power to stop time from moving forward, although it wasn't due to a lack of trying. As people began filing into the room, she focused on controlling her breathing. Jay was doing most of the presentation. All she had to do was explain the activities, but her heart was beating so hard, she didn't think she'd be able to get a single word out. Her stomach was churning too. Please don't let me have to make a mad dash to the bathroom in the middle of the workshop. She wiped her sweaty hands on her pants, hoping the moisture didn't show. That's all she needed. Sweat marks on her pants *and* gas. She stole a quick glance around the room. They didn't look all that scary, so why did her face feel so pale?

She hoped once Jay got started, she'd calm down, but as her part grew closer, nausea threatened to overtake her. When Jay introduced her as Agent Apocalypse, her breath caught, but when she looked at his encouraging face, she was able to spit out the first sentence. Her voice wavered, but after a moment, her breathing steadied and she was able to lead them through the activity. Jay's humor and teasing helped ease her nerves. His staff seemed to enjoy their banter and eagerly joined in the activities.

Nearly half an hour had flown by when Jay announced the Appropriate/Inappropriate game. Brandon grinned as Kricket explained how the activity worked. She would show video snippets of real staff interactions and they would vote on whether it had been handled appropriately or inappropriately, then discuss how it could be better handled.

The staff burst into laughter as they watched clips of their co-workers caught in funny situations. Some had acted appropriately and some had not. They roared at a montage of Gayle's sarcastic responses to Jay, including her 'Look what you did, you big moose,' response when Jay crashed into Kricket that morning. Of course they voted all of those *inappropriate*.

Kricket laughed at the surprise on Jay's face when she showed a montage of one word clips of him snapping at Gayle. Brandon interjected they'd had difficulty finding any that didn't include profanity.

She thought the clips were over, but apparently Brandon had secretly added a repetitive clip from her morning coffee debacle. 'I'm so sorry, Kricket.' 'Stop it!' 'I'm so sorry, Kricket.' 'Stop it! Stop it! Stop it! Stop it!' Brandon strategically spliced it to emphasize the apologetic look on Jay's face and the angry one on hers. She gaped at Jay.

"I dare you," he mouthed. She hesitated for a moment, then turned around and slid her jacket down to her waist to reveal 'Man, That's Cold' on the back of her T-shirt. His team whooped and applauded as they ended the demo on that note.

"You did it," Jay said, with a huge grin on his face. "I knew you could."

"I know I didn't have a very big part, but just standing in front of a group is something I never thought I'd be able to do. Thank you for that." She could tell from his smile that he knew it was a big deal for her.

Her adrenaline had her chatting wildly as they walked down the hallway and into his office, but when he closed the door, she became suddenly silent. Up to that point, her focus had been on surviving the presentation. But now, she felt very alone with him. And very awkward.

He motioned for her to sit. "It's hard to get any privacy in this place," he said, pointing at a camera in the corner of his office.

Normally that statement might be thrilling, but right now, privacy with him was the last thing she wanted. She could sense this wasn't going to be business-related. The pain of enduring an explanation of why he never contacted her after their romantic evening ranked right up there with having her private parts waxed. Rrrrip!

After punching some buttons on his keyboard, he sat across from her at the table. "I want to talk to you about…that night," he began softly. "This morning, when I glanced at my video monitor and saw you standing in the lobby, I was—" He paused and rubbed the whiskers on his chin.

"You didn't expect to have to see me again. I get it." Her face grew hot and she looked down to conceal her expression. Why couldn't they just pretend it didn't happen?

"It's nothing personal. I just don't do the dating thing."

She glanced sideways at him. "Why not?"

He shrugged. "I travel a lot. It's just easier that way."

"So you just stalk then?"

"Yeah, I just stalk." His relieved grin told her he wasn't enjoying this conversation either. "So we're good then?"

"Yeah. We're good," she said, even though they were anything but good.

A crackling noise caused them both to turn and look at the phone on his desk.

"Now that y'all are good, why don't you stalk on out here so we can go to Happy Hour," Gayle's voice said over the phone intercom. "I'm sure Ms. Taylor could use a beer."

He closed his eyes for a moment and rubbed his whiskers again. "If Gayle wasn't so good at taking care of me, I would have poisoned her coffee a long time ago."

Kricket laughed, even though she secretly hoped the earth would open up and swallow her whole so she didn't have to watch him backpedal out of dragging her along to Happy Hour.

"You'll come won't you? You've already met some of the people who will be there. It'll be fun."

Even though his eyes looked eager, she shook her head. "I'm supposed to meet my friend Becca and her husband."

"Do you have to?"

She shrugged. "I guess not. They'll go with or without me."

He stood and held out a hand. "Please come with us?"

Against her better judgment, she nodded and placed her hand in his.

CHAPTER 10

KRICKET, GAYLE, AND BRANDON followed Jay down the back hallway to the parking garage where he and the managers parked. Jay was driving them since there was very little parking at the Pub. Pallets and boxes of alarm equipment were stacked to the ceiling of the garage. When they rounded a corner, Kricket stopped and took a deep breath. There it sat...Mud Ninja.

"Whose Jeep is that?" The wicked grin on Jay's face answered her question. She pointed her finger at him. "You almost hit me!"

"I was trying to be nice and buy you a coffee. And *you* need to learn how to do a proper Jeep wave."

She cringed. She'd forgotten about her *spontaneous* act of flipping him the bird. She hadn't even given herself credit for that in her journal.

She walked around Mud Ninja, admiring all the customizations. "Did you build it yourself?"

"Yep."

"Can we ride in it?"

He grinned proudly. "Sure."

"I am not riding in that contraption," Gayle said, with her hands on her hips.

"So you're walking then?" Jay asked wryly.

There was a short stare-down before Gayle moved to the passenger door. "Fine then. Brandon, give me a boost."

Brandon held both hands in the air. "I am not touching your butt, Gayle."

Jay shoved a box under the door with his foot. "There you go, your highness. Step on that."

"So, what's this business about a Jeep wave?" Gayle asked as they pulled out of the garage.

"When Jeepers see each other on the road, they wave," Kricket explained.

Jay smirked at Kricket. "But not usually with your middle finger."

"I'm sure you deserved it," Gayle said. "So what did you do to cause her to flip you off? And what's this I hear about Jay being at a dance club?"

Jay cocked his head at Kricket, then glared at Gayle. "I think our next course demonstration will be titled *The Mechanics of Minding your own Business.*"

"Gayle, how long have you worked at H-Tech?" Kricket asked in an effort to sway the conversation away from their Club 100 rendezvous.

Gayle's scowl morphed into a proud grin. "Eight years now. I practically raised Jay from a pup." She really didn't look that much older than Jay.

"I handle everything from his conference details to making sure he has groceries in his house, to managing his rental properties. That's practically a full-time job right there. That's how I met him. He came to collect my rent one day, and I told him I lost my job. He hired me on the spot and we've been together ever since." She reached forward and rustled his hair like he was a kid. "Even though he makes me want to whip out a can of Gayle on him half the time, he's a good egg."

He tried to look annoyed as he batted Gayle's hand away, but she caught a hint of a blush. They obviously thought the world of each other, even though they bickered like siblings.

Jay found a parking spot about a block from the pub. The walk was chilly and he fought the urge to pull Kricket close to him to keep her warm. He led the way to their usual spot upstairs, where his team had already pulled two tables together near the dartboards. In an effort to make her feel more comfortable, he quickly engaged Kricket in a game of darts. Focusing on the target and not on Kricket's butt proved challenging as she aimed and sailed a dart into the center of the bull's-eye. He wasn't the only one admiring her butt, and that bothered him more than he cared to admit. After she beat him by an embarrassing landslide, Brandon challenged her to a game, so Jay joined the group at the tables and ordered a beer for himself and a flirtini for her, chiding himself for remembering her drink of choice.

Brandon purposely flirted with her. Jay hadn't mentioned her, but Brandon could always tell when Jay was interested in someone and enjoyed trying to beat him to the punch. One of Kricket's throws completely missed the dartboard, causing her to laugh and turn red. Her infectious laugh made him want to pick her up and twirl her around, like guys always seem to do in chick flicks.

How was he going to get through this project without losing his mind...or his self-control? He would be better off just telling Mr. McKnight the deal was off, but her fresh ideas were exactly what he was looking for. Which reminded him, he hadn't responded to Mr. McKnight's email asking how the demo went. He pulled up the email on his phone and typed, 'See for yourself,' then attached a link to the workshop recording Brandon had uploaded.

A message popped up from the H-Tech security system. Mitch's security controls were annoying, but if he ignored the message, the security desk would just call him. It was an override request for a visitor sign-out breach. He'd forgotten to have

Kricket return her visitor badge before they left. Holy shit, call the National Guard. We have a major security breach.

He opened the link to view and clear the entry. 'Kristen Taylor.' It hadn't occurred to him that Kricket was a nickname. Out of curiosity, he clicked on the link to the driver's license image to see how old she was. And how much she weighed, he thought with a laugh.

The photo slapped him in the face. She was younger, with blonde hair. And she looked like...no, it couldn't be. He glanced at the name. Kristen Kelsey Taylor. Krissy's middle name was Kelsey, but her last name was Beckett. His eyes froze on the birth date. July fifth. He dropped his phone on the table and stared at it. He'd always told Krissy the fireworks show was her birthday gift. His heart drummed in his chest as realization washed through him. She's Krissy. *His* Krissy.

A million thoughts raced through his mind as he charged down the stairs. He slid onto an empty barstool and leaned on the bar with his head in his hands. His head was swimming. How did she not know who he was? The memory of kissing her surged into his mind. He squeezed his eyes shut. Thank God he hadn't taken her to bed.

"Here, you look like you need this." The bartender with a nose ring slid a shot glass in front of him.

"Thanks." He lifted the glass and threw it in his mouth.

A hand on his shoulder made him jump. "What's gotten into you?" Gayle asked from behind him. "You ran off like your pants were on fire."

"I just needed a minute."

"Don't tell me you're down here pouting because Brandon's flirting with your girl."

He stared at his empty shot glass.

"C'mon, tell Gayle what's wrong."

He picked up his phone and showed Gayle the driver's license image. "Kricket. Her real name is Kristen Kelsey. It's her. It's my Krissy."

Gayle's eyes grew wide as she took the phone from his hand. "Krissy? You found Krissy?" She crossed herself. "Lord have mercy, you slept with Krissy."

"I did not sleep with her, thank God."

"How did she not know who you were? Doesn't she know your last name?"

"I have no idea."

"Do you think maybe she was too young to remember?"

"I can only hope." He had no idea what they'd told her about why she was taken away. If she knew the truth, she'd hate him for it.

They quickly formulated an exit strategy, then headed upstairs to rejoin the group. He would make up a reason to leave so he could tell her in private. Kricket and Brandon were still playing darts, so he sat at the table and sipped his beer. It was all he could do not to sweep her up and hold her, but the last thing he wanted was to cause a big scene. His staff was well aware of the Krissy story. The part of it that could be told, anyway. Using the story of their childhood motorcycle accident in one of his speeches had catapulted his speaking career. He was known in the conference world as the *Squirrel Promise* guy.

Kricket occasionally looked his way and smiled. He searched for something familiar. Maybe her eyes…definitely her shy mannerisms. Now that he knew who she was, he could see it, but he never would have been able to pick her out of a crowd.

Kricket and Brandon walked back to the table laughing. She took the empty seat next to Jay, while Brandon slid in beside Gayle. His mouth suddenly felt dry. He couldn't sit there long without telling her. How was he going to get her out of the pub without setting off alarm bells in her head? And then how would he tell her? He tried to focus on the table conversation, but his mind was reeling.

Brandon's poke in the arm startled him. "Dude, get your head out of the clouds and pass those sweet potato fries over here. Did you even hear me? I said, do you want to take Mud Ninja to the river with me tomorrow? I'm getting a new dirt bike."

Jay stiffened. He glanced at Kricket, who was frowning.

"What's wrong?" Brandon asked her.

She shrugged. "I was in a motorcycle accident once."

Shit. Shit. Shit. Of all subjects, why did he have to bring up motorcycles? The shut-the-hell-up look he shot Brandon did no good whatsoever.

Brandon furrowed his brow at him, then turned back to Kricket. "What happened?"

Gayle shoved a plate of pita chips and artichoke dip towards Kricket. "I'm sure you don't want to talk about it, do you, hon? Here, have some of this dip before I eat it all and make myself sick."

"I'll gladly tell the story if it keeps Brandon from getting a motorcycle."

Jay's heart beat wildly. Do not do this. Not now. His mind grappled for a way to stop her, short of throwing her over his shoulder and fleeing.

Kricket selected a chip from the basket and toyed with the dip. "My neighbors had some land just outside of town. They always took me along on their Sunday family outings." Her cheeks flushed for a moment when she realized everyone at the table had stopped to listen, but she continued. "Late one afternoon, I wandered off picking flowers. It was almost dark when one of the boys finally found me. We were quite a ways from the others, so he gave me a ride back on his motorcycle, even though I wasn't supposed to ride on it. When a squirrel ran out in front of us, I screamed. He swerved to miss it and we ran through a barbed-wire fence." She rolled up her sleeve to show her scar. "It ripped the skin down both of our arms and left us with really awful scars."

Silence surrounded the table, as mouths fell open.

"I'll bet you hate him for that," Jay said softly.

"Of course not. It wasn't his fault." Her face softened into a delicate smile. "He was my hero."

"Some hero," he said. His quick glance around the table warned everyone to remain silent.

She stared into space, as if reliving it in her mind, oblivious to the silence at the table broken only by Gayle's sniffling. "We were lying on the ground with our arms split open. Blood was everywhere." She shook her head at the sight she was apparently visualizing. "He crawled to me even though his arm was hurt as badly as mine. He held me while we waited for help to come."

In the hundred times he'd told the story, he'd never considered how it would feel to listen to her tell it. He unbuttoned his cuff and began rolling up his shirt sleeve.

"He'll always be a part of me. While we huddled there waiting, he touched his torn arm to mine," she said, holding up her arm to demonstrate. "And you know what he said?"

Jay turned towards her and pressed his bare scarred armed against hers, reciting with her, "We're bound by blood. I promise I'll never let anything hurt you again."

She froze, her face ashen. She jerked her arm to her chest and stared at him wild-eyed. He watched the kaleidoscope spin in her head, waiting to see which emotion would stick when realization hit. She looked up at him with blank eyes and fled.

"Krissy, wait!" Fuck.

❧

Kricket raced blindly across the parking lot, disoriented by the patches of light flashing in the darkness. Her ears thudded like race horses, running faster and faster. Was that her heartbeat or was it footsteps behind her? Her chest grew tighter and tighter with every step. Is this what a heart attack felt like? She was going to die at the age of twenty-six. She was breathing too fast. She had to stop running, she was breathing too fast. She needed to sit down, or lie down, but she couldn't stop running. Her heart was going to explode all over the street. She heard a car horn. Someone yelled her name. There were lights everywhere. The lights were so bright. She turned away from them and someone tackled her, sending her tumbling to the ground. Pain seared through her elbow as it scraped across pavement. She tasted blood and grass in her mouth. Why was there grass in her mouth? There were hands in her hair and on her face. She shook her head to get them off. She had to get up. She needed air. She was going to die if she didn't have air.

"I can't breathe, let me go, I can't breathe," she coughed. When her arms were freed, she rolled away, gasping for air. She pulled her knees against her chest and buried her head in her crossed arms. Breathe, breathe, breathe.

"Krissy, please, baby…" The whisper was so close, she could feel his breath. "Krissy, it's me, Jayson."

Did he say Krissy? She felt a familiar jagged indentation as he took her hand and rubbed it down the length of his arm. As her brain reconnected, her breathing slowed.

When she peered at him, he rested his forehead against hers, just like he did when she was little. Warmth spread through her heart and slowed its beat. "Jayson," she whispered, melting forward into his arms.

He gathered her in his lap and rocked her as sobs overtook her body. "Shhh. It's okay. I'm here now," he whispered in her ear.

She cried a thousand tears for every year since he'd abandoned her. They shivered in the cold as he cried with her. She gulped away a sob and looked at him. "My letters…," she choked out. "Why didn't you answer my letters?" She wiped her nose on her sleeve. "You forgot about me."

In the glow of the street light, she watched his face twist into a pained stare. He gathered her cheeks in his hands. "I never got any letters." He pressed his forehead to hers and shook his head. "I never forgot you, not even for a second."

CHAPTER 11

"HOP UP HERE AND let's fix that elbow." Jay lifted her onto his bathroom vanity, then rested a hand on her knee while he rifled through his medicine cabinet. She seemed unreal, as if she might disappear into thin air if he didn't keep a hand on her. That's why he'd insisted she ride home with him. There was no way he was letting her out of his sight. Not now. Not after finding her.

She winced when he dabbed ointment on her scrape. "Sorry I had to tackle you," he said, blowing on the scrape to stop the burning.

"Sorry I freaked out."

Covering the scrape with a bandage triggered a memory. *He was in his parents' bathroom, comforting Krissy while his mom tended to her wound. Krissy's sutures had become infected because her worthless mother hadn't changed the bandages regularly. Karen had taken one look at Krissy's seeping bandage and carried her into the bathroom to doctor it. He'd kept Krissy calm by pressing his forehead to hers.* He closed his eyes as years of guilt flooded him.

"Jay? Jay, are you okay?"

He captured her face in his palms. "There are no words to describe how sorry I am."

"You had no idea I would freak out like that."

He trailed a finger down her scarred arm. "I mean for this."

"Jay, don't." Tears pooled in her eyes. "It was an accident. And it was a long time ago."

"I scarred you for life."

"Please don't." She pressed a finger against his lips. "You're scarred too."

"I used to look at mine and wonder if you were looking at yours." He swallowed hard. "And hating me for it."

"I never hated you. I hated the scar, but never you."

He tugged a tissue from its holder and dabbed her eyes. "Will you forgive me?"

"There's nothing to forgive." She held up her arm and he pressed his scar against hers.

With foreheads and scars pressed together, they let the bond wash away the heartache they had each endured for seventeen years. Their breathing slowed in unison as the healing connection they both needed enveloped them. All the words they'd longed to say to each other flowed unspoken between them.

He had no idea how much time had passed as their souls reconnected. He broke their silence with a hoarse whisper, "My Krissy."

"My hero," she whispered in return.

He reluctantly pulled his forehead away and smiled at her. "Some hero I am. So far today, I've poured coffee on you, busted your lip, and tackled you." He squeezed a bit of ointment on his finger and lifted her chin. "Stick out your bottom lip. Let's see how it looks now."

She laughed, then parted her lips and he dabbed at it. As her eyes peered up at his, the memory of kissing those lips were challenged to a duel by the memory of kissing Krissy the toddler on the forehead. It was a battle he knew his mind had only begun to fight.

"I put your gym bag on the bed. I'll open a bottle of wine while you change," he said, lifting her off the counter. "I want to know everything about you."

❦

They surveyed each other from opposite ends of his yellow leather couch. His long legs stretched out next to hers were like a furnace, making her warm inside and out. After two glasses of wine, she was thoroughly enjoying an excuse to openly ogle his gorgeousness. Was that wrong? It felt wrong. No doubt he'd been a hottie at sixteen, but she'd seen him through the eyes of a child. He looked very different through the eyes of a woman. *Stop it.*

"Your eyes are the same, but I don't think you had whiskers at sixteen." She didn't think he had two fully loaded guns on his arms at sixteen either, but they were gloriously busting out of his T-shirt now. She decided not to mention that observation.

"I should have recognized your eyes, but your hair threw me off because it's red. And it's so long."

"It's not red, it's auburn," she huffed. "I remember you being tall, but I can't believe your legs are so long."

He ran his hand across her calf below her cropped running pants. A glint of mischief crossed his face. "I can't believe your legs are so *hairy.*"

She jerked her legs underneath her and threw a pillow at him, nearly knocking his wine glass out of his hand. "It's *winter.* I skipped two, maybe three days." She knew her face was scarlet.

"Easy, killer," he said, setting his wine glass on the table behind the couch. His mouth twisted wryly. "You obviously didn't have plans to go home with a stalker tonight."

She gaped at him and felt the blood rush out of her face.

"That was a joke, Kric." His face grew serious and he studied her for a moment. "But we do need to talk about that."

"Talk about what?" She picked up a gray throw pillow and ran her fingers along the short stubby fringe. Great, he's going to lecture her about being a slut.

"We need to talk about that night. About the kiss."

Her eyes shot directly to his lips when he said the word *kiss*.
She quickly looked away, hoping he hadn't noticed. Up to that
point, she'd felt completely comfortable. Now she needed to barf.
"Can't we just pretend it didn't happen?"

"Can we?"

She considered it for a moment while she studied a picture
on the wall to avoid eye contact. "I guess not."

"That kiss was..." He paused for what seemed like an hour-
long minute.

Hot? Twisted? Unforgettable? She stole a peek at him while
adjectives swirled through her mind. His eyes were closed and his
forehead was wrinkled. Was he re-living it in his mind like she had
been for weeks?

"Unfortunate," he finished.

That word hadn't crossed her mind, but was certainly better
than twisted.

"I think subconsciously we recognized each other. That's
why I felt so...so tender towards you. We mistook it for attraction.
I'm just glad we didn't—" He took a deep breath and blew it out.
"Let's just say this conversation could have been a lot more
awkward." He paused for a moment and she knew he was waiting
for her to look at him, but she couldn't. "How does it make you
feel?" he asked with a tender voice.

How does it make her feel? Experiencing the most
meaningful kiss of her life from the most gorgeous man she'd ever
met, who just happened to be her long lost hero? She could imagine
the look on his face if she told him how it really made her feel.

She plucked a word out of the air. "Creepy?"

He chuckled. "Yeah, creepy pretty much sums it up,
sasquatch."

"Enough about my legs, already!" She hurled herself at him
and pounded on his chest. He counted out loud, one centipede, two

centipede…then pinned her in five seconds flat. She burst into giggles. "No fair, you used to count to ten so I could get in a few good punches first."

"Well, your punches are a little more solid now," he said, holding her arms against her sides with his forearms. "And you're not a little girl anymore."

The amused look swept from his face. It was so quiet she could hear him swallow as he studied her intently, his familiar eyes now darkened into the seductive eyes she'd seen the night he'd kissed her. Her heart thundered as she reluctantly held his gaze. He reached up and tenderly tucked a lock of hair behind her ear, then trailed his fingers down her jawline.

Her breath caught and his eyes flickered back to the familiar eyes of Jayson. With an abrupt kiss on her forehead, he was off the couch and on his feet in one swift move. "I'll open some more wine."

Okay, she took it back. The only thing creepy about that was his ninja move off the couch. He popped his neck in both directions on his way into the kitchen. When he reached up to get wine from the rack over the refrigerator, her eyes zeroed in on the flash of skin above his low slung sweatpants. How did someone make a T-shirt and ratty pair of sweatpants look so sexy? She was pretty sure she was not mistaking anything for attraction. She sat up and pulled a throw over her legs.

His eyes danced as he returned with a fresh bottle of wine and topped off her glass. "Let's talk about the good stuff now, little miss high school cheerleader." He lowered himself onto the couch and pulled her feet onto his lap, making a grand gesture of tucking the sides of the throw around her hairy legs. "Tell me about the first time you got drunk."

CHAPTER 12

WRAPPED AROUND KRICKET'S SLEEPING body, Jay willed the sun not to peek its unwelcome light through the window and end his bliss. He wasn't sure how late they'd talked before drifting off on the couch. At some point during the night, they'd wound up clutching each other in their sleep, and he would continue to hold her until she awakened. Hopefully that wouldn't be soon, because never again would he have an excuse to hold her like this. He shifted his hips away from her so *Little Jay*, who was fully aware of the beautiful woman snuggled against him, wouldn't bust his big brother persona.

Quietly stroking her unruly hair so as not to wake her, he pondered the countless times he'd done that when she was a child. Tara would drop her off in her little footie pajamas to stay with them while she went clubbing. Krissy always tried to stay up late with him, but rarely made it past the first fifteen minutes of a movie before her little head would fall slack on his shoulder.

Her lips parted in a small breath and she burrowed her head deeper into his shoulder. The desperate physical longing to press his heart against hers was overwhelming. He'd forgotten that feeling, or had pushed it from his mind. Until the night he'd danced with her.

He gently pulled her closer, burying his nose in her hair as waves of warmth filled his heart, smothering the hollowness he'd grown accustomed to. He could hold her like this forever, and never let her go. But he had made a blood promise to never let anything hurt her. A promise he'd failed miserably at. And now his resolve to keep that promise was even stronger. Because now he had to protect her from the one thing that could hurt her the most. Himself. "I love you, baby," he whispered, knowing he could never hold her like this again.

∽

Kricket pulled the blanket off her head and scrunched up her face at the frothy green concoction Jay had whipped up in his turbo-charged blender that not only had awakened *her*, but probably everyone within a two-mile radius. "I'm not drinking anything that's the color of my Jeep."

"Just try a sip. It tastes better than it looks." He sat on the edge of the ottoman. "Drink up. Then I'm going to show you what a real Jeep can do," he said with a wink.

She'd drink anything if it meant spending more time with him. She took a small sip, then pretended to gag. His eyes widened, then he laughed when he realized she was faking. "Okay, it's really not that bad," she said, giggling as she took a bigger sip. "Wait, a real Jeep? So what are you saying?"

"You haven't been off the pavement in your Jeep, have you?"

She huffed at him. "I've only had her a few weeks."

"Pavement Princess." He grabbed her blanket, and swatted her with it. "Get up. We'll stop by your apartment to get some old clothes." He wiggled his eyebrows at her. "We're going wheeling and we're gonna get muddy."

She stood up and stretched. "I remember watching you and Mitch when I was little. Karen never let me ride in your Jeep when you did anything fun like that."

"I can't wait until she sees you," he said with a wide grin. "She and Dad will be in town tomorrow for family day at Mitch and Meg's. We'll surprise them."

The thought of being in Karen's arms again was more than

she could wrap her mind around. "I can't wait either. Hey, Grandpa and Dot live nearby. Can we stop by for a minute on the way to my apartment? Grandpa won't believe I found you."

A shadow crossed his face as he turned away from her. He hesitated for a moment before answering. "Sure, we can do that."

❧

Dot met them at the door wearing bright red lipstick and a red sweater with a scarf tied around her neck. It was obvious she had spent the last ten minutes frantically primping after Kricket had texted them saying she was bringing someone over. "Well hello, young man," she said, blatantly appraising the full length of Jay. "My goodness, someone's been eating his Wheaties." Oh please, Dot. Do they even make Wheaties anymore?

Kricket hugged Dot. "Don't embarrass me," she whispered in her ear.

Their Golden Retriever, Biscuit, flew into the room and planted her front paws on Jay's chest.

"Biscuit, get down," Grandpa said, struggling to get out of his recliner.

"She's fine." Jay gave Biscuit's fur a good rubdown. "I used to have a dog like this. They can't get enough attention."

"Damn leg just won't work like it used to." Grandpa said, hobbling over to give Kricket a peck on the cheek.

"Grandpa, guess who this is." Kricket was so excited, she was about to burst.

He looked up at Jay and smiled. "Well whoever he is, he passed the Biscuit test."

"Remember the Hunters who lived next door to Mom and me in Tulsa? It's Jayson! Jayson Hunter." She linked her arm through Jay's. "I found him. Well, we found each other," she said, grinning up at him. It was all she could to do keep from jumping up and down like a child.

Grandpa's broad smile darkened into an unreadable emotion. A moment of chilled silence enveloped the room, cut only by the thumping of Biscuit's tail on the hardwood floor.

Dot glanced back and forth between Grandpa and Jay, then thrust her hand towards Jay. "How wonderful! It's so nice to meet you, Jayson. Isn't that wonderful, Dean?"

"My pleasure, Dot." Jay shook her hand, then turned to Grandpa. "It's been a long time, sir."

Grandpa shook his hand. "Yes it has."

"So you remember him, Grandpa?"

"Yes, I remember him." Grandpa glanced at Jay's Jeep in the driveway. "That's a pretty souped up Jeep you've got there, son. Let me grab my coat and we'll go have a look at it."

Why were they acting so weird? Surely Grandpa didn't hold the motorcycle accident against Jay.

Kricket started out the door with them and Grandpa stopped her. "You ladies stay inside where it's warm. Give your grandpa a little guy time."

The door had barely closed behind them, when Dot started in. "So how is he in the sack?"

She would never get used to the things that came out of Dot's mouth. "I wouldn't know," she said, watching them walk towards the Jeep.

"Well, from the looks of you, it's obvious you didn't sleep at home last night." She picked a tiny leaf out of Kricket's hair and held it up with a questioning look. "Must be an interesting story behind this."

"Okay, okay. I *did* spend the night at his house, but not like that. It's been seventeen years. We had a lot of catching up to do."

Dot glanced out the window at Jay. "Well as far as I can tell, he's got eyeballs and a package in his pants. And you're the prettiest thing this side of the Mason-Dixon Line, so it's a little hard for me to believe there wasn't a little hokey pokey going on."

Kricket just shook her head. Any response would just make it worse. They watched the men out the window while she told Dot the story, conveniently leaving out the part about the night at the dance club. Their families, and most especially Dot, didn't need to know about their romantic beginning.

❦

Dean was interested in the Jeep, but just as Jay expected, he was far more interested in talking to Jay alone. "It was silly of me to think that you and Kricket would never run into each other again. But I must say, it sure caught me off guard."

"Trust me, sir, you're not the only one. Thank you for not throwing me out of your house in front of her." He braced himself for Dean's reaction.

"I'll bet it felt like you were walking in the door to your own hanging, huh? I have to give you credit, you've got a pretty good poker face."

Jay blew out a breath. "Growing up with a high school counselor for a mother, I learned the skill quickly. Still comes in pretty handy."

"I imagine so." Dean opened the passenger door. "After I have my hip surgery, I'll be able to do this myself, but for now would you give me a boost, son?"

Jay helped him into the Jeep. As soon as Jay climbed in the driver's side, he looked Dean squarely in the eye and bit the bullet. "Mr. Taylor, there's no way I'm letting Krissy out of my life again. So I'd like to get everything out on the table and apologize for my role in what happened."

Dean shook his head. "It was a long time ago, son. The most important thing is, it all worked out for the best."

Jay loosened his death grip on the steering wheel and dropped his head back against the headrest to stare at the roof of the Jeep while considering his words. Apparently he needed to get it off his chest, because he found himself pouring out his heart to Dean. His outrage each time Tara yelled at Krissy. His anguish that he couldn't protect her better. The guilt that plagued him for the motorcycle accident. And the scar. And the Tara incident. Guilt overtook him as the memory flooded his mind. Just as it had a thousand times over the last seventeen years. "I shouldn't have been drinking that night. I could have stopped it before—"

"We never told her, son. Didn't see any reason to tell her something she obviously didn't remember or had somehow blocked from her mind."

If only he could block it from his own mind. When Dean's hand touched his shoulder, he looked up into a face full of compassion, not condemnation. "You're right, son. You shouldn't have been drinking while watching my granddaughter. But I won't question what happened that night. I wasn't blind where my daughter's concerned. Tara did a good job of playing the doting mother when we were around. She'd always been a little wild, but after she had Kricket we thought she might settle down. And she did until her asshole husband ran off, leaving her to raise a baby on her own."

Jay stared at the steering wheel for a moment, fighting the temptation to give Dean a play-by-play explanation of what happened. But it would do no one any good now. It was best just to let the truth lie dead with Tara.

"Kricket told me about Tara's car accident. I'm sorry for your loss, sir." And he was sorry for Dean's loss, but he wasn't at all sorry that Tara was dead.

Dean nodded a thank you.

"From what she told me, Kricket's father and stepmother weren't exactly model parents either."

Dean's eyes blazed, then he shook his head. "It took years before Kricket would even talk to us about it." He stared silently out the side window for a moment before continuing. "It was right in the middle of Ruth's chemo. We just couldn't take her in right then. The treatments made Ruth so weak, she was bedridden most of the time. I was trying to hold down my job and care for her too. We knew Kricket's father didn't want her, but—"

He pulled a handkerchief from his pocket and blew his nose. "The summer before Ruth passed, Kricket came to visit us. We knew immediately something was terribly wrong. She clung to Ruth. She would sit in the bed with her for hours, but rarely said a word. And if anyone raised a voice, she'd run and hide in her closet.

"On the Fourth of July, Ruth felt good enough to sit on the patio and watch the fireworks display in the park behind us." Dean smiled at the memory. "Kricket was mesmerized by the fireworks. It was the most animated we'd ever seen her. She asked Ruth if Tulsa was close enough that you could see them too. We told her you could see them. Just seemed like she needed to hear that."

"The Fourth of July has always been tough for me. I think of her every time I see fireworks."

"That night, as we sat watching the fireworks, she told us story after story about Jeep rides and swimming...all the things you did together. She always called you her hero. I never got to thank you for taking such good care of her."

Jay gave him an obligatory nod while maintaining his gaze out the front windshield. He didn't feel like a hero.

"After Kricket opened up, Ruth began probing about her father and stepmother. Kricket didn't say much, but enough that I called her father and told him she was staying with us for good, and if he had any problem with that, he would need to get an attorney. He didn't.

"After Tara's accident, Ruth made me promise her that Kricket would never have to live with her father. So after Ruth passed, I started the adoption process. Kricket's father eagerly signed the papers and he's been out of her life ever since."

"She told me it was Ruth who came up with the nickname Kricket."

Dean nodded. "I always said she was so quiet you could hear the crickets chirp, so Ruth got the idea to make a play on her name."

They sat in silence for a moment, lost in their own thoughts.

"Mr. Taylor, just so you know, when Kricket and I first found each other again, before we figured out who we were, there was…some attraction."

Dean smiled. "I'm not surprised. She grew up to be a beauty, didn't she? Certainly doesn't know it though."

His throat tightened and he cleared it before continuing. "I'm not going to have a romantic relationship with her. It would just end badly. And if I can manage to swallow my guilt, she doesn't ever need to know what happened that night. I can't bear to hurt her again."

"Guilt is a coffin you don't want to lie in, son. Trust me. I've harbored enough guilt for the both of us." Dean gave his shoulder a pat. "I don't want to see her hurt again either. But secrets rot away your soul." He started to open the door, then paused. "She's stronger than she seems. You'll figure out the right thing."

"Whatever it takes to keep from hurting her, that's what I'll do. She's very important to me sir."

"Me too, son."

CHAPTER 13

WHEN KRICKET'S PHONE CHIRPED, Becca grabbed it. She read the text and grinned. "I think he likes you," she sang, bobbing her head in rhythm.

"Give it." She grabbed the phone from Becca.

"How many times has he texted you tonight? It's obviously killing him to be away from you for a few hours."

"He's probably on a date. Just because I showed up after seventeen years doesn't mean he'd cancel a date to spend time with me. We spent all night and all day together. He's probably sick of me."

Becca topped off the wine in their glasses. "Who texts every thirty minutes on a date? If he said he's at the Thunder game with a client, he's at the Thunder game with a client. It's a big game. I could have paraded through the house in a leopard thong and handcuffs and Kevin wouldn't have missed this game."

"You do that anyway."

"Point taken. Anyway, you have plans with me, sister. I couldn't have waited another second to hear about your Jaynormous adventure, so here's to girls' night in," she said, holding up her wine glass.

Kricket clinked Becca's glass and continued on with her story. "Apparently, I was downgraded from *intoxicating* to *unfortunate* after he found out who I was. He made it abundantly clear I was friend-zoned."

"Unfortunate? What's that supposed to mean?"

Kricket shrugged.

"I think the downgrade came after he felt your hairy legs. Have you forgotten the three basic rules for leaving the house? Clean-shaven legs, waxed lady parts, and sexy undies. You should be glad nothing happened last night. I shudder to think of the forest growing down there," she said, sneering at Kricket's crotch. "If you haven't taken care of that already, we're marching right into my garage and getting the weed-eater."

"I handled that after we went mudding, and thank you for bringing it up again." She cringed just thinking about it. "Just call me *Miss Sexy*. I seriously wanted the earth to open up and suck me in. Which by the way, might happen. Did you feel the earthquake today? What's up with all of these earthquakes in Oklahoma?"

"Apparently tornados aren't enough to keep us living saintly. Speaking of natural disasters, what happened with his marriage? At the club when I asked him if he cheated on her, his eyes got all Clint Eastwoody." She narrowed her eyes and tried to look tough.

"I'm not sure. He clammed up when I asked him about it. Said it was a mistake from the beginning. He *did* say she was the total opposite of me."

"And what exactly does that mean? Was she bald with one eye?" Becca plucked her iPad off the coffee table. "What's her name?"

"Rachel." Why did saying that name stab her heart? Of course she couldn't expect him to make it to the age of thirty-three without being snagged by someone, but for some reason it pained her to think about him loving someone enough to get married. "What are you doing?"

"Let's call it research." Becca typed 'Rachel Hunter OKC' in the search bar. "Here she is. Wow, those can't be real."

Kricket leaned closer. "Let me see." Her heart sank at the image of Jay decked out in a tuxedo, standing by a sensuous woman in a slinky black evening dress. A tiered diamond necklace dripped into her cavernous cleavage. Chandeliers hung from her ears beneath dark hair pulled up into a sophisticated knot. She'd probably never had a bad hair day in her life. The photo apparently had been taken at a charity ball or something. The only thing missing was a red carpet and the paparazzi. And Jay's smile. "He's right, I'm definitely the opposite of that." She tried not to sound too despondent.

Becca gave her an annoyed look. "If you wore a dress like that, you'd be much prettier than her. But only if you shaved your legs." Kricket laughed at the mental image of her boobs getting lost in the draping bodice of the dress and her hairy legs sticking out of the high cut slit down the side.

"Look at the way they're standing," Becca said, tracing the photo with her finger. "Haven't you seen those photos of celebrity couples in People magazine where they interpret their body language? She's obviously posing and he looks like he'd rather be anywhere else but there."

That gave Kricket a little bit of satisfaction. At least he wasn't adoringly gazing at her.

Becca typed Jay's name into the search bar. "Look at all these conferences he's speaking at." She clicked on several links. "He's the keynote speaker at most of them. They don't let just anyone be the keynote speaker."

Kricket scooted closer. "Oh my good hotness." That was her Jayson? Now she was going to feel awkward around him again.

"Here's a link to request pricing. I'm going to fill it out and see how much he goes for."

Kricket grabbed the iPad. "Don't you dare! What if he found out?"

Becca rolled her eyes and grabbed it back. "Don't be a spaz. Look, this site groups speakers in price ranges." She typed his name in the search bar. Her mouth fell open. "Whoa. He's in the

$20,000-$30,000 range. For a forty-five minute speech?"

"Ugh." Kricket let her head fall backwards onto the couch to stare at the ceiling. "He speaks in front of a thousand people, and I nearly puked when we conducted a sample workshop for twelve of his employees. He must think I'm such a baby."

Becca touched Kricket's arm. "Say that again. You actually did one of your workshops?" Her voice was soft.

Moisture sprang to Kricket's eyes as pride welled in her heart. "I did it, Becca. I was so nervous, but I did it. He made me want to try. And he made me feel like I could."

Becca gave her a tight hug. "I'm so proud of you, girl."

"I wish Brock could have seen me. He always laughed when I talked about becoming a trainer. But at least he'll know about it. Jay said he's going to brag on me to our CEO, Mr. McKnight. You know, the one who transferred me back home after the Brock and Sutton debacle. Jay is so pissed off at Brock about this project. You should have heard him yelling at Brock on the phone. It was awesome."

"Does Jay know Brock is your ex?"

"No. And he's not going to if I can help it."

Becca snapped the iPad shut. "So, what does Jay's house look like? It must be incredible if he's a CEO *and* he makes thirty grand per speech. I wonder how many speeches he does in a year," she pondered, her brain obviously calculating.

Kricket didn't try to hide her exasperated look. "Actually, he lives in one of his rentals. It's pretty small, but it looks like it's straight off of HGTV. His sister-in-law is a decorator."

"Did you see where the magic happens?"

Kricket felt a stupid grin consume her face. "I had to force myself not to stare at his bed while I was changing in his room last night." Just thinking about it made her blush. "It was very *male*. Mostly gray with a bit of navy. I swear the comforter and all the pillows were pure washed gray linen. It was hard not to jump on it and roll around."

Becca looked duly impressed. "Were there any ladies' toiletries in his bathroom?"

"Although I would have liked to shower with something besides men's soap, I was glad to see there wasn't any. But none of this matters, because he made it very clear he's not interested in me that way."

Kricket's phone chirped again. Becca looked at it and raised her eyebrows. "We'll see."

CHAPTER 14

Sunday, January 22nd
...I could fill three journals with the events from the last two days. I'm so far outside of my comfortable box, I can no longer see the edges.

Today's Goal: Don't be shy in front of his entire family.

"I CAN'T WAIT TO SEE Mom's face when she sees you," Jay said as they waited for the security gate to swing open at the entrance of Mitch and Meg's neighborhood. He nodded and waved at the guard as they drove through. "She's going to be so surprised. I told Mitch and Meg, but they're sworn to secrecy."

The excitement in his eyes reminded her of when they were young. He'd been jabbering about surprising Karen all day. And although she would have preferred a quiet reunion alone with Karen, rather than meeting the entire family at once, she couldn't bear to burst his bubble. Her throat was starting to constrict at the thought of everyone fawning over her. She hadn't fully explained her anxiety attacks to him, but being the center of attention was definitely a trigger.

She closed her eyes and tried to picture Karen's warm face, hoping that would soothe her nerves. Karen was in her fifties now and probably looked completely different. She might have a touch of gray in her hair, or a few extra pounds. Surely she still had that dimple on her left cheek when she smiled.

Karen's eyes had always expressed encouragement, support, and pride in Kricket's smallest accomplishments. Hopefully she wouldn't be disappointed in her now, as an adult.

The sound of Jay's fingers drumming on the steering wheel broke through her thoughts. "You okay?" he asked, wheeling the Jeep into Mitch and Meg's circular driveway.

"I'm just a little nervous, that's all."

He placed a warm hand on her knee. "They'll love you."

She smoothed imaginary wrinkles from her jeans while Jay walked around Mud Ninja to open her door. She'd tried on everything in her closet at least twice before settling on black skinny jeans and boots with a light pink sweater. Hopefully she looked casual but cute, without looking like she'd tried too hard.

The impressive home loomed above them as they walked hand in hand up the sidewalk. It was a far cry from the modest neighborhood they'd grown up in. H-Tech business must be good. "Do your parents live in a home this large?"

Jay shook his head. "No. Dad's still as conservative as when he was struggling to get his business started. Although they do live on a golf course in Tulsa now. That's one thing he did spring for. He and Mom enjoy playing together."

When they reached the porch, he squeezed her hand. "Are you ready?"

She nodded, unsure if she was more excited or nervous.

Jay's eyes sparkled with excitement as he opened the front door and led her inside. The enormity of the two-story foyer with a big curved staircase took her breath away. Not only did the stairs spiral up to a second floor, but they went down another flight as well. She peered over the banister to see what was below.

"There's a wine cellar and safe room down there, but Mitch uses it as his man cave. It's where we hide out to watch games. We can drink beer and yell at the TV screen as much as we want without catching any crap from Meg," he said with a chuckle.

What an elegant home it was. Everything was soft gray and white. Light dove-colored carpet, a white couch with shiny silver pillows, shimmery silver drapery, and an expensive-looking sculpture in the foyer was hardly what she expected in a home with two kids.

A fire crackling in a white stone two-way fireplace that separated the great room from a large open kitchen gave the room a warm glow. She stopped to check her shoes. Tracking in mud on Meg's white carpet definitely would not get her off to a great start.

Footsteps barreled down the stairs, sounding like a herd of buffalo. Madi stopped in her tracks, wide-eyed. "Kricket!" She threw her arms around Kricket's hips and squeezed hard, nearly knocking her over. "Remember me?"

Kricket grabbed Jay's arm to steady herself. "Of course I remember you. Madi, right?"

Madi grinned and nodded excitedly. "Mom and Grandma are in the kitchen making lasagna. Wanna come upstairs, and play Barbies? I have one that looks just like you." She tugged on Kricket's hand.

"Hold on, Madi," a short blonde woman said, walking towards them through the great room. "You can't commandeer her three seconds after she sets foot in the door." Madi gave her mom an exasperated look and let go of Kricket's hand with a huff.

"Sorry about that. I'm Jay's sister-in-law, Meg." Kricket felt the familiar rise of color course up her neck as Meg gave her the once over. It wasn't a critical review, just a curious one. Meg was barely as tall as Kricket's shoulders. Supposedly Mitch was an inch taller than Jay, so they undoubtedly were an unusual looking couple. And sex must be challenging. Why did that always cross her mind?

Jay led her towards the kitchen, motioning for Meg to follow.

The eminence of the moment filled her stomach with butterflies. When they rounded the fireplace into the kitchen, her breath caught at her first glimpse of the woman she'd longed to see for seventeen years. Karen's back was towards them, but Kricket recognized her immediately. Her hair was the same. The way she stood was the same. She was still Mama Karen.

"Mom, I brought someone for you to meet."

Karen shut off the kitchen faucet. "I didn't know you were bringing a guest." She dried her hands on a dish towel before turning around. "And my hair looks frightful today," she said, smoothing her hair.

Tears welled in Kricket's eyes the moment she saw Karen's face. She blinked rapidly to keep one from trickling down her face. Do not cry. Do not cry. Do not cry. Her legs felt wobbly and she had to force herself to breathe.

Jay's arm tightened around her shoulders. "Mom—"

Madi popped between them. "Grandma, this is Kricket," she announced proudly. "She's the girl Uncle Jay was afraid to talk to at Starbucks."

Meg laughed at the exasperated look on Jay's face.

Karen suppressed a grin and patted Madi on the head. "Out of the mouths of babes," she said, extending a hand towards Kricket. "Welcome dear, I'm Karen."

The warmth of Karen's hand and her familiar smile filled her heart until she thought it would burst. She couldn't speak. All she could do was gaze into Karen's eyes.

Karen's forehead wrinkled as concern crept across her face. "Oh dear, your lip is bleeding."

She tasted blood. Her hand flew to cover her mouth. She'd obviously been chewing on her lip so hard she'd reopened the split from the coffee mug incident.

Karen grabbed a dish towel from the counter, then tilted Kricket's chin up with her thumb and dabbed at her lip. The remembrance of the mother's love she saw in Karen's gaze warmed her soul, causing a tear to escape and roll down her cheek.

Karen stopped dabbing. Her eyebrows knit in concentration as her eyes searched Kricket's. Suddenly her eyes grew wide and her face turned ghostly white. "Dear sweet Jesus." Her hand flew to her heart. She glanced at Jay. His face broke out in a wide grin.

A sob escaped Karen's throat as she folded Kricket in her arms. "My baby, my baby, my baby," she repeated, rocking her gently back and forth. Sobs shook both of their bodies as they clung to each other.

Kricket closed her eyes, soaking up the love that swallowed her entire being. How many times had she imagined this very moment, never allowing herself even a glimmer of hope that it would ever happen?

Jay's steady hand on her shoulder only seemed to make her weepier. "Come on, you two," he said after a time. His voice was tender. "Let's sit down before you both collapse."

As they wiped their eyes with tissues Meg provided, the back door flew open. "Krissy!" Mitch reached her in three broad steps and swung her around in a circle. Her burst of giggles helped extinguish her tears. He was likely the largest man she'd ever seen, dwarfing Jay in height and bulk. His bulk was more around his middle than in muscle though.

"Look at you, you gorgeous thing," Mitch said, lowering her to the floor before pulling her into a hug that nearly caved in her lungs.

When he released her, she caught a glimpse of Tom, wiping at his eyes with the back of his hand. Tom was still handsome, just a tad grayer than she remembered. It was obvious where Mitch and Jay had got their looks. He moved towards her and gave her a brief but warm hug. She hadn't been particularly close to Tom as a child. He always seemed to be at work. And when he was around, he always seemed to be reprimanding Mitch or Jay for something, which scared her a little.

"I never thought we'd see the day," Tom said, draping an arm around Karen.

"This is the most wonderful day of my life," Karen said.

"Well, apart from when you boys were born of course." She gave Jay a fake stern look. "You big sneak. Now I see why you asked me to bake a German chocolate cake."

Miles rounded the corner. His eyes grew wide when he saw her.

"Look, Miles, it's Kricket!" Madi shrieked and grabbed her legs again. Suddenly everyone was hugging her and talking at once. She was trapped by Madi, who clung to her legs trying to talk above everyone else, trapped by Jay steadying her, trapped by a hundred arms hugging her. And so many voices. Voices, voices, voices, fusing together in a deafening roar.

"Madi let go, you're going to trip her." "So how did you find her?" "Madi get back!" "Can you believe how grown up she is?" "Mom, why does everyone call her Krissy?" "Guys, you're smothering her," Jay's voice boomed above the rest. "Will you come play Barbies now?" "Mom, why is she so white?" "Jayson, she needs some air."

The noise thundered in her ears. She had to get away from the noise. She couldn't breathe. Too many people were too close, consuming all of her air. The walls moved towards her now. People and walls smothered her. Her lungs cried for oxygen. She gasped, searching for one tiny breath of air. Please, no, not in front of everyone. There was no air left in the room and she was going to die. Right there in front of everyone. The spinning in her head pulled her towards the darkness. She tried to push it away but the spiral sucked her inward. Into the darkness. There was air in the darkness. And silence.

She found herself sitting on a bed atop a puffy cheetah print comforter. Jay was kneeling in front of her with his hands on her shoulders, and Karen was sitting next to her. Their eyes were full of concern.

"It's okay, it's just us. Me and Mom."

She stayed motionless for a moment, while her mind fully transitioned from the darkness. "I'm okay," she whispered, glancing at Karen, then back into Jay's worried gaze.

"Tell me what happened. How do we help you?" She did this when I told her who I was too," he said to Karen.

"It's just stupid social anxiety. When too much attention is on me, sometimes I freak out. I'm okay now." She wasn't really okay. She wanted to bury herself in the pillows and never leave the room. Now everyone would fawn over her asking what happened, making it ten times worse. "Everyone probably thinks I'm a freak," she said into her hands.

"Of course they don't. Many people would feel a little overwhelmed to be surrounded like that. We'll be more mindful of your personal space until you get used to us again." Karen gave her a side squeeze before standing. "I'll go help Meg finish dinner. You stay here with Jay as long as you need to."

She nodded.

Jay's face was riddled with guilt. "Kric, I'm sorry. I didn't know," he murmured as he shook his head. "The workshop...I shouldn't have coerced you into doing that." He paused, brows furrowed. "So why didn't the workshop trigger it?"

"I'm not sure. Maybe because it wasn't focused on me personally. After I got started, I just got into it and didn't think about it so much."

"I'm really sorry," he said, resting his forehead against hers. She looked up just as he went to kiss her nose, causing his kiss to land on her mouth. They both sucked in their breath and jerked away.

"She's okay. He's kissing her," Madi squealed from the other room, followed by Meg's voice saying, "Madi, put down that iPad. You know better than to spy."

"Mitch and his effing cameras," Jay muttered. She followed

his eyes to the smoked glass dome on the ceiling. "He has security cameras everywhere, except in the bathrooms," he added quickly.

She was slightly creeped out by the cameras, but glad for the distraction from their unintentional mouth kiss. "So you're saying I can't pee until I get home or a hacker might post my toilet activities on Girls Gone Wild?"

He chuckled. "No worries there. Remember? The Hunters are in the data security business." He lifted her hand to his lips, then stood, giving her that come hither grin that he obviously had no control over. "Come on. I'll make sure they give you some space." Why did he have to be so freaking sexy all the time?

Karen and Meg were preparing dinner, while the rest of the family lounged around the dining area and great room watching a football game. The kitchen, casual dining, and living area were one big room, making it a cozy place for gathering.

Meg handed her a glass of wine as if nothing had happened. Karen expertly took the focus off her by putting her to work peeling potatoes at the sink while Jay sat at the dining table to relay the events of the last two days. The family laughed at the funny parts, gasped at the exciting parts, and hurled questions one after the other. Everyone except Miles, that is. He listened intently to the story, but was familiarly quiet. Occasionally she caught him glancing at her, but when she smiled he quickly looked away and turned red. Her heart went out to him. She knew that feeling all too well. Sitting among a group of chattering people, longing to join in, but having no words.

By the time they'd finished dinner, the entire story had been told and Kricket felt much more comfortable around everyone. Having spent most of her youth living with only her grandpa, she'd had very little exposure to big family gatherings. She found it loud, and exciting, and scary all at the same time. And she had a feeling she could become very used to it.

After dinner, they gathered in the great room, watching football and besieging her with questions. There was so much to catch up on. She shared an over-sized chair and ottoman with Jay, who hadn't strayed two feet from her all evening.

Madi stood behind them braiding Kricket's hair. "This is lot's more fun than braiding my Barbie's hair." She leaned around the chair with a big grin. "Want me to teach you, Uncle Jay?"

"Sure."

Kricket's face flushed at the thought of his hands in her hair, especially in front of everyone. Madi made a show of explaining exactly how to select a piece and lay it over the other one. Kricket's eyes drifted shut as Jay's fingers glided through her hair, pulling sections away from her face and into the braid. It was far better than a shampoo massage at the hair salon. When a sigh escaped her lips, she opened one eye to see if anyone had heard. Mitch was watching Jay with the same tight jaw Jay got when he was angry. Meg, who was sitting next to him, smiled and winked. Kricket looked down to study her fingernails.

Jay dropped her hair rather abruptly. "This is too complicated, Madi. Kricket, would you like to see the rest of the house?"

"Sure," she said, running her fingers through her hair to unravel the partial braid.

Madi led the tour like a docent in a museum, pointing out features she'd obviously heard her mother highlight when working with decorator clients. Afterwards, they stood on the terrace outside the upstairs game room watching golfers smack away their cabin-fever on the eighteenth fairway. It was one of those glorious 60° afternoons that Oklahoma was occasionally blessed with in the middle of a typically arctic January.

"I'm going to call you Aunt Kricket, okay?" Madi asked, climbing on the iron rail like a monkey.

Kricket nodded, touched that Madi already felt such an attachment to her. Since she had no siblings, she'd never thought about being an aunt. She liked the sound of it.

Madi pointed across the fairway. "Aunt Kricket, see that house over there on the other side of the pond...the third one from the corner? That's Uncle Jay's new house."

Jay grinned when she looked at him, somewhat surprised. "I've had my eye on that house for a few years and it finally went on the market last fall. It's on the perfect lot, just like this one, with a view of the fairway and pond. And the pool is surrounded by landscaping, so golfers can't see it from the cart path. It's bigger than I need, but it's far from being ostentatious like this house. Meg's completely gutting it." She could see the excitement in his eyes. "She won't let me see it until it's finished. They're still four to six months out."

"If it's your house, why can't you see it?"

"You don't know how bossy my mom is," Madi said.

"She's not kidding." He gave Madi a knowing look. "I've been through building a home once. It wasn't a fun experience. I'd rather wait and see the result instead of being in the middle of the process. Meg knows what I like, so I'm just letting her work her magic."

Mitch joined them on the terrace. "Why don't you girls go in and help get dessert ready." She sensed Mitch was trying to get rid of them, so she followed Madi back into the game room. Miles was sprawled on the couch typing on his phone.

"Whatcha doing, Miles? Texting your *girlfriend*?" Madi asked in a sing song voice, trying to snatch the phone from his hands.

"Leave me alone, Madi." His eyes flicked towards Kricket before focusing again on his phone. She knew that look. Anything and everything was embarrassing around strangers.

She touched Madi on the shoulder. "Madi, will you tell them I'll be there in a minute?"

Madi skipped out of the room, singing. She was the complete opposite of Kricket as a child. Oh, to be so outgoing and carefree.

When Kricket sat on the couch next to Miles, he stiffened, so she inched away a bit. She sat quietly for a moment, contemplating how to draw him into a conversation without scaring him to death. "It's a little hard to get a word in edgewise in this family, isn't it?"

He shrugged, but didn't look up. The movement of Mitch waving his arm outside on the patio caught their attention, and they both turned their heads to look out the sliding glass door. She couldn't hear what they were saying, but Mitch was blasting Jay about something. "I remember them arguing a lot when we were kids. Apparently some things never change." she said, more as a question than a statement.

"They can get into some doozies, for sure. Dad's mad because he thinks Uncle Jay's going to hurt you."

That was the last thing on her list of guesses as to why they were arguing. "Why would Jay hurt me?"

"He won't. Dad doesn't know that, but I do." He watched them out the window. "Quiet people watch and listen. We see things other people don't."

She smiled to herself, impressed that at fourteen, he was so self-aware. "I'm quiet too, but I'm not that good at figuring people out." She glanced at the patio out of the corner of her eye. Jay was in Mitch's face now with that piercing look that she hoped was never directed at her.

"Do you have a twitter account?" Miles asked, then turned bright red.

She smiled, proud of him for having the courage to ask. "I sure do." She pulled up her Twitter account on his phone. "That's me. Follow me and I'll follow you back."

"You're a co-founder of the Jeep Mafia?" he remarked, scrolling through her feed. "That account is awesome!"

She could tell her coolness factor just skyrocketed. "A group of us run the account. We have a blast. I've actually met a few of them too."

He glanced up with a shy smile. "You're a lot nicer than Aunt Rachel was."

Even though she soooo wanted to go there, she could hardly grill Miles about Jay's ex. Okay maybe just a little.

The terrace door opened, blowing her opportunity. Mitch and Jay walked inside. "Let's go," Jay snapped.

He looked pissed. But she'd made a grand entrance and there was no way she was going to allow him to turn it into a grand exit as well. "I'm not going anywhere until I have a big piece of that German chocolate cake."

CHAPTER 15

JAY'S SILENCE ON THE drive home from Mitch and Meg's made her realize something. Even though he was her Jayson, she had to admit, she really didn't know him at all. What was going on inside his mind? And why would Mitch think he would hurt her? As a child, she trusted him completely. And she still wanted to, but a lot could happen to a person in seventeen years. Enough to change them entirely. So far he'd been far from forthcoming about things that happened during the years they were apart. What if getting to know him completely wrecked the image she'd built up of him in her mind? That was hard to even think about.

After whipping into a parking space in front of her apartment, he turned to her. "Come to Houston with me tonight," he blurted.

"What? I can't just—"

"You already said your office is closed tomorrow for Martin Luther King Day, right?"

"Yes, but—"

"Then you can come. You need to see first-hand what D-A-S-H is all about anyway."

She sat speechless while he climbed out of the Jeep and walked around to open her door. On the spur of the moment, he wanted her to hop on a plane and go to Houston? Just like that? He obviously didn't know her very well either.

"Stop frowning," he said as he helped her slide out. "We can catch an early flight home Tuesday morning and still be in the office by 8:30."

She dug in her purse until her fingers finally located her house keys. "Jay, I really don't think—"

He snatched the key from her hand, grinning wickedly. "I won't give it back until you say you'll go."

"What? Jay, you can't do that!"

"Watch me," he said, dangling the key just above her reach. She jumped up, trying to swipe it from his hand. After tugging on his arm to no avail, she poked him in the ribs. He nearly knocked her down when he doubled over, and they ended up laughing in a tangle by the door. Her cranky next door neighbor peeked out his window and scowled at them. They tried to regain their composure, but ended up laughing so hard she nearly peed her pants. When they finally regained control, her abs were sore.

"C'mon Krissy, please say you'll go," he pleaded. "I just found you. I can't be away from you yet."

Did he have any idea how convincing his eyes could be? Probably, because he certainly used them to his advantage. In all honesty, she couldn't bear the thought of being away from him yet either.

"Okay, on one condition," she said in her best negotiator voice. "Stop calling me Krissy."

"Deal." His face lit up and he spun her in the air, just like Mitch had earlier. "I didn't realize I called you Krissy," he admitted, after setting her down. "It's just a habit, I guess. So, *Kricket*, let's get you packed."

Once inside, he wasted no time. He walked straight to her bedroom and into the closet. "Where's your luggage? We need to leave for the airport in forty-five minutes."

"Forty-five minutes! I can't be ready to go in forty-five minutes. I need to check my weather app...I need to know what kind of conference it is, where we'll be staying, where we'll be eating..."

"You're killing me." He reached for her luggage on the top shelf of the closet. "I'll help you, I'm a packing pro," he said, yanking the handle of her suitcase. The overnight bag resting on top of it slid off and bonked her on the head, knocking her against the wall.

"Krissy, I'm sorry. Are you okay?" She lay completely still.

He leaned over her, cradling her head in both hands. "Krissy, talk to me!"

She couldn't keep a straight face, so she thrust open her eyes like she was waking up from an exorcism. "Boo!"

He jumped. "You little shit."

"I told you to quit calling me Krissy."

The scowl on his face told her she'd succeeded in making her point. When he stood, he pulled her up with him and pointed his finger in her face. "Don't think I've forgotten how much you hate being tickled. You're just lucky we're in a hurry."

Hopefully the naughty thought that flickered through her mind and tingled her lady parts didn't show on her face.

He glanced around her closet, apparently oblivious to the fact that tickling her at this age would be an entirely different ballgame than when she was eight. "You color code your clothes?"

"Doesn't everyone?" she asked, knowing full-well her fondness of organization was slightly on the obsessive side.

He responded with a smirk. "I'll find something for the conference tomorrow and you grab something to wear back on the plane that you can wear straight to the office on Tuesday." He thumbed through her dresses, then stopped and snapped his fingers. "That dress you wore to the club. It's perfect. I don't see it in your *green dress* section," he said with a smirk.

Her eyes darted to the dress, still crumpled in a dejected symbolic heap on the closet floor. He looked at the dress, then looked at her with a furrowed brow.

"Dry cleaning pile," she offered, stepping in front of the bright yellow dry cleaning bag hanging on the door.

If he noticed, he didn't pursue it. He pulled out a cream knit dress. "How about this one?" She nodded then held up a pair of shoes to match.

"Perfect. Now, where's your pajamas?" He opened a drawer, then quickly closed it. A wry grin spread across his face as he slowly reopened the drawer. "Your underwear is color coded?"

"Get out of my undie drawer." She shoved him out of the way, wishing she'd listened when Becca encouraged her to sexify her underwear collection.

"Easy, killer. I was just looking for your PJs." He surrendered with his hands as he backed out of the closet.

Cabinet doors opened, then banged shut in the bathroom. "Do you have one of those little cosmetic bags somewhere in here?"

Seriously, was he going to pack her tampons too? She stuck her head in the bathroom and pointed towards the living room. "Go! I'll be ready a lot faster if you will just get out and leave my stuff alone."

"Ten minutes," he said, holding up both hands. "I'll be in the living room making sure your magazines are alphabetized."

✍

"How do you do this in front of so many people?" Kricket asked, peeking at the crowd through a slit in the curtains while the sound guy helped Jay adjust his mic. Just standing on the side of the huge stage made her nervous.

Jay swung his arms over his head a few times, pacing the small backstage area where they waited. "I didn't start out with audiences this size. You have to build up to it. At first it's intimidating, but it gets easier with practice. Before long you fall in love with it to the point of getting a speaker's high." He was obviously well on his way to that high, because he couldn't stand still.

The mic guy held a finger to his lips to quiet them as the Master of Ceremonies began Jay's introduction. "...and now please welcome successful entrepreneur and founder of the D-A-S-H business management system, Jay Hunter."

Jay kissed her on the forehead, clicked on his mic, and strode onto the stage looking perfectly at ease. And perfectly hot in a long sleeve blue shirt and gray flannel slacks that fell gracefully over his stallion legs. "Good morning," he said, flashing a smile that undoubtedly melted the heart of every female in the audience.

She watched in awe as he expertly drew in the crowd, keeping their attention with examples, stories, and more than a little self-deprecation while explaining the fundamentals of D-A-S-H. His energy was contagious, and he had the crowd laughing, gasping, and clapping throughout his presentation. So that's why they pay him the big bucks.

After concluding with a summary of the four components of D-A-S-H, he checked his watch. "We have a few minutes left. What questions can I answer for you?"

An attractive woman in the front row raised her hand.

"Yes?" Jay said, pointing at her.

"I'm disappointed that you didn't tell your Squirrel Promise story. It's such a memorable example of the *Humanity* factor in D-A-S-H."

Jay glanced towards Kricket as if pondering something, then turned back towards the audience. He stared at the stage floor for a moment before continuing. "It's ironic that the most important aspect of my business model is remembered by the story of my biggest failure. A promise I made at the age of sixteen to a little girl who looked up to me through eyes that saw no imperfection."

Kricket felt the blood drain from her face.

"I hurt her in a motorcycle accident," he continued. Caused by a squirrel trying to commit suicide. And by my recklessness. While we waited for help, I made a promise to never let anything hurt her again. I made that promise because I wanted so badly to be able to keep it. But I couldn't keep it. And the course of our lives were forever changed."

Kricket watched the spellbound faces of people listening to his story...*their* story. Listening to him tell it made it seem surreal.

"I set up an unreasonable expectation because I wanted it so badly...so very, very badly. And she trusted me and expected me to keep my promise." He paused again.

"I tell this story because there will be times when you are tempted to make an unattainable promise to a customer because you want the business so badly. Perhaps it's a deadline you can't possibly meet, or a product you typically don't offer. Or maybe it's a new customer you've been courting for years, and they finally give you a shot, but their request is unreasonable."

He took a moment to look around the room. "Don't make a squirrel promise in your business. If you can't meet a customer's request, don't say that you can. A customer may not be happy, but will respect you for being honest. But if you make a promise, and then break it, it could cause a domino effect that your customer won't forget."

Kricket's breath caught when he unbuttoned his cuff and began rolling up his sleeve. "I have this scar on my arm that reminds me every single day of my broken promise. And unfortunately, she has one just like it." Gasps circled the room, followed by utter silence as he stood with his arm raised, displaying his scar. He made eye contact with each side of the room. "A broken promise can last a lifetime." The lump forming in Kricket's throat threatened to choke her.

The woman in the front row raised her hand again. "Did you ever try to find her?"

He rubbed his chin. Please don't point me out. Please, please, please.

"No, I didn't."

"Why not?" someone else asked.

Even from a distance she could tell he swallowed hard.

"I was afraid of the reflection I'd see in her eyes."

A vice gripped Kricket's heart. After a short pause, he cleared his throat. "Thank you for your attention. I trust you will enjoy the conference." He walked off the stage, handed his mic to the sound guy, grabbed her hand, and strode towards the side exit. Before opening the door, he stopped and took her hands in his face. His eyes bore into hers. "I never wanted to tell that story in front of you. To us it's tragic and personal, but to them, it's a story that will make them remember. A story to drive a point home. I'll never invade your privacy by disclosing that I found you. I tried to leave it out, Kric. I'm sorry."

And that was the end of the discussion, because he flung open the door. "We have to get to the exhibit booth quickly," he said, leading her briskly down the hallway. "The Jessicas are there, but it's important for me to be there after my speeches."

"Who are the Jessicas?" she asked, struggling to keep up with his long stride.

"Our sales reps. They man the exhibit booths when I speak at conferences."

She was out of breath when they arrived at the exhibit hall. He introduced her to Jessica A. and Jessica B. At first she thought it was just a letter to distinguish them, but actually the A. was for Allenton and the B. was for Brookshire. Jessica A. had long blonde hair, and Jessica B. had shoulder length dark hair, but otherwise they were two bookends. Both sported short skirts, low-cut blouses with surgically enhanced cleavage bursting forth, and spiked heels that would make her feet scream after about twenty minutes. She glanced down at the cream dress and boots Jay had packed for her. Before leaving her hotel room, she'd admired her outfit in the mirror, satisfied that she looked cute. But the Jessicas looked hot. Cute, hot, cute, hot. Ugh, they win.

Jay stationed her inside the booth to form a barricade from the crowd. Her task was to keep the baskets of freebies replenished, while Jay and the Jessicas stood out front mingling with the visitors. She was perfectly content behind the booth, organizing the pens, golf tees, and koozies bearing the D.A.S.H. logo. The Jessicas made full use of their feminine wiles as they worked the crowd…innocently touching men on the shoulder, hovering head to head over iPads to demonstrate the D-A-S-H software, and pretending that everything a male customer said was clever or funny. She would rather have her finger tips sloughed off with a cheese grater than have their job.

And naturally, while the men focused their attention on the Jessicas, the women flocked around Jay. Although most women clucked about the Squirrel Promise story, or asked about the D.A.S.H software, a substantial number seemed more interested in Jay's hardware than in his software. They batted their eyes at him and puffed out their breasts like Tom turkeys. A few bold ones pressed a business card into his hand instead of dropping it in the box for the iPad raffle. The whole scene made her nauseous. Not that it was any of her concern. But she did notice that when their fingers lingered a little too long on his, he deftly removed his hand, smiled casually, and moved on to the next person in line. So this was Jay's life.

The crowd thinned as attendees stuffed the last of the freebies in their conference tote bags and shuffled off to their next session. Jay deposited his handful of business cards in the raffle box, then headed to the refreshment table to grab some bottles of water.

Once he was out of earshot, the Jessicas surrounded her. "So you're the famous Squirrel Promise girl," Jessica B. said, hungrily.

"And you both grew up to be hotties," Jessica A. threw in. "How lucky is that? So, are you guys together or what?"

"Oh, no, we're just—" She shook her head, unable to control the flush she knew crept up her cheeks. "He's always been like my big brother. I don't think I'm really his type anyway."

Jessica B. made a show of looking her up and down. "You're definitely not his *normal* type, but he is all about you, trust me."

Jessica A. jokingly punched Jessica B.'s shoulder. "You should know. You've won our bet how many times in a row now, four?" She eyed Kricket and smiled wryly. "So you two really aren't together?"

Kricket shook her head.

"Hmmm, then maybe tonight I won't have to buy drinks. Want in on our bet, Kricket?"

"What bet?" she asked, glad they were making an effort to include her.

"Well, in case you haven't noticed, Jay gets his own collection of business cards from horny conference women who aren't interested in winning an iPad," she said with a smirk. "When someone catches his eye, he puts her card in his pocket, and ta-da, she's the lucky winner of breakfast in bed with the hot speaker. We make bets on who he'll choose. Want in?"

A jagged brick of air lodged in her lungs. Kricket let the pen she was holding slip from her fingers onto the floor so she could lean over to pick it up and discreetly regain her composure. She pretended to search for it a moment under the table while sucking in a few deep breaths. She plastered a smile on her face before standing to face them. "Sure, I'm in." She was in, alright…way too deep.

Jay returned with a bottle of water for each of them. So that was it. There wasn't a woman in his life, there were *women*. As in a different one every week, or ick, maybe even every night. And if he hadn't left her standing on her doorstep, she would have been just another notch. As his lips touched the water bottle for a sip, the memory of his soft kiss flashed in her mind. How many women dwelled on that same memory? Thinking about him being with someone made her stomach knot. She pressed her temples to force out the image that invaded her mind.

For the remainder of the day, she observed Jay from her secluded spot behind the table and although a few more business cards were pressed into his hand, if he put one in his pocket, she didn't see it. And for that she was thankful.

After a dinner fielding question after question from the Jessicas, the four of them perched at the hotel bar. Kricket listened to them chatter excitedly about the strong leads they received at the exhibit booth, which had been bustling all afternoon.

"So what do you think of our conference world?" Jay asked, resting his arm on the back of her barstool.

She spared him the details of what she really thought. "You were right. Hearing your speech and observing the sales pitches at the exhibit booth really helped me understand the components of D-A-S-H. I can see why it's so popular."

Before he could respond, Jay's phone dinged with a text. She glanced at the message out of the corner of her eye, which was obviously from a number in his contact list because it displayed the name 'Victoria.' The message was short, but to an obvious point, '9:30, Room 724.'

She pulled her purse from the back of her barstool and pretended to rummage through it to disguise the fact that every drop of blood in her face had dissipated.

Jay looked at his watch, then patted her arm and stood. "I

need to go review some footage of my speech before turning in. I'll walk you to your room."

"You go ahead. I'm just going to finish my drink," she said, without looking up from her purse. There was no way she was going to let him deposit her in her room on his way to a booty call.

"It's late and we have an early flight."

"Seriously, Jay," Jessica A. said, rolling her eyes. "Let the girl finish her drink. We promise not to keep her up late and corrupt her."

She could tell he was annoyed, but he didn't press it, and told the bartender to put their tab on his room. When he looked at her with knitted eyebrows, she knew he was struggling with how to say goodbye in front of the Jessicas. He'd been giving her a hug and a kiss on the forehead when they parted, but this was work-related.

"Well, goodnight, ladies." He touched her on the arm and she could tell from his face he felt her flinch. "Kricket, will you text me when you get in your room so I know you made it safely?"

She nodded, wondering if he'd excuse himself from his bed partner to read her text.

After he left, Jessica A. eyed her over her drink. "He's a teensy overboard on the big brother thing, don't you think?"

"I'll say," Jessica B. replied. "Guess no one wins the bet tonight. He's meeting Victoria. He doesn't pick a lucky bed partner when she's around," she informed Kricket.

"So...who's Victoria?" Kricket asked as nonchalantly as possible.

"His sure thing. She's another conference speaker. They review each other's speeches...and everything else," she said, raising her eyebrows up and down. Jessica A. held up her wine glass. "Here's to Victoria saving me bet money."

৯

Kricket lay in bed, staring at the photograph in the conference schedule. Victoria Frasier, CEO of Frasier Marketing Consultants. Sleek short blonde hair and red lips curved with an air of superiority. The epitome of a sexy, sophisticated executive woman. The epitome of the type of woman who captured Jay's attention.

Of course he'd had girlfriends when she was little, lots of them. Undoubtedly he slept with at least some of them, but back then she didn't even know what that meant. She just knew he was her Jayson. But he wasn't Jayson anymore. And he wasn't hers anymore. And until now, she hadn't fully admitted to herself that she wanted him like she'd never wanted anyone before.

The dagger of reality carved a hole in her heart. He was in bed right now. With a woman named Victoria. Slowly undressing her, running his fingers over her skin while his smoldering brown eyes devoured her. Kissing her deeply until their passion was so intense he had to have her right then. And he did have her. And tomorrow, or next week, he would have her or someone else again.

She switched off the lamp on the nightstand, letting the darkness swallow her whisper. "You promised me, Jayson. You promised." As much as she longed for him to hug her and make everything all right, he couldn't. She rolled onto her side, pulling a pillow into the raw pit of her stomach. And cried. For what they had been, but would never be again. For what they were now, and what they weren't. Because the flawless hero her mind had clung to for seventeen years wasn't flawless after all. And because he would never know that he'd broken his Squirrel Promise again.

CHAPTER 16

KRICKET WAS PROUD OF her acting skills. She'd done a pretty good job of pretending everything was just fine on their early morning flight home. And she *was* fine, for the most part. This morning she'd given herself a stern lecture. They'd spent three glorious days in their own little bubble getting to know each other again. But bubbles eventually pop. And now that she'd had a glimpse of Jay's world, she knew Mitch was right. He would hurt her. In a way that Miles was too young to understand. She had to accept what he was. And love him…like a brother. No sister cares if their brother is a man-whore, right?

She called her boss Deidre when they arrived at the H-Tech office to let her know that Jay asked her to start on the project first thing this morning. Deidre suggested they discuss it with Brock since he and Mr. McKnight were flying in for a meeting with Jay this afternoon. So cue up the acting skills again. She was now in the same building with not one, but two men who preferred to screw someone besides her.

"Vic…tor…eeee…uhhh." Kricket rolled the name off her tongue while she touched up her makeup in the H-Tech ladies' room. Even Victoria's name sounded sexy, as Becca had so kindly pointed out when Kricket called her last night to whine about Jay being a man-whore. Becca's advice was to wear something slutty and hoe up her hair to make Jay forget all about Vagina Victoria and the business card bitches. Becca was always so helpful.

"Kricket, Kricket, Kricket," she said into the mirror. Not exactly what you'd call sexy. Her name even *sounded* like an annoying insect. It definitely wouldn't roll off your tongue in the throes of passion. She pulled the tie from her hair and fluffed some curls with her fingers. Seeing Brock's reaction to her new auburn hair color was the only thing about this meeting she looked forward to. She had to admit, it did make her look kinda sexy. She did a supermodel pose in the mirror. "Do you boys want it?" She smacked her lips together. "Can't have it."

A movement caught her eye. She turned to see Gayle leaning against the doorway with her arms crossed.

"How long have you been standing there?" she asked, squeezing her eyes shut in an attempt to make either herself or Gayle magically disappear.

"Long enough," Gayle responded knowingly. "And what exactly are you doing?"

She sighed loudly. "Everyone's fawning over me now that they know I'm the Squirrel Girl. I just needed a breather. And a pep talk before I have to meet with my ex, I mean with the V.P at Pinnacle." Stop talking, you idiot. Just stop talking.

Gayle raised an eyebrow. "So, the V.P from Pinnacle that Jay is going to annihilate today is your ex? I'll bet you'd like to be a fly on the wall."

"You have no idea," she said, dropping her lipstick back into the pocket of her purse.

A proud smirk curved Gayle's lips. "Never underestimate the power of knowing your boss's password. I was just grabbing a soda before I log into the security camera feed to watch the showdown. Care to join me?"

"More than words can possibly express." This was going to be good. Really good.

Gayle pulled up the video feed of Jay's office on her computer and positioned the monitor so they could both watch. Mr. McKnight and Brock were sitting in the guest chairs at Jay's desk.

Kricket had no doubt Jay had purposefully held the meeting in his office instead of the conference room as an expression of his authority. Although there certainly was no need. He was the epitome of intimidation. She couldn't help but snicker at Brock, who looked like a ten-year-old sitting in the principal's office. The last time she'd seen him, he was sitting naked on her couch, smirking. He wasn't smirking now.

Jay took a slow sip of coffee and eyed Brock, then turned to Mr. McKnight. "I've already expressed my disappointment in how this project has been handled, Cecil, so let's skip the recap and get right to a resolution."

Mr. McKnight nodded. "Of course, Jay. Going forward, Brock will personally handle this project. He will ensure you get exactly what you are looking for."

Jay opened his mouth to speak, but Brock jumped in. "Mr. Hunter, please accept my apologies for Ms. Taylor's lack of preparation and unprofessional performance. The video you sent of her sample presentation is grounds for dismissal. Rest assured she will be relieved of her duties. That preposterous T-shirt stunt at the end in no way represents the quality of work my department produces."

Kricket's face grew hot. Not with embarrassment, but with anger. She stared at the screen with her mouth open.

Jay's eyes narrowed as he leaned back in his chair and crossed his arms. He maintained relentless eye contact while Brock babbled on about the many hours he and his staff had spent thoroughly analyzing the D-A-S-H business model before customizing the workshops. It was all she could do not to burst in Jay's office and call Brock out. Okay, who was she kidding, she would only do that in her imagination.

After Brock finished, Jay eyed him with those wolf eyes that came out when he was pissed. About the time Brock looked like he was going to spontaneously combust, Jay turned to Mr. McKnight. "I'll get right to the point."

Gayle waggled her head at Kricket. "Preppy boy's gonna be hanging upside down by his balls in about ten seconds."

"Mr. McKnight, I must apologize for neglecting to include a detailed message when I emailed you the video of the workshop Kricket and I conducted. When I typed, 'See for yourself,' I meant, 'See for yourself how perfect the workshop was.' I see now that the message was misconstrued."

Jay looked pointedly at Brock. "Her workshop design was exactly what I've been asking for but couldn't get from your team. Ms. Taylor was given no information about my company, no time to prepare, and yet she figured out exactly what I wanted in thirty seconds…by looking at my coffee mug. How's that for research?" He picked up his ninja mug and took a slow deliberate sip. "And the *preposterous* T-shirt stunt was at my request."

Brock stared in stunned silence.

"The first trainer's presentation was the complete opposite of what I asked for. It was as if he knew nothing about my company." Jay leaned forward and rested his arms on the table so his face was only a few feet from Brock's. "So here's my question, Brock. In your *thorough* analysis of D-A-S-H, I presume you and your team reviewed my website and watched a few of my speeches, right?"

Brock glanced at Mr. McKnight, then nodded. "Of course."

Jay rubbed his chin. "You see, here's what baffles me. My Squirrel Promise speech is on the homepage of my website, and yet, you didn't think it was important to tell Ms. Taylor about it? In fact no one on your team put two and two together about her scar?"

Brock looked confused.

Kricket scooted closer to the computer screen. She didn't want to miss a single syllable of this.

Stone faced, Jay rolled up his sleeve and held up his arm to display his scar in Brock's face.

Brock's eyes grew wide. "That's…just like Kricket's scar. You're the motorcycle guy."

Jay kept his arm extended in front of Brock, maintaining his stone faced expression. "So I'm going to ask you again, Brock. Did your team research my company website?"

Mr. McKnight looked completely befuddled. "What's going on here, Jay? What does your accident have to do with this?"

"You don't know Kricket, do you?" Jay said to Mr. McKnight.

"I've met her once. Get to the point, Jay."

Jay punched the button on his speaker phone. "Gayle, do you know where Kricket is?"

Kricket shook her head wildly at Gayle, mouthing 'No,' but Gayle ignored her. "Yes, she's here with me."

"Please send her in," Jay snapped.

Kricket dropped her head in her hands. Why did he have to involve her in this confrontation? Gayle nodded towards Jay's office and smirked. "Time to help bury your ex."

Her heart beat wildly as she forced herself to stand and walk towards his office.

Jay mouthed, "I'm sorry," when he met her at the door, then led her to the edge of his desk. "Kricket, I apologize if this seems somewhat personal, but would you mind pushing up your sleeve?" His firm yet gentle eyes locked with hers, which somehow made her feel like she was stripping for him. She slid up the sleeve of her sweater, hoping her face wasn't as red as it felt.

Mr. McKnight's face turned white. "The Squirrel Promise girl." He stared at her for what seemed an eternity. "All this time, she was right under my nose," he said shaking his head. "Jay, if only I'd known."

Vengeance was sweet, but being that close to Brock made bile rise in Kricket's throat. She fought to keep her face from looking like she'd just bitten into a lemon. She couldn't step back without being obvious, so she let gravity contort her body as far from him as possible without actually moving.

Jay glanced at her, then at Brock, then at her again, his eyes squinted slightly. His expression darkened with an unreadable emotion. "Thank you, Kricket. I'll be out shortly."

Mr. McKnight smiled and shook her hand, before turning to Brock with eyes of fire. "Brock, if you will excuse us, I'd like to talk to Jay in private."

CHAPTER 17

AFTER MR. MCKNIGHT AND Brock left, Jay asked her to wait in his office. He'd been gone for half an hour. Now he stood like a mountain in the doorway, wearing those wolf eyes she'd hoped would never be aimed at her. And now they were. He slammed the door behind him. "He's had you, hasn't he?" he said through gritted teeth.

"What?"

"You've slept with him." His eyes looked like they could crack ice. "Is he the one who screwed your friend?"

She crossed her arms and stared back at him. Who'd had a front row seat to his harem call at the conference yesterday? Not to mention witnessing his Victoria booty call. "I don't see how that is relevant to this project."

"It's relevant to me."

"Why?" She couldn't wait to hear Mr. Man-whore's response.

He walked towards the window and stared outside at the rain, his body rigid with anger. She silently watched as the tightness in his shoulders gradually loosened. When he finally came and sat across from her at the conference table, his eyes were gentle again. "Because he doesn't deserve you and because he hurt you," he said softly. "And I wasn't there to protect you."

Her fury at his nosy outburst melted into mush. "You said yourself that was an unattainable promise. Even if you were around, there are some things you couldn't protect me from."

He sighed. "I want to though."

She nodded. "I know. But I'm not as delicate as you seem to think."

His response was a thin smile.

"How did you know it was him?"

He looked away for a moment in an apparent act of anger management before turning back towards her. "I could see your skin screaming when he stood by you."

He was dead on, and the fact that it was so obvious made her laugh.

His eyes took on a twinkle again as he slid a document from the folder he'd brought in. "I want you to come work for us."

"What?" She forced herself to take a breath. "What do mean? Why? Because I slept with Brock?"

He leaned over the table towards her. His warm hands grasped hers. "Just listen for a minute. Pinnacle didn't meet my expectations. *You* did. If I continue going through them, I won't be able to get what I want when I want it. Your workshops are exactly what I'm looking for, and I can see so much more potential with them than I initially planned. We won't stop at just developing the workshops my client requested. You can design the training for onboarding new D-A-S-H clients. And all those ideas we talked about on the plane...we can do them. You and me, together." His eyes grew wide with excitement and his hands waved wildly as he spoke. "We'll create a new business line. An online training portal of employee soft skills. It's the perfect spinoff of D-A-S-H. And we can—"

"So you want me to quit my job and come work for you?"

"Not for me, for H-Tech." He turned the document to face her. "Mr. McKnight agreed to release the rights from any workshops you've developed that Pinnacle hasn't used. And he provided me with your current salary, so this is what we're offering you."

"You've already spoken to Mr. McKnight about it?" She wasn't sure if she was more surprised or angry.

He clasped both her hands, crumpling her fingers in his excitement. "We can do great things together, and neither you nor I will ever have to deal with that ass-wipe Brock again. Because if I see him again, I'll end up in prison."

Apparently he wasn't kidding, because he didn't smile. She glanced at the document and nearly fell out of her chair. "Jay, I can't accept this offer. It's way too much money."

Releasing his stronghold on her fingers, he patted her hand gently. "D-A-S-H is sponsoring an HR conference in July. That's the perfect time to introduce a new learning portal spin-off. After you see the time commitment it will take to be ready by then, you'll probably demand a raise." A hopeful smile spread across his face. "So, will you do it?"

It wasn't a hard decision. Working for the Hunters. Having her creativity encouraged instead of squelched. Eliminating any need to see Brock again. "Okay," she said. "Let's do this."

"Yes!" He stood up and held out his arms. She'd barely pushed her chair away from the table when he swooped her up and twirled her around, an action the Hunter boys seemed to enjoy. Her foot hit the conference table and his coffee mug flew across the room and smashed against a filing cabinet. As he set her down, they both looked silently at the broken pieces of the ninja mug that had inspired this entire endeavor.

"What in the devil?" Gayle exclaimed, barging through the door. "What is it with you two and coffee?" she exclaimed after seeing the remnants of the mug on the floor. She put her hands on her hips and gave Jay a head-bob. "And I guess you expect me to pick that up?"

"I suspect you've been sitting at your desk doing your nails and they aren't dry yet, so I'd hate for you to mess them up," he said wryly. "Kricket's joining H-Tech, so take her to HR for new-hire paperwork, then help her get set up in the office next to Dad's."

A slow grin spread across Gayle's face as she looked back and forth at the two of them. "I'd love to. But why are you putting her in the bat wing?"

"It's quiet and she's going to be busy."

"Barren is more like it. Maybe she'll put some life in that wing."

So her office was in a bat wing. This was certainly going to be interesting.

Jay stooped to pick up the handle of the broken coffee mug. "Kricket, meet me in the lobby conference room at 4:30 for a board meeting. Gayle, shut my door on your way out and don't let anyone bother me. I have some preparation to do for the meeting."

❧

Kricket arrived in the conference room fifteen minutes before the board meeting started. She needed a moment alone to talk herself down from the ledge her mind was barely clinging to. She had no idea who was on the H-Tech board or why she was attending, but a board meeting wasn't even a speck on the horizon of her comfort zone. Her journal undoubtedly was sitting on the kitchen table rubbing its hands together and licking its lips in anticipation of her next entry.

She studied the primary colored fish chasing each other around their ten foot by five foot glass prison on the conference room wall. Fish had no stress. Or did they? Did the yellow fish really want to catch the blue one, or was it just enjoying the chase? Was the blue fish scared of the yellow fish, or was it playing hard to get? And after the yellow fish caught the blue one, would it suddenly decide it preferred the striped fish? Kricket blew out a deep breath. Brock was gone…history…completely out of her life. When she looked up, Jay was walking towards her through the lobby wearing that grin that made her heart do a back handspring, back handspring, back somersault. And may history not repeat itself.

She was relieved to see the board consisted only of Tom, Mitch, Jay, and a kind looking gentleman who Tom introduced as their General Counsel, Randall Johnson. He had sad eyes like a beagle. Tom called the meeting to order with the smack of a gavel, causing her to jump in her seat. Was he serious with the gavel? It hardly seemed necessary when there were only five people in the room. But she'd never been to a board meeting before, so maybe that was a requirement. All she knew was her stomach just tightened up another notch.

Tom explained to her that all new business ventures must be approved by the board. "We are a small company, but we don't act like one. Family is family and business is business." His tone was even more stern than normal. "When we are in this room, it's all business." Which was pretty evident by the gavel.

Jay presented a detailed outline of their online training portal idea, including budget and resource requirements, with an aggressive goal of launching it at the D-A-S-H sponsored HR Conference in July. She was astounded he'd been able to gather so much data in the few hours since he'd inserted Brock into his Jayanator and turned it on high. Overhead would be minimal, because they already had the technical staff on hand who was just wrapping up a project.

After Jay described his vision of how the training portal would function, Tom turned to her and asked what her vision was. Her brain blurred into fuzzy static. She hadn't expected to be asked her opinion in a board meeting. A chirp on her phone indicating it was her move in an ongoing word game she played with Dot snapped her mind back to attention. It garnered her a stern look from Tom for not having her phone muted, but it also gave her an idea.

"It's a great idea, but we need something to make employees *want* to complete the modules." She held up her phone. "People like to play games. They like to earn points and brag about the levels they achieve. I don't know if your developers can do it, but maybe we could create a game." She glanced at Jay, who smiled and cocked his head, urging her to continue. "It could be a simulation where they earn points for completing levels of learning and handling various office situations. Employees could create an avatar and a gamer name, like *Office Ninja* or something like that, maybe even interact with other staff. Player statuses could be posted on the company's homepage, and winners could be recognized in newsletters and such. Maybe even offer real prizes."

After saying all that in one long breath so she wouldn't lose her nerve, she peered cautiously around the room. Each of them stared at her with knitted brows. They hated it. She should have just agreed with Jay and kept her stupid mouth shut.

"I like it," Jay said, nodding his head. She couldn't tell if he really did or he was just trying to save her from the silence that enveloped the room. "I think you've really got something there."

The others remained silent.

"*Skill Hunter*," she said, causing everyone to turn towards her. "We could call the game *Skill Hunter*."

She would never forget the startled looks on their faces. Followed by big smiles. Big smiles for her.

CHAPTER 18

Tuesday, February 14th
...When you're single on Valentine's Day, you just want to make
yourself invisible, so today's challenge definitely won't be
practicing eye contact or smiling at people. Probably not going to
attempt the 'banishing negative thoughts' challenge either...

JAY WAS AT A conference, so undoubtedly he and Vagina Victoria or the lucky winner of the business card lottery would have a romantic dinner followed by non-stop Valentine sex. She pictured his woman of choice in a thigh high fire-engine red dress, matching lipstick, and the fierce look of a tigress who'd claimed the most desirable mate...much too vivid of a mental image on an empty stomach. She grabbed the white paper bag from her passenger seat and pulled out the red frosted Valentine's Day donut she'd treated herself to on the way to work.

Max the H-Tech security guard eyed her hot pink angora sweater through the monitor as he buzzed her in the parking garage door. "Morning, Ms. Taylor. You look just like a valentine today."

Her office was near the entrance to the parking garage, at the mouth of Tom's executive suite. It hadn't taken long to figure out why they called it the *bat wing*. Tom, Kricket, and the Legal Beagle were the only occupants of that hallway. Like Gayle had warned, it was pretty desolate. Tom was only in Oklahoma City on Mondays and Tuesdays and the staff tended to avoid him anyway, so the only time anyone came down that hall was to go to the basketball court or the parking garage. And you had to be a Hunter to park in the garage. Or a pseudo-Hunter like her.

She switched on the light in her office. Perched on the center of her desk was a single pink rose in a slender vase. She nearly dropped her coffee trying to get to the card poking out of the vase. She yanked the card out of its tiny envelope. 'Happy Valentine's Day - Jay,' it said. She ran her finger over the writing on the card and breathed in the heady fragrance of the bloom. A single rose was such understated elegance.

She pulled a small black gift bag from her humongous purse that doubled as a briefcase and fluffed up the red tissue paper. She'd ordered the perfect Valentine gift for Jay. A black coffee mug imprinted with *Mud Ninja*. It was meaningful, but couldn't be misconstrued. And she'd filled it with Hot Tamales, which admittedly could have been misconstrued if it weren't his favorite candy.

She practically skipped down the hallway towards his office. When she turned the corner into Jay's wing, her feet skidded to a halt. A single pink rose stood on the desk of every female employee. She now knew exactly why they coined the phrase, 'knocking the wind out of your sails.' Her body withered. Before reaching Gayle's desk, she took a deep breath and forced her shoulders to straighten.

"The roses are beautiful," she said, plopping in Gayle's visitor chair as if she hadn't a care in the world.

"Jay and Mitch do that every year for their staff. Of course, guess who had to get here at six-thirty this morning to set them out?" Gayle said with a fake yawn. She raised an eyebrow at Kricket's fuzzy pink sweater. "That sweater may as well say 'touch me, touch me' on the front of it. Somebody must have a date after work."

Kricket smoothed her hand down the front of her sweater with a flourish, like the models do on QVC. "Actually I haven't made my final selection yet. The line of men began forming outside my front door last week. My neighbors were complaining, so I borrowed those posts with the little velvet ropes from the movie theatre to keep the prospects lined up in an orderly fashion." She tried to keep a straight face, but couldn't keep from laughing as she spit out the last few words.

Gayle shook her head. "Well, I don't doubt that. And *you-know-who* would be at the front of the line if he wasn't away at a conference."

"Whatever," she said, picking an imaginary fuzz ball off of her sweater. "He needs velvet ropes around his exhibit booth."

"Good point. Maybe I'll order one of those number dispensers," Gayle said with a laugh. "Now serving number fourteen. Number fourteen, please report to the Penthouse Suite."

She wanted nothing more than to pump Gayle for information. Did he keep in contact with his conquests? Did he even know their names? Had Gayle ever met Victoria? Did he talk to Victoria outside of the conference world? With even a hint of prodding, she knew Gayle would spew information like a shaken can of soda. The two sides of her head battled each other. Naturally, Miss Goody-Goody won, so she swallowed her questions and changed the subject. "I'm having lunch with Becca today. I haven't seen her in weeks."

"Good for you. Jay's been working you way too hard. He just called and said he has back-to-back speeches all day and asked me to make sure you'll be in your office at 6:30 for a web conference." Gayle smiled wryly. "If you ask me, he's just making sure you don't have a Valentine's date."

She gave Gayle the raised eyebrow *mom* look. "He just wants to make sure I'm on schedule with my SkillHunter edits." She stood and handed over the gift bag. "Will you put this on his desk? It's a coffee mug, so no need to peek."

"I would *not* peek," Gayle said, clutching her hand over her heart like she was insulted.

"Yes you would," she said, turning to leave. "And don't eat the Hot Tamales inside it," she called over her shoulder.

❧

At exactly 6:30, Kricket's computer bleeped. Jay's image popped on her screen. "Hey you," he said with an easy smile.

"Hi, yourself. Thanks for the rose." She picked it up and drew in a long breath through her nose. "It smells fantastic. It's really nice of you to do this for everyone."

He gave her a sheepish look and changed the subject. "You look nice in that sweater. I'm sorry I had to schedule this call so late. I hope I didn't interrupt any plans."

She rolled her eyes at him. "Are you kidding? I'll be here until at least nine. For every script I edit, five new ones land in my inbox."

"I told you the hours would be horrendous. I know it's hard work, but it will be worth it in the end."

"I wouldn't trade it for anything."

He grinned then his face grew solemn. "I got you something."

Her heart jumped. All day, she'd been second-guessing her decision to give him the mug. If Gayle hadn't seen it, she would have secretly removed it from his desk. "You did?"

He nodded towards her credenza. "Pull out the lower left drawer."

She swiveled her chair around and opened the drawer. Her hand flew to her chest. Atop her stash of file folders sat a silver box with a blue bow. The kind of box that screams 'jewelry inside.' Her heart beat against her fingers as she stared at the box.

"Pick it up, silly."

She plucked out the box and gently placed it on her desk. She'd never received such a beautiful package.

134

He tapped on the screen. "Quit biting your lip and open it."

"It's too beautiful," she whispered.

"Just open it."

She tugged on both ends of the ribbon and let it fall on the desk, then carefully unfastened each piece of tape to free the box from its wrapping.

"You're killing me, you know it?"

She grinned at him, knowing he would have ripped the paper off like a two-year-old. As she lifted the plastic case out of the box, the scene from Pretty Woman where Richard Gere snapped the lid on Julia Roberts' fingers flashed through her mind. In the movies, there's always something magical about the moment right before the woman peeks into the box. She paused to fully absorb her moment. As she opened the lid, the glimmer of silver made her breath catch. A TAG watch, just like his. Silver with a dark blue face. "Oh, Jay, it's beautiful." Her eyes met his in the monitor.

"There's a note in the box," he said, with a nod.

She found the small folded note and opened it. All it said was 'Nine Million Minutes.' She questioned him with her eyes.

"Seventeen years is nine million minutes," he said softly. "I wanted to get you something as a symbol of the time we lost. And the time we now have. I couldn't wait until your birthday, so...happy Valentine's Day."

She bit her lip to keep it from trembling. "I don't know what to say."

His lip curved in a lopsided grin. "Say you like it."

"I love it." She put it on her wrist and rotated her arm back and forth to watch it catch the light. "I love it because it's just like yours."

His phone dinged. He looked at the text, but ignored it. "If I were there, I'd take you to dinner."

She considered using the movie theatre ropes joke again, but changed her mind. "I left you a gift on your desk." She glanced at her new watch again. "But now I'm embarrassed for you to see it."

"You got me a gift?" His face lit up like a child's. "I won't be back until Friday. Will you go get it and open it for me?"

His excitement was hard to resist, even though it totally ruined her opportunity to find something better before he returned. "Okay, I'll be right back."

She flew down the hall, grabbed the gift, and rushed back. As she neared her office, she heard him talking. Just as she opened her mouth to tease him about talking to himself, she heard him say, "Drop it, Victoria," in a snippy voice.

She stopped dead in her tracks and stood completely still so he couldn't hear her.

"How many times have I told you I'm not involved with Kricket? She's like my kid sister, okay? End of conversation. I'll see you at seven."

Kricket sat the gift bag on the edge of her desk, waited a few seconds, then slapped on a big smile before sitting in front of her computer. His eyes flicked up from his phone when she sat down.

"Your office door was locked, so I couldn't get your gift. You'll just have to wait until you get home." She hoped her smile didn't look as fake as his did.

CHAPTER 19

Sunday, March 12
...Between my journal challenges and my Jay challenges, the layers of my shyness are slowly peeling away. I'm nowhere near where I want to be, but I'm much closer. Jay encourages me to stretch myself at my own pace.

Today's Goal: Tell Jay how much I appreciate him. That counts as "Giving a Compliment."

LOUNGING AROUND WITH THE Hunters watching a movie was Kricket's favorite part of family day. Leaning against Jay, sharing a bowl of popcorn, with Madi sprawled across his legs on the ottoman made her feel like part of the family. Miles was right there on the couch beside her too. After several family days and about three hundred texts, Miles was finally comfortable around her. He even asked her for advice on how to talk to girls—well actually just one girl named Breanna—so last Sunday she secretly gave him a Confidence Journal. He'd eyed it warily until she unveiled a small combination safe to keep it away from you-know-who.

The contented look on Madi's face brought back memories of how it felt being eight years old and surrounded by the Hunters. It was a feeling she'd clung to during the awful months that she'd lived with her father. On Sunday evenings, when her father and stepmonster had fancy people over for dinner, she'd been forbidden to leave her room. Not that she would have anyway. She much preferred the seclusion of her room where she could crawl into bed and watch a movie, surrounded by stuffed animals that she pretended were Jay, Mitch, Karen, and Tom.

And now she really was surrounded by them. Jay's fingers

mindlessly twisted a tiny lock of her hair. For whatever reason, no matter what he did with other women, she hoped he didn't play with their hair. She liked to think it was their special thing.

She was comfortable with their relationship and their routine. Since they worked such long hours and lived so close to each other, he picked her up for work on the days he was in town, always bringing her a tumbler full of his green breakfast concoction. Strangely, she'd actually started to like it. They typically worked until seven or so, then grabbed dinner on the way home, making a game of trying out the different hole-in-the-wall restaurants that kept popping up near H-Tech. They spent most of their free time together as well. She and Gayle watched the H-Tech team play soccer on Friday nights, Jay took her mudding on Saturdays, and Sunday was family day.

In the office, he was strictly professional, but outside of work, most people would probably think they were a couple. Unlike her, he was affectionate by nature. When they parted, he always hugged her and kissed her forehead, then raised his arm for a scar bump. Okay, it was more meaningful than a scar bump. Maybe scar *touch* was a better word. It replaced the forehead touching. Their desperate need to reconnect made it acceptable that first weekend, but there had been no further face to face forehead touching or body to body snuggling since. She missed the closeness, but knew it was for the best. They worked together. They were like family. Not that she needed to define their relationship. Why did girls always need to define their relationships? He was hardly the kind of guy she needed anyway.

Jay's chest rose and fell behind her in a deep breath as he pulled her head towards him and kissed her hair. Not a peck. More like a hug with his mouth on her head. And just about the time she was comfortable with their undefined relationship, he'd go and do something like that. She would give up German chocolate cake forever to know what went through his brain when he did that. He did it to Madi too, so it definitely wasn't sexual, although it sent delicious shivers down her neck that unfortunately made a crash landing in her happy spot. It was more…what was the word? Not intimate. Affectionate, maybe? Like when you see a cute puppy and you can't help but kiss its head. Perfect, she was his puppy.

For reasons she couldn't quite put her finger on, it seemed normal for him to show affection towards her, but she wasn't comfortable instigating it. Sure, she hugged him back, but kissing him on the forehead or hair? Well first of all she couldn't reach his head, and second, okay maybe this one should be the first reason…what if he took it the wrong way? What if he rejected her touch? No one would be surprised to hear she had rejection issues.

When she glanced up at him, he tilted his head and smiled. A stray curl of hair fell helplessly across his forehead begging her to rescue it. It was so dark and shiny. She longed to pick it up and let it glide through her fingers to see if it felt as silky as it looked. Oops, there's that tingle again. It would be so much easier if her body was a little more on board with the whole *puppy* concept. She leaned against his chest and snuggled in a little bit. He kissed her head again, and she crossed her legs to squelch the tingle.

As soon as the movie was over, Mitch turned off the TV. He stood, held out his hand to Meg and pulled her off the couch to stand against him, completely enveloping her tiny frame in his broad arms. "Meg and I have something we want to share with everyone." They both literally glowed. As soon as the room was silent, he continued. "We brought home another souvenir from the Caymans." They looked at each other and grinned. "We're going to have a baby," he announced.

Jay stiffened beside her.

"A real baby?" Madi flew off the ottoman and wrapped her arms around her parents' legs.

Karen touched Jay's shoulder on her way by to give Meg a hug.

"That's wonderful news," Tom said, moving to shake Mitch's hand.

Miles' face scrunched up like he'd just tasted doggie doo. "That's gross you guys. You're like way too old to be—"

Kricket slugged his shoulder and gave him a stern look. She stood, pulling Miles up with her. "Be nice," she whispered in his ear.

There was hugging, and laughing, and a few tears as Meg showed them her tiny baby bump and told them the due date was in September. Jay heartily congratulated them, but his smile looked forced. Like when someone accidentally steps on your toe and it's throbbing, but you smile and say 'It's okay' because you don't want them to feel bad. When he hugged Meg, she smiled almost apologetically through teary eyes. Mitch and Tom kept a worried eye on him and Karen slipped her arm through his. Kricket had the uncanny feeling she'd walked into a movie theater fifteen minutes late and was trying to catch up on the plot.

After toasting the news with a bottle of champagne that Mitch opened, the women migrated to the kitchen to talk about baby clothes and nursery colors, while the men stayed in the great room talking about whatever guys talk about. It wasn't long before Jay came into the kitchen and put a hand on her shoulder. "Are you about ready to go? You said you wanted to get to your grandpa's."

She nodded. "I'm sorry to run out after such big news, but I really do need to go. Grandpa's doing well after his hip surgery, but we're worried he'll try to overdo it and fall. Dot's in San Diego visiting her new grandbaby, so the neighbor is checking on him during the day, and I'm staying overnight."

As they said their goodbyes, Karen seemed to give Jay an extra-long hug and Tom patted him on the shoulder, which was not something she'd ever seen Tom do before. What in the world?

Jay hardly said a word on the way home. At her door, he held her for a long time. When he pulled away, she put both hands on his face. "Tell me what's wrong," she whispered.

"Nothing."

"It's me, Jay. You can tell me if something is wrong."

He shook his head, kissed her forehead, and left.

CHAPTER 20

"YOU SHOULD BE OUT on a date, not spending your Sunday night babysitting your crippled grandpa."

Kricket set his water glass and sleeping pill on the nightstand and handed him his book. "You're my date tonight, Grandpa. And for the record, I don't spend the night with just any date." She held up her hand to stop the protest she knew was on the tip of his tongue. "I know you don't need me, but I don't want you falling down while you're here alone. Besides, can't a girl spend a little quality time with her grandpa?"

He winked at her. "Maybe you should try spending the night with a date sometime. Might help you get a second one."

"Grandpa! Dot's rubbing off on you." She wasn't about to tell him she hadn't been on a single date since she moved back from Dallas. "I'll let Biscuit out before I go to bed. Night Grandpa," she said, pecking his cheek. "C'mon Biscuit, let's go watch something gooey and romantic on Lifetime."

Biscuit followed her into the living room and curled up in her doggie bed, watching with hopeful eyes as Kricket settled on the couch under a furry blanket.

"C'mon girl. I won't tell." Biscuit landed on the couch in one leap, thanking her with a big wet slurp on the face. "Yuk. You're welcome." She wiped her face off with the blanket and shoved Biscuit towards the end of the couch. "Go keep my feet warm, you hairy monster."

The movie did a poor job of keeping her interest, since she couldn't keep her mind from worrying about Jay. Her eyes were heavy and it was after eleven, so she found the remote and clicked off the movie. "We know how it ends anyway, right girl? Let's check on Grandpa and then we'll go outside." Biscuit's ears perked up and she jumped off the couch. She left Biscuit spinning in circles at the back door while she tiptoed to Grandpa's room. He was fast asleep with his book sprawled across his chest, so she eased off his glasses and turned off the lamp.

"Okay, okay, I'm coming." Biscuit was wearing a hole in the floor by the back door.

Biscuit barged out the door like a racehorse out of the gate. Kricket stuffed her feet into Dot's glittery pink slippers that were sitting by the back door, zipped up her hoodie, and grabbed the blanket off the couch before following Biscuit outside.

The only thing visible in the sky was a perfect half-moon. She stared at it, as she had so many times as a teenager, marveling at the vastness of the universe and contemplating her place in it. She didn't know how long she'd stood there before the cold made her shiver. She whistled for Biscuit, who flew out of the darkness and bounded onto the porch, wagging her tail. "Good girl." She patted Biscuit on the head then turned the doorknob. Nothing happened. "No, please no," she said out loud. She rattled the doorknob and pushed on the door, in hopes it hadn't latched. It had. She rattled it again, then leaned her forehead against the door. This can't be happening.

She sat on the back step, encasing herself in the blanket she'd thankfully grabbed, and buried her head in Biscuit's thick fur. "What are we going to do now, girl?" Grandpa took mind–bending sleeping pills, so he would never wake up, even if she beat on his window or rang the doorbell repeatedly. She had no keys to the house or to her Jeep, and no cell phone. This was a stage four crisis.

She rubbed Biscuit's fur like it was a genie bottle that would magically produce a solution as she pondered her options. The frigid night air hurried her decision. There was only one thing she could do. Jay's house was only a mile and a half away. She wasn't crazy about the idea, but her options were few. As in that was the only one. Jay had been in such a foul mood after hearing Meg was pregnant, she was fairly sure he'd be home.

"Come on girl, let's go." She headed down the street, with Biscuit trotting happily beside her. "I'm glad you think this is an adventure." Her eyes scanned the darkness, half-expecting a zombie or the Grim Reaper to spring from behind a shrub. The neighborhood was safe, but nonetheless she began to trot. For whatever reason, trotting made her feel safer than walking. Besides, work had kept her from getting in a good run for more than a week. Dot's slippers were hardly suitable for running, but her body got into the rhythm and before she knew it, she was standing in Jay's drive.

The sight of him standing in his bedroom window gazing out at the sky made her breath catch. A lamp in the background illuminated him just enough to see that his chest was bare and his hair was messy. He couldn't see her in the dark, so she watched him for a moment, wrapped in the blanket. There was something forlorn about him. Maybe the absence of his normally proud stance, or the way he blankly stared. His guard was down. She felt she was invading a private moment. A vulnerable moment. If only she could draw back the curtains around his soul and coax out whatever burden or heartache was torturing him at this very moment…use her thumb to gently smooth the crinkle between his eyes and make his world right again. A car turned the corner, lighting her up like a Christmas tree. Jay's head jerked towards her. When he turned away from the window, she assumed he was headed for the front door.

He opened the door, wearing only a pair of knit boxers and a frown. "What are you doing out here?" he asked gruffly.

Until this very second, it hadn't even crossed her mind that he might not be alone. And now the reality of it nearly knocked her to the ground. He had a woman in his bedroom.

Biscuit bounded into the house, so she couldn't turn around and run, even though that's exactly what her body wanted to do. "I'm... I'm sorry," she stuttered. "I didn't mean to bother you, I know you're not alone, but I'm locked out of the house, so if I could just use your phone." She looked down at her feet. Now would be a great time for one of those stupid earthquakes to open up and suck her in.

"I'm alone," he said, running a hand through his hair. "I didn't mean to sound so gruff. You just surprised me, that's all. Come in. You must be freezing." When she stepped inside, he gathered her against his bare chest, blanket and all, resting his chin on her head. "I'm not sure why you're here; but I'm really glad that you are."

Her nose pressed against the clean scent of his bare chest melted her body into a pool of liquid on the floor. "I went outside with Biscuit and got locked out of Grandpa's house," she said, when she caught her breath. "Running here was the only thing I could think of doing."

"I'm glad you did," he whispered into her hair. "I couldn't sleep. Now maybe I can." When he looked at her, the redness of his eyes was startling. She'd never seen him like this. He'd either had too much to drink, had been crying, or possibly, both.

Her eyes were drawn to his chest. She'd never seen him without a shirt and although she knew he worked out, she had no idea his chest and abs were so ripped. The tattoo at the top of his arm caught her eye. She studied it for a moment, deciphering the shapes. Pain seared through her heart when she realized what it was...and what it stood for.

"Oh Jayson, I didn't know you had that." Her index finger

cautiously reached forward and touched the infinity symbol resting inside a bleeding heart at the top of his scar, then traced the swirls of tears flowing down each side. She rested her forehead against his chest, tears rolling down her cheeks. For as long as she lived, no matter where they were or what they were to each other, she would never forget this moment.

He silently held her, rocking gently.

After a while he pulled away and looked at her. She brushed a stray lock of hair from his sad eyes. "I wish you would tell me what's wrong."

"It's nothing," he said, shaking his head. "Just something I need to work out myself."

There was no sense pressing him. If she'd learned anything about men, it was that you can't nag them into spilling their guts.

After borrowing his phone to text Grandpa, she pulled the furry blanket from her shoulders and spread it on the ottoman. "Is Biscuit okay here?"

He nodded. "You can sleep in here with me," he said, turning towards his bedroom. "Miles and Madi stayed over last night and built a fort out of the sheets in the guest room, so it's a mess." When she didn't follow, he stopped and turned around. "It's a big bed. You'll be safe."

Following a droopy, bleary-eyed Jay into his bedroom was not at all how she'd pictured this moment. There was no question she would be safe. She patted Biscuit's head, who was already curled into a ball on the ottoman. "Night, girl."

Jay was pulling a T-shirt over his bare chest when she came through the door. A weak grin broke through his stone face as he surveyed her. "Somehow you always manage to make me smile," he said, shaking his head. "That's quite an outfit."

She'd completely forgotten she was wearing the 'Topless and Dirty Jeep Girl' hoodie Dot had given her, which coordinated perfectly with her 'Moooove over' cow print jammie pants and Dot's pink glittery slippers. It was a proud moment indeed. And of course, when she unzipped her hoodie, her nipples stood out like fog lights through her thin white T-shirt. She knew what Becca would do at this moment. But she wasn't Becca, so she turned away and slipped off her hoodie, then quickly crawled under the washed-linen covered bed that had invaded her dreams on more than one occasion. Jay slid in the other side and they lay three feet apart with their backs to each other, like a bickering married couple.

The memory of her face pressed against his bare chest consumed her thoughts. And his tattoo was etched in her mind. She wanted to ask about it, but what was there to say? It spoke for itself. Beautiful, yet heartbreaking. She wondered how many women had seen it, and what he told them it represented. Everyone knew tattoos have a story behind them. Something impactful on one's life. So she'd impacted his life. Or the accident had.

Falling asleep was impossible while he shifted around on his side of the bed. When his breathing finally became heavy, she curled herself around a pillow and pulled the covers under her chin waiting to drift off.

A sound made her jerk. "Kric?" He said it softly, but she was in that stage just before falling asleep when any noise sounded like an explosion in your head.

"Hmmm?"

"Can I hold you?"

"Of course."

His arm curled around her waist and slid her into his awaiting spoon. His hold was tight. Desperately tight. Not in a sensual way, but the way a frightened child might clutch a teddy bear. With her free hand, she stroked the scarred arm that covered her, hoping he found comfort in it. It was all she knew to do.

After a time, he loosened his embrace and lay chastely curled around her, with his arm resting across her waist and his pelvis a safe distance from her hips. She longed to ask him again what was wrong, but dared not risk provoking him to withdraw and turn away, so she silently basked in their closeness.

When the absence of his warmth sent a shiver through her, she realized he'd rolled away. The moon cast just enough light through the window to see his outline. He lay on his back with his hands resting beneath his head.

The sound of his voice startled her. "I always wanted kids," he said softly. "A little girl...like you, I guess. Rachel never wanted any. I thought she'd change her mind." His sigh filled the room. "One evening I was emptying the bathroom trash and I noticed a pregnancy test. It was positive."

Kricket forced herself not to gasp as a meteor crashed into her head. A baby? How could she not know he had a baby?

"I was ecstatic, but I didn't say anything because I figured she wanted to surprise me. Our marriage was...well, it wasn't in the best place. But a baby...that could change everything." An hour-long minute passed before he continued.

"I thought she would tell me at dinner, but all she talked about was a project she was working on that would require her to be in Chicago for a month. That's where she was from, so she was pumped about it. When we got into bed, I couldn't wait any longer, so I told her I found the pregnancy test."

The sound of his hard swallow filled the room. "She said it wasn't mine."

Kricket covered her mouth to stifle a gasp. "Jay, I'm so sorry," she said, rolling onto her side to put her hand on his arm.

He pulled her tightly into his chest, burying his head in her hair. "She killed it, Kric. It could have been mine, but she killed it." He took a deep shuddering breath. "I would have raised it without her if she had just given me the chance. It's not right that the father of the baby has no say in it. She didn't even give me the chance."

"I know. I'm here," she whispered into his chest. She tried to be strong for him and not cry, but his T-shirt grew wet from the tears as her heart bled for him. At that moment, she realized that watching someone you love struggle with pain was far worse than being in pain yourself.

Wrapped in each other's arms, they rocked as she whispered soothing words to him. As the rocking continued, their hips began moving in rhythm. A tingle shivered through her as his lips grazed her ear, hesitated, then slid down her jaw and devoured her mouth. He kissed her hard, and she responded with the desire she'd long suppressed. His hands were everywhere…on her face and in her hair…running under her T-shirt to cup her breasts…slipping into her pajama pants to pull her hips against his hardness. Her hand slid under his T-shirt, melting into the smoothness of the chest she'd touched so many times in her mind.

"Raise your arms, baby," he said, then lifted off her T-shirt and tossed it on the floor. His hands slid into her hair and pulled her mouth to his in a hungry kiss. "I need you, baby." The words were barely spoken when he tore his lips from hers. "Fuck!" As suddenly as it started, he was off the bed and out of the room.

Curled around a pillow, she listened for his return. But all she heard was her own heartbeat pounding in her ears. She didn't fight the darkness, hoping to be swallowed into the void between knowing and not knowing. Anything to distract her from the ache in her arousal and the emptiness in her heart. The darkness threatened, but the darkness didn't come. Her breathing slowed and her mind cleared, leaving her to fully face the gut punch of reality.

Shame devoured him. His mom was right. Someday his demons would cause him to hurt someone he loved. Why did it have to be the one person more important to him than life itself? Kricket was trying to be there for him, her sweetness consoling him. And he'd thanked her by pawing at her like a hormonal teenager in the backseat of a car.

It was obvious from the thump of Biscuit's tail on the ottoman that Kricket was standing in the doorway, but he didn't look up. He knew she wouldn't come to him on her own. She wouldn't want the confrontation. And he couldn't bear to see the devastated look on her face.

If only he could wrap her in his arms and go back in time to when they were kids. Before all the hurt happened. Before the scars. Before she was taken away. Before Brock. Before Rachel. Before the baby that never got to be.

But if he touched her, or even got close enough to hear her breathe, he would sweep her off to his bed and finish what he'd started. Which would only hurt her more. He let out a deep breath, forcing his voice to be soft when he spoke. "Go back to bed, Kric," he said, without lifting his face from his hands.

She didn't move and she didn't speak. He could almost hear the tears he knew were rolling down her cheeks. "Please, just go to bed."

After she slipped quietly back into the bedroom, he went into the garage. The punching bag hanging from the ceiling had been on the receiving end of his frustrations for nearly two years. He punched until his knuckles were raw. But it failed to take away even a fraction of the pain he felt in his heart. The pain of reality.

~⑤~

The grinding sound of the blender whirling in the kitchen woke her. The last time she'd checked the clock, it was four a.m. She hadn't cried, well okay, she hadn't sobbed. She'd lain there, torn between hating him and loving him, and between feeling sorry for him and feeling sorry for herself. For someone who liked to get things out in the open, he'd certainly managed to keep something important from her. He'd been hurt badly. And she wanted to be there for him. She wanted to be the one who broke down his walls. Instead, he'd shunned her. Again.

The thought of facing him made her stomach knot. But she was worried about leaving Grandpa alone all night, plus she had to get ready for work, so she climbed out of bed and pulled on her hoodie. If they'd actually had sex, she wouldn't feel so self-conscious, but now it felt like facing a stranger who had accidentally caught her naked.

Biscuit greeted her when she walked into the living room. Kricket patted her furry head, then pulled the blanket off the Ottoman and wrapped it around herself before sitting down.

"I let her outside already," Jay said, walking into the room with two shakes. She turned away when he held one out to her. She wasn't in the mood for green goo.

He placed both drinks on the coffee table and sat on the couch facing her. She knew he was waiting for her to look at him, but she couldn't.

"I'm sorry, Kric."

She stood and walked to the window, then gazed out at the gloomy gray morning. "Sorry for what?"

"You know what."

She whirled to face him. "No, I don't know what," she spat. "I laid in there all night wondering what the hell happened. So I'd like to know exactly what it is you're sorry about." Her anger made her voice shake. "Are you sorry for keeping something like that from me, or sorry that you broke down your wall and told me about it? Are you sorry you tore off my shirt then stomped out of the room like I had leprosy, or are you sorry I wasn't someone you could just leave in a hotel room and never see again?" Her chest heaved while she waited for his response.

"Yes," he said, resting his head in his hands.

"Yes? To what? All of the above?"

"Yes…I mean, no. Not the leprosy part." He rubbed his face in exasperation. "I'm sorry that I nearly took advantage of you for comfort sex."

She thought her head was going to explode. "Comfort sex?"

"I'd had too much to drink. I'm sorry. That wasn't about you."

And there it was. She was just some chick laying in his bed…easy access to a quick lay. If they'd seen it through to fruition, how would this conversation be going right now? Would he treat her like his other one-nighters? And what did he say to them anyway? Thanks for the fuck, have a great life? Her gut was rotting.

She started towards the door. "I need to go check on Grandpa. You can take me or I'll walk, but I'm going now."

He started to say something then obviously thought better of it and walked to the kitchen counter to grab his keys. She avoided his eyes as she followed him into the garage and helped Biscuit into the Jeep.

The only sound during the five minute ride was Biscuit's paws excitedly racing back and forth across the back seat. Before the Jeep had completely stopped in Grandpa's driveway, she threw open her door.

His hand on her arm stopped her. "I'm sorry if I hurt you," he said quietly.

Her teeth clenched as she turned to glare at him. "Well, you're pretty good at that, aren't you?" She jerked away her arm and climbed out. After Biscuit jumped out of the back seat, she slammed the door and stomped towards the house.

Less than five steps into her retreat, regret overcame her. Oh, that was mean, Kricket. That was really, really mean. She berated herself as tears streamed down her face. But she couldn't take it back, so she kept walking. Like a coward. And even though it took Grandpa forever to get to the door, she didn't turn around.

He stayed in the driveway for some time after she went inside. She watched him through the curtains, just sitting with his forehead against the steering wheel. She wanted to run back out and tell him she was sorry. That she loved him. But she didn't. Again, like a coward.

He finally raised his head and looked towards the house, then left.

CHAPTER 21

Monday, March 13th
...They say that after you make love to someone, everything changes. But it also changes when you don't...

Today's goal: *To just breathe...*

THE WARM BEADS OF water pulsated against her head and streamed down her body, creating a sultry mind-numbing cocoon. She closed her eyes and soaped her body, moving slowly down her neck, across her collar bone and circling each breast, imprinting the memory of Jay's touch in her mind. The daydreams that had enveloped her since that first night she'd danced with him were now replaced with a taste of the real thing. A sumptuous morsel leaving her starving for more. The entanglement of their bodies, his commanding hands, his greedy lips...oh his lips. Her mind languished in the feel of his soft whiskers grazing her skin.

The sudden coldness of the water jolted her back to reality, banishing the memory of desire in his eyes, and replacing it with his look of devastation after she spat out those hateful words. She thrust the shower knob to the off position, wrapped herself in a towel and sunk to the bathroom floor. She'd obviously thrown him a gut punch, because he rarely showed emotion on his face. Except when he smiled. She tried to picture the way his eyes softened and one corner of his mouth turned up a tiny bit more than the other, but the image imprinted in her mind was the slack in his jaw and the droop in his eyes, as if his heart had ceased beating.

How had last night ended so badly? They'd had such a tender moment when he finally opened up to her. Of course she didn't want to be another one night stand, but she refused to believe there wasn't something more. So what had she done wrong? He'd always loved her, she knew that. And the way he'd kissed her that first night, and last night...there was definitely attraction. Why couldn't he just let it happen?

By the time she hoisted herself from the bathroom floor, her hair had half-dried into a wavy mess. Oh, what she'd give to stay home from work and barricade herself from the world beneath her comforter. But the programmers had worked all weekend on the latest round of SkillHunter changes, so she couldn't possibly stay home and coddle herself. At least she'd have an excuse for holing up in her office and avoiding everyone...meaning Jay.

She grabbed her phone off the bathroom counter and pulled up her calendar, praying her schedule was clear for the day. All the air spilled from her lungs. A 2:00 p.m. Board meeting. How could she bear that? Her stomach curdled just thinking about sitting near Jay for two hours trying to pretend like all was right with the world. Why did Tom still include her in their stupid board meetings anyway? She twisted her hair into a knot, pulled on a sweater and pants, and rushed out the door.

Jay's Jeep was already in the parking garage when she arrived, which didn't surprise her, since she was nearly an hour late. She slipped down the hallway to her office and partially closed the door to ward off anyone who dared to venture into the bat wing.

By noon she'd only made it through a few pages of the SkillHunter changes. Her concentration was thwarted by the continuous replay of last night in her head...and of this morning. Poor Grandpa hadn't seen her cry like that since she was a child. She couldn't help but wither into his arms and release tears of anger, disappointment, embarrassment, and most of all, tears of regret for what she'd said. Somehow Grandpa had known exactly what she needed. No questions, just silently holding her and stroking her hair while she cried it out.

Gayle's voice startled her. "You and Jay should call a meeting so you can stare into space together," she said, pushing the door open with her foot. She plopped a box of pizza and two bottles of water on Kricket's small conference table. "I grabbed the Canadian bacon and pineapple before the programmers got their paws all over it." She scooted a chair out from the table and patted the other one. "Come sit. You look like you need a break. And I need a place to hide out for a little while. Jay's in a mood," she said, rolling her eyes. "When he's not staring into space, he's barking orders at me like I'm a dancing poodle."

Well that answered her question about how Jay was handling it. At least he was angry. She'd much rather see him angry than hurt.

Gayle was already firmly planted at the table, so even though she was hardly in the mood for chitchat, she pasted on a smile and pushed away from her desk. Food sounded vulgar, but Gayle would know something was up if she didn't eat anything, so after sitting down, she selected a small piece of pizza.

Gayle eyed her over the rim of her soda. "Did you go to family day yesterday?"

She nodded.

"How was it?"

She took another bite and chewed slowly. Gayle knew Jay better than anyone, so she decided to throw out some bait. "Meg's pregnant," she said, closely watching Gayle's reaction.

Gayle pinched the bridge of her nose and shook her head. "Jay didn't take it well, did he?"

"Not at all." Kricket dropped a half-eaten pizza slice on her plate. "I didn't know about the abortion until last night. Why would he keep that from me?"

"Don't take it personally, hon," Gayle said, patting her hand. "You know how men are. They don't like to talk about stuff. He hasn't told many people outside the family."

No doubt he'd told Victoria. The thought of Jay confiding in her while they were in bed, and then letting her console him with her body made her nauseous.

"Does he ever see her? Rachel, I mean?"

"No. She left for Chicago the very next day. That's where she's from, and that's where the man she was having an affair with lived. She traveled there a lot on business, so…" She raised her eyebrows knowingly. "The divorce was handled through their attorneys, so Jay never saw her again. Just like that, she was gone," she said, snapping her fingers. "I imagine she was pretty shocked though. She got very little out of the divorce. Tom could see the writing on the wall before Jay married her—we all could—so he insisted Jay have a pre-nup to protect the ownership of the company."

"What was she like?"

Gayle thought for a moment before responding. "In a word? Unsatisfiable. That woman wouldn't have been happy if Jay's fine white ass was made of pure gold."

Kricket laughed for the first time that day. "Unsatisfiable isn't a word, but you certainly painted a picture in my mind." A moment of levity felt good.

"He's lucky to have you, you know. He may not admit it, or even know it yet, but he needs you."

Kricket hoped her wince at those stinging words wasn't visible. 'I need you,' he'd said. That was when everything went horribly wrong.

CHAPTER 22

JAY'S EYES BURNED FROM lack of sleep. He gave in to their plea and closed them for a moment while half-listening to Mitch present the February sales results in the Board meeting. Jay was sure Mitch and Meg hadn't planned another baby, but they seemed thrilled. Now their perfect lives would be even more perfect. They'd only dated six months before getting married, but apparently Mitch knew he had chosen well. Meg was smart as a whip, beautiful, and just feisty enough to keep Mitch on his toes.

He, on the other hand, had picked a certified card-carrying cunt. Sure, Rachel's affair had been a nut-punch, but the abortion had sucked him into the depths of an icy black sea. He'd drifted in the comfort of its numbness for nearly two years. Until Kricket.

He rather liked the wall he'd built around himself, but the moment he'd caught a glimpse of her at Starbucks, something warmed inside him. She was a soothing summer rain slowly melting his icy barricade. He was helpless against the gentle way she moved, her flowery smell, and that shy smile that spread easily across her face when she saw him. Until last night.

He glanced across the table at her for the hundredth time, hoping to catch her eye so he could at least mouth that he was sorry. But her eyes were focused on the handout Mitch was reviewing. Board meetings still made her nervous, but she was slowly becoming more and more confident in expressing her opinion—both in and out of the board room. He'd certainly witnessed that this morning. Her words had hurt him to the core. But she had every right to be angry. What man fucking jumps out of bed right when things are getting hot? She's probably sitting there counting the things she considers wrong with her perfect little body.

Her movement caught his eye, as she stretched her neck from side to side with her eyes closed. He couldn't help but picture her head tilting back to give him full access as he trailed kisses down her collarbone. She'd suck in a soft sigh when his lips reached her breasts. He closed his eyes and pictured her breasts. The light of the moon had reflected their beauty; small and silky with a perfect sized pink nipple perched proudly on the end. And her butt. His fingers ached to release that fiery mane from its bondage and watch the curls slide down her back until they rested just above her naked heart shaped butt. He'd felt its tight smoothness. But he longed to see it in the light of the moon as well. And somewhere on it was a cricket tattoo he wanted to see up close and personal. She may be shy on the outside, but her little body had lost all control when he'd touched her. He pinched the bridge of his nose to cast out the image. This was Krissy. But now that he'd felt her body pressing against his, would he ever be able to look at her again without wanting every inch of her? An image of Tara's makeup smeared face popped into his mind, sneering, "She'll never have you."

Mitch slugged his arm. Jay looked up to see Tom's penetrating stare. "I asked if you agree, Jay."

Shit. He glanced around the room, trying to gauge his expected response from their expressions, but he saw nothing but annoyance in their stares.

"Yes sir, I agree."

Apparently that was the right answer, because Tom said, "We all agree then," and moved on. Hopefully he hadn't just agreed to trade in his Company Range Rover for a Prius.

On the chance Kricket was watching out of her peripheral vision, he crossed his arms and slowly traced the length of his scar with his index finger. Without lifting her eyes from the handout, she crossed her arms and did the same. Not absentmindedly like she sometimes did when she was nervous, but slowly and deliberately. She glanced up at him. Only for a moment, but long enough for him to know they would be okay. They had to be okay. The taste of having her was nothing like the taste of losing her. And he simply could not lose her. Not again. Family members could scream and yell and even hate each other sometimes, but in the end, they were still family. Tom and Karen considered her a daughter. Mitch and Meg considered her a sister. And Miles and Madi called her Aunt Kricket. As long as he treated her like a little sister, there was no risk in losing her. And if that was the only way he could have her, then so be it.

He could tell by the angle of her body that her legs were outstretched under the table, so he reached with his foot and gently rested his ankle against hers. The leg jerked away, and Mitch stopped in the middle of his presentation, giving him a 'what the hell' look.

Shit, wrong leg. He pulled back his leg and sat up straight just as Tom slammed the gavel on the table. Kricket jumped, then sat up straight, wide-eyed.

"This meeting is adjourned until tomorrow morning," Tom barked, glowering first at him, then at Kricket. "And I expect the two of you to have settled whatever is keeping you from focusing on the matters of this board meeting." He picked up his folder and marched out the door, followed closely by the Legal Beagle.

"Well, fuuuck me running," Jay mumbled, leaning back in his chair and clasping his hands behind his head. His brother laughed, and Kricket's face looked like she'd just watched someone shoot a puppy.

"Relax, Kricket," Mitch said. "Dad just likes to use his gavel. His bark's worse than his bite." He winked at her and grinned.

"I've got to admit, it was a little hard concentrating on my report while both of you were playing footsie with me."

"I was just stretching my legs, Mitch," Kricket said, glancing at the table.

Mitch pushed himself away from the table and stood up with a smart-ass grin on his face. "I'm just glad Dad called the meeting before Kricket slid her hand under the table and accidentally grabbed the wrong dick."

Kricket's mouth fell open. Jay had never seen her turn so red, but he couldn't help but laugh.

Mitch gathered his papers, then stood and winked at Kricket. "My legs aren't the only thing longer and easier to find," he said, before heading towards the door.

"Hey, Mitch, you forgot something," he said. When Mitch turned around, Jay gave him the one finger salute. Mitch smirked as he closed the blinds, then punched the off button on the room monitor keypad. "There. You kids can kiss and make up now." He was still laughing as he closed the door behind him.

Jay moved to the chair next to Kricket so she wouldn't have to look at him while they talked. He lay his hand on the table in front of her with his palm up. She stared at it for a moment, then covered his palm with hers. He could feel her heartbeat in her thumb when they laced fingers. He couldn't imagine not being able to touch her. Even if it was only like this.

"I hurt you," he said, after silently absorbing her touch.

"And I hurt you."

They both started speaking at the same time, then stopped.

He squeezed her hand. "This was my fault. Can I go first?"

She bit her lip and nodded. He'd give anything if she would look at him, but he knew she wouldn't. This was too serious.

He brought her hand to his lips and held it in a soft kiss for a moment as regret squeezed his heart. "You, in all your gentleness and kindness, tried to be there for me. And I repaid you by hurting you. I'm truly sorry."

"What I said this morning was so ugly," she said, obviously fighting back tears. "I didn't mean it and I had no right to say it. You've been nothing but wonderful to me…for my entire life."

He held up his scarred arm. "Forgive?"

When she pressed her pale arm to his, he fought hard not to sweep her up and tell her he'd never hurt her again. But if he'd learned anything in his thirty-three years, it was that promises get broken and people get hurt. And hurting her was simply not an option.

She nodded, then surprisingly, fully met his gaze. "Promise you'll tell me about your demons instead of keeping them bottled inside?"

He nodded, wanting to pull her close and breathe in the scent of her hair, feel her heart beat against his, and keep her there forever. But he couldn't.

The silence in the room surrounded them as he carefully considered his next words. Based on the passionate way she'd returned his advances last night, she obviously wanted more than he could give her. He brushed a strand of hair from her face. "I don't want my mistake last night to become a thorn in our relationship. You are, and have always been, an essential part of my life. Even while we were apart, there was a piece of you that I just couldn't let go." His mind grasped for an alternative to the word *but*. The one word that would contaminate everything else he said.

"I want to be sure that never changes." Well, hell. Now it sounded like he was proposing. He took another breath and blew it out, forcing himself to say what needed to be said.

For once, he was the one who couldn't meet her eyes. He couldn't bear to watch their hopeful look wilt. "I realize I've been monopolizing your time. SkillHunter will soon be at a point where you don't need to work as many hours, so I want you to go out and have some fun. You know, date someone." His heart screamed as the words left his mouth, and it took every ounce of skill he'd mastered to wipe all emotion from his face.

CHAPTER 23

Wednesday, April 12th
...Do something courageous. I'd say working alongside Jay with
a smile plastered on my face for the last month surely counts as
doing something courageous.

Today's goal: Quit being a fool.

SHE HADN'T PLANNED ON going for an evening run, but her lunch time therapeutic shopping trip resulted in a pair of lime green running shoes. With work slowing down, she was finally able to get out of H-Tech at a decent hour, so it was time get back into her running routine. Instead of driving to the running trails at the park, she headed towards the edge of town. The streets for a new housing development were being grated, so the only thing she had to share her run with were the idle dump trucks and backhoes patiently waiting for their drivers to start them up again on Monday morning.

The lowering sun was slowly giving way to a slightly damp chill in the air. The wind had picked up, so she dug under the seats of her Jeep, hoping to find a stray ball cap. Naturally all she found was a hot pink rhinestone 'Princess' cap, meant for a nine-year-old, that Grandpa and Dot had brought her from Disney World. She thread her ponytail through the hole in the back, tucked her key in the hidden pouch of her running pants and took off, emptying her mind of everything except the sound of her feet hitting the pavement and the steady in and out of her breath.

But images of Jay crept in to taunt her. How was she supposed to ignore her feelings when she had to see him every single day, either in person or on Skype? She wanted him in the worst way. And even though he was strictly hands off, it was impossible to remain oblivious to the quickening of her heart when their heads were hovered together over a SkillHunter proof, or to his crooked grin when they shared an inside joke, or to the sexy way he held his mouth while mulling over an idea. Even the sound of him clearing his throat made her lady parts tingle.

And at night as she lay in bed willing herself to fall asleep, when would she stop checking her phone every five minutes for his goodnight text? 'Sweetest of dreams, Kricket.' She longed to see those words again. But it was clear that anything he considered affectionate or intimate was now inappropriate. She was beyond little sister-zoned now. She was employee-zoned.

Besides, in his eyes, she would always be a shy clumsy kid. Maybe she could never live up to the high heeled, short skirted business women who boldly vied for his attention. But the longer she ran, the stronger her resolve became to show him—to show everyone—that she wasn't a delicate little shy girl anymore. Jay, Grandpa, Becca, and yes, most of all...herself.

Her legs felt like noodles when she finally made it back to Grasshopper. She grabbed a water bottle out of the cup holder and perched on the front bumper to scroll through Twitter while her body cooled down. Her Twitter Jeep Mafia friends thought Grasshopper was a beast. They didn't need to know her off-roading experience solely consisted of riding shotgun in Jay's Jeep, and that half the time she hopped out because he was going to try climbing something that might not end well. She was surprised how close she'd become to the others who helped run the Jeep Mafia account. They were spread from Washington to Florida, and everywhere in between, but she hoped to meet them all at a Jeep event someday. Actually, now would be good. Being away from Jay for a while might be just what she needed.

The sun was dipping low, so she stood and stretched her back from side to side before climbing into Grasshopper. Just beyond a *Road Closed* sign, an enormous hill piled high by the dirt movers caught her eye. A photo from the top of that hill would make a great tweet. She glanced around to make sure she was alone, then inched Grasshopper between the sign and the dirt movers and stopped at the bottom of the hill to size it up. From this angle, the hill was more than a little daunting, but a small price for a great photo. And even more importantly, no one would ever again be able to call Grasshopper a *Pavement Princess*.

"So are we going to do this or not?" she asked Grasshopper. Since she was climbing a hill, she assumed she needed to shift into 4-wheel drive, because after all that's what it was for, right? She shifted into drive then pulled on the 4WD knob, but it didn't move. Pushing aside the fear she'd break something, she jerked the knob really hard. It lurched into place. "Ah, there we go." Her heart was beating ridiculously fast. Why was she such a wimp?

"Are you ready, girl?" She cranked up her stereo for moral support and pressed on the gas pedal. Grasshopper's front end started climbing, but the back tires spun in the loose dirt at the base of the hill. She pressed harder on the gas pedal, but the tires just dig deeper. The last thing she needed was to get stuck, so she let off the gas. Grasshopper rocked back slightly and stopped in the cavern the tires had dug.

"This is not a problem, this is not a problem, this is not a problem," she told herself, forcing her mind to concentrate. She shifted into reverse and stomped on the gas, proud of herself for thinking to turn the steering wheel so the front tires didn't end up in the ruts dug out by the back tires.

She sat at the bottom of the hill gazing upwards. It was hardly a large hill. One might even call it a dirt pile. It was certainly climbable. This hill was not going to win. She just needed to get a running start. Her heart was pounding, but she could hear the hill calling to her, "C'mon chicken. A real Jeep girl would do it." Her mind dwelled on a number of other things that could go wrong. She had no idea how fast to go. If she went too slowly, she might get halfway up and get stuck, or worse, roll back down and possibly flip over. And if she went too fast, she might take flight off the other side. Neither possibility was appealing. But it was time to stop being a little girl and start taking some risk.

She backed up about fifty yards and started moving slowly towards the hill, then yanked the knob into 4-wheel drive and stomped on the gas. This time the rear tires dug in and Grasshopper chugged up the hill. When they reached the top of the hill, she gunned it a little to be sure they made it over, then cruised down the other side. She made a wide circle and stopped to face the hill and revel in her victory. In her glee, she forgot to snap a photo from the top. She could hear her Twitter friends now..."Pics or it didn't happen."

She lowered all four windows, scanned through her *Bad Girl* playlist, cranked up her favorite song, then floored it. The wind whipped her ponytail as they forged up the hill at the perfect pace. She'd never been an adrenaline junkie, but this victory felt sweet. At the crest of the hill, she brought Grasshopper to a stop. The blood drained from her face. Sitting at the bottom of the hill was a motorcycle cop, watching her. And waiting.

She was going to be arrested and she was going to jail. She punched the radio button to squelch her blaring music, hoping to appear like the law-abiding citizen that she was instead of a reckless thrill seeker. Her heart pounded as she gripped the steering wheel and inched Grasshopper down the hill. Of course this would happen a week after she bought a gun to keep in her Jeep. Why had she chosen *that* to fulfill the 'Do Something Brave' step in her journal? Rule number one from her concealed weapon certification class popped into her mind as she pulled up beside him. They made it abundantly clear that if you get pulled over with a gun in your car, you must notify the policeman immediately. She practiced what to say while she watched him get off his motorcycle and walk to her window.

"I have a gun," she blurted, turning to pop open her center console.

"Stop," he said firmly. "Put your hands on the steering wheel."

She slammed the console lid shut and gripped the steering wheel.

"Please step out of your vehicle."

As she slid from the Jeep, visions of herself skulking in the corner of a jail cell while three burly women played rock, paper, scissors to see who got to have her first whirled through her mind. She hadn't had sex in nearly a year and now she was going to be a shared love slave.

"That, Ms. Taylor, is how you get yourself shot." He took off his sunglasses and looked at her pointedly. "Is that what they told you to say in your license to carry class?"

"No sir," she squeaked out. "It's what they told us *not* to say." Was it a good thing or a bad thing that it was the same cop? Second offense...bad. The fact that he had a slight grin and remembered her name...potentially good.

He pointed towards the sign. "Did you notice that large sign as you drove around it? The one that says 'Road Closed' in large letters?"

She nodded, fixing her eyes on a pile of beer cans a few feet in front of her, undoubtedly left by some teenagers who had sought out this secluded place for a Friday night party.

"Do you remember the speed limit signs we talked about last time?"

"Yes sir."

"They're not kidding with these signs either." He took off his sunglasses, then leaned inside the Jeep and looked around. "So what else do you have in here? Hand grenades? Drug paraphernalia? Dead body?"

When he turned back towards her with a broad smile, relief washed through her. "Would you mind telling me exactly what you're doing out here?"

"I came out here for a nice solitary run, and then I saw the hill. And, well I'm just tired of everyone telling me my Jeep's a mall crawler, so I climbed it." She crossed her arms, immediately realizing that she looked and sounded like a pouting child.

"I like what you've done to your Jeep," he said, admiring Grasshopper's new wheels and bumper. "And if it's any consolation, you hardly looked like a mall crawler when I saw you scale that hill." He tweaked the brim of her ball cap and grinned. "You know, it's not a good idea for a *Princess* to be out here running by herself."

She'd completely forgotten she was wearing the stupid Princess hat. "This was a gift from my grandparents. They forget that I'm not still in junior high," she said, adjusting her hat. "And I wasn't expecting to see anyone out here."

"My point exactly. We may live in a safe town, but running in a secluded area is never a good idea."

She shrugged her shoulders. "I just needed a little reality escape."

He nodded with a knowing smile. "Running's good for that."

"You run?" Flirting obviously wasn't her strong suit, but maybe a common interest would get her out of a ticket. Her going to jail worry had dissipated.

"Not as much as I'd like, but I try to get in one good run a week." He paused for a moment as if considering what to say, then pulled his wallet out of his pocket. "If you ever want a bodyguard when you run, here's my card." He smoothed the bent corners before handing the card to her. "I'm Levi, by the way. Levi Somers."

"Cops have business cards?"

He laughed. "I work as a personal trainer on my days off. I'm going for a run around Lake Hefner Saturday afternoon, if you're up for it."

She shrugged. "Thanks, but I'm having lunch with my best friend and we usually end up shopping afterwards."

"Maybe another time then." He smiled and opened the door. "If you'll just scoot back around that Road Closed sign, I'll pretend I never saw you." He held the door as she climbed in, then shut it behind her and stood with his hand on the door handle. "Although that won't be an easy feat," he added with a wink.

She felt her face flush as she started the engine. What was she supposed to say to that?

"And Ms. Taylor?" he said, after stepping away from the Jeep.

She looked into his face, soft with empathy.

"Whatever it is you're escaping from. It'll work itself out."

CHAPTER 24

Saturday, April 15th
...I'm pretty proud of myself for not completely making a fool of myself with the cop, who I'm pretty sure was flirting with me...

Today's goal: *Practice flirting...*

BECCA TOOK A DAINTY bite of her egg white omelet. "I can't believe you turned down a date with the hot cop. Just think how much fun we could have shopping for it today."

"He didn't ask me out. He asked me to go running," Kricket said, waving down the waiter to ask for another napkin. Her caramel drizzled chocolate chip pancakes were orgasmic, but messy. "He offered to be my running partner, that's all."

"You said he offered to be your *body guard*. And how can you pour that much sugar into your body so early in the morning?" Her face contorted with disgust. "After that breakfast of champions, you *need* to go on a run."

Kricket wiped a drip of caramel from her chin and slowly licked her finger. "I have a ridiculously healthy green shake every weekday morning, so I deserve this. You should try it. Maybe you wouldn't be so uptight all the time, and Kevin would want to have sex with you more often."

"He's just really stressed in his job right now. Nothing a little new sexy lingerie can't cure," Becca said with a flip of her hair. "Perhaps you should focus that sass on flirting, and check off a journal challenge instead of bashing your friend." She nodded towards a table across the room. "That guy's been eyeing you. Although he probably lost interest after watching you attack those pancakes like a piranha."

She casually glanced at the table then shook her head. "Not my type."

"Who cares? Jay said you should date, so that's exactly what you need to do. Jealousy is a great motivator."

"I'm not going on a date just to make him jealous. It wouldn't work anyway."

"Do you consider the cop your type?"

"Maybe. He's good-looking. But he was just being nice."

"Open your eyes, *Princess*. Despite your atrocious fashion sense, he's obviously interested or he would have hauled your ass to jail for climbing a stupid pile of dirt. "What's his name again?"

She fished his card out of her purse. "Levi Somers," she read, pretending she didn't remember his name. In one fell swoop, Becca snatched the card from her hand and plucked Kricket's phone from the table.

"Don't you dare," she said through gritted teeth. She grabbed at her phone, but Becca leaned back out of her reach. "Becca, please don't," she pleaded.

Becca held up a finger to shush her while she punched in the number. There was nothing she could do short of leaping across the table and gripping Becca's neck in a stronghold, but she wasn't interested in making a scene. Please don't let him answer. Please don't let him answer.

"Hi Levi," Becca said in her most sexy voice. "This is Kricket. You know, the Jeep girl who likes to break the law."

Kricket polished off her mimosa in one gulp.

Becca laughed daintily at his response. "I was thinking of going for a run later, and I'm looking for a bodyguard. Know anyone man enough for the job?" Becca winked as Kricket contemplated stabbing herself with her butter knife.

"That sounds perfect. I'll see you at four-thirty. I'm looking forward to it too."

Becca held out her phone. "Close your mouth, Kricket. You said your goal today was to flirt with someone."

Kricket glared at her. "That was hardly what I had in mind."

Becca turned on her innocent look. "I was just trying to help."

"Maybe I don't need your help. Besides, it doesn't count unless I do it myself."

"Tell you what. I'll let you go on this date all by yourself."

"It's not a date," she corrected. Her stomach was beginning to ache. And not because of the pancakes.

CHAPTER 25

CONVERSATION HADN'T BEEN NECESSARY while they were running, but now that they were settled on the patio at the lakeside tavern, she searched her mind for something, anything to say. The moment the waitress brought their beers, Kricket downed half of hers to fill the empty silence.

"The run was great," he said. "Thanks for inviting me." A shy grin slid across his face. "I was surprised when you called."

"I have a confession to make. It wasn't me who called. It was my friend Becca. In case you haven't noticed, I'm way too shy for that."

At first his brow furrowed, but then he grinned as realization hit him. "I thought the conversation seemed a little out of character for you. Well, I'm glad Becca called."

They ordered beers and burgers, then sat in silence watching the windsurfers on the lake. "Do you—" They both started talking at the same time, then stopped and laughed.

"Go ahead," he said.

"No, you go."

He took a quick sip of water, a move she easily recognized as an attempt to cover the feeling of awkwardness. "I was just going to say that I'm a little shy too."

"Really?" She grinned. "You certainly didn't seem shy when you were chiding me about being a lawbreaker."

"Well, you *were* breaking the law, and it *is* my job to enforce it."

"Thanks for not enforcing it to the extreme. You looked

pretty bad-ass sitting on that motorcycle." She blushed when she realized she'd basically admitted his hotness.

"It's an illusion, trust me. I'm pretty low-key when I'm not in uniform."

She nodded towards the windsurfers on the lake. "Have you ever done that?"

His face clouded. "No, I used to be a big wakeboarder, but I took a bad fall and messed up my rotator cuff about five years ago. I haven't been able to wakeboard since."

Once the beer kicked in, conversation flowed easily. He asked questions about her job and her family, and before she knew it, they were laughing and trying to one up each other with tales of their exes' faults.

She glanced at her watch, shocked at how long they'd been talking. "It's after midnight. I really should get going."

He waved down the waitress and insisted on paying the tab.

"I have a confession to make too," he said as they crossed the parking lot to her Jeep.

Aaaand here it comes. He's married, gay, or some kind of sex freak. She knew it. He was way too nice to be just a normal guy.

"When you called this morning, I had just finished a seven-mile run," he said, rubbing his leg. "I probably won't be able to walk tomorrow."

"Oh, you poor thing. Why didn't you tell me? I mean, why didn't you tell Becca?" They both laughed.

"I was so surprised when you called, I couldn't say no," he said with a shrug. "My legs will definitely be complaining tomorrow, but it was worth it."

The realization that he might want to kiss her goodnight smacked her. As did the realization that she wasn't ready to kiss anyone, so upon reaching Grasshopper, she thrust open the door so it was between them. "I really had a good time. Thanks for the burger and beer," she spat out a bit too abruptly.

The touch of his hand made her jump. He blushed and moved it away. "I'm sorry, I'm a touchy person. My whole family is." He stuck his hands in his windbreaker pockets. "I enjoyed our run. Maybe we can go again next week."

"I'd like that," she said. And she wasn't just being nice. She really would.

CHAPTER 26

Sunday, May 13th

...They're not my family and I'm not obligated to go. So why did I turn down Levi's invitation to go to an afternoon movie? Is it because after three weeks I can't keep avoiding his kiss? Or is it because Family Day is the only time Jay lets his guard down and treats me like he used to? I don't think I want to answer that question.

Today's goal: *Avoid a potential kissing situation. I know, I know, that's the opposite of a journal goal...*

"Where's Kricket?" Jay wiped his hands on his shirt before opening the refrigerator door to grab two beers.

Meg looked up from the iPad she was hovered over at the kitchen table. "She's in Miles' room, giving him romance advice. Are you guys finished putting the soft top on her Jeep?"

"Not yet." Mitch wrapped his arms around her from behind and patted her belly. "We spread it out in the sun for a little while to loosen the fabric. It's a really tight fit the first time, but after it gets stretched out, it's a lot easier to get it on."

Jay laughed at Meg's raised eyebrows.

"At least that's the way Kricket described it to us," Mitch said, laughing. "She said that's the advice the guy at the off-road store gave her.

"I hope that's not the romance advice she's giving Miles." Jay twisted the cap off his beer and glanced at the iPad as he took a swig. "Wait, you're watching them? What happened to the no spying rule?" He frowned at Meg, then gave Mitch a WTF look. "Seriously guys, don't you think it's time to scale back on the monitoring cameras, at least in Miles' room? He's fourteen. Have you considered what you might catch him doing in there?"

"Surely he's smart enough to beat off in the bathroom," Mitch said.

"Honey! That's my son you're talking about."

"Well he's my son too, full of powerful Hunter testosterone," Mitch said, nuzzling Meg's ear as he slid into the chair beside her. "So, Kricket is giving Miles romance advice, huh? This should be entertaining."

"I think it's sweet," Meg said. "It's nice that he has someone to talk to who isn't full of Hunter testosterone and understands his shyness. Don't you think it's hard on him being around you two big-mouthed beefcakes all the time?"

Mitch wiggled his eyebrows at her. "So, you think I'm a beefcake, huh?"

She rolled her eyes at him. "Is that all you got out of this conversation? Your son needs romance advice. Aren't you remotely curious about that?"

Even though Jay chastised them for stepping over the privacy line, he found himself peering over Meg's shoulder at the screen. Kricket was perched on the arm of a gaming chair, facing Miles who sat cross-legged on his bed. She had on those heart-stopping yoga pants and a lime green running shirt, but it was the compassion in her smile that got him. She had no idea how beautiful she was. He forced a picture of her as a child into his mind to tame the dragon that Meg would surely notice, given the proximity of her eyes to his crotch.

"You're grinning," Meg said, looking up at him.

"So?" He took a swig of beer so he could break eye contact without looking guilty.

"You do that when you watch her."

He gave her a silent stare to show he wasn't amused, then looked back at the screen.

Mitch eyed Jay as he took a swig of beer. "It's painful watching you and Kric's hormones screaming for each other. Why don't you just man up and take her for a ride in your bed instead of in your Jeep?"

Meg swatted Mitch's arm, then turned towards Jay. "What he means is why don't you tell her how you feel?"

"You know why." He glared at her then eyed Mitch. "And when did you decide I was good enough for her?"

A rare show of empathy washed over his brother's face. "I see how you look at her, man. And rumor has it you're breaking conference ladies' hearts left and right with your sudden disinterest in the treasures they offer up."

When Jay gave him a go-to-hell look, Mitch held up both hands resignedly. "I can't help it if the Jessicas like to talk."

He made a mental note to have a sit down with the Jessicas in the morning. "Maybe I got tired of being a *man-whore*," he said pointedly to Meg. "Your eight-year-old daughter called me that by the way." He fully enjoyed the transition of Meg's facial expression as it moved from shock to guilt. "You might want to change the password on that iPad, or at least take it with you into the bedroom at night. Hopefully she hasn't already seen a demonstration of how *that* happened," he said, pointing his chin at her belly.

To his satisfaction, Meg looked horrified. Ahhh, paybacks were great. "Kricket's going out with that cop. She's happy. That's all that matters."

"His name is Levi," Meg reminded him. "And how do you know she's happy?"

Levi, the guy Kricket was falling for. The guy who kissed her goodnight, and hopefully nothing more. His jaw tightened. The thought of a man touching her made blood spew from his ears. Kricket's voice brought his attention to the screen.

"C'mon Miles, of course you know how to kiss a girl," she said. "You kiss Madi, and your mom, and Grandma Karen, don't you?"

"I don't kiss them, they kiss me!" Miles screwed up his face like he'd just eaten brussels sprouts. "Besides, that's different. I need to know how to french-kiss," he said, wiggling his tongue.

Kricket's face screwed up like a prune. "Miles! First of all, no girl wants to see a guy coming at her tongue first. And secondly, you don't need to be french-kissing at fourteen! I didn't get my first kiss until I was eighteen!"

Jay laughed to himself at her innocence. How she'd made it that long without some guy sticking his tongue down her throat was beyond him.

Miles looked at her wide-eyed. "Eighteen? Were you fugly or what?"

He cowered when she raised her eyebrows at him. "No, I wasn't, and don't use that word."

"Sorry. So you haven't kissed that many boys then. Do you even know how?"

"Yes I do, thank you very much," she said, resting her hands on her hips and sticking out her chin in the same manner Gayle did no fewer than three times a day.

Miles leaned forward, wide-eyed. "How many boys have you kissed?"

"*That* is none of your business."

"So who was the best kisser? I want Breanna to think I'm the best kisser."

Kricket's sassy look vanished.

Miles slid off the bed and leaned against the edge. "I know you've kissed Jay. Is he a good kisser? Does he kiss better than Levi?"

Meg touched his arm. "Do you want me to turn it off?"

He shook his head. The memory of their first kiss was emblazoned in his mind. The way Kricket's hesitant green eyes had peered up at him, fearful, yet wanting. He pushed the memory away again, just like he did every time he saw her, every time he heard her voice, every time he got close enough to breathe in her scent, every time he closed his eyes to sleep, every effing hour of every effing day.

"Jay's the best kisser," Kricket said quietly, jolting him back to the present.

The sound of his name rolling off her lips caused the blood to drain from his face into a pool around his heart. The haunted look on her face startled him.

"What makes him a good kisser?" Miles asked

She rolled her eyes. "Do we really have to do this?"

"Please? I really like her."

Jay could relate to the lovesick desperation on Miles' face.

After a moment, she squared her shoulders. "Okay, fine. But only because I know you really like Breanna." Her face was red, but full of resignation as she began. "Your first kiss should be whisper-soft."

Miles scrunched his forehead. "What's whisper-soft?"

She paused for a moment, apparently fighting a case of the giggles. "I'll demonstrate using my hand. But I'm not showing you a french kiss, just a regular kiss. A good regular kiss can be…well never mind." She shook her head. "Hold up your hand like this and make a fist," she said, demonstrating.

Miles snickered and turned red, but held up his fist.

"Now, work your thumb like the mouth of a Breanna puppet." She moved her thumb up and down as if it were talking. "See? Now, close the puppet's mouth and pretend your thumb is her bottom lip. Open your mouth just a little and close it slowly around her bottom lip."

Miles watched intently as she slowly raised her fist and gently took her thumb between her lips in a kiss.

"Ho-ly shit." Jay's dick pressed against his zipper as he stared at the screen in horror. Her intention was good, but she had no idea what she was probably doing to poor Miles, and to him.

"Hell, *I'm* getting a boner watching this," Mitch said, shoving Jay. "Get in there and handle that, bro, before Miles popcorns the ceiling and humiliates them both."

The look on Meg's face was priceless. He set down his beer and jogged upstairs to Miles' room, taking a moment to adjust his jeans to give himself a little more crotch room.

The door was partially ajar, so he knocked softly before pushing it open. "Hey, we're taking a beer break, so I just wanted to see what you guys were up to."

Kricket and Miles jumped and turned beet red. It was all he could do to keep from laughing at how guilty they both looked.

"Nothing," Miles said quickly. "We were just—"

"We were just talking about girls," Kricket interrupted. "Miles has a few girls chasing him, and he wanted some advice. Did you have any trouble with my soft top?" she asked brightly,

It was apparent she was trying to change the subject, so why not have a little fun? "We're taking your advice and letting it stretch out in the sun." He leaned against the wall and crossed his arms. "So, Miles, you think Kricket has better advice on handling the ladies than I do? Have you already forgotten who taught you the secret Hunter move?" He immediately regretted bringing that up.

Kricket jutted out her chin, challenging him with her eyebrows. "Maybe he wanted to learn how to kiss instead of stalk."

"Two points for Kric," he said wryly.

Miles looked at Jay, then at Kricket, then grinned. "She was going to show me how to kiss. Using her hand," Miles threw in quickly, apparently realizing what that sounded like. "Maybe you could show me, Uncle Jay…on Kricket. You know, pretend she's one of those CPR dummies."

A bright flush ran up her neck, but she pulled off a quick recovery by making a face at Miles. "Gee thanks for making me sound repulsive. Perhaps you've forgotten that his *special* Hunter move demonstration was less than stellar."

Miles held up four fingers and grinned. "Two more points for Kricket."

She was now four points ahead, and *that* was something he had to rectify. If she wanted a duel, she was going to get one.

"I'm confident he won't be disappointed in my performance this time. Nor will you," he said, wishing he could throw a T-shirt or something over the security camera without being obvious. Mitch and Meg were undoubtedly laughing their asses off right now.

Although she tried to mask it, her body tensed as he closed the gap between them. Miles leaned forward on the edge of the bed, wide-eyed.

"The important thing to remember is the *anticipation* of the kiss should be almost as good as the actual kiss." Although he was speaking to Miles, he kept his eyes on her. "Your every move should be slow." He reached out and tucked a strand of hair behind her ear, trying to ignore her fresh scent swirling around them. "Right now, she thinks you might be moving in for a kiss, but she's not certain. Her heartbeat quickens."

When she peered up at him, he locked eyes with her, wondering if her heart was beating as fast as his. "Gaze into her eyes. Make her crave your kiss." He had to congratulate her, she hadn't broken eye contact yet. "Run your thumb down her jawline and lightly tilt her chin towards you." His movement mirrored his words. "Place a light kiss on one side of her mouth." His heart lurched as he felt her smooth skin against his lips. "Then wander over to the other side." It was all he could do not to devour her, but he willed himself to move slowly as he'd instructed. "Graze the tip of her nose lightly with yours, tilt your head a little and take her top lip gently between your lips." Her lips parted slightly as he mimicked his words. "Slowly drag your lips away and then take her bottom lip." He felt her intake of breath as he captured her pouty bottom lip then gradually released it. "And, the finish is key. Rub your nose lightly on hers, and say 'goodnight' as you kiss her softly one last time." He lightly brushed her lips, then turned towards Miles, forcing himself not to gulp in a breath. "See? It's that simple. And then you just turn and walk away, leaving her speechless."

He winked at Kricket, who stood there…speechless.

Miles crossed his arms and frowned at him.

"What? Miles, it's not that hard," Jay said, struggling to suppress his frustration. Not his frustration with Miles, with the frustration building in his pants.

"But I need to know how to *french* kiss. I don't know what to do with my tongue."

Well fuuuck. Jay ran a hand over his face and glanced at Kricket to make sure he hadn't said that out loud. She toyed with the zipper on her running shirt, which did nothing for the carnal thoughts running through his head.

Miles looked up with a sheepish yet calculating grin on his face. That little shit was doing this on purpose. She was officially four points ahead, so he couldn't backpedal now. In fact, he was going to leave her four points lying in the dust with his next move.

"So, Kricket." He cocked his head and looked at her with narrowed eyes when he said her name, knowing it gave him the unfair advantage he needed. "Miles came to you for advice, not me, so why don't you tell him what to do with your tongue?"

He could see her battling a blush as she searched for a smart-ass comeback.

"Fine." She set her chin and looked straight at him. "Think of it as eating the best ice cream cone you've ever had and savoring every single lick."

His mind went places he hoped Miles hadn't heard about yet. All those years of practicing control over his facial expressions were being put to the ultimate test right now.

"Show me what you mean on Uncle Jay." Miles' voice yanked his thoughts out of the gutter. His grin hovered somewhere between curiosity, challenge, and a hint of voyeurism.

"Miles, no...just no." Kricket said. "You couldn't see anything anyway."

"Yes I could. You said not to go in tongue first, so show me how you get there."

He could tell from her stance she was nervous. Was she afraid he wouldn't kiss her? Or was she afraid he would? Was she worried about what the cop would think? Was she even thinking about the cop? Fuck the cop. He was kissing her.

"I'm not going to describe it this time, so watch closely," he said to Miles.

When he stepped towards her again, she surprisingly met his gaze. He was unsure if she was preparing for his kiss or preparing to slap him. She wavered slightly when he swept his fingers up her cheek and through her hair. He narrowed his eyes into the predator look that had worked like a charm since he'd perfected it at fifteen. Her eyes grew wide, and her lips parted as she sucked in a soft breath. Two points for Jay.

"What flavor of ice cream?" he whispered lightly as his lips brushed across hers.

"German chocolate," she whispered. "Your favorite." The come hither look in her eyes made him nearly lose his balance, and he knew from her haughty grin that his mouth was hanging open. He had to remind himself that not only was a fourteen-year-old taking studious notes, his brother and sister-in-law were glued to their SpyPad.

"Game on," he mouthed, re-harnessing his predator look. If that's the way she wanted to play, then step back, little sister, you have no idea who you're sparring with.

With her head cradled in his hands, he gazed at her until he felt the heated anticipation rise in her body. She closed her eyes and breathed in deeply as he stroked his thumb across her cheekbone. Her lips were readily awaiting his kiss, but he made her suffer. After a few moments, she opened her eyes.

"Anxious?" he whispered.

"Very."

She was playing hardball now. Figuring their score was now six to two her favor, he grazed the bridge of her nose with his, then pulled the wildcard and rested his forehead against hers. That mistake completely sucked his breath away. Cautiously nudging her lips apart with his, he took his first taste. The moment his tongue touched hers, fireworks ignited inside his head, but he forced himself to savor this stolen kiss, exploring slowly and gently. She tasted of red wine, which explained her sassiness. Everything inside him begged to devour her as he felt her lips respond, but instead, he pulled away, slowly releasing her bottom lip as their mouths parted. At the sound of her breath hitching, his lips greedily found hers again.

"Whoa," Miles said, ripping him back to the reality that he'd completely lost control in front of his family and a security camera recording to three backup files.

He tore his mouth from hers. "Got it?" he said to Miles through gritted teeth.

Miles nodded, mouth hanging open. Jay turned and left

without looking at her. Because if he did, he would take her in his arms and carry her away to the nearest private place and show her all the naughty things going through his mind. As he bolted from the room, Miles giggled and said, "I think he likes your flavor of ice cream."

He headed down the stairs two at a time towards the sound of Mitch and Meg laughing.

"Nice job, little bro. You just turned my son into a perv." Mitch said when he reached the bottom of the stairway.

He strode into the kitchen and slammed his fist in the SpyPad, shattering the screen, then grabbed his beer and stormed out the back door.

❧

Kricket stared at the doorway Jay had just escaped through. That was no tutorial kiss. He'd kissed her hard. And if he thought he could kiss her like that and just walk away, he was wrong. She grabbed Miles by the shoulders and gave him a smack on the forehead, making him turn red. "Thanks, Miles," she said, then sprinted out the door. Her long legs scaled the stairs two at a time, which worked out nicely until she reached the wood floor at the bottom, and her feet skidded out from underneath her. Her butt landed firmly on the bottom step.

"Easy, Huntress," Mitch said from the kitchen with a mixture of concern and amusement.

She used the banister to hoist herself up. "Where is he?" she asked, stalking into the kitchen.

Mitch and Meg both grinned and pointed out the door to the patio. She opened the door and marched outside. Only a few minutes had passed, but he was nowhere to be found. She walked to the edge of the patio and surveyed the golf course. Surely he hadn't made a break for it. But where did he escape to so quickly?

Mitch tapped on the window and pointed to the second story balcony. She darted to the spiral staircase and climbed them one at a time to avoid another mishap. At the top, she spotted him, leaning on the rail, surveying the golf course with his fine butt pointing right at her. Oh how she loved that man. And she was going to do everything in her power to make him admit he loved her too.

"Don't you dare kiss me like that and run away, you coward." The penetrating look on his face did nothing to dissuade her. She'd seen it too many times to let it intimidate her now.

"That look is not going to work on me," she spat, holding his gaze with her own fierce stare. The one she'd been practicing on pesky mall kiosk workers who flagged her down for a lotion sample.

He took a sip of beer and turned his gaze back towards the golf course. She would mark this date on her calendar. Jay Hunter broke eye contact first.

She basked for a moment in the heady power, then strutted towards him and propped her hands on her hips. "Look me in the eye and tell me you don't want to kiss me again."

When he didn't respond, she pushed his shoulder, as if she could actually move him. He pushed up from the balcony railing and looked down at her. Not with his intimidating look. With something else she couldn't decipher. Anger? Pain?

She took a step towards him. He moved backwards until he was pressed against a brick pillar. Her prey was cornered; who's the hunter now? He could pretend her closeness didn't make him want to kiss her, but she knew better. When she ran her hands up his chest, he caught her wrists, locking his elbows between them as a barricade.

"Kricket, don't. You have no idea what you're doing," he said through gritted teeth.

"Don't I?"

In a matter of seconds he picked her up, carried her across the balcony, and planted her firmly on a patio chair, then stood facing her with his chest heaving up and down like he'd just run a half marathon. He laced his fingers in his hair and closed his eyes.

"What in the hell is wrong with you?" she spat as angry tears sprang to her eyes. "Why can't you just let yourself love me?" A tear leaked down her cheek, but she didn't care. She swatted it with the back of her hand and glared at him.

He sat on the ottoman in front of her chair with his knees spread wide so hers fit in between them. His mouth tightened, and his forehead creased as he took her face in his palms. "Don't confuse love with being in love. The kiss was a simple demonstration for Miles, nothing more." His eyes bore into hers. "Is that clear?"

Her jaw was clenched so tightly she couldn't respond. Why was he doing this?

"Answer me, Kricket. Am I clear?"

The moment she nodded, he stood and walked away.

CHAPTER 27

Friday, June 2nd
... I'm not sure I want to continue this journey. Every time I step outside my comfort zone, it slaps me in the face. I know growth is painful, but seriously...

Today's goal: *Just be normal quiet Kricket...*

KRICKET WASN'T SURE IF Jay intentionally had stayed out of town for the majority of the two weeks since the *kissing incident*, or if his conference schedule was just heavy, but the time away from him gave her an opportunity to sort out her thoughts. Although it had taken several sleepless nights to get there, she'd finally come to the conclusion that if a man tells you he'll hurt you, he probably will. Most men don't come with a warning label. And even if he *did* want her, his access to women at conferences was too easy. And one cheater in her lifetime had been plenty.

The sound of his long stride descending down the hallway of the bat wing made her heart quicken. Not because she missed him, but because she was anxious to show him a last-minute tweak she'd made to SkillHunter. At least that's what she told herself as she grabbed her lip gloss out of her top drawer and quickly ran it over her lips, then chided herself for it.

"Hey, Kric."

"Oh, hi Mitch. I thought you were Jay. Your footsteps sound alike."

He glanced at the lip gloss she was attempting to hide in her hand. "Sorry to disappoint you."

She tossed the lip gloss in the drawer, ignoring his remark

while he plunked his colossal body in a chair in front of her desk. He pointed at her computer screen with his chin. "SkillHunter looks great. Are you ready for your big debut?"

"I'm pretty nervous. I wish Jay wasn't so eager for me to be involved in conferences. Even though this is a small break-out session, there's a vast difference in doing a workshop for ten people here at H-Tech and being on a stage in front of 100 strangers." Strangers who came to see him, she thought, as images of women fawning over Jay invaded her mind.

"He knows you can do it. We all do."

She smiled to cover her doubt. She could not, would not disappoint them. "He thinks after a few of these, I'll be comfortable enough to join him onstage for the big SkillHunter launch. As if that will ever happen."

"Don't sell yourself short. The audience will love the two of you together." He ripped open a bag of almonds and studied her while he chomped on a few. "You're good for him, you know," he said after swallowing his mouthful.

She shrugged. "He's done so much for me, I—"

"You've done a lot more for him," he interrupted. "You have a calming effect on him. I don't have to jump in his face nearly as often as I used to," he said with a grin.

"It's probably because we're almost finished with SkillHunter. We've all been pretty uptight the last few months."

He popped another handful of almonds in his mouth. Lines of concentration deepened between his brows as he continued his study of her while he chewed.

"What?" she asked.

"Are you still seeing that cop?"

Was Mitch seriously trying to talk to her about her love life? Meg must have put him up to it. "We spend some time together." She wasn't about to go into detail with him. The Hunter family didn't need to know that she'd friend-zoned Levi, and their outings consisted solely of running together.

"I know it's last minute, but I have four company tickets to the Thunder playoff game tonight. Meg's not feeling well, so you're welcome to use them. You could take your cop friend and another couple with you."

Levi would pass out if she asked him to the game. Not only because it was the Thunder playoffs, but because she'd turned down several of his attempts to do something other than go on a run. But there were six company tickets. "Who has the other two tickets?"

"Gayle. I think she's taking some new guy she met." He chuckled. "Maybe you'll get the chance to pull the poor unsuspecting fool aside and give him a warning."

"That sounds fun. Levi will be thrilled. I'm sure my friend Becca and her husband will jump on the chance to go too. Thanks for thinking of us, Mitch."

He paused at the door as he was leaving. "Kric?" He looked uncomfortable, which was odd. "I'm glad you're a part of our family again. You're good for all of us." He turned and left before she could respond.

Becca sprayed a stream of sticky goop into Kricket's roots and scrunched it up with her fingers. "This is your first real date since Brock, so we've got to hoe up your hair a little bit. Give Levi a peek at your inner skank."

Kricket eyed herself in Becca's full-length mirror, tugging on the sides of the bright Thunder blue skirt Becca insisted she borrow. "I'm afraid Levi and everyone else is going to get a peek at my inner thighs in this skirt. She fiddled with the neckline of her also borrowed billowy silk top. "Do you have any double-sided tape? If I move the wrong way, my boobs are going to flop out of this blouse." She looked longingly at her skinny white jeans and cute sequined Thunder T-shirt, lying lifeless on the floor where Becca had discarded them.

"Your boobs aren't big enough to flop anywhere." Becca stepped back to size her up. "Now that is some sexy boom-boom. If Levi doesn't want you, every other man in the arena will."

"I look like a slut."

"No you don't. You look hot. There's a difference."

"Kevin," Becca yelled. "Come here, hon."

As expected, Kevin dutifully appeared in seconds.

"How does Kricket look?"

"She looks like a slut," he said with a frown.

Kricket kicked off the blue peep toe pumps she could hardly walk in. "See? I told you. I'm changing."

"Those are my clothes, Kevin. She does not look like a slut."

"She just doesn't look like Kricket, that's all." He shrugged. "It's better without the heels, though." She knew Kevin was just trying to backpedal, but she had to admit, without the heels, she didn't look quite as overdressed and slutty. So with her own clothes crumpled on the floor, and Levi ringing the doorbell, she had no choice now but to throw on her flats and just go with it.

Levi's blush made it apparent he was pleasantly shocked when she walked into the entry hall after Kevin answered the door. Naturally, Becca made her wait a few moments so she could make a grand entrance. He'd never seen her actually dressed like a girl. Her outfit definitely sent a message. Hopefully not too much of one, because there would be no *inner skank* activities tonight.

Levi seemed somewhat timid on the drive to the arena, although anyone would be with the endless questions Becca asked him. Kevin swatted her leg and called her Detective Becca, but that didn't faze her.

Once they arrived, Levi's cop demeanor took over as he

skillfully led them through the crowd towards the entrance. She liked the way he assumed control when needed, but otherwise was pretty laid-back. Like Jay, she thought, then kicked herself. Levi insisted on buying a beer for each of them, then they traveled down the long flight of steps towards their seats near the arena floor. She would have never made it down those steps in heels.

Becca and Kevin entered the row first, then Levi motioned for her to follow them. She shook her head. "Go ahead. You and Kevin will want to talk about stats or whatever guys talk about at games. He'd been questioned enough by Becca on the drive, so there was no way she'd let him sit next to Gayle and her date.

"These seats are unbelievable," Levi said, scanning the arena. "Thanks again for inviting me. I usually sit up in Loud City. The players look like ants from up there." He laughed, then his face grew solemn. "You look amazing, by the way. I'm sorry I didn't say that earlier, but you basically left me speechless."

She wasn't sure which one of them was blushing more. "I'm glad you could come on such short notice." Say thank you, stupid. Why is it so hard to acknowledge a compliment?

His mouth turned up in a crooked smile. "I would have canceled a trip to Europe for this." From the look in his eyes, she wasn't sure if he meant for the Thunder game or for her.

While the guys leaned forward chatting wildly about the game, Becca made suggestive gestures about Levi behind their backs. Becca's laughter suddenly stopped. Kricket turned towards the aisle to see what had caught her attention. Instead of seeing Gayle, as expected, she was looking at a man's crotch. A crotch she'd looked at more times than she cared to admit. Jay's crotch was less than three feet from her face. Standing behind him was Brandon, doing a poor job of hiding a smirk.

She followed Jay's eyes first to Levi's confused face, then to Kevin's open mouth, and finally to the gleam in Becca's eyes that said she was going to enjoy watching this turn of events much more than watching the game.

As if his intruder radar was triggered, Levi's cop demeanor took over again as he stood to shake Jay's hand. This was going to be a long evening. And Gayle or Mitch, or whoever was behind this, was going to die on Monday. She would make certain of that.

Brandon leaned around Jay, looked her up and down, and grinned. "You look scandalous, Kricket."

Jay's head swung around and she knew exactly the look he was giving Brandon.

"I borrowed some of Becca's clothes," she said, pressing her knees together when Jay's eyes flicked towards her legs. His jaws were clamped together when he looked up.

"Well you should do that more often," Brandon said, smirking when Jay glared at him again. She didn't look at Levi, but assumed his glare was similar.

When they took their seats, she made a point of turning towards Levi. Although trying to ignore Jay was impossible when the warmth of his shoulder against hers sent tingles down her spine. The touch of Levi's shoulder against her other side did nothing. She spent the first half of the game standing when Jay sat and sitting when Jay stood, because every time they both touched her, the contrast made her heart sink. Levi was the sweetest guy in the world, and good-looking to boot, and she knew if she gave him half a chance, he would fall in love with her. But she also knew she could never fall in love with someone as long as she felt like this about Jay.

Three minutes before half-time, she and Becca headed to the ladies' room so they could beat the line that would quickly form. On their way out, she saw one of the programmers from H-Tech.

"I'll be in line at the bar," Becca called over her shoulder when Kricket stopped to meet his wife. "Kevin and Levi are going to the Thunder gear shop, so come help carry their drinks back when you're finished talking."

After several minutes of uncomfortable small talk, she excused herself and headed towards the bar to find Becca. When she turned the corner, she spotted Becca standing at a bar table with Jay. It appeared they were in a heated conversation, so she hid herself in the crowd as she walked towards them, then stationed herself within earshot behind a large man eating a paper basket full of nachos at the table behind them.

Jay's voice rose above the chatter around her. "What do you mean, what am *I* trying to do? What are *you* trying to do?"

Becca's voice was sharp. "If you're not going to man up and admit your feelings for her, quit toying with her. I've spent the last eighteen years encouraging her and protecting her, so don't think for a minute that I'm going to let *you* waltz back in her life and mess it up."

"*Me* mess it up? *I'm* the one encouraging and protecting her. *You're* encouraging her to be a slut. That outfit she's wearing tonight was all your idea, wasn't it? She never dresses like that. She looks like she's putting it all out there for anyone who wants it."

"That's the kind of girl you like, isn't it?" Dead silence followed, and she knew they were having a staring contest.

"And I suspect it was also your idea her first journal goal was to *get laid*? And I believe that's a direct quote," he spat.

Kricket sucked in a breath. He'd read her journal? That was it. She flew around nacho man. "Why don't you both quit trying to run my life for me?" She put her hands on her hips and glared at them. "I am perfectly capable of taking care of myself."

They both gaped at her. Her face was hot and her heart was beating wildly, but she couldn't stop now. She pressed her hands tightly against her hipbones so they couldn't see her shaking. She would not back down this time. "And you," she said, sticking her finger in Jay's face. "You had no right to read my journal."

Jay's shoulders dropped, and he closed his eyes for a moment. His voice was barely a whisper when he spoke. "Baby I didn't mean—"

"Don't...call...me...Baby," she said through clenched teeth. She looked him directly in the eye, picked up his drink, turned it around and drank from his side, then slammed it down in front of him. After grabbing two beers from the table, she stomped towards the arena.

Jay called her name, but she didn't stop until reaching her seat. She tried to appear calm and force a smile when she handed Levi his beer. By the time Jay and Becca arrived, she'd sucked half hers down. Becca climbed over their legs without waiting for them to stand up and let her through. Levi leaned back and turned red when her short legs practically straddled him as she struggled to get by. Some of her drink sloshed out on Kevin's knee. He scowled while wiping it off with his hand, then motioned for her to give him the drinks. Brandon raised his palms in a what-the-hell motion, but Jay just shook his head and stared at the court.

Levi patted her leg. When she tensed, he jerked it away like he'd touched a hot coal. She rested her hand on his knee in an attempt to make up for it.

"You okay?" he whispered in her ear.

She nodded, then leaned against him so her other shoulder was as far from Jay's as possible. The score was close, so she tried to focus on the game, clapping when the Thunder scored, and standing and yelling with the crowd when the announcer told everyone to *get loud*. Becca sat solidly with her arms crossed. When Becca was mad, she was mad. Covering it up to make a situation better for others would never cross her mind.

During a timeout, a tap on her shoulder from behind startled her. "Hey, that's you," the guy said pointing to the Jumbotron. When she looked up, she watched her own mouth fall open on the screen. The Kiss-cam was focused directly on her and Jay. She shook her head, but the camera didn't move. Even though she wasn't thrilled about kissing Levi in front of eleventy billion people, she pointed at him so they would pan over. But instead of moving the camera, they displayed a little comic character pretending to push her head towards Jay. She'd seen them do that before and knew they were relentless, even when people mouthed something like, 'It's my sister.'

She glanced at Jay, hoping he wasn't making her look like a fool by cringing. With a cocky grin, he put his arm around her shoulders and pulled her in for a long kiss on the lips. Everyone gasped, then cheered. Everyone except Levi and Becca.

As soon as the camera had moved on, she swatted Jay hard on the shoulder. "What in the hell was that?"

He held up his hands in exasperation. "What did you want me to do?"

She decided not to answer that.

CHAPTER 28

JAY CARRIED HIS FAVORITE pair of wheeling jeans into the garage where Mud Ninja was waiting. Waiting to take him into the darkness. He unfolded them and surveyed the battle scars. He'd had these jeans almost as long as he'd had Mud Ninja. The hem was permanently mud-stained and ragged on the back from rubbing against the floorboard under his boot. And there was a hole in the knee from a tree branch that had grabbed him on a tight trail. He turned them over to look at the back pocket that had torn loose when he'd crawled out of Ninja after flipping over. A reminder that every dare was not worth attempting. He stared at the familiar red label in the seam of the pocket. Levis. Now they were a reminder of the man Kricket was seeing. The man who might be touching her right now. He lifted the garbage can lid and chucked his memory-filled jeans inside. He would never stick his ass in a pair of Levis again.

He should have known something was up when Gayle suddenly couldn't go to the Thunder game. On his slow hike down the arena steps, his heart leapt when he'd first seen the flash of Kricket's hair, her head thrown back in laughter. Then he saw who had made her laugh. Lord knows it had been way too long since he'd made her laugh like that. Levi seemed like a nice enough guy, and it was obvious he'd fallen for her. And of course he wanted her to find someone who made her happy. He just didn't know it would hurt so much.

After unfastening the bolts on his hard top, he used the pulley to hoist it off the Jeep to its storage spot on the garage ceiling. Mud Ninja had seen him through some rough times. Taking it from a stock Jeep to a bad-ass machine had kept his mind occupied after Rachel left. Maybe it was time to build another one.

He tossed a cooler of Guinness in the back and climbed inside. Before starting the engine, he punched the password in his phone one last time to see if she'd responded, then tossed his phone in the cup holder and leaned back against the headrest. His stupid Kiss-cam stunt had angered her even more. She wouldn't even look at him the second half of the game, then left without as much as a goodbye. He'd sent her a message saying how sorry he was. What else was there to say?

He grabbed his phone again to send one more message, 'Sweetest of dreams, Kric.' If only he could tell her that in person. He started the engine, cranked up the stereo as loud as it would go, and backed Ninja out into the night.

The crisp air numbed his face, but the music did nothing to numb his mind as he headed out Highway 74 towards the land where Brandon's family ran cattle. Trails snaked through the ranch, and he would run each and every one of them before the night was over.

Pulling onto the dirt road entrance to the ranch, he switched on the LED light bar that stretched across the windshield of his Jeep, then slid out to unchain the gate.

He and Ninja descended into the night. His light bar lit the way like a beacon, although he hardly needed it. Over the years, he'd run these trails a hundred times.

After a few hours, he stopped at the center of the ranch where they always gathered after a day of wheeling. And where they used to have some pretty crazy parties back in their college days. With a crackling fire in the pit and two beers in his hand, he climbed onto the hood and settled himself against the windshield to watch the night sky.

The full moon sent his thoughts back to the first night he'd kissed her. From the moment he saw her at Starbucks, he was mesmerized. But that night after leaving the club, when he'd lifted her chin to kiss her, the desire mixed with fear reflected in her eyes by the moonlight had sucked him in completely. Until then, he'd successfully avoided feeling anything for any woman.

He'd fallen in love with Krissy, the tiny pink baby, the first time he'd held her. And he'd fallen in love with Kricket, the intoxicating woman, the first time he held her. Why did they have to be one and the same?

He closed his eyes, hoping the darkness would seal out the vision of her. Was she with Levi tonight? He could tell by the way they interacted, she hadn't slept with him yet. They didn't have that casualness of touch that came after sleeping with someone. But his stupid spat with Becca had probably sent her straight into his bed.

Levi was clearly wary of him. He'd been friendly but observant of their interaction. Men could sense things and Levi was no fool. He stared at the fire, letting the dancing flames lull his mind. Maybe she was in bed with him right now. Or maybe they were huddled in front of a fire sharing the secrets of their souls? Both possibilities disturbed him. He wanted to be the one, the only one, she felt close enough with to share her fears, her dreams, and her desires.

A large crackle in the fire jolted him awake. The temperature had dropped, so he slid off the hood and walked to the back of the Jeep to grab the jacket he kept stashed behind the toolbox. When he shrugged it on, the scent of Kricket's shampoo, mixed with the smell of a campfire, surrounded him. It seemed much longer than four months since their Jeep Club outing when he'd kept her warm in his jacket while they listened to wheeling stories around the fire. With his eyes closed, he could almost feel the tickle of her hair against his neck and hear her sigh as she snuggled against his chest.

CHAPTER 29

Monday, June 29th
...I don't know if I'm more nervous or more excited to actually be taking part in a conference presentation this week. Okay, yes I do know. Nervous wins by a long-shot...

Today's goal: *Picture myself giving an awesome presentation...*

FOR THE LAST HOUR, Gayle had been slowly sinking further and further down in the chair across from Kricket's desk. "How many times are you going to walk through this presentation, girl? I've heard it so many times, *I* could give it in my sleep."

Kricket pointed her presentation clicker at Gayle and pretended to zap her with it. "In case you've forgotten, you're still paying your penance for your little Thunder game conspiracy."

"I was doing you a favor. *Jay's* the one who turned it into Rockem-Sockem Robots with Becca. I don't see *him* paying any penance. Or was that behind closed doors?" Her eyebrows flew up and down suggestively.

She stared at Gayle, unamused.

"Apparently, Levi isn't satisfying your womanly needs, because your sense of humor is screaming, *I need to get laid*," Gayle said, waving off her stare.

"And *that* is what is considered inappropriate office talk. Apparently, *someone* hasn't been paying attention in class," she said to change the subject. "Maybe they should withhold your diploma next month. I'm not sure you learned anything about HR Management."

"After seven years in school, I am walking across that stage swinging a hot pink boa," Gayle said, pretending to flip her hair.

"Besides, we're talking as friends. No co-worker would sit in here for hours listening to your nonstop practice. Now, why don't you put that clicker down and go let Levi make you tongue-tied?"

When she didn't respond, Gayle tilted her head and eyed her. "You haven't slept with him yet, have you?"

She turned towards her computer to restart the presentation slides to hide her expression from Gayle.

"Does the poor boy know you're in love with someone else?"

Luckily Gayle's cell phone rang, giving Kricket a chance to recover from her sudden lack of oxygen.

"The security desk needs me," Gayle said, after hanging up. "It's nearly six o'clock. Promise me you will run through this presentation only one more time, then take a breather. Go have a drink with your friend. What's her name, Becca?" That wouldn't happen until Becca apologized. This time Kricket had held out. She was tired of always being the first one to apologize.

Kricket waved her off and restarted the presentation. She'd made it through a few slides when she sensed someone's presence behind her and spun around to promise Gayle she'd go home after this last run-through. In the doorway stood Becca, holding a bottle of Chocolate Mint schnapps. Their first attempt at drinking had been shots of Chocolate Mint schnapps. It had ended badly, but had become their secret bond, their go-to drink when they were in a reminiscing mood.

Becca's face bore a downcast look she'd rarely seen. Kricket didn't say a word as Becca walked in and sat down across from her. Becca pulled two shot glasses from her purse and silently filled them, then slid one glass towards her. "I'm sorry, Kricket."

Kricket looked into the moist eyes of her dearest friend. The friend who would hold her hair out of the way if she were puking, or stay awake all night to talk her through a crisis. The friend who would go to battle for her without hesitation. And the friend who had crushed her heart more frequently than any man. Becca's methods might not always be the most appropriate, but her intentions were good.

Kricket knew how difficult those words were for Becca to say. But they were all she needed to hear. She picked up the shot glass and held it up for a toast. "Friends forever."

CHAPTER 30

Thursday, July 2nd
...My presentation is tomorrow. 100 people in a room staring at me. That fulfills almost every journal challenge all in one fell swoop.

Today's goal: *Do absolutely nothing that involves any amount of stress...*

KRICKET WATCHED THE FLOORS tick off as the hotel elevator descended from the twenty-sixth floor to the lower gates of hell. It was her own fault for mentioning to Jay that she admired Victoria's commanding presence. So what was she supposed to say when he sprung on her that Victoria had agreed to a last minute coaching session over a drink? She glanced sideways at Jay, who looked so good in his jeans and untucked black shirt, it hurt her eyes. He smelled good too. So he was either planning to escort Victoria back to his room later for *dessert* or hook up with the business card slut behind door number two.

He reached over and tucked a strand of hair behind her ear, then rested his palm on the hand she was using to trace her scar. That certain smile he gave her—the one he gave only to her—was normally comforting, but not even a Valium would calm her now. "Victoria's very easy to talk to," he said softly. "You'll like her, I promise."

It was inconceivable that she would *like* a woman who later would be tangled in hotel sheets with Jay. She swallowed hard to tame the bile rising in her throat. Although they were in Caesar's Palace, she halfway expected to hear the song 'Welcome to the Hotel California' as the elevator slowed to a halt. Jay took her hand as the doors opened to spit them out into the hallway to hell.

Heels clicked sharply across the marble floor. She knew before looking up, it was Victoria. The closer Victoria got, the smaller Kricket felt. Her sleek blonde bob glimmered against a black pantsuit that likely cost more than a sofa. Her blood red silk blouse perfectly matched suede pumps that were undoubtedly Jimmy Choo. A gigantic garnet necklace that screamed David Yurman lay against her cleavage. Boobs. Of course she had boobs. She was a walking, talking Nieman Marcus mannequin.

Kricket fingered the tiny diamond necklace her grandpa gave her last Christmas. Even though Jay had assured her the slim gray slacks, emerald blouse, and black flats she had on were perfect, next to Victoria, she looked fifteen.

Surprisingly, Victoria's starkness disappeared when she smiled. "Jay, it's good to see you," she said, extending her hand adorned with, yes, more David Yurman.

Watching them shake hands was odd. A hug between old friends seemed more fitting, even if they were trying to hide the fact that they knew every inch of each other's bodies.

"Victoria, I want you to meet Kricket," Jay said, giving her shoulder a gentle squeeze of encouragement.

Victoria's smile widened as she clasped Kricket's hand in both of hers. "It's lovely to finally meet you, Kricket. Jay speaks fondly of you and I'm eager to get to know you myself." Her voice was soothing and her smile seemed genuine. She looked much kinder up close…and younger. She was probably a few years older than Jay, but not the cougar she'd originally pegged her as.

"It's nice to meet you." She forced herself to meet Victoria's eyes. "I enjoyed your speech this morning and…well, I hope to be as good as you some day." An embarrassing flush rose up her neck.

"Thank you. I'm certain you will be." She patted Kricket's hand before releasing it, then turned to Jay. "Now that you've introduced us, I believe we can manage on our own."

Over the last few months, she'd learned to detect Jay's nearly imperceptible body language and facial expressions. Although his expression didn't change, his slight head tilt showed her that Victoria had surprised him. Apparently, he'd planned on joining them. Honestly, she wasn't sure if she preferred talking to Victoria with or without him. Either way was a sneak preview of hell.

They challenged each other with their eyes for a moment before Victoria dismissed Jay with a flick of her hand. Watching Victoria tame Jay with one look was unsettling. This really was Hotel California.

After giving Victoria a stern look, he put his hands on Kricket's shoulders, magically transforming into his soothing puppy dog eyes. "I'll see you shortly. We can have dinner later."

Victoria led the way through the lobby and into the hotel bar, completely bypassing the hostess stand. A wave of her hand told Kricket to have a seat in a gray leather booth that overlooked the crowded sidewalk. She dutifully complied while Victoria glanced expectantly around the room until she caught a waiter's eye and signaled him over.

"They make a wonderful lavender martini. Would you care to try one?" Victoria asked after sliding into the other side of the booth with the grace of a Persian cat.

"That sounds great. Although martinis usually kick my butt." She squeezed her eyes shut at her country music lyric response.

Victoria laughed. "In my opinion, a drink is pointless unless it kicks your butt." She turned to the waiter. "Two lavender martinis and a fruit and cheese plate. And when our drinks are half empty please bring another. Otherwise we expect to be left alone."

"Of course," the waiter said with a bow as he turned to leave.

Apparently Victoria turned everyone into an obedient dog, which definitely altered the images in her mind of Victoria and Jay's bedroom activities. Ugh. Please tell me she's not his Dom.

"I hope you don't mind that I sent Jay away," Victoria cooed, as if she were the most docile person in the world. "I thought you might be more comfortable with just the two of us."

She nodded. There was nothing comfortable about this at all, but it was clearly better than watching secret lover looks pass between them.

Victoria nodded an acknowledgment to the waiter as he delivered their martinis, then hurried away. "Jay showed me a video of one of your practice presentations. He's very proud of you."

She quickly took a sip of her drink since she had no idea how to respond. The hint of lavender mingled with lemon was like nothing she'd ever tasted before. "This is beyond amazing."

"I knew you'd love it. Now, bottoms up," Victoria said, raising her glass in a toast. "It can't be easy talking to a woman who has slept with the man you're in love with."

Her head imploded, annihilating any possibility of responding. She knew her mouth was hanging open, but she had no control over any aspect of her body. She wasn't certain she was even breathing.

Victoria reached across the table and gently pried her fingers loose before she crushed the stem of her martini glass. "I'm sorry I shocked you. In case you haven't noticed, I'm very direct, but it's a situation we need to address so it isn't an impediment to your coaching session. Now, take a deep breath and take a drink."

Kricket killed her drink in ten seconds, set down her glass a little too forcefully, then crossed her arms and stared out the window. Was it that obvious? Was she making a fool of herself in front of everyone? Or just Victoria? And Jay…what must he think of her? She could picture them lying in bed together tonight, peeling with laughter.

"You do love him, don't you?" Victoria asked gently.

She knew her expression gave her away, so there was no need to answer. She bravely looked Victoria in the eye. "Do you?"

"Gawd no!" Victoria said so loudly it startled her. "He's an overgrown teenager who still plays soccer for heaven's sake." Her nose wrinkled like she'd just been slimed. "And his idea of fun is driving that ridiculous Jeep around in the mud. We're very good friends...who occasionally satisfy each other's physical needs. Nothing more than that."

"So, how long have you two—?" That came out before she could catch herself.

"We've been coaching each other for five years. No matter how many times you deliver a speech, it's important to have someone critique you," she explained. "Over the years our friendship grew, but the sex didn't begin until after his divorce." She smirked over the rim of her martini. "Not because I didn't try." Her wry smile acknowledged the silence that hung in the air. "I can tell by the look on your face what you must think of me."

Luckily, the waiter's arrival delayed the need for a response.

Victoria nodded her approval as he placed an artistic display of fruit and cheese on the table and swapped out their empty glasses with fresh martinis. "Perhaps I'm not quite as terrible as you think," she said, after selecting a tidbit of Havarti cheese and placing it on a cracker. "Jay used to confide in me about his relationship with Rachel. It was obvious she was cheating on him, so I figured he was fair game."

Kricket plucked a stem of grapes from the plate and twirled it between her fingers. "You're not his only one, you know." She had no idea why she felt the need to say that. The martini obviously was taking control of her mouth. "Women slip him business cards and—" She fell silent as her breath caught.

Victoria's eyes softened as she placed her palm over Kricket's hand. "I hope you never learn the difference between having sex and making love. I suspect you have no experience with the first one and very little with the other."

She choked out a small laugh. "Is it that obvious?"

"Jay wouldn't be in love with you if you did."

Her eyes fell. "I know he loves me, but not like that. More like a little sister...an obligation." She focused on folding and refolding the napkin in her lap. "I thought he was attracted to me when we first met at the dance club, but after he found out who I was—"

"He may be fooling you, and he's obviously trying to fool himself, but he definitely does not see you as a little sister. I could tell he was in love with you the first time I saw you with him at a conference in Houston. I wanted to meet you then, but he wouldn't hear of it. He protected you like a baby bird." She tossed her head back and laughed. "I teased him mercilessly about it." She leaned forward as if telling a secret. "And for the record, he hasn't been in my bed since he found you again. Or in anyone else's, I assure you."

She looked out the window to keep from meeting Victoria's eyes. She'd actually begun to trust Victoria, but that was a flat out lie. Her face grew hot. "I know you met him that night," she blurted out. "I saw your text," she said, her voice trembling from her own outburst.

At first Victoria looked puzzled, then a sly grin spread slowly across her face. "So you do have claws."

She grabbed her purse and rose from her seat. She had baby claws and was not about to take on Victoria.

"Kricket, stay. Please? Let me ease your mind."

She blinked rapidly, but couldn't stop the tear that rolled down her cheek.

"Please," Victoria said. She pulled a tissue from her purse and offered it. Her eyes were full of empathy, not condemnation.

Against her better judgment, she accepted the tissue and slid back into the booth.

Victoria placed her palm on Kricket's hand. "I see you've met my good friends, insecurity and jealousy. Always waiting in the wings to fill our minds with negative assumptions when we only see a piece of the picture. Trust me, I know them well," she said with a distant look.

Kricket dabbed at her eyes so her mascara didn't smear.

"For the record, Jay has not been in my bed since January. I would not tell you that if it weren't true. When we are at the same conference, we meet after our presentations to review video and critique each other while it's still fresh in our minds. That's what my text was about. I remember that night well. We reviewed the videos and then we talked about you." An amused smile slid across over her face. "I told him you were beautiful and he actually blushed. And when he didn't come to my room afterwards, that told me everything I needed to know."

Relief, regret, and embarrassment washed through her body at once. She nearly bit through her bottom lip as she tried to think of something to say.

Victoria interrupted her thoughts. "Does Jay know you saw the text?"

She shook her head.

"So he has no idea that you know about us."

"No."

Victoria appeared deep in thought for a moment. "He's still healing. And he's trying to process his feelings for you. You're all he talks about. And the way he looks at you—" Her eyes grew dreamy as she took a sip of her martini. "I'd love to see a man look at me that way."

It was hard to picture Victoria as a hopeless romantic. "Have you ever been in love?"

Victoria waved her hand in dismissal. "We've all been in love. We've all been cheated on, and we've all been hurt. But men tend to take it harder. When a woman is cheated on, she thinks, 'if only I was younger or thinner, or my hair was blonde—' But for a man who discovers his wife cheating, it's a direct hit to his virility. It means she had to go elsewhere to get fulfilled, so he assumes his penis is too small, or he doesn't know how to use it properly." She ran a finger around the rim of her martini glass. "And in Jay's case, that couldn't be further from the truth."

Kricket winced, knowing her face was as scarlet as Victoria's blouse.

"Too much?" Her lips pursed in a teasing grin.

"Just a tiny bit," Kricket said, indicating with her thumb and forefinger. After realizing what she'd done, they both started laughing. It felt good to let go of some tension.

"Wait," Victoria said, holding up both hands. "You said you met Jay at a dance club? He conveniently neglected to tell me that." Her breasts shook as she chuckled. "Jay Hunter at a dance club. That's a story I've got to hear."

Victoria leaned forward, popping nuggets of cheese in her mouth like a kid watching a scary movie as Kricket described their encounter at Starbucks, how he followed her to Club100, their magical dance, and the tender kiss goodnight.

"But apparently, I have the sex appeal of a roll of toilet paper, because he walked away from the one and only sex proposition I've ever made." She knew she sounded pouty, and she wasn't at all sure why she had just confided that to Victoria, the walking, talking sex goddess.

Victoria put her hand on her heart. "He said you were intoxicating? Now that *is* sexy. And that kiss...hook-up kissing isn't tender like that," she said, shaking her head. "It's more ravenous, a function of lust. It's a means to an end. It's—"

"Okay, okay, I get it," Kricket said, holding her hand up traffic cop style. "It's pretty obvious I don't evoke that kind of passion in him."

"You are gently beautiful, without trying to look sexy. Not at all easy to walk away from."

Walk away. Those words stabbed her directly in the heart. Every man she'd ever loved, except her grandpa, had walked away from her.

The cricket chirp text alert on her phone startled her from her somberness.

Victoria held out her hand and snapped her fingers. "Let me see your phone. One hundred bucks says it's Jay. I'm sure he's been pacing the floor worrying about what vulgar things I might be disclosing to you."

She placed her phone in Victoria's waiting palm. So far Victoria had done an excellent job of demonstrating commanding presence. It was nearly impossible not to comply with her mandates.

Victoria glanced at the text then dropped the phone in her purse. "We'll let him stew for a while."

"Wait, what are you doing? What did it say?" Did Victoria seriously just steal her phone?

"I'm going to prove that he's in love with you." She extracted a credit card from her wallet and held it in the air to signal the waiter for their check.

"What? How?" Kricket's heart was beating fast.

"You'll see. Let's go to the restaurant across the street and have some dinner, shall we?"

CHAPTER 31

VICTORIA SLIPPED THE HOSTESS a fifty dollar bill and asked for a table overlooking the Bellagio fountains. Fifteen minutes later they had a table, drinks, and between them both, four texts from Jay. Victoria read aloud Jay's texts from Kricket's confiscated phone.

"Kricket, are you OK?"

"Hello?"

"I'm worried, please answer me!" she mocked in a cartoon voice. She popped the lime green phone back into her purse prison, then pulled out her own gold covered phone and flipped through her messages. "Mine are worded a little differently," she said, turning her phone around to display the messages.

"Where the hell is Kricket?"

"ANSWER ME VICTORIA!!"

Kricket's fingers dug nervously at her scarred arm, but neither that nor the two martinis were doing a thing to calm her racing heartbeat. She pictured Jay pacing the room, running his hands through his hair. He was going to be furious, and she had no desire to be involved in a battle between the King of Confrontation and the Queen of Bluntville.

Victoria opened her menu with a flourish. "I recommend the arugula and pulled chicken salad. They dress it with a divine lemon tarragon vinaigrette."

She nodded. She hated tarragon, but all she could think about was easing Jay's worried mind. What if he called the police? Her phone rang inside Victoria's purse. Victoria dug it out and flicked it on silent.

"Don't you think we should answer it? I know he's worried," she said, gnawing on a fingernail.

"I'm certain that he is. Now take your finger out of your mouth and drink your martini. You need to relax."

She took a sip of her drink, watching Victoria over the rim.

"Do you always do everything you're told?"

Her initial reaction at being called out on her submissiveness by the most domineering woman she'd ever met was to freeze, but she couldn't help but chuckle at herself. "Pretty much," she said, nodding her head. "I learned at a very young age that following the rules made life a lot easier."

"But not very much fun." Victoria's face softened. "Tell me a childhood story about Jay and yourself."

She gazed across the street at the dancing water display while clips of her childhood paraded through her mind. "Jay used to take me for top-down rides in his red Jeep. I'll never forget the rush of the wind in my face and the music so loud I could feel the bass beating in my stomach." She felt a silly grin consume her face as the feeling came back to her. "We had a ritual. We always headed towards this big river in the middle of town. He knew right when to start counting so we would be in the middle of the bridge when he reached the number ten. Then he would stick his head out the top of the Jeep and let out a loud yell. I was very reserved, but he continued to coax me until one day I finally joined in. Once I tasted the exhilaration of complete abandonment, I was hooked. After that, every day I sat waiting for him on the front porch, hoping—"

The ringing of Victoria's phone interrupted her story. Please, please answer it this time.

Thankfully, she lifted the phone to her ear. "Victoria Frasier," she answered in a businesslike tone, as if Jay wouldn't know who it was.

She could hear Jay yelling through the phone, "I'm in the bar, where are you? And why isn't Kricket answering her phone?"

Victoria held the phone away from her ear as he spoke, then responded in a calm voice. "We're having a lovely time, thank you for asking."

"Hand the phone to Kricket. I need to—"

"We're having dinner. She's regaling me with fascinating stories about her childhood."

"Where are you? I'll come join you for dinner."

"You asked me to coach her. Do you want me to or not?"

"Of course I do, but—"

"Then leave us alone."

"Let me talk to Kricket."

"She's in the ladies' room."

He sighed loudly. "Fine, I'll call her."

"She left her phone here on the table."

"Victoria, are you fucking with me? Is she OK?"

"What are you so worried about?"

The phone was silent for a moment except for his huff. "Don't start, Victoria. You know why."

"No, Jay, I don't. Please enlighten me."

"Fuck you."

"See? I knew you were in love with her."

Kricket held her breath waiting for his response. But all she heard was his breathing. "Victoria, please. Just don't," he finally said, resignedly.

"I see her coming back now. Hold on to your panties for a moment and I'll put her on." Victoria waited briefly, then handed her the phone and said in a loud voice, "Kricket, Jay's been trying to reach you."

"Hi," she said enthusiastically into the phone, hoping her voice sounded peppy instead of guilty.

"Why didn't you answer my texts? I was worried."

"I'm sorry. I guess my phone was on silent. I didn't mean to worry you." She hated lying to him, but what was she supposed to say?

"How's everything going? Do you want me to join you?"

She shook her head, even though he couldn't see it. "We're fine. Victoria is great. She's just getting ready to start coaching me."

His silence was followed by a huff of resignation. "Okay, but I want to see you before you go to bed." Victoria raised an eyebrow and Kricket rolled her eyes at her. "You have a big day tomorrow, so please don't stay out too late." His voice sounded more pleading than commanding.

"I won't. I'll call you when we're finished."

A Cheshire cat grin slid across Victoria's face as she took back her phone. "See? I proved he's in love with you."

"No, you proved he sees me as a child who needs to be chaperoned."

❧

Instead of coaching her over dinner, Victoria asked endless questions about her childhood, work, and her family. Victoria carved off a bite of the chocolate lava cake she'd insisted on ordering, swirled it in the dollop of whipped cream and slid it in her mouth. "Mmmm," she groaned, then sat motionless with her eyes closed before easing the spoon from her mouth. Great, now she knew what Victoria's 'O' face looked like. How long would *that* be imprinted in her mind?

Victoria's eyes fluttered open. "You must try this. It's divine," she said, tapping the dessert plate with her spoon.

If it was *that* good, maybe they should order another one. She scooped up a small bite and stuck it in her mouth, then quickly grabbed her napkin to wipe off the drizzle of caramel she felt dangling from her lip. A perfect demonstration of the difference between a Persian cat and a hound dog.

Victoria placed her spoon on the table and pushed the dessert away from her. "One bite is all I'm allowed. Any more than that and I may as well apply it directly to my ass." After they laughed for a moment, Victoria changed the mood with a steeple of her fingers under her chin. "I've noticed that you rub your arm a lot."

Kricket's hand flew away from the scarred arm she didn't realize she was rubbing. "When I was a kid, I rubbed my scar when I was nervous. For some reason it calmed me. Apparently I still do it. It's silly, I know."

"It's not silly, it's sweet. But fidgeting is the number one transgression against having a strong presence, both in personal interactions and during presentations. You've watched Jay give speeches and interact with people. What do you think gives him his presence?"

She knew a stupid grin spread across her face as images of Jay flooded her mind. "If I had to put my finger on it, he's big. I mean, he's obviously a giant, but the way he stands and the way he carries himself, is…well, big. But he's a man, so —"

"Exactly. To have a strong presence, you don't have to be a big person, you just have to act big. Stand tall and take up space, like a man does." She leaned forward as if her next comment was a deep, dark secret. "Doesn't it drive you insane to sit beside a man? They take up the space of two people with their legs spread apart like a five-dollar whore."

"Exactly, if Jay is sitting anywhere near you, his Jaynormous legs are all over you. Which isn't necessarily a bad thing, I suppose," she added with a laugh.

Victoria threw her head back in laughter. "Jaynormous, I love it."

"That's my friend Becca's term for him. She's barely five

feet tall, but she acts like Bigfoot." She sighed. "She's naturally confident, like you and Jay."

Victoria's laughter subsided to a compassionate smile. "No one is as confident as they appear. Everyone has a story and everyone has a demon that renders them self-conscious to some degree. Next time you're chatting with someone, try to figure out their story. It forces you to listen carefully, which helps take the focus off of yourself, which keeps you from fidgeting. See? You're not fidgeting. You're listening carefully because we're talking about Jay."

Kricket laid down her spoon. "Maybe I'm not fidgeting because I'm busy stuffing my face with this chocolate ecstasy."

"Chocolate does cure everything," Victoria said, with a yearning look at the dessert. "Jay may be naturally confident, but like everyone else, he has a story. What do you think his story is?"

"That's easy. He grew up in the perfect family, built a successful company, and married a beautiful woman who cheated on him."

"So Rachel is Jay's demon?"

"Duh."

She paused for a moment. "You've heard his Squirrel Promise speech, right?"

"Yes."

Victoria smiled and shook her head. "You're not listening to his story."

CHAPTER 32

Thursday, July 3rd
...In seven hours, it will all be over. That is if I make it through the next seven hours...

Today's goal: *Be big. Take up space. Be big. Take up space...*

BETWEEN WORRYING ABOUT HER presentation, considering the validity of Victoria's speculation about Jay's feelings, and analyzing Jay's mood when he met them for one final cocktail last night, she'd hardly slept a wink. She knew he would be angry, or at the very least annoyed at Victoria's phone antics. But she'd been around him long enough to know that anger made him loud, not quiet like he was last night. And she'd felt strangely awkward around him. Like a secret hung in the air.

Her fingers grazed over the David Yurman bracelet he'd given her at breakfast this morning. Her birthday wasn't until tomorrow, but he said he wanted her to have it for the presentation. She wasn't sure if he'd purchased it weeks ago, or if he'd seen her gawking at Victoria's jewelry last night, but she had to admit, this tiny version of Victoria's cuff bracelet did make her feel more confident. Not because it was an expensive bracelet, but because Jay had obviously put some thought into selecting it. Instead of her ruby birthstone, which seemed obvious for a birthday gift, the bracelet was flanked on each end with two peridot stones. He knew she loved green.

The small silver wrapped box he'd placed on the table had caught her off guard. He'd cautiously watched her open it. And of course she'd dropped it right into her bowl of cranberry nut oatmeal. Normally they would have hooted with laughter over her bumble, but he just grimaced and reached over to rescue it. No wonder he still saw her as a little girl. She tilted the bracelet and watched it sparkle in the light. He wasn't in love with her. It would be foolish to even entertain the thought. But what if he was?

She slipped on the bracelet, grabbed her purse, and headed out to meet Victoria at the entrance to the mall adjacent to the hotel, as instructed by a text she received first thing this morning.

"You need something fabulous to wear to boost your confidence," Victoria said when she arrived. "I saw the perfect dress in a store window yesterday." Victoria's idea of *fabulous* probably entailed a short dress and a pair of slutty pumps. Now she could add 'tripping on stage and landing with her dress hiked up to her navel' to her list of worries. She glanced desperately in store windows as they walked, hoping to spot what *she* considered the perfect outfit.

"Here it is," Victoria said, waving at the Versace window with a flourish. "What do you think?" Victoria's eyes implored her to say she loved it.

The light pink dress on the faceless mannequin was exactly the opposite of what she had anticipated. It was pretty, but slightly feminine for her taste. And although feminine was better than sleazy, it was sleeveless. She took a deep breath. "It's lovely, really, but..." She touched her scar. "I need something with at least three-quarter sleeves. I'll feel self-conscious enough in front of that many people. Plus we're trying to avoid anyone recognizing me as the Squirrel Promise girl."

Victoria eyes softened. "Of course. Let's look inside."

After hearing the details of their mission, the sales girl led them straight to a mannequin wearing a sea green silk shirtdress. There should have been violins playing, because it was the exact color of Kricket's eyes. The sales girl looked her up and down, then selected the two smallest sizes on the rack and led them to a palatial fitting room. Please dear God, don't let Victoria come in here while I change. She'd shared a fitting room with Becca a thousand times, but she had no desire for a woman who sleeps with Jay to see her half naked. As if reading her mind, Victoria matter-of-factly parked herself in the fitting room chair, making it clear she was staying.

Kricket resignedly inched off her clothes. Why hadn't she at least worn a bra and undies that matched?

Victoria made no attempt to hide that she was watching in the mirror. "Has Jay ever seen you in a swimsuit or—?"

"No," Kricket cut her off.

"Look in the mirror and tell me what you see."

She peered in the mirror and shrugged. With shoulders slumped and arms wrapped around her body, she hardly exuded a strong presence. But then again, she was standing half-naked in a dressing room with Jay's bed buddy. Any sane person would be uncomfortable in that situation.

"I see a butterfly," Victoria said gently.

Her hand flew to her hip. "Oh, no, that's a cricket. You know, for my name. It's dumb, I know."

"I'm not talking about the tattoo on your ass." Victoria rose from the chair and stood behind her. "Stand up straight. Chin up," she said, meeting her eyes in the mirror. Her warm smile twisted into a wry one. "Jay is going to fucking die when he sees you naked."

Kricket's blouse slipped from her fingers onto the floor. Not only was she stupefied by the F-bomb leaking out of Victoria's sophisticated mouth, but how do you respond to a comment like that?

She fumbled to free the dress from its hanger, then quickly stepped into its silkiness. After fastening the pearl buttons and the belt, she glanced in the mirror. It looked and felt incredible.

Victoria's eyes reflected her approval. "It has the sexy appeal of a woman in a man's dress shirt, yet it's cut to accentuate a woman's body." Victoria adjusted the belt and smoothed the dress over Kricket's hips. "I'd need some spandex under this, but your butt is as firm as an unripe peach. All you need is a sexy thong and you're in business," she said, smacking Kricket on the rear. "Slip it off and I'll take it to the counter while you get dressed."

After the few moments it took to regain her composure, Kricket tilted her head to peek at the price tag hanging under her armpit. The dress cost more than a month's rent. No matter how perfect it was, and no matter how confident it made her feel, she simply couldn't justify it.

Apparently, her face reflected her thoughts, because Victoria flipped open her Prada handbag and plucked out a Prada wallet. "Hand me the dress and I'll go check out."

"But I can't let you—"

"Of course you can. Jay will pay me back."

In response to her grimace, Victoria lifted an eyebrow. "Meaning H-Tech will reimburse me for it." She waited until their eyes met in the mirror. "I am absolutely certain that I will never enjoy his company in my bed again. Now, get dressed while I check out. Then we'll go find a lingerie store. Nothing makes you feel more confident than a leopard bra and thong."

CHAPTER 33

THE AUDIENCE WASN'T THAT large, maybe seventy-five people. Jay would carry the load of the presentation. All she had to do was cover three bullet points. She checked to make sure all her buttons were fastened...again, and straightened her belt...again, as she and Victoria stood on the side of the stage watching Jay begin the break-out session. Her stomach churned, threatening to send her to the ladies' room for the third time in the last hour.

Victoria's touch on her arm made her jump. "These few minutes before you begin are the worst. Even for those of us who've done it hundreds of times. Once you get started, you'll forget your nervousness."

"What if I forget what I'm supposed to say?"

"You won't. But I'll be sitting on the front row. If you have any trouble, look at me, and I'll raise my hand and ask a question to get you back on track."

"I can't begin to tell you how comforting that is. And how much I appreciate all you've done to help get me ready for this." The extent of Victoria's support was astonishing.

Victoria rested both hands on Kricket's shoulders like a proud mom. "Walk out there with your head high, knowing that every man in the room wants you. And every woman in the room wants to be you."

"Thank you," she said, unsure if that statement made her more or less nervous. More. Definitely more. She took a deep breath and met Victoria's eyes. "You know...I really wanted to hate you."

A laugh erupted from Victoria. "Honey, you certainly wouldn't be the first." She nudged her towards the stage. "Now, go. Go and be wonderful."

Her legs felt like wet bags of sand as she forced them one in front of the other onto the stage towards Jay. Focusing on his smile was the only thing that kept her from turning and running the other way. She knew she'd eventually have to look at the audience, but right now she focused on one thing. Walk towards his smile, walk towards his smile, walk towards his smile.

Jay winked as he placed the slideshow clicker in her palm, then moved aside to watch from his perch on a stool. They had agreed he would remain on the stage so she wouldn't feel abandoned. It didn't work. She felt completely abandoned.

She took a deep breath and squeezed the clicker to display the first slide in her presentation. Her palm was so sweaty the clicker nearly squirted out of her hand. When she turned towards the enormous screen behind her, she froze. Her slide didn't appear. She clicked again and nothing happened. She stared at the screen, clicking, and clicking, and clicking, then looked at Jay in desperation. He hopped off the stool and strode towards her with a calming smile that did nothing to calm her. He took the clicker and tried it himself. Nothing happened. They'd tested it before the workshop. Why didn't it work now?

The A/V guy jogged onto the stage and handed Jay another clicker. When he pressed the button, her slide appeared. Jay held up a hand towards the audience. "Sorry folks, my bad. I grabbed the wrong clicker." He pointed the first clicker towards the audience. "This one is for zapping anyone who falls asleep."

Laughter erupted from the audience. She took that opportunity to peek at the first few rows of people. They seemed a lot less scary when they were laughing. Jay handed her the correct clicker and resumed his position on the stool.

After taking a deep breath to steady her voice, she began. "There are three important steps to help ensure the success of new employees. After I reveal them, I'll cover each one in detail," she said, hearing her own voice shake. She pressed the button on the clicker and turned towards the screen. Her first bullet point didn't appear. No, please, not again.

Her panic-stricken eyes sought Jay's. He signaled something with his hands, but she had no clue what he was trying to tell her. She shrugged her shoulders and stared at him as he once again plastered on a smile and hopped off the stool to rescue her.

When he showed her the correct button to click, the audience burst into laughter again. She didn't even need to look at the screen. She knew exactly why they were laughing. The first two bullet points showed on the screen.

1. Make sure the employee has the right tools.

2. Make sure the employee knows how to use them.

Their eyes met and they both grinned at the opportunity before them. They couldn't possibly have staged a better setup than this.

She put her hands on her hips. "Well, I don't know what you expect—"

He pressed the clicker button to show the next bullet.

3. Make sure the employee knows what you expect of them.

Jay shook his head, holding up his hands in surrender. "And that, my friends, is an example of what happens when your new hire training plan fails to include these three steps."

After covering the steps in detail, they exited the stage together to thundering applause. Her feet barely touched the ground. When they got behind the curtain, he lifted her up and spun around, sending her into a relieved burst of giggles. The look of pride in his eyes when he lowered her back to the floor matched the sense of accomplishment she felt.

"You were amazing," he said, with an enormous grin. The sparkle in his eyes made her heart sing. "I'm so proud of you," he said, sweeping her into a long hug.

When he pulled away, his eyes were commanding. "I've got to rush to the exhibit booth. The crowd will want to interact with you, but I don't want you to get overwhelmed so I booked a massage for you in the spa. You can slip out the side door."

"It's okay. I can handle it," she said, even though she'd rather have her knees busted with a sledgehammer.

He shook his head. "You've had enough excitement for one day. Go relax and we'll celebrate over dinner. Just the two of us," he added. His smile made her knees buckle. Just the two of them. That sounded really nice.

CHAPTER 34

VICTORIA REACTED EXACTLY AS he expected. "Jay, you can't miss a promotional opportunity like this," she implored, easily keeping up with his long stride as they weaved through the crowd towards the exhibit hall. "Everyone in that audience will be clamoring to meet Kricket."

"Which is exactly why she's not going to be there," he snapped.

"Imagine the frenzy you can create before SkillHunter debuts if you announce her as the little girl in your Squirrel Promise story. Your overprotection of her is going to cost you sales."

"I said no. Period. End of conversation." When he shot her his best shut-the-hell-up look, he was surprised when she actually did. Normally she took it as an invitation to push him even further.

"By the way, thank you for taking her shopping this morning." he said, ensuring the subject was closed. "She looked amazing. I think the dress helped boost her confidence."

"I suspect it had more to do with the leopard bra and thong she's wearing."

He whipped his head towards her then kicked himself for responding exactly as she'd intended.

"Or, perhaps it's what I told her," she challenged.

He stopped abruptly and pulled her into a corner of the hallway. "What did you say to her?" He clenched his fists to keep from wrapping them around her throat.

"I just told her that you have a little prick and you suck in bed."

"You did not tell her about our relationship," he said through his teeth, as if he could make it so by speaking it.

"Oh come on Jay," she chided. "Don't you think the Jessicas talk?"

Why didn't he think of that? Of course the Jessicas talk. No wonder Kricket wasted no time hooking up with the cop. "I have no reason to hide that from her," he said, forcing a nonchalant shrug.

She regarded him quizzically for a moment. "Then why are you so worried I told her about us?"

"I'm *not* worried. She just doesn't understand the concept of having sex purely for sex."

"She does now."

"What?"

"I explained it to her."

"You explained *what* to her?"

"The difference between sex and making love." Victoria's face showed how much she was enjoying this. "She knows about the business cards too."

The realization of what Kricket must think of him hit hard. He shook away the image of her disappointed face. "It's best that she knows I'm not capable of falling in love again."

"That's not what I told her."

"What did you tell her?" he snapped. Controlling his anger was no longer possible.

"I told her that you're in love with her."

"Why in the hell would you tell her that?" He was breathing as hard as a racehorse.

"Because you are."

He glared at her, not trusting himself to speak.

"I see it in your eyes when you look at her. I see it in your face right now because you think I've ruined it for you, which I haven't. Just admit it, Jay. You're in love with her." She reached for his shoulder, but he shrugged her hand away. "And if you're not in love with her, then why haven't you been in my bed since you found her? You haven't been in anyone's bed have you?"

"Suck me, Victoria."

"Gladly. Come see me tonight," she responded to his back as he stalked away.

As expected, their exhibit booth was crawling with visitors. Victoria was right. Everyone wanted to meet Kricket.

"I'm sorry, she had to catch an early flight home," he lied to another disappointed attendee. They would have to eat dinner somewhere off the strip to avoid running into anyone he'd disappointed with his lie.

His promise of a celebration with just the two of them didn't seem like a very good idea now. He couldn't have her thinking it was a romantic dinner. He'd invite the Jessicas to join them. And Victoria, since he was feeling suicidal.

With a smile plastered on his face, he tried to focus on the barrage of visitors instead of the anger at Victoria seething within him. How dare she spout her assumptions to Kricket and ruin the façade that took everything within him to carry out on a day-to-day basis?

He was jolted back to the present by an all too familiar graze on his hand. "I'd love to learn more about SkillHunter," a redhead with a silicone rack purred, pressing a business card into his hand. Her smoldering eyes told him exactly what she'd like to learn more about.

"Jessica will be happy to walk you through a demonstration." He handed her card to Jessica B. and turned his attention to a balding man selecting a flashlight keychain from their freebie basket. "Good afternoon, sir. We're giving away an iPad in about ten minutes. If you have a business card, I'll get it in the drawing."

As the man fished out a business card, Jay glanced across the aisle. The brunette manning the Paycom booth didn't bother to look away when he caught her staring. She tucked a strand of hair behind her ear, then slowly ran her fingers down the length of her hair.

"I found one," the balding man said, handing Jay a ragged-edged business card that he'd probably used in a pinch as a toothpick.

"Perfect. We'll be drawing a lucky winner in just a few minutes." Jay held the card by the edge to drop it into the entry jar, then wiped his hand on his jeans.

He looked up to find the Paycom brunette standing in front of him. Like the Jessicas, she dressed to capture attention, short skirt and lots of cleavage.

"Your booth has been stealing my thunder all afternoon, so I thought I'd see what's so exciting over here." Her gaze roamed up and down the length of him in one of the most flagrant ogles he'd experienced in some time. "I mean other than the obvious," she added, foregoing subtlety.

"We're introducing a new interactive staff training software soon," he said addressing her first comment instead of her last. "People are curious about it."

"Sounds intriguing." She plucked a pen from the table and twirled it in her fiery-red manicured fingers. "Some of the vendors are meeting at Delmonico's for Happy Hour after the exhibit hall closes. Maybe I'll see you there."

"I'm meeting my team for dinner as soon as we pack up our booth."

She found his hand, placed her business card in it, folded his fingers over, and squeezed. "Then maybe, I'll see you afterwards."

He glanced next door at Victoria's booth and saw that she

was watching. Her voice echoed in his mind. 'You haven't been in anyone's bed, have you?' He blatantly ogled the Paycom brunette as she swished back to her booth, then looked directly at Victoria and stuffed the business card in his back pocket.

CHAPTER 35

KRICKET FOLDED AND UNFOLDED her napkin for the fortieth time. Her elation over what was supposed to be an intimate celebration with Jay had long faded to a colorless gray. Somehow 'just the two of us' had turned into a party of five. Of course she was elated over the success of the presentation, but listening to the Jessicas prattle excitedly about the potential sales it had garnered was hardly the image that had floated through her mind during her spa treatment. And even worse, the tension between Jay and Victoria hung in the air like a rancid smell. She couldn't help but wonder if Victoria was the reason their intimate dinner had been hijacked. But why, if there was really nothing between them? She stuck a freshly manicured fingernail in her mouth and tried not to watch them as she counted the seconds until dinner was over.

"We just opened a new club on the top floor," the waiter said, presenting Jay with the dinner check. "You'll love the atmosphere and you ladies can get in free until ten."

Jessica B. looked excitedly around the table. "It's supposed to be amazing. We have to go."

Jay handed his credit card to the waiter. "You ladies go ahead. I have some work to do before morning."

"Don't let us keep you, then," Victoria said, shooting him a nasty look.

"Party pooper," Jessica A. said. "We're not finished celebrating, right Kricket?"

She was in no mood to go dancing but Victoria's eyes implored her to agree. "Sure," she said, laying her neatly folded napkin on the table. Jay could be a butt if he wanted to, but this was supposed to be a celebration, so she was going to go have some fun. Even if it killed her.

Several rounds of martinis had significantly altered Victoria's foul mood, and Kricket's concern over her spoiled evening was disintegrating into a nice rose-colored fog.

"Drink up, sister," Victoria said, sliding onto a barstool after dancing to the last three songs. She slid Kricket's martini glass towards her. "Come on, this is a celebration."

Kricket downed the rest of her second flirtini, then nodded towards the Jessicas who were talking up two nicely dressed young businessmen. "You and the Jessicas certainly have no trouble talking to guys."

"It's easy. Quit worrying about how you're standing or sitting, or what you're going to say and focus on the other person." She shifted on her barstool and glanced around the club. "Let's practice. See those four guys over there?"

Kricket nodded, hoping this wasn't going to be too painful.

"Watch them closely. I'll bet you a hundred dollars one of them touches his package before I can count to ten."

She nearly spit her flirtini on the table. "What?"

"I'm serious, men can't go thirty seconds without fondling their nuts. Ready? One, two, three, four, five, six. Ding, ding, ding, there's our winner." Victoria raised her hand for a high five.

The laughter escaping from her mouth felt good. Victoria was even more fun when she was wasted. She pointed towards a table of three guys. "Okay, let's do them now."

Victoria raised her eyebrows. "Why you little tramp. All of them…at once?"

She rolled her eyes. "I mean let's watch them now."

That group took to the count of twelve before a middle-aged

guy in wrinkled khakis reached for his crotch. Victoria set her drink on the table. "Now, tell me what you were doing with your hands while we played the game."

"I have no idea, I wasn't paying—" She stopped midsentence when she realized what Victoria had done. Not only had she taken her mind off of her self-consciousness, but more importantly, off of Jay.

"Ladies, would either of you care to dance?" Kricket glanced up to a kind-faced man of about thirty-five.

Victoria dismissed him with a brisk wave. "If you can't decide which one of us you'd like to dance with, then no."

His crestfallen look was unbearable. "I'd love to," Kricket said, hopping off her bar stool. The appreciative smile that crept across his face warmed her heart. Asking a woman to dance had to be excruciating.

He was a terrible dancer, but he tried hard, and when the dance ended, he thanked her profusely. Apparently he had broken the ice, or she'd had enough flirtinis to loosen up and appear more approachable, because she danced the next three songs with three different guys. Not necessarily attractive guys—most of them were over forty—but it was fun, and gave her a chance to practice eye contact on men. It was much easier when they weren't attractive.

Since Victoria was doing some serious flirting with an extremely good-looking and extremely *young* guy at their table, Kricket headed towards the bar for a water. Between the flirtinis and the dancing, she'd managed to keep her mind off of Jay, for the most part. She was determined to spend the rest of the evening celebrating. After weeks of worrying about it, her presentation was over. And even if it hadn't gone exactly as planned, at least she didn't die.

A warm hand pressed against her back. "There you are."

She closed her eyes for a moment before turning around,

letting her mind bask in the memory of the first time she heard that same voice saying those exact words.

"There *you* are," she said, turning to face him. She didn't even bother trying to squelch the silly grin that spread across her face. "I thought you had work to do."

"I hurried through the emails that were pressing and left the rest until tomorrow. I wanted to come celebrate with you." The gentleness in his eyes cast a hint of sensuality. Did he have any idea what that did to her?

"I'm sorry about dinner," he said. As if on cue, the pulsating music slowed to a romantic tempo. His mouth curved with tenderness as he offered his hand. "Dance with me?"

The familiarity of the moment was spellbinding. Her heart applauded, and her head scolded her as she took his hand. When they stepped onto the dance floor, he twirled her once before collecting her loosely in his arms. "I was watching you from the doorway when I got here," he said, smiling down at her. "It's nice to see you're having some fun after a stressful day." One side of his mouth twisted into a lopsided grin. "I'm just glad you were dancing with an old bald guy."

Why did he care? She tossed her hair, trying to appear nonchalant. "Always the big brother, aren't you?" She watched his eyes to gauge his reaction, but saw nothing. "I was practicing a tip that Victoria taught me. She said if you focus on reading the other person's story, it helps keep your mind off your awkwardness."

"Is that what you're doing now? Reading my story?"

"I'm trying to."

A little crease formed between his eyebrows. "What do you see?" he asked softly.

A myriad of responses swam in her head. What *did* she see, besides a man she loved with all her heart? She could hardly admit that.

"Do you see a man who danced with a girl and knew at that very moment his life would never be the same? A man who would give anything to change the past so he would be worthy of her?"

Tears sprang to her eyes like she'd been punched in the nose. She slowly shook her head in response.

He leaned so close she could feel his breath against her face. "Then you're not reading my story very well."

Her heart beat wildly as he brushed the tip of his nose across hers. The moment his lips touched hers, everything around her melted away. Nothing existed outside the slow massage of his tongue to the rhythm of the music. Her heart reached for his as her lips responded to his deepening kiss. When he pulled her closer, she slid her hand lazily down his back and tucked it into the back pocket of his jeans.

The edge of something stiff stuck under her fingernail. Her hand instinctively jerked away from the stinging prick, then realizing what it was, she thrust her fingers in his pocket and pulled out a business card. The perfume wafting from it was a dead giveaway.

She thrust away from him and held the card between them like a plate of armor. "Your room or mine," she mocked, reading the scribble on the back of the card. She waved the card in his face. "This tells me everything I need to know about your story." Every ounce of faith she had in him now lay in a messy pool on the floor. She glared at him while the full power of her hurt and anger sank in.

"Kric, please, it's not what you think. Let's just go somewhere and I'll explain," he pleaded.

"You don't need to explain a thing. I know exactly what's going on here." Her voice was too loud, but she didn't care. "Miss Business Card Bitch was a no-show, so you thought you could sweet-talk me into being your slutty one-night-stand fill in." She grabbed his hand and slapped the card in his palm. "I know you don't hear this very often, but *no thank you.*" Blinded by tears pooling in her eyes, she bolted in the direction of their table. She had to get her purse and get out of there.

Victoria sprang from her barstool when Kricket stormed up to the table. "What's wrong?" When Kricket didn't respond, Victoria grabbed Jay's arm. "What in the hell did you do to her?" That three second head start was all she needed. She snatched her purse from the table and fled. Fueled by rage, she dashed through the hotel lobby and flew out the exit without looking back.

CHAPTER 36

WRAPPED IN THE COCOON of her comforter, Kricket glanced around her disheveled bedroom. Wads of tissue dotted her bed and the surrounding floor like puffy white dandelions. The contents of her purse were strewn across her dresser. Her expensive new dress, shoes, and leopard undies lay dejected on the floor where she'd cast them this morning after swapping them for the comfort of pajama pants and a T-shirt.

With the aid of some leftover muscle relaxers, she'd slept half of her birthday away, but she certainly needed the rest after holing up in a bar last night until she was certain Jay had gone to bed. After he stopped texting around two a.m., she snuck to her hotel room, grabbed her things and headed to the airport. There was no way she was going to be trapped on a two-hour flight sitting next to Jay, so she caught the early flight out. Monday she'd have to face the wrath of Simon, the accounting department Nazi, for the outrageous cost of her last minute flight change, but that would be nothing compared to what she had to face today. If only she could stay huddled under her blankets forever.

She'd ignored Jay's thirteen texts, seven phone calls, and two visits to her front door, but this evening she had to face him in front of everyone and pretend that everything was fine. Because tonight was the Hunter family Fourth of July celebration. And Madi had let it slip that they were also celebrating Kricket's birthday. All the Hunters would be there. Grandpa and Dot would be there. And even though it was the last place she wanted to be, the birthday girl had to be there.

Her body was stiff from lying in bed and she stretched the kinks out before trudging to the bathroom. One look in the mirror proved that her magic red-eye erasing drops would be no match for the amount of crying she'd done. She tilted back her head and flinched as the droplet splashed against her eyeballs, then blinked rapidly, bathing them in the coolness of the liquid. The corners of her raw eyelids stung when she dabbed away the excess liquid with a tissue.

The steam from the hot shower helped clear her stuffy nostrils and soothe her tense neck muscles, but it did nothing to numb her mind. How could she have been so naïve? He'd been playing her all this time, dangling seductive tidbits of attention until she got too close, then knocking her down. *Here Kricket, swat. Here Kricket, swat.* All in an attempt to keep her ready and willing to service him in case Victoria or one of his business card bitches didn't pan out.

And just like he'd been slowly preparing her to service him in a moment of need, he'd been slowly preparing her to be on display. His encouragement to participate in conferences wasn't to help her realize her dream. All these years, he'd exploited their accident to audiences by pretending it was a life altering experience. Finding her had been a real boost to his earnings potential. He'd probably already ordered a gilded cage to display her in during his next round of conferences. 'Step right up folks for a closer look at the Squirrel Promise Girl. And for an extra $100 you can even feel her scar.'

She held her soapy arm under the shower head and watched the bubbles slide off, leaving her scar sparkly clean. "Well game over, Jay Hunter," she said out loud, as she stepped from the shower and grabbed a towel.

After drying her hair and twirling it up in a knot, she patted concealer around her puffy eyes, then sponged on a layer of foundation. Levi had been so understanding. Maybe she *could* fall for him now. He was kind and funny, and easy on the eyes. She threw her makeup sponge at the mirror. And he didn't fuck everything that walked.

CHAPTER 37

THE BUZZ OF CHATTER around the dinner table worsened her headache, and the smell of food wafting up from her plate made her stomach churn. She'd completely underestimated how difficult today would be. Even the sound of Jay's voice hurt. She tried to force a smile and pretend to care about the table conversation, but gravity pulls hard when your heart is hurting. The muscles in her face felt lax, making the corners of her mouth and eyes seem heavy. And a fog blanketed her head, muffling sound as though she was hearing the world through balls of cotton.

As she poked at the food on her plate, reality swallowed her. Karen, Jay, Meg, Miles, all of them had so completely immersed her in their everyday lives, she'd lost sight of the fact that she wasn't really a Hunter. And she'd never be a Hunter. And yes, in the recesses of her heart, she had to admit, she longed to be a Hunter, a real one. Mrs. Jayson Kyle Hunter. It was unlikely there would ever be another one of those. And even if there was, it wouldn't be her.

The thought of someday sitting at this table with Jay and some woman who'd managed to break through his walls—a dream she'd been unable to achieve—was inconceivable. It was time to start unraveling the threads of her life with them. Karen would be hurt. And Miles. How could she abandon him just as he was beginning to make some progress in his shyness? She wanted to hate Jay for the far-reaching effects of his behavior. But Victoria was right. She'd listened, but hadn't heard him. He'd been abundantly clear they would never have that kind of relationship.

"Who'd like more of my pistachio salad?" Dot asked, holding up the green foamy concoction she faithfully took to every potluck event. It was difficult to look at, much less eat. Everyone at the table masked a cringe, except Madi, who groaned loudly.

"I'd love some more," Karen graciously offered.

Dot handed the bowl to Miles to pass down the table. "You're a handsome young man. I'll bet you have to fight off the girls with a stick."

Miles' body tensed, and his eyes dropped to his plate.

"And a shy one too," Dot said, ruffling his hair. "Girls always like the shy ones, don't they?"

"Miles," Mitch said sternly. "Let's see some manners, son. Answer her."

The familiar look on Miles' face made her die a little inside. The only thing that had broken through her fog today was Mitch's repeated pounces on Miles about his quietness. And with every scolding, she saw a little bit more of the progress he'd made fly out the window. She knew all too well how devastating it felt to have your shyness pointed out in front of others.

On Mitch's face, she saw the haughty look of disappointment cast upon her as a child. The demanding look that completely voided your mind of words. The look of her stepmother.

"Dot's question sounded rhetorical to me," she said, meeting Mitch's eyes.

"Yes, of course it was," Dot said, patting Miles' arm. "I'm just a silly old woman who likes to tease."

"He needs to learn how to carry on a conversation," Mitch said.

Meg touched Mitch's arm and silenced him with her eyes.

"He's too quiet for girls to like him," Madi said, sticking a forkful of ham in her mouth. "He had a girlfriend named Breanna, but she likes Caleb now."

"That's enough, Madi," Meg said quietly.

Madi batted her eyes at her mother's glare. "Well she does."

Miles chewed on his bottom lip. She could tell his mind was begging him to flee.

"What's for dessert, Karen?" she asked in the happiest voice she could muster. "German chocolate cake, I hope." She avoided Jay's eyes and the look she might see in them. Was he reminded of their Friday afternoon ritual of splitting a German chocolate cupcake? He'd never said it, but she knew he started it to commemorate the Friday they found each other again. Losing those little traditions, the things only the two of them shared, that's what would hurt the most.

"Of course I made your favorite cake," Karen said with a twinkle in her eye. "Kricket, why don't you help me clear the table while the others go enjoy the patio."

Jay stood so abruptly, he nearly overturned his water glass. "Mom, you go sit outside with the others. I'll help Kricket with the dishes."

Her breath caught. So far this evening, she'd successfully avoided being alone with him. Even though her heart screamed for him, she had no desire to listen to his excuses or apologies. If he thought he could sweet talk her out of being mad, he was dead wrong.

Karen gave him a don't-argue-with-me-look. "I'd like to spend a little time alone with Kricket on her birthday, if you don't mind."

Jay threw his napkin on his plate and followed the others out the back door.

As soon as they were alone in the kitchen, it became apparent Karen had an ulterior motive. She should have known Karen could sense something was wrong. She picked up a dishtowel and resigned to the impending inquisition.

Karen swirled the soapy sponge around a gravy-soaked saucepan and handed it to her to dry. "A mother always knows when her kids are hurting," she said softly. "And two of mine are hurting."

Kricket silently dried the pan, long after any moisture was present.

"You know I'm always here to listen, right honey? I consider you my daughter and hope you feel that you can talk to me about anything. Even if it involves my son."

The acknowledgement that Karen considered her as one of her own widened the crack that etched down her heart. She swallowed the lump that filled her throat. She longed to throw herself in Karen's soothing arms and feel Karen's fingers lovingly stroke her hair while she poured out her heart. But she wasn't a little girl. And Karen would always be Jay's mom, not hers. She focused on the pan she was drying. If she tried to speak, she would turn into a blubbering mess.

They washed and dried a few more pans in silence before Karen spoke again. "So, this young man, Levi. Is that getting serious?"

She shrugged. "Not really. We have a lot of fun running together, and he's one of the nicest guys I've ever met."

"I want you to be happy, honey, but I'm glad you're not rushing into anything." Karen dried her hands before gently brushing away a lock of Kricket's hair from her eyes. "Things are not always as they appear."

She knew Karen wasn't talking about Levi. But Karen had no idea what Kricket's eyes had seen.

After the dishes were done, Kricket followed Karen out to the patio. She wasn't surprised to find Dot entertaining the family with a funny story about a couple she and Grandpa met last summer on an Alaskan cruise. Dot could tell stories for hours and hold everyone's interest, but she also tended to dominate conversations.

Madi bounced out of the rocking loveseat she was sharing with Jay to wrap herself around Kricket's legs. "Hooray, you're finished, come sit by me!"

Madi pulled her towards the loveseat and sat on the end, patting the center for her to sit down. "You can sit by Uncle Jay. But be careful, he's the tickle monster," she said, her eyes filled with glee.

Dot paused in the middle of her story and turned towards them with a sly grin. "Is that kinda like Santa Claus, but with a longer line?"

Everyone laughed. Everyone except her and Jay. Knowing Karen was watching their every move, she forced a smile and sat down on the spot Madi was patting. With three of them on a loveseat for two, the entire right side of her body was squashed against Jay. And the longer she sat there, the more annoyed she became at the rush that rocketed through her every time she felt him breathe.

Miles was engrossed with his iPad. She noticed Mitch frowning at him, so when Dot finished her story, she casually stood and walked over to sit by Miles, hoping to engage him before Mitch went berserk.

"Miles, what's your favorite subject in school this year?" Grandpa asked, undoubtedly trying to distract Dot from beginning another tall tale.

She appreciated Grandpa's attempt to engage Miles, but she could tell by his stunned silence it caught him off guard. She nonchalantly nudged him with her elbow. "You like algebra, don't you, Miles?"

"Miles," Mitch barked. "Can you not answer a simple question yourself?"

She felt Miles body freeze next to hers, and she knew from the look on his face and from her own experience that his mind was completely blank from the public reprimand.

Mitch glared at him, waiting.

Within seconds, she was off the couch and in Mitch's face. "Do you really think that's how you help someone overcome a debilitating fear? Do you have any idea what it feels like to have someone command you to speak when your brain refuses to send a single word to your mouth? Do you?" She glared at him, unconcerned with the scene she was causing. "Of course you don't, because you've always been a big ballsy brute who has more to say than anyone even cares to hear!" Her index finger was inches from his face. "I'll tell you what it feels like. It feels like your brain is completely numb and time stands still while everyone watches you, waiting. All you can see are faces staring at you while you try to force your mouth to speak. But your brain can't think of one tiny word to say." She blinked back the tears of anger-filled memories brimming in her eyes. "Are you afraid of anything, Mitch? Or are you too big and tough to admit it?"

She held his eyes so he would know she expected an answer. "Are you?"

From the corner of her eye, she saw Tom start to stand, but Karen put her hand on his arm and shook her head.

"He's afraid of spiders," Madi offered.

She stepped closer to Mitch with her hands on her hips. "So you're afraid of spiders? How about we find a great big hairy garden spider and let it crawl up your arm so you can just *get over it*," she taunted, motioning towards the flower beds. "Do you think that would cure your fear of spiders, just…like…that?" she asked, snapping her fingers in his face.

She was vaguely aware of everyone's eyes following her as she paced in front of him. "I can assure you, the answer is no. It's no different than leaving a shy little girl in the middle of a department store and telling her she had to ask someone for help or she would never get home. Then turning on your heel in your big fur coat and marching away. Leaving her standing all alone, surrounded by strangers." Her voice caught as the memory washed over her. Too scared to talk to anyone, she'd hidden in a bin of stuffed animals for what seemed an eternity until some nice lady noticed her and led her to the store security office. Her stepmother had put on quite a show pretending to be distraught over losing her child in the store.

Jay rose from his chair and came to stand beside her, but she stepped away from him. She didn't need a big brother now, or ever.

Mitch closed his eyes for a moment. Her chest heaved with deep breaths. The realization that she was standing in front of everyone berating Mitch rendered her silent. Everyone stared, stunned and waiting. Waiting for Mitch's response or waiting for someone, anyone, to break the silence.

When Mitch's eyes opened and met hers, they were moist. He first looked at Meg and Madi huddled together in a chair, then held out a hand to Miles. "Come here, son."

Miles eased off the couch and slinked over to Mitch, who knelt down on one knee and rested his hands on Miles' shoulders. "I'm sorry, son. I didn't know that's how it felt." He pulled Miles into his chest. "I didn't know."

The patio was silent with the exception of a few sniffles and the sound of Tom and Grandpa clearing their throats. Mitch held Miles for a long time, then stood and held out a hand to her. "I'm sorry, Krissy," he said, pulling her into his bulky body. "And I'm sorry for what you went through after they—" He paused and turned towards Grandpa. "She's lucky to have you, Mr. Taylor. You've done a great job with our little Krissy."

Grandpa nodded.

He gave her a side squeeze. "You surprised me there, tigress. Press the right buttons and those claws come out like a switchblade," he said with a chuckle, which eased the tension and prompted everyone to gather around them in a hug fest. Between Karen, Grandpa, and Miles, she thought she was going to be squeezed to death. But instead of feeling suffocated by their fawning, she felt warm.

Grandpa patted Mitch on the back. "I think your little brother deserves some credit as well," he said, extending a hand towards Jay. "Just look at our girl. Not only is she telling off Bigfoot, but six months ago I would have bet you a million dollars she'd rather have a root canal without anesthesia than speak before an audience."

Jay's face bore a mixture of pride and pain as Grandpa gave him a pat-on-the-back man-hug. "She had it in her all the time. She just needed a little nudge," he said. His droopy eyes caught hers. "We all do sometimes."

She pulled away from Mitch and escaped into the house, leaving Jay's impending hug hanging. She knew it was obvious, but she didn't care. She couldn't fall back into his trap. And if she felt his heartbeat against hers, she would.

CHAPTER 38

CHOCOLATE AND COCONUT WAFTED through the air when Karen
lifted the glass dome off of the antique cake stand, revealing a
castle of chocolate cake with coconut caramel icing oozing from
each of the four layers. "Who's ready for birthday cake?"

Tom leaned over the cake and took in an overly dramatic
breath. "Smells wonderful as always, hon."

Karen glanced towards the kitchen table where Kricket was
playing a word game on the iPad with Miles. "Kricket, do you
remember the first time I made one of these for your birthday?"

Her eyes welled up, and all she could do was nod and return
Karen's smile. How could a cake make your heart hurt so much?

On her sixth birthday, Karen had invited a few neighborhood
kids for a small party...her first real birthday party with kids. She
didn't know any of them very well. The attention while opening
the gifts they brought overwhelmed her, so Jay sat on the floor
beside her and played tug-of-war with McGruff, their Scottish
terrier, to distract the kids so she didn't feel like they were
watching her. To this day, she still hated opening gifts in front of
people.

Meg set a stack of dessert plates next to Karen, then turned
towards the family room. "Madi, run out to the garage and tell your
dad and Jay we're cutting the cake."

"But Mom, I'm drawing a picture for Kricket's birthday,
Madi whined from her perch on Dot's lap. Madi already had Dot
and Grandpa wrapped around her little finger.

Miles rolled his eyes and switched the iPad from the word

game to the security app. "If the garage monitor's on, I'll ask them on here," he said. After he punched in the password, an image of Mitch and Jay standing on the passenger side of her Jeep popped onto the screen. She couldn't help but stare at Jay's bulging muscles as he lifted the front passenger door off its hinges. She'd concocted the idea of asking them to take off her doors for the long weekend to get Jay into the garage and away from her.

Just before Miles' finger hit the unmute button, Jay's voice boomed through the iPad speaker. "I can't help that I fell in love with her."

The house fell silent. Her face grew hot as she stared at the iPad. She knew it. Jay was in love with Victoria, and she had to hear about it with seven pairs of eyes staring at her.

Mitch took the door from Jay and set it against the wall. "Well it's about damn time you finally admit it. You'd better hurry up and tell her before Levi shows her what a real man's like in the bedroom." He laughed and slapped Jay on the back. "I'm just kidding, brother, it's pretty obvious Kricket's in love with you too."

Kricket stared at the screen. It was her? Jay was in love with her? She glanced up at a mixture of shock and grins on everyone's faces.

Meg stepped towards the table. "I think maybe we should turn the iPad off and let Jay and Kricket talk in private."

Jay's voice came through softer this time. "I have to tell her about Tara."

Meg's hand flew towards the iPad, but Kricket quickly snatched it off the table. Holding it out of Meg's reach, she watched Mitch close his eyes for a moment, clearly disturbed by Jay's announcement. "Tara's dead, Jay. Kricket never has to know. What would you say anyway? Please pass the salt, and oh by the way, I fucked your mother?"

The roar in her ears was deafening. She couldn't move. She couldn't breathe. She stared at the screen, but saw nothing. The sound of the iPad hitting the table as it fell from her hands startled the fog from her vision and she glanced across the room. Tears filled her eyes as she first met Karen's gaze, then Tom's, then Grandpa's. Their faces were ridden with guilt. She knew without turning to look, that Meg's was too. Everyone knew. Everyone but her.

Miles grabbed the iPad and punched a button. "You just told her, you asshole."

Jay's head swung towards the garage monitor. Their eyes met screen to screen. She'd seen enough Animal Kingdom episodes to know that in that split second when the hunter and the hunted lock eyes, the moment she moved a single muscle, the chase would ensue.

She leapt to her feet and barreled towards the front door. After grabbing Jay's keys off the entry table on her way out, her feet flew one in front of the other, her mind completely focused on getting to his Jeep before he sensed what she was doing. She hopped in and jabbed the key at the ignition, but her hands were shaky, and the keys slipped from her fingers and fell to the floor.

"Kricket!" When she glanced up, Miles was running out the front door, with Jay and Mitch on his heels. Her hands scoured the floorboard until her fingers found the key ring. Fumbling through them, she found the right key, stuck it in the ignition and started the Jeep. The transmission groaned as she slammed in the clutch and threw it into reverse. After lurching backwards into the street, she ground the gear into first and stomped on the gas just as they got to the edge of the driveway. "Kricket wait!" Jay reached for the door, but jerked his arm back as the Jeep took off. When she glanced in the rear view mirror, he was standing in the middle of the street, with his hands on his head, watching her drive away.

CHAPTER 39

STATIONED IN GRASSHOPPER IN front of her apartment, Jay kept his eyes fixated on the little red dot that was Kricket, thankful for the GPS tracker he'd installed on Mud Ninja. With the exception of his heartbeat, his body felt numb. At least she hadn't run to Levi. She'd headed north towards the city limits, where the only thing the blaring stereo would annoy were cows. He pictured her hair whipping about in the wind, with strands sticking to the tears streaming down her face. Knowing she was doing the exact thing he'd done with her when she needed to escape from the wrath of Tara gave him no comfort. "Please be careful, baby," he said to the dot.

As badly as he'd wanted to chase her, his family was right. If she saw him, she might endanger herself trying to escape his tail. She had to come home eventually, and he would be there waiting when she did.

He could only imagine the details her mind was conjuring up to fill in the missing pieces of the story. He'd been an idiot for thinking he could, or even should, keep it from her. There was no need using this time to plan out what he would say. He would simply tell her what happened—no excuses, no fluff, just the truth. Instead, as time dragged by, he tortured himself with memories of her. Memories from their childhood. The day he first saw her at Starbucks. How soft her lips were—the stricken look on her face as she drove away slammed into his mind again. He pounded his fist against the steering wheel, then shook his stinging hand. The pain from the smack was nothing compared to the pain in his heart.

The sky darkened as two hours passed. He wasn't at all startled by the thunderous boom over his head at the stroke of ten p.m. He'd been dreading it, hoping she would return before it happened. But as he watched the first burst of sparkling red and blue lights from the fireworks display fill the sky, he was alone. Very alone.

At least a dozen firework shows were visible from the parking lot where he sat, the largest being only a mile away at the university. Was Kricket watching them too? He leaned his head against the head rest and watched the show out of the top of Grasshopper. Normally a fireworks show seemed short, but this one seemed to go on forever, plunging each burst of color deeper into his heart. Of all the fireworks displays he'd watched wishing she were there, never had he longed for it as badly as this one. He lay his head against the steering wheel and wept.

When he finally lifted his head to glance at his phone, the little red dot was headed back towards town. Please don't go to Levi's, he pleaded to the dot, willing it to stay on course towards her apartment. He held his breath as she approached the turnpike entrance. If she got on the turnpike, she was going to Levi's. If she stayed on the frontage road, she was coming home.

When she passed the turnpike entrance, he leaned his head back and released a long sigh of gratitude. She's coming home. He slid out of Grasshopper, walked around the parking lot a bit to get the blood circulating in his legs again, then sat on her doorstep to wait.

Apparently seeing Grasshopper, she hesitated at the apartment complex entrance, as if contemplating another flee. He leapt up, digging the keys from his pocket. If she turned around, this time he was going after her. Another car pulled in behind her, giving her no choice but to continue towards her apartment. She inched into the spot next to Grasshopper. Without a word or even a glance, she got out of Mud Ninja, threw the keys at him, unlocked her door and walked in. But she left the front door open. And that was all the invitation he needed. She might be unwilling to face him, but she was obviously unwilling to turn him away.

She went through the motions of arriving home as if he weren't there. He stood in the entryway while she hung her purse on the hook behind the door, removed her shoes and placed them in her closet, then grabbed a bottle of water from the refrigerator without offering him one. Without even a glance his way, she sat on the couch and flipped on the TV. When she pulled a big pillow into her lap and wrapped her arms around it like a security blanket, he wanted to gather her in his arms. Deep down she might long for his comfort, but right now she would fight him. He eased himself onto the other end of the couch as if the mere movement of the cushion might cause her to flee, then leaned forward and rested his forehead on his steepled fingers.

He could feel her inside his heart, and knew she could feel him too. They always could. It was one of those things that was hard to explain. Even when they were apart, they could just feel each other. And if he waited long enough, hopefully that connection would soften her barrier.

When her tense grip on the pillow loosened, he knew that, just like him, she was powerless over the instinct of their souls to reach out for each other. It didn't mean she'd forgive him, but it meant she'd listen. And that was all he could hope for.

She picked up the remote and muted the TV, but kept her eyes fixed on the now silent rerun of *Friends*. "I'm listening," she said quietly.

He took a deep breath before beginning the conversation he'd dreaded for seventeen years. "After our motorcycle accident, I didn't think anything could ever make me feel as repulsive as hurting you and causing that scar on your arm." He touched the rough line of his own scar as he spoke. "But that promise I made you, that stupid, stupid promise—keeping it ended up hurting you even more."

He rose and walked to the window, staring at their Jeeps sitting side by side in the parking lot while his mind groped for the right words. "That night...before your dad came and took you away...you don't remember what happened do you?"

In the reflection of the window, he watched her almost imperceptibly shake her bowed head.

"Mom had the flu, so I watched you at your house while Tara went clubbing. After you went to bed, my T-shirt was bothering my arm, so I took it off. It was just a few weeks after the accident and our arms were healed to the point where the itching was unbearable."

He began pacing behind the length of the couch to tame his adrenalin. "I drank a few beers from the refrigerator. More than a few, actually. To be honest, I was pissed that I had to babysit you instead of going out with my friends. I mean, I would have done anything for you, but babysitting wasn't what a sixteen-year-old guy wanted to do on a Friday night. So I got drunk and fell asleep on the couch. Tara must have come through the back door because I didn't hear her come in."

He forced himself to continue. "I woke up to find Tara naked and all over me." He grasped his Adams apple to keep the bile from rushing into his throat at the memory of Tara grinding on top of him, forcing her margarita basted tongue into his mouth.

"She was drunk, Kricket, really drunk...worse than I was." He could still smell her sickeningly sweet perfume mixed with cigarette smoke. "I didn't want it, Kric, but when you're sixteen, you wake up with a hard-on—"

Kricket's hands flew to her ears, and she shook her head. "Please stop! I don't want to hear any more."

He rounded the couch and sat on the ottoman in front of her, then gently took her hands from her ears and held them. "I didn't want it. You have to believe me, I didn't want it."

She snatched her hands away and buried her face in them. "Don't touch me, Jayson."

"You must have heard the struggle, because the next thing I knew, you were in the room yelling at her to stop hurting me and trying to pull her away. Her arms were flailing, and she knocked you across the room." He clenched his teeth against the anger as he re-lived that horrendous moment. "Your head hit the coffee table and when I saw the blood and your crumpled little body, I thought you were dead."

She looked up at him incredulously, her eyes glazed with torment, her breath exhaling in shudders.

"She was drunk, Kricket. She didn't mean it, she was just really drunk." He wanted to stop and console her, but he had to finish.

"I picked you up and ran home. Dad took you from me at the door. You came to as he laid you on the couch. There was a gash on your forehead where you'd hit the edge of the coffee table when you fell. It didn't need stitches…and only left a tiny scar." He lifted his hand to touch her forehead, but she turned away.

"I held you while Mom cleaned your face. And then I rocked you, and rocked you, knowing I was going to lose you forever."

Kricket slid off the couch and walked to the window, standing with her back to him. More than anything, he wanted to rush to her, pull her close to his chest and hold her until her pain went away. Just like he used to. But he couldn't make this go away. So he sat silently, waiting for her to say something, anything. But she just stared out the window.

"I love you, Kricket. I always have. And now I'm in love with you. I need you to know that."

She turned and glared at him through wet eyes. "So were you in love with me last night when you were going to fuck that Paycom girl at the conference?"

Her words slapped him in the face. A dull pain pulsed in his temples. She would never believe he took that business card to make a point to Victoria—to prove that he wasn't in love with Kricket. It even sounded lame to him now.

"I haven't touched another woman since I found you again. You have to believe that."

She closed her eyes for a moment then turned back to the window. "I said I'd listen and I did. Now I just need you to go."

He stood paralyzed, absorbed by the gravity of the situation. He couldn't leave. Not now, not until he made her believe him. "Kricket, please, just let me—"

She moved towards the front door and opened it. "It's too much, Jay. It's just too much. Ever since we found each other again, it's just been *too* much."

The mixture of anger, pain, and fear he saw in her cold stare strangled his heart. He closed his eyes for a moment, waiting. Waiting for her to change her mind, for her to see in his face how much he loved her, for her to say, 'I love you too. Please don't go.' But she didn't.

"Goodbye Jay."

Reluctantly, he picked up his keys from the coffee table and walked towards the door, pausing to look in her eyes one more time in search of a glimmer of forgiveness. If she closed her eyes, he'd know she was faltering and maybe there was hope. But she didn't.

"I love you, Kric," he said, then stepped through the door into the harsh reality of life without her.

CHAPTER 40

KRICKET WASN'T SURE WHY she ended up at the cemetery the next morning. She hadn't been to her mom's grave in years. Grandpa always took her on Memorial Day to put flowers on the headstone. But after junior high, going to the lake for a long weekend with friends became more important than leaving plastic flowers on a gravestone, simply to become covered in red dust and blown askew by the Oklahoma wind.

Unhurried to reach her mother's grave, she ambled thru the cemetery, straightening a spray of flowers here, or reading a headstone there. A twig was lodged in a bright pinwheel stuck in the ground near a tiny grave. She paused to remove it.

Emma Hope Randall
Born 2/7/15
Died 2/9/15

Two days in this cruel world. Just long enough to experience love, but short enough to avoid the heartbreak of it. She stood for a moment watching the pinwheel spin freely again before moving on to her mother's grave and plopping herself cross-legged next to her mother's small headstone.

Tara Amber Taylor
Daughter and Mother

And apparently, *skank*. It was easy to understand why Grandpa hadn't told her what happened when she was young, but someone should have told her after she and Jay found each other again. They had to know it would come out eventually. Karen's silence probably hurt more than anything. But how could she fault her for being loyal to her son? She stared at the headstone of her own mother who lay there in the cold ground, unable to protect her, comfort her, or even apologize if she so chose. What was her mother's story? Not the story of what happened, but the story of who she was. She refused to believe her mom was just a bad person. If only she could gaze in her eyes once more, maybe she could see the pain that caused her to act as she did. She had a broken heart. And a broken heart can change you.

Overwhelmed by the stress of not only the last few days, but the last few months, she buried her head in her hands. How was she going to live without Jay, or Karen, and all of the Hunters? She'd finally found them again and now—

The sound of a car door jolted her. She raised her head to see Grandpa hobbling towards her. Of course he knew to look for her here.

He slowly made his way towards her, grimacing against the hot sun. The cane and his limp from hip surgery made him look older than he really was. She was relieved to see he'd come alone. Dot would try to fuss over her. Fussing wasn't what she needed right now. As Grandpa grew closer, she stood and brushed the grass from her shorts.

"I thought I'd find you here." He jabbed at a few leaves with the tip of his cane. "I'm sorry honey. I should have told you. I just didn't know how, and I thought maybe—"

She hushed him with a hug. "I know," was all she could manage to say.

An expansive oak tree towered over a nearby bench, providing a much needed barrier from the sun. She used her sleeve to brush away the few tears that leaked from her eyes as they walked arm in arm to it. They sat silently, gazing at the headstone.

"I wish Mom were still here, so I could ask her what happened."

"I wish she were too, honey," he said, his eyes moistening.

She studied his face as he watched a hawk circling overhead. She'd never really considered the pain Grandpa must feel from losing his only child.

"If your mother's story differed from Jay's, who would you believe?" he asked quietly.

"I don't know," she said resignedly. "I don't know anything anymore." She leaned against his shoulder while a fresh round of tears slipped out.

He gave her arm a squeeze. "I know you love him. I could see the stars in your eyes that very first day you brought him to the house. And the stars in his eyes were just as bright. But what matters most in a relationship is trust. Only you can decide if you trust Jay enough to know that he told you the truth. Then you have to decide if you can deal with that truth."

She nodded against his shoulder. "But how do I know?"

"Ask yourself what kind of man he is. Is he a man of his word? Has he otherwise been truthful to you?"

And that was the question of the century. Jay was a man of impeccable character in every manner, except where women were concerned. And that, of course, was the most crucial aspect.

They sat together until the heat became unbearable, then walked arm in arm back to the parking lot. Grandpa, always the gentleman, opened Hopper's door and held it while she climbed in.

"It's a funny thing," he said as she fastened her seatbelt. "Sometimes the most valiant effort to protect someone you love is the very thing that ends up hurting them the most."

CHAPTER 41

Monday, July 6th
... 'Do something brave' should read 'Do something painful.' It's time to start over...again.

Today's Goal: *Start over.*

TOM WOULD ARRIVE AT work in exactly three minutes, which was just enough time to rush out of his office before he saw her. But Kricket forced herself to stay planted in his guest chair. She stared at the little green mermaid lady on her half empty latte cup, mentally rehearsing the speech she'd prepared. She'd thought about it all night and knew what she had to do.

Her stomach clenched at the sound of Tom's footsteps in the hallway. His long stride was similar to Jay's, but his pace was quicker. When he reached the door and saw her, his black thermos of coffee nearly flew out of his hand.

"Kricket," he said, quickly resuming his stoic demeanor. "I wasn't expecting you."

"I apologize for the intrusion, Tom, but I need to talk to you. I hope you don't have an early appointment." No one ever had an appointment at 7:00 a.m., but she didn't want him to think she was disregarding the protocol of scheduling a meeting.

He set his thermos on his immaculate desk and placed his briefcase on the credenza. "I always have time for you, Kricket."

"Thank you," she said, watching him unscrew the lid of his thermos and pour coffee into a large H-Tech mug. She inhaled deeply, hoping the soothing aroma would ease her pounding heart.

After pressing the remote button under his desk to close the office door, he pulled out a chair and joined her at the small conference table. "What can I do for you?" His forehead was creased, but his smile was warm.

She swallowed away the lump in her throat with a quick sip of her lukewarm latte, then cleared her throat and began before she could change her mind. "You and your family have been more than generous to me by giving me this opportunity at H-Tech. I want you to know how much I appreciate it. But, I think it's best for everyone that I find another job." The moment she spoke the words, her nose tingled like someone had smacked it. She blinked away the moisture that filled her eyes. "I'll stay until the end of the month. That will get us through the launch. Then it should be easy enough to replace me with someone to provide the new client training and manage any needed updates." She took a deep breath and focused on her latte cup. She'd made two pacts with herself this morning. One, not to give in, and two, not to cry. "I have enough in savings to last a few months while I find another job. I hope I can count on you for a recommendation."

"As your employer, I would be disappointed to see you go," he said, peering over his glasses. "SkillHunter is already seeing tremendous success with our existing client base. Your idea and your dedication is what built SkillHunter. It would be a shame not to see the fruits of your efforts."

He removed his glasses and worked on adjusting an earpiece. "I've never been much for sentiment. And when you were small, you probably thought I was an ogre. You may still think that," he added with a smile. "But I consider you like one of my own, so I'm going to speak to you as a father, not as an employer."

Touched by his unusual show of humor and affection, a small grin slipped through the heavy weight of her misery.

"One thing I've learned over the years is, whether in business or your personal life, any decision you make in the throes of a crisis is probably a bad one."

She cringed at the expected lecture.

He surprised her by covering her hand with his warm palm. "I know you're hurting and you're angry. And you undoubtedly feel betrayed by all of us. That's why I won't accept your resignation right now."

Betrayal. His validating words reached into her soul and christened her agony. She looked away, blinking rapidly against the tears they incited.

"I can't believe Mama Karen didn't tell me," she murmured.

"It broke her heart to keep something like this from you. She worried about it constantly. Secrets eventually surface, but it wasn't her place to tell you."

"I feel as though all of you whispered behind my back, trying to keep a secret that everyone knew but me." She used her thumb to wipe at the lipstick mark on the plastic lid of her latte. "I feel like a fool."

"It wasn't like that, kiddo. I know it's a tremendous shock, and it's going to take some time to wrap your mind around it. You're an important part of our family, and we'll support you both while you get through this."

His words felt heavy on her shoulders. She wasn't a part of their family. And now she never would be. As much as she loved all of them, no matter how hard they tried, things would never be the same.

His voice broke through her thoughts. "You're not aware of this, but when you were young, you helped Karen and me through a difficult time. Let us do the same for you."

"How did I do that?" she asked, looking up at him.

His pained expression caught her off guard. She'd never considered that, smothered beneath his stiff demeanor, could be a story of disappointment, tragedy, or pain. She searched his eyes as he silently regarded her. They were a lighter brown than Jay's, with tiny flecks of gold around the edges. She'd always thought them to be stern and intimidating, but they were actually rather gentle. And deep within them, she saw love, and a hint of pain.

"Karen and I lost a baby…a little girl," he said abruptly, as if compelled to spit it out. "She came way too early and never had a chance. Her name was Emma."

The pain echoing through his voice tightened the already suffocating vise around her heart. A whispered "Tom," fell from her mouth.

He acknowledged her with a faint nod, and continued. "I truly didn't think Karen would get through it. She'd hardly get out of bed, and became rail thin. She lost interest in nearly everything, including the boys for a while. And poor Jayson…he'd been so anxious for a baby sister. While Karen was pregnant, he would rub her belly and talk to the baby. Then after we lost her—" His eyes closed in a memory-filled wince. "Jay couldn't understand why we didn't bring Emma home from the hospital. He thought we didn't want her."

A tumble of thoughts and feelings assailed her. The despair over her own situation compounded by a deep sorrow for Karen and Tom. Her hand flew to her mouth. And Rachel's abortion. That had to be more than Jay could possibly endure, more than any of them could endure.

"You came along about a year later," he continued after a sip of his coffee. "I'll never forget the first time Tara asked Karen to babysit you." A slight smile touched his lips as his mind slipped into the past. "The moment Tara placed you in her arms, Karen glowed. As if the sun reached down and kissed her shoulder. And Jayson," he said with a chuckle. "We couldn't keep him away from you. Mitch was crazy about you too, but at sixteen, he was off doing his own thing, so he wasn't around much. Jayson was proud to be the big brother for a change, and he took his role very seriously." He rubbed his clean-shaven chin. "I'll admit, at the time, I was a little concerned about the family becoming so involved with you. You needed them as much as they needed you, but I knew it would be devastating if you moved away or..." He took a quick sip of his coffee.

"Or if something happened."

He nodded, and they both sat in their own thoughts for a moment.

"Just talk to him, kiddo. You owe yourself that."

She kept her gaze on the table.

"You and Jay can work this out. Give yourself some time to digest it, then talk to him."

She stopped twirling her empty coffee cup and stared at it, shaking her head. "There's just too much between us that's painful. I need to start trying to put it behind me. I can't do that if I am constantly around him, and your family, and your business. SkillHunter belongs to Jay. Your family belongs to Jay." Saying the words out loud left her hollow inside.

"That's where you're wrong," he said gently.

She shook her head, vowing resolve. "Tulsa's not too far from Grandpa. I'm sure I can find a job there. I just need to get away...from everyone."

"SkillHunter is yours. You're welcome to run it from our Tulsa office, if you decide to move."

She laughed at his attempt to add a little humor to this painful conversation. "Thanks for the vote of confidence, but Jay's doing a fine job of running his own company."

"I don't think you heard me." He pulled a notepad from a drawer and drew four pie charts, labeling each with an H-Tech company name. "While each of my sons has majority ownership in his company, we make major decisions together because we all have a vested interest. That's why you've been included in our board meetings." He wrote her name in the biggest piece of the pie chart titled 'SkillHunter.' "You are the majority owner of SkillHunter."

She stared at the picture, trying to absorb what he'd just said. SkillHunter was hers? Her thoughts volleyed between feeling thrilled and grateful, to feeling trapped. Owning SkillHunter was far and away the most shocking and exciting news she could fathom, but—

She didn't look at Tom when he placed his palm over hers. "I consider you one of my own. I did this for my boys, and I wanted to do it for you too. Jay asked me to wait before telling you. You should know by now that his biggest fear is hurting you. If SkillHunter failed, he didn't want you to be disappointed or feel responsible."

She closed her eyes against the thought of enduring a wound that would never be allowed to heal. Somehow she had to convey her appreciation, yet politely decline.

"I know what you're thinking, so let me put aside that thought right now. Your interest in SkillHunter is not negotiable. It's a gift. But whether you want to stick around here or not is completely your decision. If you decide you need to move away, you can either run SkillHunter remotely or we'll hire someone to run it for you. It wasn't meant to trap you in our family, only to recognize you as a part of it."

"I don't even know what to think." Her mind swirled with fear, mixed with excitement, and dread.

"You don't need to make any decisions right now. Everything is ready for the SkillHunter launch next week, so why don't you head out to San Diego early? You can take some time for yourself without anyone bothering you. Jay's worried about flying in the morning of his presentation anyway. This way you'll already be there to take care of any last minute issues."

"But I'll miss Gayle's fortieth birthday party." The thought of trying to socialize while pretending everything was fine wasn't at all appealing, but Gayle was her friend. Jay was even breaking his always-arrive-the night before-the-conference-rule, just so he could be at her party.

"I think Gayle will understand that having you onsite to oversee the conference prep is more important than a birthday party," he said. "She's flying out with Jay the next morning to help with the launch before she heads out on her birthday cruise. You could take her to a nice birthday dinner on the wharf before she ships off."

She knew Gayle would understand. "You're right. And I do need some time by myself."

He smiled and patted her hand. "I'll ask Peggy to change your flight arrangements. Go pack, and I'll see you in a week."

She nodded once, then stood.

"And Kricket?

"Yes?"

"Your presentation. You'll be great."

CHAPTER 42

Tuesday, July 14th
...Sometimes I feel like the only thing constant in my life is this wretched journal, forever taunting me to do something I don't want to do...

Today's goal: I'm taking a vacation from goals. I have plenty of stress in my life right now...

JAY WAS THE LAST THING on her mind before falling asleep and the first thing on her mind when she woke up. She'd seen a tweet about that and didn't like what it had asserted. The truth was, she missed him desperately. And even though he'd promised to leave her alone until he arrived for the conference, she couldn't help but check her phone for a message the second she woke up, and again throughout the day more times than she cared to admit. Never make a promise you can't keep. Why did she wish so badly he wouldn't keep this one?

She tried distracting her mind with work, or lounging by the pool and entering someone else's life in a good book. But everything she read became a blank page as her mind drifted back to thoughts of him. Attempting to distract herself with sightseeing made it even worse. The only thing she thought about on her whale-watching excursion was how he would have teased her by pointing out a non-existent whale and acting shocked that she couldn't see it, or pretending to push her overboard. And while she perused the shops dotting the boardwalk, she wished he were there to share a cheese-covered pretzel, or try on silly hats and take funny selfies.

On her way back to her room, she stopped in the hotel gift store for a package of crackers or something that would sit well on her stomach. She refused to sit in another restaurant and order another beautifully presented piece of freshly caught fish only to push it around with her fork. With her carb overloaded selection of overly-orange cheese crackers and a package of butter cookies, she stood at the counter while the cashier waited on a young boy of about six and his mother.

"Mommy, can I have a cupcake?" the little boy asked, eying the glass case of baked goods strategically placed by the cash register to tempt customers into a spontaneous purchase.

Watching him bounce up and down in ecstasy after his mother nodded her consent made her smile. The grin felt odd on her face, as if the muscles around her mouth were straining against it.

"Strawberry or German chocolate?" his mother asked.

The all too familiar pain stabbed inside her heart, causing her eyes to mist. She blinked rapidly and surveyed the colorful candy neatly arranged on the shelf beside her. Anything to distract her mind. Anything to keep that first tear from falling. As a tear slid down her cheek, she quietly set the crackers on the counter and left.

❧

Hotel bathroom mirrors don't lie, and this one told her she needed to get a grip. Her eyes caught their own reflection as she wiped the mascara smudge from her eye. At first she looked away, but then she forced herself to study them. Looking *into* your eyes was very different than looking *at* your eyes. The story she saw in them nearly instigated the tears again. And *that* wasn't happening, so she flipped off the light and walked into the bedroom area.

Since she'd abandoned her cracker and cookie purchase, dinner was going to be a package of M&Ms and a tiny bottle of wine from the mini-fridge, while watching a romantic comedy from the comfort of her hotel bed.

As she changed into a cami and pair of boxers, her guilty conscience chided her about skipping her run for the third day in a row. If Levi knew she was skipping an opportunity to run along the boardwalk in the ocean breeze instead of around the small windy lake at home, he'd think she'd lost her mind. Or her heart.

She barely tasted her M&M dinner as she scrolled through her list of text messages. Two were from Becca, four were from Levi, and one was from Victoria, which she opened immediately. 'Meet me for lunch tomorrow at 1:30 in the hotel lobby.' It was just like Victoria to command instead of ask. Although she was tempted to respond "no," just to show Victoria she'd grown a pair, in all truthfulness, she was anxious to talk with her. No one knew Jay's mind better than Victoria. Plus, in her own brazen way, she was rather comforting. 'See you then,' she typed.

She took a few sips of wine straight from the little bottle before opening the messages from Levi. No response from her for days surely had him worried sick. She felt bad, but the last thing she wanted to do was tell the story and dredge everything up again. Plus, she wasn't sure how she'd feel about Levi criticizing Jay after she told him.

But it wasn't just that. Levi was such a good friend to her. Like the night he skipped a friend's birthday party and surprised her by bringing over a movie and a bag of caramel popcorn because she was too tired from working on SkillHunter to go out.

Guilt stabbed her in the gut as she poured a few more candy morsels in her hand. That was the night he finally kissed her. And that was the night she knew. His kiss was nice and actually rather sensuous, and if she'd never been kissed by Jay, she probably would have felt differently about it. But no kiss would ever make her forget Jay's.

She jumped when her phone rang. Levi's name glowed on the screen. She waited a few rings then dropped her bag of M&Ms on the bed and answered.

His voice was comforting after being alone for several days, and soon she found herself pouring her heart out to him, thankfully without choking up.

"Aww, Kricket, I wish I could be there to help you through this. That's a lot to deal with, and you already had plenty on your mind worrying about the launch this week."

"I'm okay, really. I'm one of those people who prefer to deal with stuff alone. I just can't believe he never told me." She picked up the little wine bottle for another sip and braced herself for the Jay lambasting. She wasn't at all sure why she suddenly felt defensive of him.

"I wouldn't have told you either," Levi said quietly.

"What? Why not?" She wiped at the dribble of wine she spit onto her cami. "That's not exactly the kind of secret you keep from someone you're close to."

"It is if it would serve no purpose other than to hurt you."

"He just didn't want me to hate him," she scoffed.

"No. He didn't want you to hate your mother." He remained silent while his words sunk in. "Kricket," he said, interrupting her thoughts that had drifted miles away.

"Hmm?"

"Don't condemn someone for wanting to protect you."

"I don't need to be protected. I can take care of myself."

His grin was audible. "Yes, you can. But that doesn't prevent people who care about you from wanting to safeguard you from pain or stress. Don't take this the wrong way, but you're the kind of girl people want to protect. It's not that you're helpless or incapable, it's just that you're..." She could tell he was searching for a word that wouldn't offend her.

"I don't use this word very often, because my balls would shrink if I did, but well, you're *precious*."

An image of shriveled balls made her snicker, which made him laugh, but then he fell silent.

"You miss him, don't you?" His voice was gentle, yet probing.

She rubbed her fingers across her scar, her lifeline to Jay, then let out a sigh. "Yes," she said quietly.

Silence hung in the air like fog. She couldn't tell if he was hurt or mad, or just disappointed in her weakness.

"You love him, don't you?"

She swallowed hard, unhappy that not only was he forcing her to admit it to him, he was forcing her to admit it to herself.

"It's okay. I already knew the answer. I could see it in your eyes when you looked at him. And in his," he added.

"Even if I do, I can't just pretend it never happened."

"No, you can't. But if you really love him, you can work through it. Don't you think he's affected by it too? Even though we men are *vagina-seeking assholes*, as my sister puts it, having sex forced on you as a teenager could be traumatic, even for a guy."

"I never really considered that," she said. The oddity of this conversation was not lost on her, but Levi's gentle concern and objective opinion felt like a salve on her heart. "I don't know. I'm not up to another dysfunctional relationship."

"Humans are dysfunctional, so you'd better get used to it," he said with a laugh. "Look at it this way. You sat at the bottom of that big dirt hill in your Jeep, knowing you'd already failed once, but you tried again anyway, didn't you?"

She felt her eyes widen. "You saw my first attempt? You were there the whole time?"

"Yep." She could hear his cocky smile in the phone.

She laughed. And it felt so good to break through her cloud of confusion and sorrow that she laughed until she was giddy. Then the volcano brewing inside her erupted and her laughter tumbled into sobs.

"I'm so sorry," she blubbered into the phone. "I'm just a mess of emotions right now." Her nose was running like a faucet, so she threw back the covers and walked to the bathroom for tissues.

"You're okay. I'm right here." He remained silent while she regained her composure.

"I'm sorry you had to witness that," she finally said with a little laugh. "It just builds up and has to come out once in a while."

"I'm just sorry you're there alone. But you know I'm always here, right? I won't deny that I'd like to be more, but first and foremost, I'm your friend. Promise you'll call me if you need a shoulder, okay?"

"I promise. Thanks, Levi."

As she ended the call, she wondered if she'd hurt his heart. And that made her cry again.

CHAPTER 43

SHE'D ACTUALLY SLEPT MORE last night than she thought she would. The puffiness would be gone by the time she saw Jay at his opening speech tonight, but lunch was only an hour away and she knew Victoria would see through the double layer of concealer she patted under her eyes. When her phone rang, she dashed to the nightstand, chiding herself for hoping it was Jay.

It was Victoria. She willed her voice to sound cheerful.

"Meet me in room 932 in ten minutes and bring your laptop," Victoria commanded, foregoing any sort of greeting.

"But—"

"There is no time for buts. Jay's flight has been delayed, and he's not going to make it in time for his opening speech. We've got to make a plan," she said, then hung up before Kricket could respond.

She bustled around the hotel room in a frenzy, throwing on a sweater and slacks and searching for a pair of earrings. She'd not been her normal tidy self this week, and couldn't find one of her black sandals. Exasperated, she forced herself to stop in the middle of the room and just breathe. When she looked again in the closet, her shoe was lying right in front of her nose. She slipped it on, threw her laptop in her bag and grabbed a granola bar from the snack basket before darting towards the elevator.

Victoria opened the door the moment Kricket knocked, as if she'd been watching out the peephole. Naturally, her room was an executive suite. Kricket had seen a few of the suites Jay stayed in.

The luxury of them never failed to amaze her. And just like being in Jay's room, she felt woefully small as she stepped in.

Victoria led her to a small table spread with papers, and wasted no time getting down to business. "It's entirely possible that Jay will arrive before the presentation is over, but we've got to plan for the worst and be prepared to fill the entire forty-five minutes. The fact that H-Tech is the premiere sponsor of this conference, and is formally launching SkillHunter tomorrow, means we've got to make this appear well-planned and in no way seem like a last-minute fix. Pre-conference opening speeches are more casual and entertaining in nature, so we have some leeway here."

The way Victoria used the word 'we' made her stomach lurch.

Victoria suddenly paused, her face softening. She reached across the table for Kricket's hand. "I know you're hurting, and I'm sorry for what you're having to deal with. We'll have a long talk about it after we handle this situation, but I need you to put that aside for today. I know it's not easy, but you're a business owner now, and this is one of those times where you have to reach inside yourself and find the tiger lurking within. Can you do that?"

She would not, could not, do Jay's speech for him. There was no tiger big enough for that.

Pep talk over, Victoria shifted back into business mode. "Jay asked me to fill in for him, and I can certainly do that. I can easily mimic his speeches. Hell, in a pinch, I could spontaneously speak on the subject of pickles, or the color orange for forty-five minutes."

Kricket blew out a breath. Her shoulders relaxed in gratitude and relief. Thank God, she didn't mean 'we' literally.

"However…" Victoria's fine arched eyebrow curved upwards in a challenge.

And here it comes. Of course there was a catch. This was Victoria after all.

"Don't give me that look," Victoria chided. "Surely you trust me enough by now not to put you in a situation where you might flounder. After all, I'm a graduate of the Jay Hunter School of Employee Success," she said with dramatized arrogance. "I don't just critique his speeches. I listen to them." She placed her palm over Kricket's fidgeting hands and smiled warmly. "After I tell you my idea, I will not think any less of you if you say no. Deal?"

As Kricket nodded, she felt the tiger inside her tuck its tail and run.

CHAPTER 44

VICTORIA'S IDEA WAS GENIUS. Petrifying, but genius. Who didn't wonder if a speaker really practiced what he preached? Apparently everyone at the conference was curious to hear exactly that. On the way down from her room, Kricket overheard four ladies in the elevator dishing about Victoria's teaser tweets.

"Does Jay Hunter really walk the walk?" the fortyish blonde woman said, scrolling through the tweets and reading them aloud. "Is Jay Hunter the real squirrel in his Squirrel Promise story? Hear the scoop from one of his young staff members," she read, with raised eyebrows. She opened the side pocket of her enormous yellow purse and exchanged her phone for a tube of lipstick. "Don't you always wonder what the speakers are really like?"

"I've heard he's quite the womanizer," her friend responded. "I'm disappointed that we may not get to see Jay, but this sounds intriguing."

The blonde turned towards the mirrored elevator wall to apply her lipstick. "Me too. His speeches are always outstanding, especially that one about the squirrel, but have you *seen* him?" She pressed her lips together then smacked them with a pop. "Delish."

Kricket bit the insides of her cheeks to keep from laughing. Victoria had created quite a stir by wording everything just vaguely enough to make it sound like the speech tonight was going to be a Jay Hunter roast.

Victoria's teaser tweets had certainly peaked interest. Hordes of conference attendees huddled around tables for ten eating their standard conference meal of rubber chicken doused in a frothy yellow sauce, flanked by mashed potatoes, and a mixture of limp vegetables. Just as Victoria had predicted, the audience was predominately female, not because they wanted to catch a glimpse of Jay, but because the Human Resources industry consisted primarily of women.

Kricket buried her face in the heavy blue stage curtain. She wasn't buying Victoria's assurance that the presentation would feel like chatting with a very large group of friends.

"What are you doing?" Victoria asked. "You're going to mess up your makeup."

"Praying for divine intervention."

She heard Victoria's compact snap shut, then felt warm gentle hands on her shoulders. "Remember when I said those last few minutes before it starts are the worst? All you have to do is answer my questions. It'll be a piece of cake." She squeezed Kricket's shoulders. "Now stand up straight and take a deep breath. It's time." She winked, then turned and waltzed onto the stage.

Victoria's black pencil-skirt suit and scarlet peep-toe stilettos contrasted sharply with Kricket's white sheath dress covered in enormous lime polka dots. According to Victoria, it was important she look and feel like herself. And that she did. This was by far the most perfect dress she'd ever owned. Victoria had agreed on a lime green cardigan to cover her scar, and had even acquiesced to kitten-heeled pumps to reduce the risk of tripping.

She could do this…for SkillHunter and for Jay. But most of all, to prove to herself that she could. She pressed her hand against the school of fish swimming inside her belly as Victoria announced that Jay would be late and quite possibly absent due to unforeseen circumstances. Those who hadn't already heard about it sighed disappointedly, while those who'd read the tweets waited with anticipation for the juice they expected to hear.

"I know you were eager to hear Mr. Hunter's Squirrel Promise presentation. How many of you have already heard the story, in person or otherwise?" Victoria asked the crowd.

At the sound of the crowd murmuring, Kricket peeked around the curtain into a sea of raised hands. She glanced around the room, searching for a few kind faces in the crowd to focus on when she walked onto the stage. A woman in a bright yellow dress near the front caught her eye, as did a kindly-looking man sitting on the left side. Both had comforting smiles. When she glanced to the right side of the room, her legs buckled beneath her. No, it couldn't be. A man about halfway back looked eerily like Brock.

Panic welled in her throat as she grabbed the conference booklet from her briefcase and flipped to the list of attendees. It couldn't possibly be him. Brock wasn't in Human Resources at Pinnacle. Running her finger down the pages, she prayed she wouldn't find what in her heart she knew she would. Her finger stopped and so did her heart. *Brock Strickland, Human Resources Director, Zynon Enterprises.* He'd changed jobs?

Nausea swept over her like a raging waterfall. She needed to run. She needed to run as fast and as far from here as humanly possible. She'd run until she found the end of the earth and then she'd keep going, because she simply could not deal with this, with her life, right now.

Her name booming through the microphone caught her attention. "Kricket Taylor, designer of SkillHunter, a new employee development software game H-Tech is unveiling tomorrow, is here to provide us some inside scoop on what it's like to work for Jay Hunter. Please help me welcome Ms. Taylor," Victoria announced, leading the audience in applause.

There was nothing else she could do. She forced her feet to overrule her brain and walk towards the applause, keeping her eyes focused on Victoria, who left the glass podium to meet her in the center of the stage. They shook hands, then sat together on a sleek white leather couch flanked by acrylic end tables holding a bottle of water for each of them.

The hot stage lights did nothing for her worries about sweating profusely, but they did provide the benefit of obscuring her view of the back half of the audience. So even though she knew Brock was there, at least she couldn't see him.

After warming up with a few background questions, such as her role in the company, her previous experience, and a description of the H-Tech corporate culture, her erratic breathing slowed and she was able to loosen her death grip on the arm of the sofa.

Victoria's soft demeanor calmed her, and she soon lost herself in telling stories that portrayed how Jay believed in her when she didn't believe in herself, how he'd coaxed her and led her through tasks she never thought she'd be able to do. Victoria skillfully filled in any blanks and added amusing touches when Kricket floundered for words.

But when Victoria paused to take a few questions from the audience, her comfort level plummeted. What was she doing? They'd rehearsed Victoria's scripted questions, but thinking on her feet was number 1089 on her list of 100 strong points.

After responding to a question about Jay's management style as being the type of boss who played on the company soccer team and took every employee to lunch on their birthday, the tightness in her chest eased, allowing her to breathe somewhat normally again.

"We have another question from a gentleman," the pretty conference assistant with the roaming microphone said, making her way towards the back. When the man stood and stepped into the light, Kricket felt the blood drain from her face. It was Brock. Panic-stricken, she glanced at Victoria, who cocked her head slightly, obviously bewildered by the angst on her face.

Brock cleared his throat loudly before speaking. "I'm sure Mr. Hunter appreciates the two of you stepping up to the plate to cover his tardiness." He paused in an apparent effort to let his tardiness remark sink in. Brock was also a master at speaking and understood the power of the pause.

"And your question, sir?" Victoria said, exuding calmness. You could almost see the hair standing up on the back of her neck as she morphed into mother lioness mode.

Brock cleared his throat again. "You indicated Mr. Hunter cares deeply about his employees. But Ms. Taylor disclosed to us her fear of public speaking, so I find something rather curious. Due to his failure to arrive in time to fulfill his speaking commitment, he thrust a member of his staff, who is obviously petrified, into the position of filling in for him. That seems to demonstrate the opposite of everything you just said about him."

Her face burned. How dare he insinuate that Jay was an inconsiderate ass like himself? And not only did he just point out to over seven hundred people that she looked nervous, he'd used the term *petrified*. Asshole, asshole, asshole. Her anger eclipsed her nerves. She signaled to Victoria that she would field the question.

"Thank you for bringing that up, Mr. Strickland." She intentionally used his name to ensure audience members were aware that she knew him. Her anger made her breathing erratic, so she paused for a moment, took a deep breath, then continued. "Mr. Hunter has a steadfast rule about arriving to a conference venue the night before he is scheduled to speak. He likes to meet the conference organizers, check the stage set-up, and chat with early arriving attendees to learn what concerns they might have so he can customize his presentation to their needs. As a speaker yourself, I'm sure you understand that," she added.

"Today he broke that rule for the first time. Instead of flying in last night, he scheduled an early flight this morning, which would put him here in plenty of time for this evening's engagement. But as luck would have it, Mother Nature reared her ugly head and reminded him why he made that rule in the first place. I'm sure everyone would like to know the reason he broke his own rule." She had watched Jay speak enough to recognize this was one of those moments that invited a pause to build anticipation. Heads nodded around the room. She made eye contact with a few people before continuing.

"Gayle, his administrative assistant of seven years had a dream of going back to college and earning a degree. It was a slow process, because she worked full time while attending classes at night. And believe me, keeping Mr. Hunter in line is no easy task," she added for the sake of humor. "Midway through her degree, Gayle became frustrated and was ready to give up her dream. Mr. Hunter made a promise to her that if she stuck with it and graduated before she turned forty, he would send her on a cruise...*and* dance at her birthday party in his boxers. That's why he broke his rule, and planned to fly in this morning. Gayle graduated in May, so he was fulfilling his promise at her fortieth birthday party. And I'm anxious to hear if she held him to the boxer part of that promise," she said, pausing as the audience laughed at the mental image she'd created in their minds.

"That's the kind of man Jayson Hunter is. He doesn't break a promise." She looked directly at Brock. "Does that answer your question, Mr. Strickland?" They'd better be recording this, because Jay was going to flip when he saw how awesome her speech was.

She couldn't hear if Brock answered, because applause filled the room. She twisted the cap from her bottle of water and held it to her mouth. Not because she was thirsty, but because being the recipient of applause had to be the most uncomfortable feeling she'd ever known, and she wasn't about to sit there with a ridiculous grin on her face.

"That's another promise Mr. Hunter is undoubtedly sorry he made," Victoria said with a chuckle. "Apparently he didn't learn his lesson after breaking his Squirrel Promise."

"He didn't break the Squirrel Promise," Kricket blurted, then immediately snapped her mouth shut. The room became eerily quiet and for the first time since taking her place on the stage, she felt the full impact of seven hundred pairs of eyes staring at her. Jay's words of caution spun through her head. How many times had he warned her of the public response if her identity was discovered?

"So you're saying the story isn't true?" Victoria asked.

The room rustled with whispers and the clink of forks against dessert plates as attendees abandoned their strawberry-dolloped cheesecake. A hush swept through the room like a warm summer wind and all eyes were completely focused on her.

If it weren't for Victoria's soft encouraging eyes, she would have felt as though she'd been thrown under the bus, but it was obvious Victoria would follow whichever direction she decided to take with her response.

After swallowing the golf ball-sized lump in her throat, she began. "Someone once told me that when we only know part of a story, our minds fill in the missing details with our fears, or insecurities...or guilt," she said, crediting Victoria with a smile. "If I may, I'd like to fill in the missing details of Jay's Squirrel Promise story."

Victoria placed a hand on her arm and squeezed gently. "I think we'd all like to hear that. And how is it you know the missing details of the story?"

Kricket pushed herself up from the couch, immediately feeling the absence of Victoria's nearness. She faced the audience, chewing on her bottom lip while she steadied her breath. In their faces, she saw an assortment of bewilderment, empathy, surprise, curiosity, and in a few, the lightning bolt of realization.

She shrugged her cardigan off her shoulders and let it slide down to the floor, then held her arm across her chest so her scar pointed towards the audience. "Because I was there."

CHAPTER 45

JAY SKIDDED TO A HALT when he heard the chatter spilling through the closed ballroom doors. Abandoning his trek to the back stage entrance, he flung open one of the ballroom doors to see what in the hell was going on, while plotting how to murder Victoria for turning the presentation into what sounded like a circus. Shrill voices saying "It's her," and "It's the Squirrel Promise Girl," resounded through the chatter.

Once inside, he stopped abruptly. "Oh baby, what are you doing," he said out loud.

What had Victoria done? Kricket stood in the middle of the stage holding up her scarred arm to the audience. She looked petrified, but something about her stance, and the way her eyes glanced purposely around the audience showed determination. He covered his mouth with his hand to keep from yelling. He had to get to Kricket. He could dart back out the door and head to the side stage entrance, but he couldn't bear the thought of leaving her for even a second.

Gayle, who had been rushing down the hallway a hundred yards behind him, stormed through the door. She gaped at Kricket. "Oh my soul. What is that girl doing?"

"I have no fucking idea, but Victoria is dead. Stay here. I'm going backstage." He pushed on the exit door, but the sudden hushing noises in the crowd made him stop and turn around. Victoria stood beside Kricket, holding up a hand to silence the crowd.

"I know everyone has questions. We all have questions, but since you came to hear the Squirrel Promise story, perhaps Ms. Taylor will agree to tell it."

He was going to kill Victoria for making Kricket look like a circus freak.

The crowd hushed as Victoria guided her back to the couch. His body twitched with indecision. His first instinct was to run up the aisle, jump on the stage, and kill Victoria on the spot, then carry Kricket away.

Gayle's fingers dug into his arm. He jerked towards her, ready to lash out with the desperation bubbling inside him, but the empathy in her eyes made him hesitate. "She doesn't always need rescued, Jay. Let her tell the story."

He shook his head to clear the anger and looked towards the stage just as Kricket began to speak.

"Jay leaves out a rather important part of the story," she began, her voice faltering slightly. "He neglects to mention that he was hurt in the accident worse than the little girl. His ankle was sprained, but he so desperately wanted to get to her, to make sure that she was okay, that he drug himself across the gravel road to reach her. They had to pick the gravel out of his bloody arm."

She blinked towards the ceiling in an obvious attempt to stifle the tears. He knew all too well how difficult it was to tell the story without breaking down. Over the years he'd trained himself to tell it with feeling, but without tears.

"And that's when he made the promise. The promise that he kept." She wiped a stubborn tear with her fingertip and continued. "He thinks he broke the promise because he couldn't prevent her from being taken away. He thinks it was his fault." Tears were streaming down her face now. One of the stage crew ambled nervously across the stage with a box of tissues. She thanked him and paused to wipe her cheeks.

"But it wasn't his fault," she said, shaking her head. "And what he doesn't realize is that this scar, and the memory of him in her heart, is what kept her going until the day he found her again."

She believed him. He closed his eyes, letting her declaration sink in. She may never completely forgive him or return the love he felt for her, but she believed him. A warm flood of relief seeped through his body.

Gayle's hand touched his back, and he turned towards her smiling face. "See? Sometimes you just need to let the girl talk," she said through a tearful grin.

"So, I guess it's safe to say you're the mysterious Squirrel Promise Girl," Victoria said, obviously attempting to lighten the mood.

A laugh bubbled from Kricket as she nodded. "I guess there's no denying that now," she said, touching her scar.

"So I hope you don't mind indulging us all in a little scoop," Victoria said, with a mischievous look that Jay knew meant she was going to milk this.

"Well, I'm the one who popped the top off this sparkling beverage, so we might as well drink it." She rejoined Victoria on the couch.

Victoria laughed and raised her bottle of water. "Cheers then."

A few extended arms grasping beverages popped up around the audience, then everyone followed suit. Cheers, laughter, and clinking glasses filled the room. He couldn't believe shy little Kricket was being so casual on stage. She grinned broadly as though she was actually enjoying the spotlight now. He'd nearly forgotten how beautiful she was when her face glowed with happiness. His heart struggled between elation and pain.

Victoria rested her arm on the back of the couch, settling in for what undoubtedly in her mind was the marketing opportunity of the year. He'd never hear the end of her 'I told you so' about disclosing Kricket's identity.

"How long ago did you find each other?" Victoria asked.

"About six months ago, right after the New Year."

"So, tell us how it happened." Victoria leaned forward, practically foaming at the mouth.

Kricket grinned for a moment, obviously re-living the memory. "Well, first he almost rammed my Jeep, then he bought me a coffee, then he kissed me, then he poured his coffee on me—and that was all before he knew who I was—then he tackled me, then he almost got me fired, and then he hired me." She shrugged. "I guess that about covers it. Oh, and he's given me at least two panic attacks," she added.

Gayle cocked an eyebrow at him. "There goes your reputation as the ladies' man."

He couldn't help but chuckle at himself when the crowd's laughter surrounded him. He was so proud of Kricket's quick wit. Like the rest of the audience, he found himself eagerly awaiting the rest of her story.

"It sounds like things got off to a bit of a rocky start," Victoria quipped. After the audience quit laughing, Victoria made a show of looking Kricket up and down. "You're a beautiful young woman and Jay is..." She put her hand over her heart in a swooning gesture. "Well, I think we can agree he's pretty easy on the eyes. You mentioned something about a kiss, so, I think it's safe to say, we're all wondering if you two are—" She raised her eyebrows suggestively.

Kricket shook her head. "No. After he found out who I was he didn't want to kiss me anymore."

The audience laughed, and he laughed too before the full impact of what she'd just said hit him. She had no idea how far from the truth that statement was.

Victoria patted Kricket's leg. "Well I'm sure you have men falling all over you."

"Oh yes, I'm beating off men left and right."

When he saw her lips press together to suppress her grin, he knew she realized what she'd said. Now the question was, would Victoria let it go?

Victoria camouflaged her mouth from Kricket with her hand, pretending to tell a secret to the audience. "I would go there if this wasn't an HR conference," she said.

Kricket turned bright red as the audience howled.

After Victoria let the laughter die down, her face took on a dreamy nature. "I'm probably not alone when I admit that I was hoping for a more fairytale ending to this story. You know, the two of you reunited after all those years, falling in love and living happily ever after."

As Kricket's eyes dropped to her lap, Jay's heart fell to his feet.

"I guess that's not a possibility then?" Victoria prodded.

Kricket shrugged without looking up. "It's complicated."

"Love *is* complicated," Victoria said softly.

Jay had gradually made his way down the edge of the room towards the stage. From his vantage point, he could see her eyes glisten. She pressed her lips together and blinked rapidly before looking at Victoria. "Yes it is," she said, looking down at her lap again.

"So, you do love him then?"

He stepped into the light where she could see him. "I'd like to know the answer to that question myself." His entire world balanced on her answer.

The seconds hung in the air like hours. The stunned silence in the audience gradually turned into murmurs as Kricket leaned over gasping for breath. Shit! A panic attack. His legs flew towards the stage. He was up the stairs in two steps. Kneeling in front of her, he cupped her face in his hands and rested his forehead on hers. "I'm right here, baby. Come back to me. Come on baby, I'm right here," he pleaded. "Follow my voice through the fog. You can do it." He stroked her hair and wiped the tears that dribbled down her cheeks. "Breathe, baby. You have air. Lots of air."

She took a few large gulps of air. Her eyes fluttered open, then closed again in a grimace as she sighed. "I just had a panic attack in front of seven hundred people, didn't I?"

"Yeah, you did," he said, his hands still cupping her cheeks, his forehead still pressed against hers.

"Awesome." She scrunched her nose against his. "They're still there, aren't they?"

"Yeah, they are," he said, unable to keep from grinning.

"They can hear us right now, can't they?"

"Yeah, they can."

"I guess they're still waiting on my answer, aren't they?"

"I know *I* am."

She pressed her lips together for a moment then sucked in a deep breath. He felt its warmth against his face as she slowly let it out.

"Yes. I do love you."

He closed his eyes and let the sound of her words echo through his head. "I love you too, Kricket."

"Well, it's about time," she whispered.

All he wanted to do was kiss her madly…her face, her lips, her ears. He could devour her right there on the stage, but nothing would embarrass her more. He'd do that later. Right now, he had to share her with an audience who loved her too, so he settled for a soft kiss.

Laughing and hugging, they rose together and stood arm in arm before the crowd, who obviously couldn't decide whether to laugh or cry or applaud, so they merely gazed until Victoria began applauding, then the room erupted in cheers and applause.

He stood ready to whisk her away if the attention became too overwhelming, but she stood strong against his side, and her grin was as big as the one spread across his own face.

When the room silenced, she beamed at him, then turned to the audience. "See? I told you he gives me panic attacks."

CHAPTER 46

SHE WAS GOING TO have sex with Jay. How many hours had she spent lying in bed dreaming about it? Or sitting across from him in a meeting imagining what it would be like, wanting it more than air. And now that it was actually going to happen, she couldn't decide if the bubbles in her belly were from nerves or excitement. The experience of one lousy lover, at least according to Becca, was all the knowledge she brought to the table. And it had been a year since she'd even had sex, lousy or otherwise. Well, not counting the battery powered kind.

She'd probably have an orgasm-induced heart failure the moment he touched her. Would she be a huge disappointment to him? What if he was too big for her? Or worse, what if he had a miniature penis? No, Victoria had assured her that wasn't the case. What if she did something wrong or something he didn't like? What if *he* did something *she* didn't like? She'd never had a guy kiss her down *there* before. What if she lost control and snapped her legs together on his head like a mouse trap?

His soft knock on her hotel room door made her jump. She grabbed the fluffy white complimentary hotel robe from the closet and shrugged it over her cami and boxers, belting it tightly around her waist as if to barricade herself from its impending discard. When she'd packed last week, the last thing on her mind was having sex with anyone—and most definitely not with Jay—so camis and cartoon boxers were all she'd brought. Hardly provocative, but at least he wouldn't confuse her with one of the conference women he picked up, who undoubtedly brought suitcases filled with leopard and lace. She really needed to stop thinking about that kind of stuff.

The moment she opened the door and looked into his face, the jittery feeling she'd been fighting all evening disappeared. It wasn't the desirous face of a man visiting for the night. It was the gentle face of a man who was in love with her. He dropped his bag on the floor with a thud and pulled her tightly against him.

He held her long after the door slammed behind him, as if this very moment signified the togetherness they'd both longed for. Every care she'd ever had dissolved as she stood swathed in his arms and her big fluffy robe. When he released his hold, the crease between his eyes confused her.

He took her face in his palms and tilted her eyes towards his. "I want you more than I've ever wanted anything in this world," he said with a painful yet determined look. "But our first time together will not be in a conference hotel room. It's much too important for that," he said, caressing the tip of her nose.

A tidal wave of relief and disappointment, mixed with overwhelming gratitude, rippled through her, leaving a wake of moisture in her eyes. It was as if he'd been reading her mind. She wanted him so badly, but in the thousand fantasies she'd had about this moment, none of them had taken place in a conference hotel room, where he'd had more women than she cared to imagine.

His thumb gently brushed away an escaping tear. "I hope you understand. I just—"

She stood on her toes to press her lips hard against his to shut him up. "I understand that you are the most considerate man in the entire world, and I love you," she whispered against his lips.

"I want to make it special for you." He held her for a long while, long enough for her body to transition from melting with intimacy, to sizzling with desire. Her lady parts wanted no part of this waiting business. "We have a big day tomorrow with the launch. Let's go to bed, so I can hold you all night," he whispered in her hair before releasing her.

"I thought you'd never ask," she said, in the sexiest voice she could muster, attempting to lighten the moment to avoid casting her robe across the room and latching on to him in a straddle.

"You're not going to make this easy on me, are you?"

"Wait until you see what I'm wearing, or not wearing underneath this robe," she teased.

His face went pale. "Kricket, seriously, this is going to be hard enough."

She bit her lip to keep from laughing. "I know you want to see." Wiggling her eyebrows suggestively, she toyed with the belt on her robe.

"I really need your help here, babe," he said, lacing his fingers through his hair.

Even Becca couldn't make removing a robe to reveal Jeep Girl boxers look seductive, so she seized that moment to streak towards the bed, shed the robe, and jump under the covers.

"Thank you for that." he said, laughing as he strolled towards the bed. He unbuttoned his shirt and threw it on the sofa.

She wagged her finger at him. "Oh no you don't, mister. If you think I'm going to watch you do a striptease and then try to control my womanly urges, you are wrong."

"Your *womanly* urges?" He looked amused as he leaned over the bed and placed one arm on either side of her. "I love everything about you," he said, planting a kiss on her mouth. She could feel his grin against her lips. He stood and unzipped his jeans. "Close your eyes if you don't think you can control yourself over the sight of my Superman boxers."

"You're wearing Superman boxers?"

"Of course not," he said with a smirk.

She gave him an exasperated look and pulled the covers over her head. "Okay, get those pants off. You're really not all that sexy anyway."

She tried to ignore the enticing sound of first one leg, then the other slipping out of his jeans, followed by a thud as he tossed them on the couch. She heard the swish of his T-shirt being pulled over his head and suddenly his body was under the covers. He pulled her close against him, his long hard kiss leaving her dizzy and breathless.

"We'll see if I can change your mind about that," he said, nuzzling her ear. The glow through the window lit the room just enough to reflect that famous panty dropper look on his face, making his hardness against her quickly overruling any possibility of waiting.

He pulled away and looked at her with a sly grin. "But not tonight." He reached behind her and grabbed a small throw pillow to stuff between their pelvises. "There. That will keep you from getting too turned on, because I am going to hold you this close all night long."

After they laughed for a moment, his face turned serious. "I mean it, Kric. I've wanted you for so long I can't even think straight. I don't know how I'm going to make it two nights until we get home, but I will. Then I'm going to love you like you've never been loved before." He brushed her bangs from her face. "And not to be a mood-killer, but I want you to know that I've been celibate since January. And I've been tested, so as long as you're on the pill—"

She nodded, glad Becca had encouraged her to keep taking them all these months even though she didn't need them. "I got tested too after—. He silenced her with a soft kiss.

A flash of uncertainty must have shown on her face. He touched her cheek. "What babe?"

She glanced away. If she met his eyes, he would see the insecurity that swallowed her.

"What's wrong, babe?" he asked in her ear as he pulled her closer. The tenderness conveyed in his warm embrace gave her the confidence to vocalize her fears.

"There's probably a lot of things I haven't done," she said into his shoulder. "What if I'm—?"

His fingers streamed through her hair as he turned her face to his. His gaze was as soft as a caress. "Those words are like medicine for my soul." She could tell he was touched, because he closed his eyes and grew still for a moment. "I will cherish every second of guiding you through that secret garden. I love you more than you could possibly understand."

She ran her palm down his five-o'clock-shadowed cheek. "I do understand. I've loved you my entire life."

"Me too," he mouthed, pressing his lips to hers, then taking a sharp intake of breath as he pulled away. She knew he was fighting as hard as she against relinquishing to what their bodies were ravenous for. After a deep breath of resolution, he rested his forehead against hers. She focused her entire being on the warmth of their joined temples. That familiar gesture of love between protector and child from long ago, now blended with the love between a man and a woman, was both soothing and sensual at the same time. But she knew one slight move would trigger their bodies into full on, no-holds-barred passionate lovemaking. And forever more, the memory of their first time together would be tainted by the fact that it was in a hotel conference room. Just like so many others before her.

Joined at the temples, they remained motionless until their breathing slowed. When he shifted to look at her, his dark eyes radiated love like she'd never seen before. Similar, yet different from Grandpa's love.

"Your story…I see it now," she whispered, basking in his gaze from her cozy spot in the crook of his elbow.

"What do you see?" he whispered.

"I see everything I've longed to see. I see pride in what I've overcome from the little girl you used to know. I see the love that I feel inside my own heart." She smoothed his eyebrow with the tip of her index finger. "And I see the pain of the nine million minutes that you try to hide," she said, watching his eyes grow hooded. "The pain we'll be erasing with every moment we're together."

"Yes." His breath was soft against her nose. "What else do you see?"

"I see home."

He closed his eyes for a moment and the corner of his mouth tilted up in a smile as if he were envisioning the two of them snuggled in front of a fire with a glass of wine, or lounging in bed on a Saturday afternoon, oblivious of everything but each other. When he opened his eyes again, they were smoldering with an invitation that rocketed to her core.

"What else do you see?" His eyes revealed wicked intention

"I see the wanting eyes of a lover who loves me so much that he's doing everything in his power to make sure our first time together is as special as our love."

Their gaze locked. She could almost feel his caress as she read his thoughts. His eyes penetrated hers as he slid his foot down her shin and traced delicate circles around her ankle. His gaze told her he was simulating trailing his fingers down her neck and circling her breast. As his foot traveled downward, she knew from the twitch of a smile that in his mind, he'd moved lower. The implication sent waves of excitement through her. When his chin tilted up and his breath caught, she knew in his mind he'd entered her. Her hips moved slightly in rhythm with the flicker in his eyes and the stroking of his big toe between hers. The movement of his chin in an almost imperceptible rocking motion built an ache within her. His eyes and his foot were relentless and when that look, oh that look, crossed his face, a delicious shudder swept through her body.

His mouth curved into an intrigued smile as he wrapped a leg across hers. "You're going to be fun," he said, sliding a finger down her clavicle and stopping just between her breasts. "Just wait."

If a pantomimed orgasm felt like that, she couldn't even fathom what the real thing would bring. The real thing. Her gaze fell to his chest as she traced circles on his bicep with her thumb. She wanted to say something, but she didn't know how. Talking about sentimental stuff was hard enough, but talking about sex? Ugh.

"Your mind is whirling a hundred miles an hour in there. Tell me what has it so worried."

He stroked her hair patiently while she searched for the words.

"I know there's a lot of things you want to do to please me, and…" She was glad for the dimness of the room as the familiar heated flush engulfed her face. "And I can't wait. Really, I can't. But the first time, I just want to be together. No teasing, no acrobats, no world record attempts." His expression changed from touched to amused. "Just you and I, finally together."

"Of course," he whispered, pulling her into a gentle embrace. "We'll go at your pace."

With her head tucked snugly against his chest, every stroke of his hand down the length of her hair eased her tension until she was a rag doll in his arms. She was finally home.

"I love you," was the last thing she heard him whisper before she fell asleep.

CHAPTER 47

Saturday, July 18th
*...I've accomplished enough goals this past week to fill two
journals. I think I'll give it a rest. Okay, maybe just one more.*

*Today's goal: I will not giggle when we make love, even if
something tickles...*

TWO DAYS OF ANTICIPATION overpowered the special date Jay
planned for their first night home...and their first night of making
love. While waiting for their dinner to arrive, they chatted about
the family, the conference, and about plans for SkillHunter after
the launch, but there was only one thing on their minds. When the
stiff-necked waiter presented their dinner with a flourish, he
looked insulted when Jay said, "Box it up."

Her heart raced as they fled hand and hand out of the
restaurant like two prison escapees, and hopped in Jay's Range
Rover. On the drive home, her eagerness wrestled with her
apprehension. Even though she'd spent the entire day with Becca,
getting manicured, pedicured, waxed, sugar-buffed, and above all,
coached in preparation for tonight's activities, her nerves were
slightly ahead in the battle.

"Where are we going?" she asked, when he missed the
turnpike exit near his house. Her libido was making her squirm in
the seat.

"You'll see," he said with a sly grin. Even in the dark, she
could see the twinkle in his eyes when he glanced at her.

When he turned into Mitch and Meg's neighborhood, her
heart sank. Had he lost his mind? They'd left the restaurant
because they couldn't keep their hands off each other. And now
they were going to visit his brother?

"Almost there," he said, turning into a cul-de-sac long before they reached Mitch and Meg's street.

She'd nearly forgotten about the house he was remodeling. He never talked about it. "Your house. Is it finished?" she asked, as he pulled in the driveway and punched the garage door button.

"Our house. And yes, it's finished."

When they walked through the door, the transformation was astonishing. He'd shown her the house before Meg started the remodel, but that was months ago. She had no idea a house could look so different.

"It's been finished for weeks." He led her into the black and red metallic kitchen and put their food containers in the monolithic refrigerator. "I just wasn't ready to move in," he said with a shrug. "Now it will feel like home." The gleam in his eyes when he pulled her towards him made her heart lurch into her throat. "Come on, there's something I want to show you."

"Good, because there's something I want to see," she said, attempting to mask her anxiety.

"Easy, girl." He led her towards the stairs, which she knew did *not* lead towards the master bedroom. His silly grin as they headed up the steps was disarming. He looked more like a little boy with a secret than a man eager to get in her pants. When they reached the top, he swung open the double doors to reveal a Jeep-themed recreation room covering half of the upstairs level.

She'd never seen a more inviting room. The soothing oatmeal-colored walls hosted six foot canvases of pop art. The only color on the prints were brightly colored Jeeps, which matched the pillows dotting two cozy L-shaped couches. An enormous movie screen covered the entire front wall. A stone fireplace hovered in the corner next to a well-stocked bar, complete with an espresso machine touting so many buttons and knobs it would likely require a barista to run it.

The room begged to be filled with friends and family, but she could envision a lazy weekend curled up next to Jay, with maybe a dog or two, watching a football game or movie, or doing naughty things in front of the fireplace on that big furry rug.

She ran her finger across the Jeep emblem monogrammed on the back of a saddle colored bar stool. "It's the kind of room you never want to leave," she half-whispered.

"And now you never have to." When he pressed the remote, then gathered her in his arms, the room was engulfed with the music video of the song they first danced to at Club 100. Basking in the memory of that night that seemed so long ago, she let her body sink against his as they swayed to the music.

He kissed her as the song ended, then turned her towards the movie screen, surrounding her from behind. "There's something else I want you to see," he whispered in her ear.

As the song "Story of My Life" began, the screen lit up with an image of her as a baby lying in her crib. When she turned to question him, he nodded towards the screen. "Just watch."

An eight-year-old Jay peeked over the top of the crib, as if she were a tiny zoo animal he desperately wanted to pet. One after another, photos and movie clips of their childhood floated across the screen—her face smeared with German chocolate cake at a birthday party—Jay coaxing her down the big slide at the playground across the street—a six-year-old Krissy snuggled beside him in her My Little Pony pajamas watching a movie with his family.

An image of the two of them sitting in Rascal, his first red Jeep, took her breath away—one of the rare photos of her as a child where she was actually looking at the camera and smiling. "That was one of my best memories." She peered over her shoulder at him. "You did all this today?"

He nodded with a gentle smile. "I called in all the troops.

Mom, Meg, and I dug through photos and videos, Brandon pieced it together, and Becca kept you busy shopping today."

The video turned into more recent clips, obviously pulled from security feeds at the office and from Mitch and Meg's house of many cameras. They laughed at a clip of their coffee spill mishap in the H-Tech lobby, a clip of him chasing her through Mitch and Meg's house when she took the last German chocolate cupcake, and one of her taunting him during Miles' kissing lesson. At one point she laughed so hard she threw her head back into his chest a little too hard and bit her tongue. When he paused the video to see if her mouth was bleeding, the memory of him trying to look at her tongue in the H-Tech lobby made them burst into laughter again.

As the video turned tender, she was stunned by the number of photos someone found of each of them gazing wistfully when the other wasn't looking. As a video of Grandpa sitting in his recliner, with Dot standing behind him appeared on the screen, Jay took a deep breath and pulled her closer against his chest, resting a whiskered cheek against hers.

Her eyes were riveted to the screen when she saw Jay step into the camera's view. He cleared his throat, and began speaking. "Mr. Taylor...Dot, I know that I'm as undeserving as they come, but I have known your granddaughter as long as you have, and I have loved her just as long. I will spend the rest of my life loving her, even if she says 'no,' but if you will honor me with your blessing, I will beg her to marry me."

She stood motionless as Jay paused the video and turned her by the shoulders to face him. "I have loved you since the day you were born. I love the way you make me smile, no matter what kind of day I've had. I love you for always trying to grow as a person, even though I think you're perfect just the way you are. I love you for seeing through my flaws and making me want to live up to your image of me." He reached forward and brushed a lock of hair out of her face. "I love the way you peer at me sideways through those long lashes, and how your face flushes when your eyes meet mine. And I love how when you close your mouth, there's still a tiny pursed opening that makes me want to kiss you, no matter where we are or who we're with."

The blood ran from her face as he took her hand and dropped to one knee before her. "I can't promise that I'll never hurt you again, because I will. Not intentionally, not maliciously, but no matter how hard I try, I will hurt you. And as sweet and gentle as you are, you'll hurt me too. I know I made a mess of things, and I wouldn't blame you if you said no—"

She touched her index finger to his lips. "Just ask me already," she blurted through tears streaming down her face.

His face relaxed into a crooked smile as he stood and cupped her face in his hands. "Kristen Kelsey Beckett Taylor, I can't imagine my life without you. Will you marry me?"

All she could do was nod her head and blubber.

He kissed her, snot and all. "I'll take that as a *yes*." She could feel his grin in his kiss.

"Yes," she choked out. "Absolutely yes."

Without releasing her, he leaned over and grabbed a tissue from the coffee table and gently dabbed her tear-streaked face. They held each other tightly, unwilling to tear their bodies away from each other.

When they finally pulled away from each other, his hand disappeared in his pocket. "Close your eyes," he said, his smile eager and alive with affection.

She captured his expression in her memory before pressing her eyelids shut. Her hand shook as the cool metal slid up her finger. The unexpected touch of his soft lips on the very spot the ring sat made her gasp. She kept her eyes closed, savoring the moment, before slowly opening them. Her hand flew to her mouth as she looked at the ring so familiar and dear to her heart. "Karen's ring," she whispered in awe.

"Mom wanted you to have it."

Words escaped her as she stared at the large emerald-cut diamond.

"Mom said she always wanted a daughter to pass it on to."

"But—"

He touched a finger to her lips to shush her. "She wants you to have it. She just wears her wedding band most of the time now."

Her fingers delicately traced the edges of the stone. It wouldn't matter if it were a quarter-carat piece of gravel, she would love it, because it was Karen's.

"The diamond belonged to my grandmother. Mom had it reset when it was passed on to her. We can have a setting designed that you like."

"I love it just like this." She closed her eyes to compose herself. Expressing her feelings was so difficult, but she wanted to. She needed to. As if he sensed it, he pressed his forehead to hers, and waited in silence. The comfort of that familiar gesture gave her the courage to speak her heart.

She looked into his eyes, letting their tenderness fill her before she began. "Marrying you is more wonderful than I can even find words for. And wearing Karen's ring...being a real part of your family..." She swallowed the lump in her throat as he wiped a tear from her eye with his thumb. "I never thought this moment would really happen, and now...it couldn't possibly be more special," she finished with barely a whisper.

"Actually, I think it can," he said. His voice was husky and his eyes contained a sensuous flame that crumbled her knees beneath her.

CHAPTER 48

SHE'D IMAGINED MAKING LOVE with Jay a thousand times in a thousand ways, and now the pure intimacy of being with him felt imposing. Her heart beat wildly as he unbuttoned his sleeve cuffs behind her then stepped back and motioned with his eyes for her to unbutton his shirt. The softness of his lips against her neck only worsened her shaking fingers that fumbled with his buttons. He slid off the shirt and dropped it to the floor then pulled his T-shirt over his head. Her eyes were drawn to his tattoo. She hadn't seen it since that awful night. He watched her study it.

"No more tears," she whispered, tracing the teardrops trickling down his smooth bicep with her finger.

"No more tears," he said in return, moving her hand to his heart. She held it there, letting his heartbeat fill her palm.

His eyes commanding her gaze, he guided her hand down his six pack to his jeans. When she slipped her fingers behind his waistband to unfasten the button and lower the zipper, the hardness of his bulge caused her breath to hitch. He slid his jeans over his hips, then sat on the edge of the couch to shed his shoes and jeans. When he stood, she took in his commanding presence. For such a tall man, his muscular legs were well proportioned to his wide shoulders, and his black boxer-briefs did little to hide what was underneath. Oh how she wanted him.

With a hand on each shoulder, he turned her away from him. A wake of goose bumps chased his fingers down her spine as he lowered the zipper of her dress, slipped it over her shoulders, and let it fall to her feet, exposing her skin to the crisp air.

His soft lips nuzzling her ear made it difficult to steady her wobbly legs as she stepped out of her heels and dress. The touch of his fingers toying with the lace on her bra took her breath away, and when his fingers slipped beneath the fabric to graze her nipple, her head fell limply against his chest

His kisses on her neck were soft and his movements were unhurried. Cupping both breasts in his palms, he released the center hook of her bra and let it drop lifelessly to the floor. Her nipples jumped to attention, begging to be touched. He immediately obliged her.

The gentle kneading of her breasts and circling of his thumbs around her nipples worked her into a heavenly trance. He slowly lowered his palm down her belly and slipped his pinky just under the top edge of her thong. His fingers skimmed back and forth across her abdomen, relentlessly teasing her before dipping between her legs and grazing her wetness. His gasp matched hers as he pressed his hardness more firmly against her butt.

Hooking his thumbs on each side, he lowered her thong over her hips, then knelt on one knee to help her step out. His hands traveled back up her legs to clench her butt. Her glutes contracted as her body responded to his tongue trailing up her inner thigh. "Jay, please," she gasped, fighting her growing desire.

He trailed kisses up her back as he rose from his kneeling position and encircled her in his arms. "Turn around. I want to see you," he whispered in her ear, sending a tremor of arousal and anxiety through her body.

Her desire gave way to the reality that she had to turn and face him in all her glory. Determined not to let insecurity ruin the moment, she squared her shoulders and turned around.

His face paled in a quick intake of breath. "Oh, Krissy." He lowered himself onto the couch and buried his head against her abdomen with his arms wrapped tightly around her hips.

"Jay, look at me. I'm not Krissy anymore. I'm a woman."

After a few moments, he opened his eyes, taking in every naked inch of her. "I can't believe you're so beautiful." He lightly stroked his chin across her stomach. The feathery brush of his five-o'clock shadow sent a rush of desire through her. When his lips meandered up and took her breast in his mouth, her back arched into him as his tongue licked and sucked her nipple.

"Jay, please. I'm so ready, and I don't want to… I want to do it together," she begged, gripping his hair.

With gentle authority, he leaned back and nodded towards his boxers. Her hand trembled as she slid his waistband over the bulge barely contained within. He watched her fully take in the masculinity of his nakedness before guiding her knees on either side of his thighs to settle her on his lap.

"I want to see your eyes when we make love," he said softly. "Can you look at me?"

"I'll try."

He laced his fingers in her hair and glided them down its length, watching it fall around her breasts. "You are breathtaking."

The brush of his soft whiskers perked her nipples as he planted kisses along the sensitive outline of each breast. She had no idea the sensation of whiskers against tender skin was so delicious. She closed her eyes, savoring those few moments of tenderness before her nipples begged to be taken. When his mouth closed around her nipple, her back arched, thrusting her breasts towards him. His lips and tongue danced slowly over her breasts, sending showers of electricity through her. He latched onto one breast, sucking, while using his tongue to circle the nipple, arousing a sensation like she'd never known.

She slid her hand down his chest to his penis standing gallantly between them. She slid her palm up its length, and he groaned against her breast when she stroked her thumb around the smooth skin on the tip. "I want you now," she gasped in his ear.

With a hand under each butt cheek, he positioned her over him. Their eyes locked as he sunk inside her. Foreheads together, they sat unmoving for a moment, cherishing the intimacy of their union.

"I will love you forever," he whispered.

"I will love you longer."

He brought his lips to hers with a gentleness that gripped her heart. A gentleness that conveyed his love over his need for her. A gentleness that told her this moment was as special to him as it was to her. His breath was warm against her face as his lips tenderly grazed her mouth. Every kiss was slow and deliberate. When her knees instinctively pressed into the couch to raise and lower herself, his lips found their way to her ear. "Slow circles," he whispered, pressing his hands on her hips to subdue them.

His soft, guiding words sent electric shocks down her neck, and she had to consciously focus on slowing down. His tongue beckoned hers to a slow romantic waltz in time with the circling of their hips. There was a dreamy intimacy to their kiss as their bodies moved in exquisite tempo. He stroked her face and hair while she gently kneaded the firm ridges across his shoulders.

The ability to tame her hips soon became impossible. Needing more than the slow circles now, she pressed her knees into the couch to raise and lower her body. A bright flare of desire overtook the gentleness in his eyes as he matched the thrusting of her hips.

Their kiss grew more arduous as their bodies sought each other. His throaty moans stoked the inferno inside her. When involuntary tremors overtook her, he tore his lips away and pressed his forehead against hers, moaning his own release as her body exploded in a burst of fiery sensations. She gasped in sweet agony and fell limply into his embrace. She was his now. Completely.

Unwilling to break the bond of their bodies, he stroked her hair while she rested motionless against his chest, basking in the total sense of love and protection that surrounded her. "I'll love you forever," she whispered.

"I'll love you longer," he said with a soft kiss.

Snuggled together under a throw he pulled from the back of the couch, the comforting sound of his heartbeat against her ear lulled her into a hypnotic state. Her thoughts drifted between the memory of their lovemaking and the poignant video montage. She wanted to experience both over and over. After lying for a time, she pulled away and looked at him. "Can we watch the video again?"

"Sure." He kissed the top of her head and sat up, pulling her against him.

"So did Brandon film you at Grandpa's house?" she asked, swinging her legs across his lap.

"Yes. He tried to be obscure with his phone video camera, but that didn't work out very well. Dot tried to take charge. And she flirted with him the entire time we were there."

"That doesn't surprise me a bit," she said laughing.

Watching the video the second time, she was surprised how much she'd missed. Naturally she ended up teary again. As he handed her a tissue, the video played further than they'd seen the first time. When Brandon appeared on the screen with the title "Bloopers" above his head, they looked at each other in surprise.

He answered her silent question with a shrug. "I have no idea."

Brandon grinned into the camera. "And this is how it *really* went. Roll 'em," he said with a dramatic wave of his arm.

The first clip showed Jay straightening his collar in the hallway mirror, actually looking rather nervous. You could hear Brandon snicker into the microphone when Jay snapped, "Turn that off, dickhead. I'll tell you when I'm ready for you to record."

In the next clip, Dot smiled towards the camera. "Are you taking my picture, sonny?" She fluffed her hair and posed. "You have the nicest head of hair I've seen in a long time." You could see her hand coming towards the camera. The video jiggled, as if Brandon had dodged her fondling fingers.

More clips followed, where Jay either messed up what he was going to say, or was interrupted by Dot telling him his shirt collar was crooked. Kricket laughed at Jay's flustered look. She wasn't surprised it hadn't gone quite as smoothly as the video portrayed.

Jay groaned when the next clip appeared, showing Jay, Grandpa, and Dot sitting at the kitchen table. "Please tell me he did not video this."

Kricket shushed him and leaned forward to hear. Grandpa looked uncomfortable as he cleared his throat. "Let's get one thing out on the table here, son," Grandpa said. "We both know you've dipped your toe in the ocean plenty over the last few years. How do you know you haven't acquired some sort of infestation? What do they call that?"

Kricket gasped. "He did not go there," to which Jay closed his eyes and nodded. "He did."

"It's an SDT, dear," Dot stated matter-of-factly.

"STD," Brandon's voice boomed into the microphone.

"No worries there, sir," Jay said. "I got a clean bill of health in January, and I've been celibate ever since."

Dot's eyebrows flew up. "Celibate since January?" She leaned towards Jay as if to tell him a secret. "Before you see Kricket tonight, you might want to...you know...tickle the pickle." She gave him an overly dramatic wink. "We'd hate for Kricket to be disappointed in *Little Jay*," she said nodding at his crotch, then taking another glance with a wry smile.

Kricket fell over laughing, watching Jay's eyes bug out at Dot. It was obvious he was struggling to maintain his poker face. He cleared his throat. "Thank you for that thoughtful tip, Dot," he said, as if she'd just told him a secret recipe. "I will certainly do my best to ensure that Kricket is not disappointed in…*Little Jay*," he said, glancing sideways at Brandon, who was cracking up into the microphone.

Jay paused the video. "See what I had to endure in order to marry you? Dot also informed me you were on the pill, so there would be no worries about *interrupting the mood with those burdensome condoms*," he said, mimicking Dot's voice. "Those were her exact words."

Kricket could hardly respond, she was laughing so hard. "I guarantee Dot will ask me about *Little Jay*."

He grimaced. "Maybe you can just tell her *Little Jay* ponied up to the task and leave it at that."

"Mehh." She shrugged. "I wouldn't go that far. I mean, you were okay," she teased.

He raised his eyebrows at her. "So, you're saying I should try again. Go a little *deeper* this time?"

"Maybe." She gave him her best sexy sideways glance in response to his suggestive look that would have melted her undies if they weren't already lying on the floor. "You think you can handle it?" she asked.

"Only one way to find out." He stood, slinging her naked body over his shoulder, bottom up. She swatted at his bare butt as he carried her down the stairs. Her body trembled just thinking of round two in what she imagined was a very sexy master suite.

Instead of heading towards the bedroom, he slid open the patio door and carried her outside into the cool night air. Before she could squeak out a scream, she felt the weightless freefall as they plunged into the pool.

"You did *not* just do that," she sputtered when they surfaced, swiping her hand across her eyes so she could see.

"You said you wanted to go deeper," he mocked, shaking his wet hair so water droplets flew in her face.

"That's hardly what I meant." She floated weightlessly in his arm, legs wrapped around his waist.

"Sounds like a challenge, Ms. Taylor." One dark eyebrow lifted mischievously.

She couldn't decide if he looked more sexy or adorable in the moonlight with that devilish grin on his lips and wet curls dripping on his face. She wiped a curl out of his eye and decided that, solely based on how her lady parts felt pressed against him, sexy won hands-down. "Perhaps it is, Mr. Hunter."

His eyes took on that fierce wolf look, making her wonder how many times a day they could have sex, because every time he looked at her like that, she was going to want him.

He lifted her onto the edge of the pool. The transition from the warm water to the night air sent shivers down her spine. He grabbed a fluffy yellow beach towel from the basket beside her and wrapped it around her shoulders.

She used the edge of the towel to wipe water from her face. Her body jolted when his tongue slid up the inside of her leg. She pressed the towel to her face and took a deep breath as he placed delicate kisses on the tender skin of her inner thigh.

When his tongue traveled upwards, her legs instinctively squeezed together against the side of his head. He touched her knees and peered up at her. "Let go," he whispered.

She took a deep breath, thankful it wasn't broad daylight so she didn't have to worry about what the view must look like from his end. She let him part her legs, but the second his tongue touched her, she involuntarily squished his head again.

He stood up in the pool so his face was near hers and took

her cheeks in his hand. "Don't you want me to?" His brows were creased in gentle concern.

She nodded, then watched the slow grin of realization wash over his face. He closed his eyes for a moment as if in prayer. Please don't let him be thanking God she'd never received oral sex before, because that just seemed wrong.

He grabbed a sunning mat from behind her. "Slide this underneath you and lie back." She pressed her hands against the concrete behind her to lift her butt while he slid the mat beneath her, then let him guide her butt closer to the edge of the pool. He began planting feathery kisses at her knee. As her legs relaxed, he gradually moved upwards, occasionally peering at her hungrily. She lay back on the mat and closed her eyes, savoring the delicious sensation of his lips and soft whiskers on the sensitive skin near the top of her inner thigh.

The longer he teased with his tongue, the more her hips began to reach for him. When his tongue finally tasted her, a moan flew from her lips. She pressed the towel to her mouth to stifle her moans. Her fingers clutched the mat as waves rushed through her. She tried to suppress it, but her body had far surpassed any hope of control and within seconds, she exploded in a rush of tremors. The noise she made would have awakened Rhode Island if she hadn't had the towel over her mouth.

Her arms and legs fell limply on the mat. One eyelid fluttered open when a drop of water landed on her chin. She looked up to see Jay's naked body standing over her. He knelt and kissed her nose. "We definitely need to work on your stamina, killer."

She managed a weak smile before he scooped her up in a towel.

CHAPTER 49

LOOKING DOWN AT THE drowsy, satisfied look on Kricket's face as he carried her into the house, Jay thought he had never seen a more beautiful sight. This angel had never been loved properly, and he was going to thoroughly enjoy showing her how it felt to be worshiped.

When he pushed open the bedroom door with his foot, the scent of roses filled the air. Her eyes fluttered open. He watched her wide eyes absorb every detail in the room like a princess in a fairytale.

Meg had certainly thought of everything. The carpet and bed were covered with a colorful mixture of rose petals. White candles on every surface emanated a celestial glow, and soft music drifted through the air. The dresser held a pitcher of water, a bottle of wine and glasses, and a tray overflowing with cheese and fruit. The nightstand boasted an assortment of lotions, mints, and gum.

"Meg did this for us," he responded to her puzzled look. "Apparently we were supposed to start in here."

"That was sweet of Meg," she said softly. "She'd be upset if she knew we wasted it."

"Oh, it's not wasted." He eased her onto the bed.

She pulled the sheet over her and scooted up to lean against the pillows. He bit the inside of his mouth to keep from grinning. Her shyness about being naked was refreshing, though not at all surprising. But he'd get her over that soon enough. When she looked longingly at the water pitcher on the dresser, he knew she was too modest to walk across the room naked.

"Thirsty?" he asked, running his fingers through her hair.

She nodded gratefully. She'd definitely had a workout.

He strode across the room to Meg's makeshift beverage center and poured a glass of water. After watching her suck down two glasses of wine at dinner, he had no intention of serving her more. There would be no falling asleep in the middle of his planned full-body exploration.

He turned around and caught her staring, causing an eruption of laughter. "You have a nice booty, Mr. Hunter," she said, a tide of crimson rushing up her neck.

As he walked towards her, she obviously tried to avoid looking at his penis, but her eyes had other plans. His penis had other plans too. In fact, he was pretty sure he'd be a walking hard-on for the rest of his life.

He perched on the side of the bed and handed her the water. Watching her lips close around the rim of the glass hit him in the crotch, just like it had that first night in the club. When she handed the glass back to him, he looked in her eyes, turned it around, and sipped from the side she'd been drinking from.

She laughed softly. "I nearly fell off the barstool when you made that move at the club."

"That wasn't a move. Well, it is this time, but it wasn't then."

"Oh really?" She crossed her arms with a condemning glare. "Then what would you call it?"

He brushed her lower lip with his thumb. "I wanted your lips so badly, I couldn't think straight. And that was the closest I could get at the time without sending you running off to Becca the bodyguard."

She made a show of glancing around the room. "Well, my bodyguard isn't here now. Maybe your move will work this time."

"I think my chances are pretty good." He kissed her soft lips. "Turn over and let's see," he whispered into her mouth.

Her eyes widened, but she dutifully rolled onto her tummy.

After surveying the bottles of lotions on the nightstand, he selected a purple one and poured a dollop into his cupped palm. She tensed slightly when he brushed her hair to one side and pulled the sheet down to expose her body. His eyes roamed the length of her while he rubbed his hands together to warm the lotion. How was he ever going to leave the house with this body at his disposal?

As his hand stroked the warm lotion across her shoulders, a deep breath filled her. "Mmm, lavender," she said dreamily, as her body relaxed into the mattress. Her shoulders were narrow, but the position of her hands under the pillow showed off her nice girly muscles. Spreading the lotion slowly across her iridescent skin, he traced each small ripple in her back with his thumb.

The soft moan that came from her mouth when he began kneading put his cock on the ready. This was going to be as trying on his patience as it was enjoyable. "I want to kiss every inch of your heavenly body," he whispered in her ear.

He delicately drug his lips along her neck, causing it to arch in response. When he sensed a tremor of desire sneak down her body, he pulled his lips away and continued exploring her back. He had a long slow journey of her body mapped out in his mind before he would allow her to reach her destination, and he would ensure she enjoyed every second along the way.

He filled his palm with more lotion and rubbed it on her nicely rounded biceps. He'd noticed them on more than one occasion when she'd lifted something while wearing a tank or T-shirt. "Nice guns," he whispered.

Her snicker into the pillow proved it pleased her that he noticed. Pressing his lips against the top of her scar, he planted kisses down the length of her arm. He didn't need to say a word. They both had scars, and that was that. It was something they couldn't change, and she'd made him promise to let it go. And hopefully someday he could.

He massaged more lotion into her heart-shaped butt, kneading his palms into its center. He desperately wanted to slip his hand between her legs and feel her slickness. Her hips were already flexing from his touch and his personal tour had only just begun, so he veered only close enough to make her yearn for more.

He knew the heavenly vision of her when she turned over would be the death of him, so he paused a moment to firmly secure control before leaning towards her ear. "Roll over, baby." She turned towards him, her eyes filled with desire. Her hand drifted up to his face. "I love you," she mouthed.

"I love you," he whispered into her mouth. He kissed her long and slow, letting his tongue fulfill what his cock longed to do…meld into the very depths of her.

As his lips traveled down the creamy expanse of her neck, he paused to admire her hard pink nipples perched atop her small, smooth breasts. From their earlier interlude, he knew they were wildly sensitive. He longed to take one in his mouth, but there was more exploring to be done.

He outlined her breasts with the tip of his finger, then skimmed his hand down her side, following the curve of her waist and hips. His touch was intended to pleasure, not tease. He trailed his hand past her thighs to her knees, then slid up her inner thigh, barely brushing over her folds before smoothing his hand across her flat belly. He traced that same path several times before leaving one hand between her legs, then made a path up her abdomen with his tongue. Her breasts surged towards him as his tongue explored their delicious peaks. She moaned softly, her hips moving in time with the stroke of his fingers on her clitoris.

The sheer joy of pleasing her held him for a time, but her responsive body combined with the love he felt soon made him crazy with desire. He slipped his finger inside and felt her shudders crash against his fingers. She gasped, appearing panic stricken.

"Just close your eyes and stay with it. There's more."

He lowered himself onto the bed, covering her body with his. A bright flame sprang into her eyes. Her hips rose to meet him as he entered her. The degree to which she responded aroused his hunger, quashing his plan to love her slowly.

Her body writhed beneath him. She was tight, and he worried about hurting her, but she grasped his butt and pulled him deeper. He craved the depths of her, and her surrendering moans were a heady invitation to freely thrust to her core. Their bodies moved in powerful harmony with one another. He showered her neck with kisses as he sought her deeper and deeper. Every stroke brought him perilously close to climax and at the sudden convulsion of her orgasm, he lost himself inside her with a tormented groan. She was his life forevermore.

CHAPTER 50

As THEY LAY IN bed the next morning, the doorbell jolted them out of their private universe. Jay groaned as he pulled on a pair of boxers. "Don't go anywhere. I'll be right back," he said with a wink.

"Are you two ever going to come up for air?"

Kricket pulled the covers to her chin when she heard Brandon's voice in the entry hall. Even though she was safely tucked away in the bedroom, after all the things they'd done in the last eighteen hours, she felt exposed.

"How many calls and messages are you going to ignore, dude? It's family day. Everyone's at your brother's for a surprise engagement party. Shit. Don't tell them I told you."

She'd totally lost track that it was Sunday. She glanced at the clock on the nightstand. It was after two. They were an hour late.

"Your niece wanted to ride her bicycle over here to get you, but I interceded."

"Thanks, pal," Jay said. "I'm sure Madi knows our garage door code. That's a show she didn't need to see." She heard a hint of pride in his voice.

"What are friends for? Hey Kricket," Brandon yelled. "Mind if I have a peek at the show?"

Undoubtedly, the sound of a slap followed by a laugh she heard came from Jay punching Brandon. When Jay said they would be there in fifteen minutes, she leapt from the bed. So much for a quickie in the shower. She resignedly jumped in the shower alone, and was out and dressed in twelve minutes flat.

"Surprise!" A bevy of family and friends pounced on them when they entered Mitch and Meg's house. Kricket forced her eyes to fly open in shock. After only a few hugs, Karen shooed everyone away, obviously worried they'd cause a panic attack.

"Gimme five, brother." Mitch held up a hand to Jay.

"Try seven," Jay said, smacking Mitch's hand.

Kricket cringed when she saw her grandpa's face pale and squeezed Jay's bicep to make him hush.

"Seven! Damn, little brother."

"Seven what?" Madi asked.

"In one night? I don't believe I ever made it over six," Dot said. Everyone turned towards her with mouths open. She patted Grandpa's arm. "I was much younger then."

"I like this woman," Gayle said, obviously impressed.

"Seven what? Seven what? Seven what?" Madi insisted.

"Seven cupcakes. Jay ate seven cupcakes in one day," Meg said, giving Mitch a look.

"In one day?" Madi turned to Jay with her hands on her hips. "Uncle Jay, you need to exercise some self-control. That's what Mama always tells me when I want another one."

"That's what she tells me too," Mitch said, wrapping his arms around Meg from behind. He looked at Kricket and grinned broadly. "So, where were the other six? I only saw the one out by the pool. I was getting a little fresh air on the balcony last night."

A gasp flew from her mouth. She stared at him, completely tongue-tied, her face flaming with embarrassment. The room grew completely silent, except for Brandon, who roared with laughter.

Mitch chuckled. "Relax, kiddo, it was just a lucky guess. We don't even own binoculars." He held up his hands in surrender when Tom glared at him. "I swear."

"Jay, how could you possibly eat seven cupcakes?" Madi asked.

"Because I'm way manlier than your dad," Jay responded with a smirk.

As the room filled with laughter, Kricket could see this was going downhill quickly. She had no intention of continuing any sex talk in front of Grandpa and the kids, so she smacked Mitch on the arm. "Can we please stop talking about cupcakes now?"

"Speaking of food, let's head into the dining room before everything gets too cold to eat." Karen suggested, in an obvious attempt to tame her testosterone-filled boys.

They'd hardly taken time to eat anything during their love fest, so Kricket piled food on her plate from the enormous feast covering the kitchen island. After such a whirlwind few days, it was comforting to be surrounded by her family and best friend at the dinner table. Becca caught her eye across the table, raised her spoon to her mouth and licked it very slowly, then cocked an eyebrow with a wicked grin.

Kricket knew exactly what her silent question was, and answered with a nod. When she realized Karen had seen their exchange, she concentrated on eating her potato salad. Ugh.

"So, when's the wedding?" Dot asked. "We went to a wedding last fall that took place right over there by the clubhouse." She pointed out the back window. "They brought the bride down in a white golf cart that looked like a mini-limousine. Wouldn't that be lovely? And you can be the flower girl, Madi."

"A big wedding is not my style," she said quickly to prevent Dot from jetting down the wedding plan runway. "I don't like having that much attention on me. I nearly passed out when I was Becca's maid of honor. Walking down the aisle with everyone staring at me…" She shuddered just thinking about it. Her feet had refused to move forward. If she hadn't locked eyes with Grandpa sitting in the second row, she would have turned around and bolted out the back door.

"But you just spoke in front of seven-hundred people," Dot said.

"I can't explain it, but that's different. I want something small and intimate. Just you guys, no more than that." She glanced at Jay. They hadn't discussed it, but she assumed he wouldn't want a big wedding either.

He squeezed her leg and smiled. "That sounds perfect."

"How soon do you think you'll plan it?" Karen asked.

"As soon as possible," Jay said. "I can't wait to marry this girl. He put his arm around Kricket's shoulder and kissed her cheek. "We can have it out there on the patio." He cocked his head and looked at her with a wide grin. "Next weekend?"

She answered him with a smile.

EPILOGUE

Two years later

KRICKET WATCHED JAY PACE across the airport lobby. Every so often, he'd look at his watch, then rake his fingers through his gorgeous head of hair. Waiting was not one of his strong suits. But who could be patient while waiting to meet the child he thought had been aborted? She gazed at Oliver's photo on her phone. Although a paternity test confirmed it for legal purposes, there was no question that Oliver belonged to Jay, with his dark curly hair and those deep brown eyes she knew so well. Except unlike Jay's penetrating eyes, Oliver's were pensive.

Of course the entire family wanted to come greet little Oliver at the airport, but Rachel's attorney suggested they pick him up alone so as not to overwhelm the little guy. A snicker escaped her as she remembered the look on the attorney's face when he gravely warned them that Oliver was an extremely shy child who rarely spoke. Jay had grinned at her and said, "We've got this."

"What are you smiling at?" Jay asked, settling into the chair beside her. She knew it would be only a matter of minutes before he'd pop up again to pace.

"Just thinking how lucky I am to have two of you to love."

"You're going to be a great mom," he said, rewarding her with a warm smile that didn't quite conceal the stress of the last few months. After receiving the call from Rachel's attorney, he'd been afraid to tell her. Afraid that she'd balk at being made a stepmother after they'd decided to wait four or five years to start a family. She had to admit when she first learned about Oliver, insecurity had swallowed her. Not only because Jay had a child with another woman, but because she didn't know what kind of mother she might be. Her experience with children was minimal, and she worried that her own mother's lack of parenting skills might have rubbed off on her. But Jay's confidence had turned her fear into excitement.

She was certain she'd be a better mom than Rachel. After doing a little digging, Jay had learned that Rachel wasn't exactly an attentive mother. She'd convinced her Chicago lover that he was the baby's father, but when their relationship ended after she hooked up with some guy in Switzerland during a business trip, the man demanded a paternity test. When the test came back as a non-match, Rachel's attorney contacted Jay. Since Rachel had jetted off to Switzerland two months ago, leaving Oliver in the care of his nanny, it didn't appear Jay would have any trouble gaining full custody.

Oliver's nanny—she'd asked them to call her Nan—was accompanying him to Oklahoma and would stay with them through Oliver's transition.

Jay burst from his seat at the announcement of the arriving flight. His eyes sparkled as he held out his hand to her. "Let's do this, babe," he said with a nervous grin.

Stranger after stranger descended down the escalator as they waited at the bottom for their first glimpse of Oliver. Each time she saw a toddler in a woman's arms, her heart jumped.

Jay anxiously shifted back and forth on his feet. He suddenly stilled. "There he is. There's Oliver," he whispered, squeezing her hand.

Perched in the arms of a grandmotherly type woman was little Oliver Owen, clutching the neck of a stuffed Panda bear, fully experiencing his escalator ride. The closer they got, the faster her heart beat.

Nan smiled warmly at Jay's wave, and they met her near the bottom of the escalator. Their first glimpse of Oliver was short, because the moment they greeted Nan, he buried his little head in her shoulder.

"Hey buddy," Jay said, gently placing his hand on Oliver's back. Oliver's little body tensed and his grip on Nan tightened.

Nan cautioned Jay with her hand and winked. "We've been looking forward to our visit. I know Oliver is anxious to play with the new toys you have for him, aren't you, sweetie?"

Oliver opened one eye and looked at them, keeping his head buried in her shoulder.

Of course Jay was dying to hold him, but he took Nan's cue. "You're right, Nan. We have lots of toys at home. Let's get your luggage off that merry-go-round so we can go home and play."

Kricket walked behind Nan, hoping Oliver would peek up at her. "I think I have one of Oliver's new toys in my purse," she said, as they waited for the luggage to start spilling out of the wall onto the conveyor belt. "Jay, why don't you see if you can find it?"

Jay reached in her purse and pulled out the toy she'd stowed there. "It's a Jeep. Do you like Jeeps, Oliver?" he asked.

Peering from the haven of Nan's shoulder, he curiously eyed the toy Jeep, but when Jay held it out to him, he buried his face again.

Kricket's heart sank at the disappointment on Jay's face. "It'll be okay," she whispered. "You know how to do this. Just give him a little while to get used to you."

When the buzzer sounded and the light began flashing on the luggage carousel, Oliver's head popped up, giving them a peek at his precious face. He was more adorable than she ever dreamed possible.

They watched him until he buried his head again. "Nan, if you'll point out your luggage, I'll grab it when it comes around." Jay handed Kricket the toy Jeep.

"Nan, I wonder if Oliver will help me with this Jeep while

you and Jay find your luggage." She casually held it out to entice him. "I can't get the wheels to turn." She knew from experience that being spoken to indirectly seemed less threatening to a shy child.

"Oliver loves to help, don't you Oliver?" Nan asked.

He peered at Nan, glanced at the toy, then the carousel, then at Kricket. She could see his little mind carefully weighing the option of receiving the toy versus the fear of being held by a stranger. He pressed his tiny lips together and reached towards her. The moment she felt his warm little body in her arms and looked into that miniature face of Jay, her heart swelled to overflowing. She immediately and unconditionally loved this child as if he were her own.

The look on Jay's face when he turned and saw them was priceless. He could hardly keep his eyes off them while he and Nan waited on the luggage.

Most shy children were more wary of men than women, so she tried warming Oliver up to Jay by saying that he was the one who bought the toy and pointing out how nice Jay was for helping Nan with the luggage.

Oliver allowed her to continue holding him all the way to the car. She could tell he was interested in, yet wary of, Jay's vastness. As they watched Jay load the luggage into the back of the Land Rover, she pointed out that Jay was tall and strong, which made her feel safe.

Nan loaded Oliver in the car seat, then sat with him in the back. Kricket drove so Jay could pay attention to Oliver during the ride home. Jay told Oliver they had real Jeeps at home that he could ride in, but Oliver would hardly glance at him.

"Here we are," she said cheerfully, pulling in the driveway. "Oliver, we have a nice cozy room for you and Nan." Meg had outdone herself decorating one of the spare bedrooms in the same

Jeep theme as the recreation room. Kricket attempted to retrieve Oliver from his car seat, but he wouldn't have any part of that, so Nan lifted him out.

Oliver's eyes immediately latched on to Grasshopper, sitting topless in the driveway. He pointed and said, "Jeep." It was the first word he'd spoken.

"Do you like the Jeep, Oliver?" Kricket asked.

He clamored for Nan to put him down. As soon as his little feet hit the pavement, he dashed towards Grasshopper. "Jeep," he said, patting the bumper.

Kricket signaled with her eyebrows for Jay to play along. "Jay, here's the key to Grasshopper. I think Oliver wants to drive her."

Nan lifted Oliver over the door and stood him in the passenger seat. He latched on to the grab bar on the glove compartment and bounced up and down with an enormous grin.

Oliver eyed Jay cautiously as he opened the door and slid into the driver's seat. Keeping one hand on the steering wheel, Jay dangled the keys in front of Oliver's cherubic face. "I'll bet Oliver wants to drive."

She held her breath as Oliver surveyed the keys. Nan made a show of aiming her phone. "I'm going to take Oliver's picture while he drives the Jeep."

His eyes roamed back and forth between Nan and Jay. The seconds slowly ticked by as he considered it. With the smallest of grins, he reached for the key and crawled into Jay's waiting arms.

Kricket couldn't see the joy on Jay's face because her eyes were full of tears. But she knew that she'd just witnessed one of the happiest moments of his life.

ACKNOWLEDGEMENT

To my husband for graciously allowing me to put writing before anything else for a much longer period of time than we ever fathomed.

To Diane and Janetta, who helped brainstorm ideas early on, building my excitement to actually follow through with penning a novel. To my draft readers, Lindsey, Amy, Karen, Diane H., Diane P., Cori, Kelsey, Kim, Troy, Kristi, Tiffany, Marjorie, Jean, Teri, Christina, Ashley, Marcia, and Ken for honest feedback and encouragement throughout the process. To Kathy, Alice, and Callie, of the Oklahoma Romance Writers of America, who were always willing to give advice, no matter how busy they were with their own writing projects. And to William Bernhardt for his valuable writing workshops and books.

To my *virtual family*—my friends and fellow Jeepers in @TheJeepMafia— for supporting Kricket and Hopper with your wit, encouragement, and Jeep knowledge. I hope to meet each of you one day.

And finally, to the man who parked his Jeep Wrangler in a bank parking lot near my house with a "For Sale" sign in the windshield. Purchasing my first Jeep triggered the writing of this novel. A Jeep is so much more than just a vehicle to drive. If you own one, you know exactly what I'm talking about.

ABOUT
LEIGH ANN LANE

In her "day job," Leigh Ann Lane enlightens audiences as a workshop leader. Her passion is encouraging people to gradually step outside their comfort zone to a richer, brighter world. Nine Million Minutes, along with the So Awkward Journal, a step-by-step diary to aid in overcoming shyness, are the first steps down passion's path.

The *So Awkward Journal* is available on Amazon.com.

Website: LeighAnnLane.com
Blog: SoAwkwardJournalblog.wordpress.com
Twitter: @KricketJeeper @SoAwkwardJournl @TheJeepMafia
Facebook: Leigh Ann Lane
Instagram: @KricketJeeper_

If you enjoyed the love story of Kricket and Jay, please consider telling a friend and posting a short review. Word of mouth is an author's best friend and would be much appreciated.

Thank you,
Leigh Ann Lane

44268992R00201

Made in the USA
Middletown, DE
05 May 2019